The Strong Stuff
The Best of The Fictional Café
2018-2020

Mike Mavilia Rochester
Editor

A Fictional Café Press Book
Boston, Massachusetts

Printed in the United States of America.
First Edition

ISBN: 978-0-9840369-5-0
LCCN: 2023903242

A Fictional Café Press Book
An Imprint of www.fictionalcafe.com
Website: www.fictionalcafe.com/the-strong-stuff/
Publisher: Jack B. Rochester
Editor: Mike Mavilia Rochester
Assistant Editor: Cori Sims
Cover Design: Melanie Marston
Cover Art: Amanda Grafe
Interior Design: Sophie Hanks

The Fictional Café is an online magazine of the arts, publishing fiction, poetry, creative nonfiction, audio arts and fine art. It was founded in 2013 by Jack B. Rochester and Caitlin M. Park. The Fictional Café is an all-volunteer organization of eight devoted creators, or baristas, and selects a Writer-in-Residence and a Poet-in-Residence every two years.

Grateful acknowledgement is made to the following authors and publishers:
Cracks of Light, copyright © 2021, by John Charles Reedburg. Published by Valorous Books. Excerpted by permission. All rights reserved.
"Nothing Against Ms. Johnson, But . . ." Copyright © 2020 by Patricia Callahan
Secret Shepherd, copyright © 2018, by James Osborne. Published by Solstice Publishing Inc. Excerpted by permission of the author. All rights reserved.
"Prisoners of the Multiverse" is excerpted from a story collection entitled *The Liar's Asylum*, published by Black Lawrence Press. Copyright © 2017, by Jacob M. Appel. It first appeared in the *New Orleans Review.* Excerpted by permission of the author. All rights reserved.
Love Poems from New England: reflections on states of mind and states of heart, copyright © 2020, by Jon Meyer. Published by Brilliant Light Publishing, L3C. Excerpted by permission. All rights reserved.
Setting the Family Free, copyright © 2019, by Eric D. Goodman. Published by Loyola University's Apprentice House Press. Excerpted by permission. All rights reserved.
The Night at the End of the Tunnel, or Isaiah Can You See?, copyright © 2018 by Mark Greenside. Published by Weasel Press. Excerpted by permission. All Rights Reserved.
Vogel, copyright © 2019 by Dave Lincoln. Published by Yellow Flower Productions. Excerpted by permission. All rights reserved.
"Wind in the Washline" and "The Prevaricating Day," copyright © 2021, by Wayne D. King, Published by Moosewood Publishing. Excerpted by permission. All rights reserved.

The Strong Stuff
The Best of The Fictional Café
2018-2020

Mike Mavilia Rochester
Editor

Introduction

Jack B. Rochester
Editor-in-Chief
August, 2023

The Fictional Café turned ten years old in May of 2023, an accomplishment to be sure, but of even greater note was the day in June 2022 when we registered our 1000th Coffee Club member, the artist and writer Martha Clarkson. Our readers reside literally around the world, in 73 countries. We publish about ten times each month: fiction, poetry, creative nonfiction, audio arts, and fine art. Everything we do is free, except for the bound-book anthologies for which we need to offset printing and mailing costs. We intend to remain free, always.

Caitlin Park and I came up with the idea for The Fictional Café over lunch in a little Thai café one sunny April afternoon in 2013 in Sonoma County, California. At the time, Caitlin was a creative writing grad student at Cal State, Sonoma. I had flown in from Boston to award her the Joshua Tree Interactive Working Writers Scholarship. We hit it off from the moment we met, and knew The Fictional Café, "FC," meant great literary things were in store for us both. And possibly the literary world. We became the first two baristas. Today, we are 10 strong.

You're holding in your hands the second edition of *The Strong Stuff*. The first edition was published in 2017 by and for the creators who appeared in its pages, as well as our readership. It sold out. I anticipate this new volume will do the same for this simple reason: the art, the poetry, the stories are darned good. The baristas who help choose what we publish are so discerning and have given so much of their time and thought to choosing great work for FC. The *crème de la crème* of what we publish in the online 'zine is what you see here in these print pages. FC, in all respects, is a collaborative enterprise. We depend on you, the creatives, for your submissions. We're only as good as what our baristas select. They don't get paid for their work. No—let me correct myself. The coin of our publishing realm for all our baristas is love: the love of artistic expression, the love of working to see great work published, and feeling loved in return for what they give to The Fictional Café.

Foreword

Mike Mavilia Rochester
Anthology Barista
Managing Editor

A lot has happened in the world since we put together our last anthology in the summer of 2017. As I sit in my now well-worn home office, it's hard to imagine a world before COVID-19, before the assault on the U.S. Capitol, before the summer of Black Lives Matter, before the #MeToo movement. Yet these events provide the backdrop in which the works you are about to see were created.

Even the process of putting together this anthology was impacted by current events. As I began reaching out to potential contributors in late February, 2022, one member, whom I had to track down on Facebook, informed me I had reached him just in time. He lives in Russia; the government was blocking Facebook and other social media platforms that day. Had I waited a few more days before writing, my message would not have reached him. The ripples of Russia's invasion of Ukraine reached even our seemingly insular literary magazine community.

Indeed, the fiction, poetry and art we present in this volume reflect the turbulence of the times, with topics covering dystopian alternate realities, social injustice, physical and sexual violence, excessive indulgence and withdrawal from the world as a whole. Now, more than at any time in recent memory, the collective seething of society has seeped into the wool of our creative works, resulting in the powerful emotional tapestry you hold in your hands.

I would like to thank every one of our featured creatives whose work we published on our "FC" website during this period. There was so much quality work that we had to expand the book to twice the size of the first. Even so, we had to make some extremely difficult decisions, but we feel this truly is "the strong stuff." Keep creating, keep submitting, keep following us. We thank you for making the dream of The Fictional Café truly come to life.

Words From Our Baristas

Jason Brick
Book Consultant Barista

I've been in publishing for a while now—not as long as Jack, but longer than many. One thing I've learned is how difficult it is to make a fiction magazine or website succeed. The competition is so strong, and the money is so tight. It has been a deeply humbling privilege to be part of The Fictional Café's success in an area where few projects enjoy that distinction.

Ruby Fink
Audio Arts Barista

One day in 2015, I received a message from Jack B. Rochester about my podcast, "Mickie McKinney: Boy Detective." I'd sent it to The Fictional Café a couple months before and hadn't heard back, but Jack was reaching out to tell me he loved the story, thought it had a lot of potential, and wanted to feature it on the website. Well, I was thrilled that someone finally liked my work and a friendship was born. Soon after, Jack hired me to produce his first audiobook. One audio book led to two, which led to six and started my career in audiobook publishing.

A year or so after I started working with Jack, he hired me on to be the Audio Arts Barista for The Fictional Café. My job was to find audio productions/podcasts I thought were a lot of fun and post them on The Fictional Café, just like Mickie McKinney. I have been finding the rough gems and pearls of audio adventure for the last three years.

Since meeting Jack, I have helped create more than a dozen audiobooks, given lectures on the benefits of creating your own audiobooks and how to do them, showcased the stories of others on Audio Arts, and built a reputation as someone with expertise in a career I had stumbled upon by chance. My experiences have been rich and my lessons priceless, thanks to Jack and The Fictional Café.

Rachel Gonzalez
Writer-in-Residence, 2023-2024

Over the years The Fictional Café has given me so many opportunities. It started with the publication of two short stories and just a few years later I landed the spot as their Writer-in-Residence. Now I have the chance to show how much I've grown as a writer and to keep growing as part of this team. It's so great to get to share this process with people who value stories and their power as much as I do.

Jennifer Green
Consulting Content Management Barista

As an editor and former educator, I am continually in awe of human creativity and passion. When I joined The Fictional Café, I had no concept of the larger role it would play in both my personal and professional growth. I've had the pleasure of reading inspiring and moving pieces of fiction, viewing poignant and original works of art, and glimpsing our shared world through the eyes and experiences of others. The Fictional Café provides an opportunity for authors and artists wishing to share their art with a wider audience, and I'm grateful for my part in helping them reach their goals and achieve their dreams.

Derrick R. Lafayette
Author and Writer-in-Residence, 2021-2022

What can I say? The Fictional Café invited me in with open arms. The bonds I made with the staff, especially Jack, will live on forever. We even came together to put out a book that sold out at the Cocoa Village Book Fest in Florida. The experience was paramount in my growth as an author. There was a big sigh of relief when I learned FC editors truly enjoyed my more off-beat stories, surreal stories, nearly anything I wanted to experiment with was ever turned away. Instead, we worked on it, polished it, and put out some of the best content I've ever produced. I'm still on the journey to continue writing the best stories I can, and The Fictional Café has cemented themselves in this trek to my becoming the best author I can be. I'm truly grateful, thankful, and humbled by all the kind words. We're family now.

Victoria Orifice
Submissions Barista

Interacting with The Fictional Café members and writers this past year has been a privilege. Reading the work selected for this anthology has been even more so. I congratulate the talented writers and poets chosen for this publication and encourage readers and new writers to put themselves out there and submit their work if they haven't already! The Fictional Café exists for those of us impassioned by the written word in all its myriad forms. Here's to what the future holds!

Caitlin M. Park
Co-Founder and Barista

I recently came across a certificate from Sonoma State University for having received the Joshua Tree Interactive Working Writer's Scholarship in 2012. I was beginning my master's program, hoping to pursue a life and career as a writer or editor—ideally, both. Jack's scholarship gave my plans and dreams a big boost. Another followed the next year, when he and I founded The Fictional Café together. I cannot say how happy I have been to be a barista on this wonderful online magazine. It has made my dreams come true, and I know many more will come true for all of us, baristas and members alike.

Cori Sims
Barista

As a newer addition to The Fictional Café, the advisors and keepers have only extended wide-open arms from the beginning. Notably, this media community embraces the breadth of memorable creative writing and upholds thoroughly written composition, particularly from a writer's lens. Co-editing the presentation of The Fictional Café's second anthology of select art, poetry, novel excerpts and short stories was an absolute pleasure. I look forward to serving The Fictional Café's horizon of archiving pleasurable and provocative literature. A special thank-you to co-founder Jack for this collaboration. Cheers!

Yong Takahashi
Content Management Barista and prior Poetry Barista

It has been an immense pleasure to work with The Fictional Café. I am truly honored to play a small part in introducing emerging writers to the world. And I would like to extend a heartfelt thank all of you for continually supporting my work. I look forward to continuing our partnership in the years to come.

Vera West
Poet-in-Residence, 2022-2023, and Poetry Barista, 2024

My time as Poet-in-Residence has moved at lightning speed but in that time I've grown so much! When given the opportunity to work with The Fictional Café, I decided to do something uncommon for me: I marched far out of my comfort zone. I began exploring the depths of my own creativity and lassoed it to emotional themes and topics that were hard for me to talk about but felt decidedly necessary to write about. It was challenging and often left me feeling raw and exposed but also stronger, and that gave my writing the bold edge readers have found relatable and engaging.

And our thanks to these former Baristas who helped acquire, review, edit and publish the works in this book on the FC website/'zine from 2018-2020: Susi Bock, Editor; Amanda Grafe, Fine Art; Mallori Luna, Submissions; Lorraine Martindale, Editor-at-Large; Michael Piekny, Editor; Steve Sangapore, Fine Art; and Ruth Simon, Editor.

Table of Contents

Fiction • Poetry • Fine Art

The Strong Stuff
Volume 2

The Lighthouse

Derrick R. Lafayette

A clump of snow slid from the plunging power lines and splattered atop the coffin. Utility poles leaned on both sides of the road. When Maverick looked up, the empty white sky was blocked by rubber cables. For miles ahead, the snow sparkled untouched. No tracks, nor footprints, completely uncharted. Behind Maverick and Goose were two sets of footprints and sled marks. Thick rope was cutting into their shoulders, dragging the wooden tomb. Its imprints creased the burly coats they'd been wearing for two months. Goose pulled down his wool scarf. The first exhale billowed into a cloud of frost. His nose was beet red, poking out from a black garden of unkempt facial hair, dripping with sweat. A limp rolled cigarette dangled in his mouth before he added the flame.

"So, how'd you do it?"

Maverick struggled to catch his breath, wheezing between the coughs. When he pulled at his wool scarf, a thin line of blood ran down his nose. The scarlet spread into his thick black mustache, making his hair look reddish brown.

"Well, we'd been talking about it for months in advance. She chose the diamond. I was never good at fashion and all that," he coughed into his glove.

"No shock value, huh? Marsha put me on a damn deadline. Counting down the days to our fourth year together."

"She seemed like the type. No offense."

"None taken. I made her wait past the deadline. Let that fury brew. You could've cooked hamburgers on her forehead."

"She the type to grab the kitchen knife, too?"

"Nah, she never was a good cook." Both men laughed a bit, and their clouds of frost combined. "I shocked the hell out her, front of her whole family."

"That's nice. Women love surprises."

Goose let the cigarette fall in the white snow. He tugged on the rope, readying his grip to pull. Maverick's chest rose and fell; reluctantly he did the same.

"You ready?" Goose said.

A strong gust of wind shot down the road, hitting them directly. Maverick squinted to look Goose in the eyes before nodding his head. Like oxen, the two men pulled the rope attached to the sled with the wooden coffin on top. Carved into the wood read:

Lawrence McKay, widower, father of two

A blanket of tiny snowflakes began descending from the sky, collecting on the ten-inch-high pile below. Their destination was far into the vanishing point, a tiny blip on the white horizon. Everything was about reaching a lighthouse near the coastline. The two men picked up the pace and within ten minutes, the coffin was covered in snow.

Maverick's knee buckled at the top of the hill. He caught himself in the fall, sticking his arms out. Goose let the thick rope sink into the snow. He stretched his back, lowered his scarf, and let another cigarette dangle. Maverick desperately gasped for air, coughing up phlegm. Goose stayed quiet, allowing the smoke to escape through his nostrils. He peered down at the cityscape below. All the abandoned buildings. Streetlights lying in the streets, trees resting with them. Car roofs popped randomly out from under the snow. A nearly buried sign that read:

Welcome to Bonebury
Population 120,365

The entire world a sheet of white. Not a soul below the hill. Once again, no footprints, no wheel tracks before them. Goose gathered both ropes, placed them atop the coffin. He patted Maverick on his back, offered his hand in assistance. Maverick shook his head, and slowly climbed on top of the coffin.

"I pushed last time," he said.

"Fair is fair," Goose responded, before nudging the sled over the edge.

He sprinted after it, snow exploding near his legs. Maverick pulled him on the coffin, right as the slope went deep, and they took on speed. For a glorious one-hundred-eighty seconds, neither man had to walk. Riding into Bonebury on the coffin of Lawrence McKay.

The sled came to a halt, stopping in front of an abandoned brick church. The huge cross on the roof had snapped and now lay flat in the parking lot. The long, snowy staircase was littered with baby strollers, hard-bottom shoes, and ruined Bibles. Sticking out from the blanket of snow was a crown of brown fur. Goose grabbed it, looked: a one-eyed teddy bear. He stared at the missing eye, the array of strings jutting out. A thick snowflake landed on its nose, melted into the cotton. Above, the blizzard raged on, and visibility grew worse.

"Did you have any kids, before all this?" He waved his hand at the desolate city.

"Lisa was barren, but the dogs made up for it."

"Hmm, Marsha and I had twins."

"Yea? So what happened?"

Goose realized he was out of cigarettes. He dropped his backpack, unzipped it, and put the teddy bear inside. Before closing it, he whipped out a silver flask. Maverick waited patiently for the answer, watching Goose slowly gulp the harsh, warm liquor.

"Same thing that happened to Lawrence," he stuffed the flask in his pocket. "Let me know when you're ready."

Maverick's knee popped when he bent it standing up. He wiped the blood from his nose onto his collar. The wind came in strong, cutting straight through his coat; he felt every prick of the unrelenting cold. Soon, all of Bonebury looked like the inside of a snow globe. Another Nor'easter on its way. Maverick could feel it in his body. Similar to a pain people feel in rainstorms.

"My headache's back. I'm only mentioning it in case I get snappy. Nothing personal, Goose," he bent his other leg and like clockwork, that knee popped as well. "Think anyone's alive in Bonebury?"

"No, just those in the lighthouse. That's what the letter said. So far, every word's been true."

"You know I got it, right?" the inflection in his voice meant it wasn't about the letter.

"Yea, I know you do."

"If I air-swigged the bottle, technically, my lips will never—"

"Can't risk it, Maverick. And I can't share it, nothing but a few drops left. Besides, you'll last longer without it."

"I'm not sure I want to."

Goose looked at him. All six feet, two hundred pounds of him. He gripped the rope, signaling it was time to go. Maverick covered his mouth with his wool scarf, stained with blood droplets. He grabbed the rope and never made eye contact with Goose. When he walked forward, tugging the rope, Goose didn't move. Confused, he glanced at him, pointed to the city, and pulled again.

"I want to make this clear, right now. There's only enough room for one body in that coffin."

"Lucky him."

They trekked deeper into the city, marveling at the historic landscapes. A bell tower that was still standing in the center of downtown. Whenever the wind blew hard enough, it would ring in a harrowing E flat. Famous coffee shops with glass walls shattered into crystals so small, one could mistake it for frost. Frozen water fountains, with long icicles on the chins of stone cherubs playing harps. Schools were missing letters in their names. Fallen skyscrapers, poorly architected and unable to withstand the harshness of the ongoing blizzards, blocked route after route, causing the men to zigzag throughout the district. On the side of a dilapidated brick wall, written in graffiti, the message:

What's Worse? The Black Plague or The White Plague?

Finally, they located a path on the train tracks. The train itself poked out from the frozen lake, the water so clear one could see the sunken cars beneath the sheet of surface ice. Like a mechanical snake stuck in time.

Up ahead was another incline. Goose pulled down his scarf but was unable to share a syllable. Maverick simply grunted, tugging with all his strength. Goose lowered his head and joined him. The two barely made it, feeling frozen grass crunch beneath their feet as they reached the brow. Straight ahead, towards the edge of the city, stood the lighthouse, protruding from the earth like a red and white stripped finger. Shining its light on the ocean near the coastline. A giant eye desperate to find life. Just like the letter said.

Goose let the rope go and sat on a flat rock. The sky above grew darker. Maverick stood there, still clinching the rope. Goose put out an open palm to him, signaling a five-minute break. Maverick leaned against the coffin, glancing up at the ghostly white sky.

"Pretty sure, with the frostbite and all, a few of my toes are broken," Goose said, swigging from the flask.

"You said that yesterday. By now, it's probably autoamputation."

"What's that mean?"

"Spontaneous detachment of an appendage from the body."

"Where I'm from, we call that early retirement."

They laughed.

Maverick found a tree stump to squat on near Goose. He coughed badly and covered his mouth. Goose handed the flask to him.

"Finish it."

Maverick looked at it, then at Goose, before downing the liquor. He smacked his lips loudly and hurled the flask towards the city below. Goose pretended he was holding a shotgun to shoot it out of mid-air. Maverick made an explosion noise with his mouth. Goose turned the pretend shotgun on Maverick and fired again. Maverick fell backward off the tree stump, landing on the snow. When he stood up to look at him, Maverick was laughing, making snow angels. Goose joined him, and both men watched the sky transition to full darkness. For a blissful moment the snow ceased and the wind stopped. They basked in the silence, overjoyed. Wondering what would happen after the lighthouse. If everything in the letter was real. If the vexing journey was worth frostbitten toes.

Maverick sat up first. Goose followed and they continued on their passage down the hill. Then they were finally upon it. The lighthouse stretched into the heavens. Resting above a huge piece of rock that edged the frozen sea.

"We made it," Maverick said between coughs.

"Looks like it."

"What's the boy's name again?"

"Xavier."

"Xavier McKay."

"When it's your time, I'd be honored to take you back to your dogs," Goose smirked.

"Have me cremated first. Otherwise, I'd be dog food," he joked back, his smile a red hue on his teeth.

"If I go first, lay me flat on my back and let the snow cover me whole."

"No dogs to go back to?"

"None at all."

Maverick opened his book bag, pulled out two sausage links. They ate at the foot of the lighthouse, inches from the door. Procrastinating, both a bit frightened about going inside, chewing slower than normal. Far in the distance, shadows were walking across the frozen sea. Fishermen were trying to make it to the shore. Grabbing onto the person next to them for balance, slipping every other step. Goose yelled out to them,

"HURRY UP BEFORE THE FOOD RUNS OUT!"

"THERE'S ONLY ONE MORE BLOOD SAUSAGE LEFT, AND I AIN'T

SHARING! DON'T LISTEN TO THIS JACKASS!"

"IF I WERE YOU I'D TURN BACK AROUND!"

Their joyous laughter echoed in the darkness.

"There's more than one left, right?"

"Of course," Goose revealed his own sausages in his backpack. "But by the time they get here, the sun will be coming up."

A strong thud hit the wall as the lighthouse door flew open. Maverick dropped his food, and it tumbled down over the short cliff. A thin young man, covered in worn, shabby, garb, stepped outside. He had long black hair that shielded his face, and his arrival seemed to bring back the harsh cold winds. He dropped to his knees when he laid eyes on the coffin. Goose finished eating and walked over to him.

"The White Plague took him quick, from what I heard."

"Coffin's been nailed shut since before we got it. The body's in the best shape you could ask for."

"Thank you . . . we must -" the thin man couldn't finish his sentence. Instead, he went into a violent coughing fit.

Goose and Maverick looked at each other with confused eyes.

The thin young man finished and cleared his throat. "Thank you. Please, let's get it upstairs."

"It?" said Maverick.

Carrying the coffin up the spiral staircase was cruel punishment for Maverick's knees. The plight seemed infinite until the thin man kicked open a wooden door at the top of the stairs. The coffin was carefully placed on the floor and pushed. Inside the room were tables filled with beakers, tongs, Bunsen burners, and boiling flasks. Liquids of all colors, ranging from purple to blue to burgundy. The thin man grabbed two hammers and handed them to Maverick and Goose, claw-side up.

"Quick, remove the nails."

"You're taking out the body?" Maverick asked.

"There is no body," the thin man confessed, scrambling for a third hammer.

"Are you Xavier McKay? Son of Lawrence McKay? Writer of the letter?"

"I'm afraid everything in that letter is a lie. It was the only way to hire you. I have the money, that part is true."

"What's in this coffin?" Goose inquired, gritting his teeth.

"The cure!"

Goose doubled over laughing, slapping his knee, almost in tears. Eventually he stopped and held his stomach, but every time the thin man attempted to speak he laughed again, drowning him out more and more dramatically, until the laughter sounded like madness.

"You hear this chicken shit, Maverick?" he leaned on his shoulder, all smiles. "The White Plague has no cure. Take a look around, doc. Only footprints in the snow is ours."

Maverick pushed Goose's hand off his shoulder.

"Maybe he's telling the truth, Goose. Maybe there is one. You don't know everything," Maverick mumbled.

"You sound like Marsha, gullible, naive. You're right. I don't know everything. But I know that much."

"I'm Lawrence McKay," the thin man interrupted.

Silence blossomed between the three men. The only sound was the cutting wind outside. Maverick's eyes ping-ponged from the coffin to the thin man, briefly believing him to be an apparition.

"You the body we been slaving for all this time? Dragging all the way to the coast for forty-five days?" Goose said.

"Please, let me show you."

All three men pulled out the long nails and pushed off the top. Inside the coffin were yarn, hay, and cloth surrounding big jugs of liquid. Maverick's jaw dropped and Goose flexed his neck to the side, in awe of what they saw. The thin man scrambled, began picking up the jars, mixing their contents with the other chemicals, concocting a potion. Maverick and Goose watched him work, tweaking the beakers, heating the flasks.

Out of a dark corner came a high-pitched sound of coughing. The thin man's ears perked up and he rushed to the corner, letting one of the boiling flasks bubble over the top. Maverick rushed towards it and took it off the flame.

"Don't touch that, Maverick. It's probably poison."

"Sometimes you don't make any sense!"

The thin man carried the tiny boy from the darkness. Feeble, malnourished, sunken dark eyes, dried blood on his lips, no older than ten. The thin man caressed his hair. Tears bubbled in his eyes.

"Just hold on a little longer," he said as he placed the back of his hand on the boy's forehead. "You're burning up."

Goose's face blanched; he started rubbing his coat, scanning the rest of the room.

"That boy's your son?" he asked painfully, without looking at him.

"This is Xavier."

"I'll hold him," Maverick said, moving his arm under the boy's head.

Lawrence showed his gratitude, then went back to finishing his chemical work. He opened a drawer beneath the wooden table top. Two syringes rolled out. He loaded one with an aquamarine liquid, then turned back to his son.

"Lift his head," Lawrence ordered, and stuck the needle into the child's neck, pressing his thumb on the plunger.

Maverick witnessed the whole ordeal in a state of wonderment. A fireworks display of miracles. Optimism surged in his old bones. Deep in his gut, he decided to believe in the cure. To believe in Lawrence. They laid the boy on a bed of blankets, and he didn't make any more noise. But as the silence grew and Lawrence prayed, you could hear him wheezing through his nose.

"Thank you," Lawrence said, reaching into the same drawer where the syringes had been and taking out an envelope. "Here's the money. It's all there, just as promised."

Goose snatched it from his hand. "A liar is a liar," he replied, thumbing through the dollars. "Ok, come on, Maverick. Let's get back on the trail, make some good distance before sunrise."

Maverick lowered his head, coughed into his hand. When he opened it, he saw a small pool of blood in his palm.

"Goose—"

"Don't even say it."

"Yes, please, stay," Lawrence butted in. "I could use the support before the others come."

"What others? You got more kids in here?"

Lawrence struggled to pick up another heavy jar from the coffin. Maverick came to his aid, smearing blood on the side of the glass. Together, they began concocting another batch. Goose felt betrayed, turned his sights on Xavier.

"Shit didn't even work. So, after all this, you gonna stay with a liar, Maverick? Help him make magic?"

"If I step outside that door with you right now, I go on doing the same thing we been doing for the last ten years. Telling the same stories, picking up the new bodies. I'm tired. I'm going to die, Goose."

"Of course you are! I am too, and so is he!" Goose pointed to Xavier.

Heavy pounding on the door broke the rising argument. A multitude of fists banging. Lawrence opened the door, but Goose pushed him out the way.

"Here come the corpses!" he screamed.

"Move out the way!"

The immense crowd of people, most emaciated, some bruised, some missing limbs, bombarded their way into the lighthouse and began climbing the spiral staircase. Goose mumbled curse words under his breath, stomping hard on the floor on his way past the immense crowd pouring in. He began wading through the sea of them, down the stairs, and as he got closer to the bottom, every face he passed looked like Maverick from different places in time. Ranging from their glory days to them being seasoned. From Maverick in perfect health, stubble on his chin, bright eyes, to Maverick with a thick beard, dried blood under his nose, and deep dark circles under his eyes. Every memory flooded his mind and before he let himself bawl, he made it downstairs and toward the door. The crowd left him behind, no one saying a word, no one introducing themselves.

Goose stepped into the dark white abyss on the outskirts of the lighthouse. He sat on the ground, unzipped his bag, and pulled out the one-eyed teddy bear. He wrung its neck, pretending it was Maverick. A small tear grew on the side of its neck and a tuft of cotton sprung out.

"You dumb old fool," he cried.

He buried his face into the bear, let the breeze carry his thoughts until suddenly his face jerked back and he coughed. A little spray of blood flew out his mouth. He wiped his lower lip with his sleeve and peered into the frozen sea. A great shadow appeared in the distance, multiplying in size, slowly taking on the form of humans. An army of darkness coming closer and closer.

Poetry

Mbizo Chirasha

Presidential Griot

Sometimes memories smell like a dictator's fart
We once jived to our own shadows under the silver moon and our shadows
danced along with us, we rhymed to the nightmares of hyenas and
hallucinations of black owls. Our desires sailed along with gowns of
fog back and forth at village dawns. Wood smoke smelt like fresh baked
bread. Time bewitched us, we ate William Shakespeare and John Donne.
We drank lemon jugs of Langston Hughes and Maya Angelou.
Soyinka's lyrical whisky wrecked our tender nerves.
We bedded politics with boyish demeanor and dreamt of the black
cockerels and black Hitler's

Sometimes time is stubborn like a sitting tyrant
Last night, commissars chanted a slogan and you baked a dictator's
poetry language. Zealots sang Castro and Stalin and you brewed a
socialist crank, the president is a stinking capitalist. I never said
he is Satanist. Back to village nights, hyenas are laughing still,
black owls gossiping, silver moon dancing still over rain beaten paths
of our country dawns.

Sometimes time stinks like a dictator's fart

Your lyrical satire sneaked imbeciles through back doors. Your praise sonnets recycled suicidal devils and polished revolutionary rejects
Back then, smells of fresh dung and scent of fresh udder milk were our morning brew and under the twilight the moon once disappeared into the earthly womb, Judas, the sun then took over and every dictator is an Iscariot.

I never said we are now vagabonds
Sometimes time smells like a dying autocrat
Mwedzi wagara ndira uyo tigo tigo ndira – the moon was once sour milk silver white and fresh from the Gods' mouth and sat on its presidential throne on the zenith of bald headed hills and later with time the moon was ripe to go mwedzi waora ndira tigo tigo ndira
Sometimes wind gusts whistled their tenor through elephant grass pastures, we sang along the obedient flora Chamupupuri icho . . . oo chamupupuri chaenda chamupupuri chadzoka
Chamupupuri icho . . . oo!

Our poverty marinated, yellow maize teeth grinned to sudden glows of lightening, the earth gyrated under the grip of thunder, then Gods wept and we drank teardrops with a song mvura ngainaye tidye makavu , mvura ngainaye tidye makavu . . . Pumpkins bred like rabbits, veldts strutted in Christmas gowns. Wild bees and green bombers sang protest and praise. I never said we are children of drought relief.
Sometimes time grows old like a sitting tyrant,
Tonight the echo of your praise poetry irk the anopheles stranded in tired city gutters to swig the bitter blood of ghetto dwellers, gutter citizens eking hard survival from hard earth of a hard country, their rough hands marked with scars of the August Armageddon, their sandy hearts are rigged ballot boxes stuffed with corruption, they waited and sang for so long.

Chamupupuri icho . . . oo chamupupuri chaenda
chamupupuri icho . . . oo chamupupuri chadzoka
Chamupupuri icho . . . oo.

Dimples of Haiti

Haiti,

stink of sweat smelling millet slavery and the scent of blood revolutions.

Slapped in the face with sanctions mud by hands under the influence

of imperialistic alcohol. A super-concoction of propaganda maize porridge and

Media yeast.

Waterfalls of anger washing away your freedom dimples

Handmaidens and mental epileptic waiters serving political syphilis in ideological cafes

Children smelling stale ideological urine and dirt diplomatic cocaine

Identities condomised with donor culture and sexual myopia

Baboons eating colors of your flag, munching apples of your freedom

Tongues kissing bottom streams of the state under the veil of democracy gospel

Haiti, my pen is a weapon of mass instruction, I see the spreading yellow York of the sun,

gently falling over the darkness of your skin, yawning off the old skin of dust,
Regaining the lost richness of your dimples.

Dawn of Sunset

Islamophobia and *Christianophobia* drank the york of our time

Socialism, liberalism and regionalism many other *isms* made rags of us. Slaves to bitterness from imported political and religion attitudes.

The sleep laden minds of Zambezi lost in the in the thicket of ballot arithmetic.

Minds swollen by songs whose tunes crevice granite boulders of unending *chumurenga.*

Sunset Acoustics

Sing *Bamako*, sing of spiders blighting freedom tomatoes

Sing of our pimped heritage

Somalia, the dramatic irony of Africa

Ethiopia, bring back the oil of our anthems and the clay of our identity

Ivory coast, your hands are hardened by hard years of madness

Cockroaches are walking over sleeping *Zambezi*

Gugulethu, tired of scathy tongues and marijuana

Egypt bulletins drenched by Arab spring urine

Abuja, how long are you going to walk in shadows?

The Man in the Iron Hat

Audrey Kalman

The hat was a marvel, like a chastity belt or a grate over an abandoned and dangerous well. The wide curve of its bowl fit the man's head perfectly. The thick brim jutted over his eyes, hiding everything above the horizontal plane of his vision and much to either side. It was astonishing that something intended to be worn could be fashioned of a material so ancient, so dense and pebbly and so, well, *iron age*. Yet the hat seemed to him the most natural thing in the world.

He didn't wear it with pride but he didn't resent it either. It simply *was*. He put it on every morning. It sat on his head through breakfast with his wife and children, through the tedious search for his briefcase, the train ride to the city, the day in the office, the ride home, drinks, dinner, TV, lovemaking—three times a week—until, just before he laid his head on the pillow, he slipped it off and set it on the bedside table, to be picked up again the next day.

The hat wouldn't have been such an easy part of his life if everyone he encountered hadn't worn their own iron hats, including his wife and, now that they were school age, his children. The design of each was customized. His wife's, for example, was squared off to accommodate her angular skull. His children, a boy and a girl, started with half-hats that sat more lightly on their heads and wouldn't damage their developing necks. They would switch to adult versions when they reached puberty.

Behatted, the man slid easily along the grooves of his life. Yet when his daughter received her first hat and asked "Daddy, why do I have to wear this thing?" he found himself unable to articulate any reason that would make sense to an adult, let alone a five-year-old. So he fell back on the parental answer of the ages.

"Because I said so."

She persisted. "But why? Why do you say so?"

He dug himself deeper into the pit of his ridiculous response. "Because that's the way it is."

"But why?"

As she grew, his daughter's attitude grew along with her, and with her hat. Each year at the clinic, the technician would fit a new one, adjusting the calipers side to side, front to back, and jotting measurements in his little book. The man and his wife requested time off from their jobs to attend the hat fittings, time willingly granted because everyone understood and respected the gravity of this ritual. They sat together while the adjustments were calculated and a larger hat fashioned. The three of them would emerge to approving nods from other families in the waiting room admiring the new hat, which extended a few centimeters closer to his daughter's brow than the previous one, covering more of her hair.

With each passing year, it became clearer that his daughter was not falling in line. One morning, just before her thirteenth birthday, she refused to get out of bed. In an hour they were to visit the clinic for the fitting of her adult hat, a solemn but joyous occasion. Two years earlier, his son had passed this milestone with eager gravitas.

On this morning, before he knew of his daughter's defiance, the man rose early, slipped on his hat, and took extra care with his personal hygiene and dress. He stood before the full-length mirror on the back of the closet door admiring his clean-shaven cheeks, lubricated with pleasantly scented lotion, his shiny wing-tip shoes, and his still-slim figure kept in shape by regular visits to the gym—three times a week on days he wasn't having sex with his wife. And the hat, familiar, protective, a marvel of human ingenuity fulfilling its purpose of keeping at bay every insurgent thought, every bad impulse, every dark humor of the human soul and allowing him to skate along the peaceful, harmonious, and easily traveled track of his life.

Elsewhere in the house, however, life was not so harmonious. His son sat alone at the kitchen table. He would go to school while his sister and parents went for the hat fitting. The boy would celebrate with them tonight but today he had a test deemed more important than attending the fitting. There was no sign of the man's wife and daughter.

He found them in his daughter's room. His wife sat on the edge of the bed with her palm against her daughter's forehead as if checking for fever.

"She won't get up."

He suddenly remembered that long-ago day when he'd had to trot out the "because I said so," which, despite its utility and alignment with the accepted approach to answering objections, had stirred a hidden pool of discomfort located beneath the man's breastbone.

He sat beside his wife and looked down at his daughter's face. She didn't appear ill. As always, seeing someone you knew hatless, even your own adolescent daughter, was slightly unsettling. The hair sticking up every which way, the brow rising wide and vulnerable over her mud-brown eyes, the way she seemed in that moment so animal, so much part of the earth and in thrall to the base instincts and desires the hat was meant to protect against.

He would try tenderness first. Maybe she was only frightened. He'd heard some children feared switching to adult hats, feared the extra weight and the way the brim would shield their eyes. That's probably all it was. He reached under the blanket for her hand.

"What's wrong, pumpkin?" He hadn't used that endearment in years.

He began to suspect it wasn't fear but something more dire when she slithered her hand away from his, turned her wide, bare head to the wall and spat out her protest in a voice he had never heard from her.

"I'm not going to the stupid appointment and I'm sure as shit not wearing that stupid hat."

She eventually agreed to continue wearing the child-size hat and thus spared her parents the mortification of their daughter appearing hatless in public. His wife rescheduled the fitting appointment for three weeks from that disastrous morning. Surely, they would be able to talk sense into her by then.

And they tried. Oh, they tried. First, the man took her to her favorite ice-cream parlor. He ordered a super-chocolate four-scoop sundae to share. He was forced to eat most of it himself while she sat, lips sealed and eyes downcast. Her ears may have been sealed as well for all the good his reassurances did. He trotted out the *all-your-friends-are-doing-it* argument and the *you'll-be-so-unhappy-if-you-don't* argument and finally the card he had not wanted to play because it meant thinking of his little girl—his little girl!—as an adult woman, the *you'll-never-find-a-husband-if-you-don't* argument. All delivered to the lowered brim of her half-hat as she dragged a spoon through the soup of melting ice cream.

The man felt at sea, navigating a situation he had never anticipated. Luckily, there were manuals for this sort of thing. From the local library, he checked out "Counseling Wayward Children: Six Steps to Bring Them Back." Step Three suggested enlisting family members. He turned to his wife. She plied her arguments at the salon, where she took their wayward child for an afternoon of mother-daughter mani-pedis. The man knew the moment they returned, fingernails and toenails painted a subtle shade of pearl, that his wife had failed too, knew it from the defiant tilt of his daughter's head under the now-too-small hat, from the way she stalked past him silently to her room.

They tried recruiting her older brother to talk to her. "I'm sorry, Pop," he said. "I don't believe I'll have any effect on her."

Finally, with only a day left before the rescheduled appointment, the man paced the dark living room. The book's penultimate step, number five, was recommended only after all other persuasive methods had been tried. This was a grave step that might, for all its purported efficacy, result in emotional trauma to the child that could—although the manual didn't phrase it quite this way or spell out the details of the consequences—alter her for life. But they had to escalate their efforts, to implement this final attempt at persuasion, which, please God, had to work or they'd be out of viable options.

They went the next day, a Sunday, just the three of them. They left their son home. At sixteen he was old enough to stay alone and there was no reason to expose him to the depravity they were about to show her.

The potentially life-altering effects of what they were about to do consumed the man's mind as he drove the winding road through the mountains to the Settlement. On his mind, too, were visions of his daughter, like snippets spliced together for a movie trailer, of her tiny face contracted in anger as an infant, her toddler grin as she toppled an entire shelf of knick-knacks, her feet scuffing up dust as she rushed ahead during a childhood outing.

And hadn't he had moments during those carefree years before she got her first hat when the thought of covering up those sandy curls, of clapping down onto that wild and inquisitive head an object designed to keep her firmly on the track designated to her, was completely abhorrent? Hadn't he buried his nose in those curls, run his fingers through them to her vulnerable nape, kissed the naked frontal lobe?

The man shook his head now, only the slightest of movements so as not to tweak his neck under the heavy hat, and glanced in the rearview mirror. His daughter stared at the passing scenery like a sullen queen. There is nothing for me in this car, her face seemed to say. Maybe nothing for me out there, either.

The man found himself blinking back tears as the car crested the plateau where the Settlement sprawled before them.

The guide who greeted them at the gate was not much older than the man's son. He must have grown up here, the man thought because they wouldn't put a newbie in charge of greetings and tours. The guide directed the car to an expansive, empty parking lot and walked with them to a second, smaller gate. The man noticed that his wife averted her gaze from the guide's bare head, where a bush of springy hair rose like a natural hat. But his daughter never took her eyes from him.

It seemed so ordinary, like visiting the zoo or the nature preserve. The tours, the man had read in the manual, were the price the Settlers paid for being left in peace to pursue their wild and unhatted existence. They had only to stay away from everyone else, keep their barbaric ideas and pursuits to themselves, and give these scare-tours to young people who refused to be hatted at the proper time. It was sad to think of these Settlers—for they called it a Settlement and not a prison, though a prison it was, a lovely, bucolic one but a prison nonetheless—with nothing to protect them from the thoughts spilling out willy-nilly, contaminating and infecting and re-infecting them.

Their first stop was a school. From outside it looked like any school, like the school his son and daughter attended. Yet inside this school there were no neat desks, no uniformed teacher leading the children through their drills, no rows of heads bowed beneath the weight of the first half-hats. Instead, there were bright round rugs, shelves overflowing with books, and corners filled with the kinds of toys most parents put away as soon as a child began school—blocks and trucks and dolls and easels pinned with papers full of colorful drips of paint representing nothing.

The man watched his daughter's face carefully. She maintained her impassive and disinterested expression. The man, on the other hand, began feeling things he had not experienced since childhood. That pool of discomfort stirred in his chest.

They stopped at a café. Here there was no dispenser of paper numbers to keep track of who ought to be served next. No shiny coffee machine sterilized and descaled and polished each night to return it to its pristine state. No bland nutritious snacks slotted into gleaming glass cases. This café was a riot. A crowd of patrons elbowed one another to reach the counter. A proprietress took shouted orders and hustled her staff off to retrieve cups of murky brew from a tall blackened urn and to serve up ragged pastries and cakes, irregularly shaped cookies and sloppy flan, kuchen and pfeffernusse—treats reserved for only the most special occasions where he came from. Wisely, the guide did not usher them inside. They looked in from the doorway, close enough to smell burnt sugar and observe the chaos but not close enough to be swept up in it. Although maybe, the man thought, his daughter needed a bit of chaos to jostle her to her senses.

Not until they arrived at the third location, an office building housing the Settlement's newest corporation did the man begin to experience an alarming rumbling under his iron hat.

"This facility just opened. They're in the millinery business. That means"—the guide paused to pull the glass door open— "they make hats."

The building's exterior was modest brick. But inside was an insurrection of color, the lobby walls decorated with hats of every hue, size, and shape. Vermillion and chartreuse and umber, violet and ultramarine. Square, round, oval. Tall and short, made of felt and velvet, tulle and corduroy, fleece and denim. But not a one made of iron.

The man snuck a glance at his daughter's face and saw, for the first time since this debacle began, a glimmer in her eyes.

And the sounds! As they made their way past half-open doors labeled "Director of Creative Development" and "Chief Innovation Officer," the man heard a sound he had never once heard in his own brown-and-gray office from behind any of the well-ordered desks aligned precisely with the walls.

Laughter.

The laughter followed them and reverberated under his hat. A mild panic hammered in the man's chest. Wasn't the hat supposed to protect against the contaminating impulses of other people, these possibly damaging ideas, sensations, emotions, and beliefs? And yet here he was, walking alongside his entranced daughter, infected by laughter. Even his wife seemed to be feeling something out of the ordinary.

"Excuse me," he said to the guide. "I have to ask. Is there some change you've made here to . . . to disable our hats?"

The guide waited for a cascade of giggles to die down from the innovation room. "Of course not," he said. "They're functioning just as they always have."

According to the manual, the Settlement visit was supposed to scare kids straight within twenty-four hours, obviating the need for the final step. But his daughter remained as recalcitrant as ever. His wife rescheduled the fitting appointment yet again, pleading illness. They had to keep this one. The hat fitters did not look kindly on repeated rescheduling.

At home, his daughter went hatless, though she agreed to wear her too-small hat in public. That wouldn't work much longer. Anyone could see she was more woman now than girl with her widening hips, her breasts requiring a brassiere, her emerging cheekbones.

The man sat in bed with the manual open on his knees. There it was: Step Six. The step no one wanted to have to take. The last, drastic, nothing-left-to-lose step. Just reading about it made him sweat.

He handed the manual to his wife. "I can't tell you about it. Read it for yourself."

He watched as she did, saw her skin blanch and her mouth go slack, her eyes widen and her fists clench.

"I had no idea," she whispered. "Did you?"

"No."

She removed her hat. "I've been thinking."

"Thinking?"

"She never does things by halves, does she?" Without waiting for acknowledgment, his wife gently lifted the man's hat from his head and set it beside hers on the bedside table. "Let's discuss our options."

In the end, they let her go. They told everyone she had run away.

"She was always a wayward girl," they explained. "A bad seed. We never could keep her on the path. We tried everything. We woke up one day and she was gone."

And their friends—their upstanding friends with newly behatted children on the paths to the best universities and the brightest futures—nodded in empathy, or sympathy, or whatever passed for such emotions because of course, the hats prevented them from having any idea of how the man and his wife felt.

Late at night, when the man lay beside his wife trying to sleep, he would feel a tingle of energy crackling between their two minds and wonder how they had ever managed to fall in love from under their hats, and wonder further at the miracle that they turned out, hatless, to be so much alike. And as he stared at the ceiling, counting sheep, he thanked goodness for his own iron hat covering and encasing the wayward thoughts he increasingly entertained about his daughter, his admiration for her refusal to fit in, his awe at her singularity of purpose and her courage in defying her parents. He relived in his mind, and was glad the hat prevented anyone from sensing that he did, her final goodbye—for it would have to be final, since no contact was allowed with the Settlers for any reason other than to arrange a scare-tour—at the gate, where his daughter, hatless and smiling, pressed herself against him for longer than he would have expected and whispered so only he could hear.

Poetry

Abigail George

Carson McCullers

I will always love music, she said to me. Turned her
face away and became a sad ghost like all the people
that I have loved in my life. The sad ghost, dead snakes,
the religious, the ordered hide mischief in plain sight.

The geranium has a tongue and the sky appears to be
falling. The moon walks wider now. It curls up. The
red-haired sun does not know how to travel lightly in
summer. She swoons. She will fall at your feet if you
remove articles of your clothing. I travel light in these
heavy years. Waving earlier to the good women who
pass me by. With their white teeth and their sweet
breath. Bread to the soul. And the wind is sunburnt from
the form and shape of the river, to the whine of the dog.

Through mountains fall childish things. If I perish,
there will be signs of the Saviour's return. It has often
crossed my mind just for the fun of it, but where is the
challenge in that if not to compound the negative, the
silent psychological framework around the country of
my tongue? What instead of pushing the envelope, I just

concentrated on the arc of writing and perfecting crafting
the perfect short story. And from hell to eternity, there
is a memoir of madness. I read wildness in the headlines.

The mining of diversity come with us welcoming the
tigers and parading them at the zoo. In front of the ill
winter sun's fabric of bone tied to the soul of the universe.

Sibling, the second daughter, Heidi in the mountains,
your arms are bare. They are like trees searching for the
hidden flesh of a vulture that has all the culture in the
world. With their lungs smiling with roots. I melt the
blue sky. I remember your petals of blood. I remember
your fire engine red lipstick. Oracle, my wish is that the paper
tiger empress takes her strange anguish to the ward, with
all of her potential. I know how a heart can grow cold.

I know you. You're winter asleep in the back. And I dream
of the goals I had in my twenties, oh, I only wanted to
write. But I did not want to live in isolation. And I am a
woman hard at work at discovering herself, her purpose.

The stain of carrion on my lips. The river gives me the
silent treatment. It is green. I can't see my reflection
though. Perhaps it is because I too am a sad ghost. I can't
let go of the difficulties of the piggy jasmine, and how it does
not grow anymore the way it used to. I can't let go of the
milk of life, and the substitutes that taste like honey, and
there's an illusion found in everything. I just cannot let go
of the solitude. The weeping in the morning just before
I get out of bed. This feeling of losing control. Of not being
in control. And then the man is all I can think of. I am afraid
he is going to leave me. They always do, for I am too sad.

There's action in the swarm. And all the bee does is simply
remove oppression. And so, I live in the poverty of the

nightfall. I cannot bear to live anywhere else. This is a
palace compared to the other places that I have lived in life.

John Updike

He writes. He writes. He writes. He writes. And it feels
as if he is writing to me. There's the letting go of sadness,
the letting go of emptiness, of the swamp ape in the land.

Lines written after communion, and as I write this, I am
aware of growing older, men growing colder. And this
afternoon, the dust of it, the milky warmth of it loose like
flowers upon me fastening their hold on me, removes the
oppression that I know from all of life. Youth is no longer
on my side. The bloom of youth. Wasteland has become a
part of my identity. I am a bird. A rejected starling. To age
sometimes feels as if you are moving epic mountains. Valleys
that sing with the force of winds, human beings, the sun.

And he is beautiful. And he is kind. And he is the man facing
loneliness, and the emptiness of the day. And I am the woman
facing loneliness, and the emptiness of the day. But how
can you be lonely if you are surrounded by so many people.

I want to be those people, if only to be in your presence a
little while longer. Death is gorgeous, but life is even more so.

I have become weary of fighting wars. Of the threshold of
waiting. And so, I let go of solitude at the beach. I see my mother's
face in every horizon. She is my sun. And the man makes
a path where there is no path before. The minority of the day
longs for power. The light reckons it has more sway over
the clouds. And there's ecstasy in the shark, in his heart with
a head full of winter. Freedom is his mother tongue lost in

translation of the being of the trinity. Tender is the night.

The clock strains itself. Its forward motion. Its song. Its lull during the figuring of the daylight. He's my knight but he doesn't know it. He makes me forget about my grief, loss, my loss, the measure of my grief. Driftwood comes to the beach and lays there like a beached whale. Not stirring, but like some autumn life, something about life is resurrected again, and the powerful hands of the sea become my own. Between the grass and the men, there is an innocent logic. I don't talk to anyone, and no one talks to me. It is Tuesday. Late. I think you can see the despair in my eyes. The kiss of hardship in my hands. It always comes back to that, doesn't it somehow. The hands The hands. The hands. Symbolic of something, or other it seems.

Wednesday morning. It is early. After twelve in the morning, and I can't sleep. For the life of me I can't sleep. Between the two of us, he's the teacher. There is a singing sound in his voice.

I don't know why I can't read his mind anymore. There's confusion in forgetting that becomes a secret. Almost a contract between two people. And when I think of him, I think of love and Brazil, love and couples. And there's a silent call from a remote kind of land, and ignorance is a cold shroud. Some things are born helpless in a world of assembled images, and how quickly some people go mad with grief (like me), dream of grief (like me), sleep with grief on their heart (like me). Speak to me before all speech is gone. This image, or perhaps another.

His face is made up of invisible threads. Each more handsome than the last. And my face becomes, turns into the face of love.

The Trio

Nick Sweeney

Of the men in the trio, one managed a hardware store, another was a supervisor in a factory producing plastic parts for light fittings, and the other a print shop proofer. Their white collars were discolored, verging on frayed, their shirt cuffs grubby, though they had to have a Sunday best at home. They were men out of old magazines and black-and-white movies, from a different time, I sometimes thought, yet there they came, swanning into mine. Every Tuesday, Wednesday and Thursday, they converged on a corner on the edge of the industrial district, where three roads met, then, without pausing, marched into our little restaurant.

"Never call it a diner," Dad warned me, a long time before I set foot in there to work. "It's a restaurant."

But with a cook, and not a chef, and no espresso machine, it can't even be called a café; it's a diner. There's nothing wrong with that. In our ad in the local rag, it says we serve 'good, honest, home-cooked food'. Those commas are the loudest items on the page. It's not too off-the-mark to say I'm ashamed of them, the way they herald that adjective that doesn't apply to food: food—*honest*? How? The word *good* says it all; if food is good, people will like it. I hate it when people say, "Oh, we had this *delicious* meal." Sure *it was delicious*, I want to yell at them. Or, "Oh, it was tasty, tasty . . . very very *tasty*." *Of course it was*. If you're starving, you'll eat things that rot and things that wriggle—but that's not what we're talking about; it's the reporting of it I take issue with. If food isn't delicious and tasty, I say don't even mention it.

And *home-cooked—seriously?* I reminded Dad that if people wanted home-cooked food, they'd stay home and cook it, wouldn't come to our . . . *restaurant* to eat. He thought I was being *challenging*. In the background, Mom counseled me with a shake of her head.

Our food is stodge, savoury or sweet, full of calories that burn in active bodies and stagnate in those whose only movement is to go to eateries and, eventually, to dentists. It's good; Dad had that part right. One out of three, at the end of the day, is not *so* bad.

The trio always ordered the same food. For hardware man, who smelt all paraffin and wire wool and cardboard, it was tripe. Plastics man, under his layer of synthetic dust, went for liver, any kind. And kidneys for print man. I once heard him attest that printing ink was, technically, edible, what with the air full of it where he worked. It also filled his hair, and nails, and the lines around his eyes. Their food was accompanied by mashed potato, and the vegetable of the day, a graying green of cauliflower, cabbage, string beans or, sometimes, the somewhat mystifying *greens*, that I called, if I were feeling mischievous, *grays*. None of them ever noticed.

All three had dirty fingernails. I heard Mom say once that she thought they would be the kind of men who washed 'below the waist' at least once a month. I could never work out whether she approved of that or not. All of them maintained a humorless look on their faces. All talked in a practiced way that gave me the feeling that, although they heard what was said, they never listened; each utterance was greeted with faces that looked expectant, but only of giving an answer that had been long formulated in all their conversations down the years, recalled, and pulled out whenever it was needed.

They liked their offal for the strength of it, I suppose, but they never savored it. Down it went, mechanically, forgotten at once, in the times between their turns to talk.

As they spent their only free hour together three times a week, they had to be great pals. Yet they seemed to regard one another—and me, their charming, eager server—with the detachment with which they'd inspect an order of garden fork handles, the calibration of machines churning out a million perfectly identical light fittings, or the fine details that made up a print spread, with its crying, leaping commas.

Contentment settled over them only when their plates had been cleared, and they were waiting for their milky coffee. With a bit of theatrical after-youing, they each took a toothpick from the ceramic pot on the table, adopted an air of concentration, and set to picking their teeth.

When freed, the blobs of food hit the window. They hit the walls. They hit the floor, and gleamed on its tiles. They stuck to the edges of tables. They decorated salt and pepper shakers, the ones I polished every evening till they shone. They were launched onto the collars and sleeves of customers nearby. The gaps in those men's teeth had to have been the size of warehouses.

Only when the excavations were finished did the men let out their sighs of pleasure, the only signs that they were enjoying their lunch hour. The ritual was not quite over: their ease was capped with their attention to the used toothpicks. I never saw any signal given, but, in unison, they broke their picks, one as exactly in the center as he could, another carefully inserting joints into his with a black-ridged thumbnail and not breaking it, just making it into a longbow shape, and the other breaking off only the pointed ends, each seemingly oblivious of the others' handiwork. At another unheralded point in these proceedings they would look at me, as if challenging me to ask what they were doing, just so they could say, "You won't be putting *them* back in the pot." Like we would. They're cheap as air, for a start—cheaper, in fact. And Dad doesn't care about denuded pine forests or bare mountains in Scandinavia; he buys toothpicks by the truckload.

I asked them to refrain, from the careless picking, not from the breaking. The one whose turn it was to pay would look at me as if I were speaking in tongues, and pass me the check, and, as was the habit in the trio, the exact money, with a rising, strongly-voiced "Thank *you*." Dad had sent our cook, Nino, to ask them to shield their mouths when they picked. She had stood over them, broad tattooed arms folded, her tone even and patient. The one paying that day had avoided Nino's dark eyes, looked around her, and signaled to me, passing the check, and that annoyingly exact sum. Dad had asked them. They had looked at him, sized him up and slotted him into the hierarchy they saw: a man who furnishes diner food for money, nothing else. One of them had pressed the check and the money due into his hand, and looked through him.

"It's the only part of their meal they enjoy," I said to Dad. About to protest at this affront to his home-cooked, honest, good food, he was perturbed into silence at the revelation. I hoped it wouldn't pitch him into the mood that trapped him sometimes—which ended up in his doubting his entire existence, and that of history itself—and said quickly, "I got an idea."

Dad looked at me, mouth open in scorn, a finger raised. He listened to me with half an ear, but that was all I needed. I'd called Nino, and we'd huddled, and plotted.

Next day was Thursday. The men came in. I took their orders and handed the copy in to the kitchen. Nino's face appeared at the service hatch. She was nearly smiling. This was a woman who never forgot any of the numerous indignities and absurdities that had befallen her and her ancestors in the place she called the Soviet Onion, and never smiled. I nodded. She turned back, and nodded to Dad. Soon, she beckoned me to the hatch.

I picked up two of the plates, the tripe, and the liver, and brought them to hardware man and plastics man. When I brought the kidneys to print shop man, I also brought them all new salt and pepper shakers, both shining. They ignored me, as usual, until they saw that I had also brought a new pot of toothpicks. Their talking stopped, for a few seconds, and forkfuls of food were paused in front of them. Their gazes shifted to those perfect spikes of pine. Then they resumed their meal.

I usually never heard what they were talking about. This day, they mentioned a rice factory in San Saba, Italy, the use of baskets on ropes to deliver shopping to infirm, or just lazy, people who lived in the upper stories of apartment blocks in the Middle East, a holy hermit who lived on a pillar and had his food sent up to him the same way, and a man who bit off a chicken's head for a dare and ended up paralyzed with some crazy disease found only in raw chickens, in an enzyme released at the point of trauma. I couldn't work out how any of this hung together. I didn't care. I saw the trio without seeing them, almost, my eyes flicking between the cash register, my pad, and the other diners.

The trio got the food and the talk out of the way. The men no longer looked at one another. They went into a study of post-prandial indulgence, like cats stretching before a fire, not caring about anything in the imperfect world around them.

I watched them openly now from the cash register, because they were too absorbed at this stage of their meal to be aware of anything else. Dad's and Nino's faces filled the hatch, Dad's lips slightly wet, Nino maintaining the even line of the grim Soviet smile that hid her metal false teeth.

The trio, their eyes hooded as if to shield the world from their favourite part of their hour, picked their teeth. The food flew. We saw it in mid-air, spinning, arcing, or straight as an arrow, before it settled in the usual places.

The whites of their eyes bulged. Their mouths stayed open. Their fingernails whitened. A toothpick snapped, prematurely, in the hardware man's grip, and he let out a low moan. The print shop manager dropped his toothpick and added his own tone. The plastics man took it up a click. They were a musical trio: they made a chord, one of those odd ones I could never remember from my abandoned piano lessons, and turned it into a discord. The other customers, distracted, noted the unearthly music, looked at one another a little uncomfortably in a second of stillness and silence, then resumed their food and talk.

The men got up, chairs flying and falling, hands to their mouths. One of them pulled money out of his pockets on his way to the door, and threw it in my direction. I caught some of it in my apron, bent for the rest, and picked it up and counted it, put some in the cash register, and placed the surplus into the tip jar.

They didn't even take the time to break their toothpicks. As usual, we wouldn't be reusing them anyhow. *Had* we been in the habit of such a reprehensible thing, we definitely wouldn't have reused these ones.

Dad nearly smiled. Nino showed a centimetre of teeth the colour of guns. I looked past her into the kitchen, and the jar that sat on the counter, in which I'd marinated the toothpicks overnight. I didn't know for certain what was in it, but had noted it in the back of the cleaning cupboard for years. It had a skull-and—bones on it, and the stark words *Danger—Highly Corrosive*. Nino picked it up and placed it gingerly into the crusher, and daintily operated the foot switch, made the unit whirr, thrum with protest, throw up a little glass dust, and then gulp. Pulling on protective gloves, I stepped over to the trio's abandoned table, and added the discarded picks to the pot. I handed the lot to Nino, and she did her magic again, emptied the toothpicks without handling them, and threw the pot in after them, making them into dust and air.

I cleared the men's plates, and used a cloth to get rid of their other mess from the window, the floor tiles, the table top and, as discreetly as I could, from the shirt collar of a little pot-bellied man all done up in a summer-weight three-piece suit, talking to his willowy secretary as if he were addressing a public meeting.

The trio hurried along the road, hands flapping, or held up to their faces. They tottered, and almost tumbled, into the reception of the nearest dentist. I knew this because, along with Dad, I followed them.

The receptionist showed her lovely white teeth in a very professional smile.

They pointed to their faces, but their movement, and noise, was put on pause as they looked at the receptionist. What they saw was a version of me. They must have wondered for seconds whether they'd really made that painful journey down the road, or whether by some awful time-warp sorcery they were still in our so-called restaurant. One of the men let out a moan. Another joined in. The third completed their awful chord.

They were looking at my twin. She was only identical on the surface. When she was eleven, she walked smack into the door that at that time bisected our hallway, its glass thin and clear as a summer day, not a speck on it nor a mark, nor even the hint of a reflection. She had been fixed on something so intently that she hadn't seen the door; maddeningly, the shattering impact had cleared her mind of whatever it had been that was so important. I sometimes thought she would never get on with her life till she remembered what it was. Now me, I would never be so preoccupied with one single thing; I drive myself crazy by trying to see everything at the same time. Back in our hallway all those years before, my sis had stood, silent, and framed in wood, and had bled. When we found her, there were shards in her head, chest, hands and thighs, and she was the whitest creature any of us had ever seen, bolt upright in a pool of blood, a hand raised as if to ward off helpers in case they broke her concentration. She was Saint Sebastian, contemplating the power of momentum, and the reward for inattentiveness, and carelessness.

My twin was in a deep sleep for weeks, fed through tubes—bad, *dis*honest food, I suppose, and not cooked in a home, but in a lab. When she left the hospital, she moved slowly, and examined the minutest details of her surroundings before she committed herself to any action at all.

When my twin was twelve, my mum bought a blue budgerigar, and caged it. My sister hated the background noise it persisted in supplying; it was the irregularity of it, she told the psychiatrist: if it had hummed a continuous note—impossible, of course—or chirped out the same Morse-code-steady message, pursued the repetitive, solitary behaviour of any imprisoned animal, she could have lived with it. She got a rubber spider from a joke shop, a life-size bird-eater, and put it on the cage, where it sat, its lifelike eyes paradoxically deadly, regarding the bird with the implacable contentment of the diner. Startled, the poor budgerigar fell to the floor of its little prison and, mortified, lay in its own mess. It took three days to perch again properly. It didn't have a cardiac event and die, but it never squeaked again.

I'd looked into my sister's eyes many times, and had sought empathy, sympathy, sometimes, and the legendary twins' psychic bonding. I only ever got a watchful, calculated curiosity back. I settled for it. We shared a twins' smile by day, at our respective jobs, and reverted to our own faces in the evenings.

The trio noted that smile of mine on my sister's face. They were too flustered, and too needful of attention, to do anything other than throw themselves on its mercy.

My sister said, "What seems to be the problem, gentlemen?"

Our uncle once told me and my sister that the mouth was the filthiest place in the body. Just like one of those mortified chickens with its deadly enzymes, the mouth was full of bacteria that would kill us. We brushed our teeth diligently. We vowed never to kiss anybody. We do, of course—you have to—but it's nearly always accompanied by distaste and, just a little, terror. Our uncle is an expert. He's also my dad's identical twin. They had decided to corner two complementary markets: my dad prompts the stodge and sweets to be made, and fills mouths with bacteria, while, a short walk along the road, at his dental practice, his brother fixes them. There's terrible perfection in it, for sure.

The trio of diners crowded into the surgery's waiting room. They looked up when my uncle put his head into the room. They had one of their moments all over again, fancied they saw my dad standing there, a restauranteur, masquerading as a dentist.

"Who's first?" my uncle said.

They stared at my uncle, fingers pointing. Distracted by a not-so-discreet cough—mine—they looked at the doorway, at me and Dad fixed in place, having by then hurried through the side door. The trio looked at one another and, once again, came up with that chord of theirs, dreadful, diminished, and, yet, growing louder.

POETRY

SANJEEV SETHI

Mythomane's Truth

If we could retrofit ourselves?
I would not be me nor you, you.

Imagine me without infirmities.
I would no longer be po-faced,
pudgy and potbellied. My eyes
wouldn't swim sans Adam's ale.

If any of this gladdens your gut:
I reckon, you aren't for me.

Flux

From entanglements of existence
I'm in firmament of my own.
In roll-call of needs anamnesis
mitigates. Past is polished with
coats of one's inner complexion.

Peeps are like diaries different
page different piece: same smell.

Vision

When you unself
from a situation or skein:
you deliver lavish
dividends for yourself.

Opportune distancing
mends the ache:
of the eventualities
of our exploits.

Propinquity bedims
the perspective:
leaving us to lust
after our parakeet or pelt.

William C. Crawford

Two Stories

Rachel Gonzalez

Little Black Dress

Lilia walked 7,392 steps to and from her apartment on an average day. And being a woman, Lilia was, on an average day, cat-called at a new corner. A new stoop. A new shop front. Since her body became what it was meant to be, they were there, noticing out loud.

A new man. The same bullshit.

"Ay Ma, lemme talk to you!"

"Yo Shawty! Where you goin so fast?"

"Baby Doll! I got something for you!"

Day in and day out, Lilia would leave her house in any manner of outfits—slacks, skirts, blouses, shorts, dresses, blazers, heels, flats—didn't matter. Whatever it was, she shouldn't be wearing it. Whatever she was wearing was subjected to a sordid request to the men she passed. If she was outside, she was subjected to the male gaze.

"Mami! Oh my God, you're too good to be true!"

"Sweetheart! Don't run off so quick!"

"Hey Girl! I've got what you need!"

Lilia walked on by, not turning her head or throwing up her middle finger. She didn't shout back or even glance their way. This wasn't a new phenomenon for Lilia, or really any woman in the history of the world patriarchal society. None of these men or their calls were harmless, but some had more weight to them than the others.

"Fine then! Dumb Bitch!"

"Fuck you! You're ugly anyway!"

"Nasty Ass Slut! Just keep walking!"

Lilia's head stayed high. She never wavered in one of her 7,392 steps. She didn't quicken her pace or hide from the men or their "compliments." Nothing that any of these men could say, shout or scream would scare her from living her life. She didn't let their fear control her.

Lilia knew what all of these men didn't. She understood them better than they would ever know. She knew that they were scared. She knew that women terrified them. That the sheer bombastic force that stemmed from being a woman shook them to their Y chromosomes. That the thought of the power they carry within themselves turned the minds of men into garbage and their words to compost. She knew that their words could and would rise to a crescendo of violence one day. She knew they already had for so many. Just as she walked by these men daily, she walked in step with other women. Some who were taken out of step, taken all the way down. She saw the pain on their faces as plainly as she saw the lust in the eyes of men. There was no escape from either the way things had been and how they would continue to be.

It was enough to make anyone cry behind closed doors, rage against the world with a clever sign and a crocheted hat, shut themselves off entirely in misguided self-preservation plots. But Lilia wasn't worried about the men. Her body was her own, her heart too big, mind too sharp, power too much, will unbreakable. And by the end of it all they would know that, too.

On a day just like any other, for no reason more particular than the fact that it was time, Lilia donned a very special dress. A crisp sleeveless white dress that hit her above the knee. As she took it from the hanger she imagined the face of every woman who had had hands laid on her. As she tucked her breasts and body into the bodice she saw battered and broken women, torn clothing, fractured bones, and crushed hearts. And as she slid the zipper up, what she heard were the cries of help that never seemed to reach the right ears at the right time.

With her first confident step out the door she set off for a new day in her life.

"Hey Girl, how—"

"Ooh Honey, where are—"

"Baby, you gotta—"

With each step Lilia took another voice was silenced. Another mark added to her pristine dress. With each comment from a new man's mouth, the dark smudges that made up their souls appeared on her skirt. The men of the world were withering and turning to husks as the blackness of their very beings manifested on Lilia's dress. Their poison was her power.

"Hey, Sugar—"

"Angel Face, you are—"

"Beautiful, where have—"

The bodies fell at her feet with each step. As her strides grew louder, the perfect white of her dress edged its way into deep, dark black. She tossed her hair and kept her gaze forward, stepping over whoever she needed to. Lilia walked on, well beyond her 7,392 steps, until the voices were gone completely and replaced by an all-new chorus.

"Thank you!"

"God bless you!"

"You've saved us all!"

Cries of joy filled the air. Women began flooding the streets. Wearing everything from their own skin to burkas and headscarves because they knew that the sun had set on the life they had known. They were finally free. Finally free from judgment and fear and degradation.

Lilia walked proudly, in her little black dress, as she knew that the world could finally be at peace.

"Collegiate Correspondence"

Hilda and Cameron were inseparable. True love, if anyone had ever seen it. But their happiness was jeopardized by the bursting of their high school bubble and acceptance into different universities. Their one way of seeing each other before Christmas or summer was a more than three-hour train ride on a student's income, which was only an idea to be entertained but rarely executed. With cell phones being a distant and futuristic dream, Cameron defaulted to the stuff of wartime: letters. Every morning he would hand-craft a letter to his faraway love, full of sentiment and pining.

"My dearest Hilda," he would write, "I miss you deeply. I'm proud of you for following your dream of being an engineer but can't help but wish that I had studied more or forced myself to be interested in your icky engineering classes and spared myself this heartache. I started my classes today; accounting seems like fun so far. I think it will only begin to kill me after about thirty years. I've heard that oxygen has similar effects on the human body."

These letters became part of both Hilda and Cameron's daily schedules, 500 miles apart. Every morning Cameron would wake up, pour himself some black coffee, force himself to drink it like a grownup, write the happenings of his previous day and send it off. Hilda would make her morning bagel and check her mail on her way home from class. After reading his letter, she would keep it open at her desk as she penned her response.

"My loving Cameron," she would respond, "I'm glad to know that accounting will only kill you slowly; at least this way I will have that much more time with you. So far my dream is simply hours of equations and bearded professors. I would like to just skip straight to the bridge-building, but unfortunately if I bypass the bearded professors and their equations my bridges will collapse and my dream will become a nightmare."

For four years, Cameron would send his letters to Hilda and she would respond. He never missed a day, and would sometimes send extra letters on the days that he knew the mail would be stopped or delayed.

"Hello lovely Hilda, me again," he would follow up. "I am writing you again because of the impending national holiday. Make no mistake, I am writing this as a point of pride as I am on a 527 school-day hot streak for writing you letters. It has little to do with the fact that my love for you is as deep and profound as a troubadour's poem. P.S. I recently enrolled in an English course called Exploring Romance in the Renaissance."

Every now and then, when letters wouldn't suffice, Cameron would crack open his piggy bank—which he soon realized was not economical because he would then have to spend money on a new one—and get himself a train ticket. And on these trips, Cameron would always see his Hilda standing on the platform in a smart outfit and sensible heels.

"Hello stranger," she would greet him.

Without looking away from her he would reach into his coat pocket and produce a folded piece of legal paper for Hilda to take. With a bemused smile, Hilda would unfold the note and read it to herself.

"Hello Hilda," he wrote on the train, "while you are reading this I'm standing right in front of you. Please put the letter down and embrace me, Ta-ta for now."

And so they would embrace for a good long time on that platform and speak only verbally for the rest of the trip—or, sometimes, with subtle eyebrow movements. Hilda and Cameron cherished their time together, which would only make their goodbye that much more bitter. But the very next day, the letters would continue. And on they went until on the day of Hilda's graduation, Cameron handed her one last letter.

"To my engineer love," he wrote, "congratulations on your accomplishment and please know that I am proud of you. Please also know that from now on where you go I go. Because I spent a cool grand on postage over the last four years. Yours always, Cameron."

And from that day on, for the many years of their marriage, Cameron kept that promise—and the only letters Hilda had to read were the occasional apology from their daughter when Hilda found her to be too nasty.

Poetry

Barbara Lawrence

Breaking the Silence

A boy cowers in the corner
as his mother raises a belt
high into the air.

A girl clings to her teddy bear
as Daddy enters her room
in the middle of the night.

A woman fights for her life
as a stranger drags her
into a vacant alley.

So many voices

Silent.

One voice pierces the darkness,
coaxes courage.

A second voice emerges
from the shadows

then another

then another . . .

An angry choir swells:

No longer will we
remain silent.

No longer will we hide
in secrecy, shame, and fear.

Tonight is the night we shout

NO MORE! NO MORE!

Hypervigilance

She surfs the edge of dreams

dares not sleep too deep

the Bogeyman lurks
in every shadow

eager to tear
flesh from bone.

Snap of twig
outside the window

she bolts up
grasps the knife
beneath her pillow

heart racing
ears tuned
eyes search darkness.

No one's there
she tells herself,
curls down to sleep

knife in one hand
teddy bear in the other.

Prisoner No More

You sentenced me

my shackles
fear
hate
shame
self-loathing

resentment, memories
of pain inflicted
bind me to you.

I drag my chains
heavy with despair
rusted with tears

long to be set free.

Blame burns my mind.
I cannot, will not forget,
yet my heart seeks peace.

Liberation lies within.
No lock can withstand
the force of forgiveness.

I alone hold the key.

Scar

She'd forgotten you were there,
tucked between vertebrae T-8 and T-9

the memory of you brought to mind
by her lover's inquisitive touch.

He traced your circumference
near-perfect circle
barely the size of a nickel

branded into her back
by a man who would not
understand

NO!
really did mean
NO!

as he grated her body
against the carpet.

What's this scar from?
her lover asks.

I forget, she says

spoons his body
imagines her cremation—

imagines your edges
curling in on themselves
like flaming parchment.

Vampire

You were a malevolent spirit,
drawn to the purity of youth
as if it were blood.

Driven by instinct,
you sucked my last drop

of innocence.

My vitality flowed
through your veins

as you turned me into the undead.

Kung Fu Crack Baby

A Novel Excerpt

John Reedburg

Editor's Note: We featured John's story back in 2020 when it was still just a short story. It has since blossomed into a novel and we are happy to hear the news! This is an excerpt from his published, award-winning book, *Cracks of Light*.

My elementary school was an off-white graffiti spectacle of a building that looked like it was a semester or two from dying of old age. Walking down the halls made me feel I'd become swallowed alive, passing down into the belly of a fire-breathing dragon until defecated into my 4th-grade class that smelled like urine. I hated going to school. My mother was a drug addict who only made sure I went so she could get a welfare check. While most kids went to learn, I went to have a hot meal. It would have been nice to live like Richie Rich with a robot maid that prepared food and protected you from bullies. Though my reality wouldn't allow me to be a cartoon. I was Demetrius Deontay Jordan, the weirdest boy at school.

I didn't have any friends.

Older kids called me "Kung Fu Crack Baby," all because my mother took drugs and my favorite kicks were a pair of holey karate shoes that were two sizes too big. The best part of my wardrobe was a black Member's Only jacket that smelled like Old Spice, cigarettes, and cocoa butter that Momma bought from the secondhand store. A day never went by without me being clowned for wearing hand-me-down clothes. Considered a nerd because I was into karate movies and pro-wrestling, Hulk Hogan and Randy "Macho Man" Savage were my favorite wrestlers. I was into Bruce Lee because I thought he was badass and made funny noises whenever he fought.

I liked Hulk because he never backed down from an opponent, no matter how big they were, while Macho Man always screamed cool things to the audience. My favorite karate movies were the *Last Dragon*, *The Karate Kid*, and any film that starred Bruce Lee.

Last Dragon was about Leroy Green, a kid in the ghetto who trained to attain the same level of mastery as the great Bruce Lee, *my hero*. Then one night, his life changes forever when he rescues a famous television personality named Laura Charles. *The Karate Kid* was a movie about a teenager named Daniel, who was bullied until he stood up and fought for himself. Leroy and Daniel were like me, social outcasts who didn't have friends. I aspired to be like them and the heroes I looked up to. It was the only way I could get through school.

I had a hard time outside the classroom. Teachers were never around when I was being bullied.

Once, when it was time for lunch, I followed the smell of chocolate milk and country burgers into the cafeteria. Big fat cricket teeth Tommy and his crew of sixth-grade bullies pushed their way through the line I was standing in. They were shouting and surrounding me.

Tommy snarled, "You're not allowed to eat here, Kung Fu Crack Baby!"

"Leave me alone," I said.

Tommy pushed me to the ground. "Get out of my line, skinny punk!"

I fell to the floor. Tommy laughed, "That's what you get."

My voice trembled; it couldn't conceal the pain, "Why you do that?"

"Because I can," Tommy said. "I don't want you in my line." As I was still laying on the floor, Tommy looked down at me with a smug look on his face, smirking, and standing over me.

Tommy bullied me every day because he knew I was too small to fight back. If he wasn't pranking me and calling me names, he was punching me or pushing me to the ground whenever he saw me.

I even had a Hulk Hogan doll he took from me one day at recess. When I got it back, the doll's head was ripped off, and its limbs were pulled out of their sockets. Another time he stole my backpack and threw my homework all over the playground. I was too afraid to get revenge, but this time in the cafeteria, I was fed up.

Enough was enough; I was tired of being picked on; it would be the last time Wide Shorts even pushed me or made fun of me. I knew that day would be the day things happened a little differently than usual.

I was a small nine-year-old who didn't care if that jiggly Dumbo-eared lazy eyed bucktooth fool Tommy from special ed was almost 13. I had fantasies about kicking his ass, though being half his size and never having fought before, I probably couldn't bust a grape in a fruit fight.

I had a fantasy about a wrestling match between Tommy and me. It was a square-off that was identical to the war between Hulk Hogan and Andre the Giant where I played the Hulkster, and Big Drawers was the other fellow.

In the first match, Hogan stood up to Andre, even though the giant was much bigger and stronger, at one point beating up his smaller opponent. Hulk held his ground, picked up the Giant, and slammed him to the mat, pinning and defeating him.

In the bout that happened in my head, I did the same thing as Hogan, except I did it faster and better and ring girls were kissing me on the cheeks and saying that they loved me. The audience was cheering and chanting my name.

Tommy would get up from off the mat and sneak up behind me, while the ladies and a roaring crowd still adored me. The women would think I was so suave. I would be smoother than LL Cool J in his "I Need Love" music video, minus his muscles, gold chain, moist lips, and Kangol hat.

While one of the ring girls wiped their lipstick from my cheek, Tommy got closer. I sensed it and moved the ladies out of the way and flung him against the ropes. He bounced off them and ran back towards me. I threw him into a turnbuckle, came over to him, and unloaded several elbows to his frontal lobe and kisser.

The crowd yelled, "Finish him!"

Dazed, Tommy stumbled out into the center of the fight-circle.

It was the perfect time to deliver that front kick to his face. He fell to the mat, belly up with a bleeding forehead in all its gore and glory.

Spectators egged me on. They wanted me to perform a bigger and better move.

They continually shouted, "Leg, drop!"

I obliged by leaping upward, hoisting, and kicking out my leg, while in midair, tightening my quadriceps with as much pressure as I could.

A split second later, I came down hard on his throat with the rear of my calf.

BAM!

I finished Tommy with one of Hogan's signature moves.

I stood in the ring, celebrating and posing for the fans. I even had a slogan where I said, "Whatcha' going to do when Demetrius runs wild on you!"

Then one day, in the real world, I was holding my lunch tray, looking for a seat, when suddenly, I was on the ground. Wiping myself off from the spatters of hamburger, ketchup, and salad stuck to my clothing, I stood to look Tommy right in the eye.

"I'm tired of you picking on me, Fat Boy!" I shouted.

"Don't call me fat, you little four-eyed motherfucker! I'm not fat. I'm big-boned."

"Yeah, your bones are big. Just like your ass!" I yelled. Everyone laughed, even a few members of his crew. Tommy pointed at my feet.

"Get out of here with those holey karate shoes."

"There's nothing wrong with my shoes," I said.

"Fool, please, those shoes are the only shoes your Momma can afford because that bitch is a crackhead, and you're a little crack baby."

"Forget you, Fat Boy. You don't know nothing about my Momma!"

Tommy got more in my face. By now, all the kids in the lunchroom had formed a circle around us.

"I know your momma is on crack because my daddy is the dope man who sells it to her!" Tommy continued ragging on me. "I always see her walk up to him on the corner. She probably smokes it with your bony ass!"

"You don't even know what you are talking about, stupid."

"What makes me a liar, Crack Boy?!"

"Because my Momma is not on crack. She's on heroin!" I said.

The entire lunchroom erupted in laughter.

Tommy stood in front of me, dumbfounded. I couldn't tell if he wanted to laugh or hit me, but either way, I was prepared.

Not only as a wrestling fan but also as a connoisseur of martial arts movies, who would practice karate in his head, I had the perfect move saved for someone like Tommy. The move was a kicking technique called "The Butterfly" I saw in the film *The Karate Kid*. The main character Daniel got into a fighting stance, by balancing himself on one foot with both of his arms to the side moments before performing a targeted kick to his opponent's face bringing him down. I knew if Tommy attacked me, I could make that move happen. I got in my stance.

"Prepare to die!" I said. Tommy had his warning.

Even though I was mimicking a fight move from *The Karate Kid*, everything I said sounded like something Bruce Lee would say in one of his overdubbed films. I guess I had been watching too much Kung Fu Theater.

I spoke with an Asian accent, trying my best to emulate Bruce.

"My body is a lethal weapon, my fat fine fluffy friend. Any enemy that attacks me will succumb to a terrible defeat and die; I am the grandest of all grandmasters. I must warn you. My martial art is my war. If you come any closer, you will experience the wrath of my butterfly. This technique is as beautiful as it is deadly. It'll make you die a thousand deaths." I sounded crazy as cat shit.

Tommy looked at me and said, "This little nigga's crazy."

"No one's crazy, fat boy, I am just one with the wind," I said.

Focused, more comfortable, standing in my pose, I took a deep breath and exhaled. If the fight that was about to happen were a scene in a karate movie, this would be the part of the film where I glow like Bruce Lee in *Last Dragon*. I was ready to strike.

"Come get this whooping! My foot must become one with your behind."

Ole' fatty fat moved in close to pounce.

Still standing in my stance, I executed the kick. Except I didn't hit my target. Instead, my shoe flew off and hit the school principal, Dr. Jackson, in the face as he headed over towards us. Jackson, a balding man with a receding hairline that complemented the longish dried-out Jheri curl he sported with his frequently worn pin-striped polyester suits. Funny thing is that he reminded me of Leroy's archenemy Shonuff in *Last Dragon*. Shonuff was an evil Kung Fu Master who gave the protagonist a hard time. So, when my shoe struck the principal's face, it was a score for Leroy and a blow to all bullies.

But as usual, when I came back to reality. Everything wasn't the way I imagined.

All the kids were laughing. Dr. Jackson now stood in front of me and Tommy, sneering, fuming, and growling under his breath in his Jamaican accent. The only thing I could say was, "Sorry." But that wasn't going to cut it.

Dr. Jackson replied waving his finger at me. "You, little one, your tail in serious trouble, boy. Bring forth yourself, and the overgrown big one. Him no still be in as much trouble as you. Back home, they would make you find your stick. Then beat you under a plantain tree with it."

I wish I could've stopped my shoe from coming off. But the funniest part is that despite envisioning myself in a scene from *Last Dragon* and performing a kick from *The Karate Kid,* I had a moment where I saw myself as a wrestler yelling from the top buckle inside the fight circle after a match, pointing to the audience and celebrating my victory. Though in reality, kids were standing around, watching me scream, flexing my scrawny muscles in the middle of the cafeteria like, "Demetrius the Conqueror is now your champion. I'm a bad man." I held my make-believe belt in the air, yelling out for the next challenger, "Who else wants some of this whoop ass?" Dr. Jackson came over, pulled me by the arm and yanked me out of my dream. "Come here, you fool." Holding Tommy with his other hand, he dragged us in tow to his office. I tried to pull away, but Jackson was too strong.

"Stop! Dr. Jackson, I have another move I saw Bruce Lee do it in *The Chinese Connection."*

"Small one, the fight's over, and you're too black to be Chinese."

Tommy blurted, "Dr. Jackson, it wasn't my fault."

"Yeah, it was," I said. "You're always picking on me."

"Oh, I see," Jackson noted. "We'll figure it all out once we get to the office," he confirmed, still pulling us along as we argued.

Sounding innocent as he could, Tommy spewed out another tale, hoping Jackson would believe him. "Demetrius pushed me to the ground, and he talked bad about my mother."

I refused to let that to ride. "He's not telling the truth, Dr. Jackson. He's the one who started everything."

"I know little one." Jackson looked over at Tommy, smirking, "Big one, mon. I don't believe you. Your lies are bigger than the size of your pants. Maybe, if your mother didn't feed you so much, you wouldn't be so large for your britches."

"But I'm not lying. That little punk pushed me," Tommy said.

"Child, I was born at night, not last night. That little one, he don't push a big mon like you. Hush up with your tales, boy, or they come haunt you. Understand? Off to the office you both still come."

As Tommy and I were being hauled away to Jackson's office, Tommy looked over at me and uttered the words, "I hate you."

"I hate you, too," I said back.

It was the last time I ever got picked on.

Poetry

Keith Kennedy

Too Busy for Suicide

I'm awfully sorry to be awful
It was the camera – you see it, in the corner

I was afraid that if I didn't fall in line
They'd make me wear a rose-colored shirt
They'd make me kill my family

So I said what they wanted to hear
I told them of your discretions, making sure
Not to elaborate too far, so they
Didn't find out what horrible things you've done
To my ass, in my mouth, while the others watched

They are sorry, too, for doing what they had to.

When Pink Was Heart

I craved your body like a mind
No matter where the dead birds fell

I changed my course to walk behind
I stared at skin 'till I grew blind

And when
you dressed
I felt
the flames
of Hell

To watch your exit, so content
Was horror that I couldn't quell
To know your sweat, your devil-scent
Was to lose myself, trapped by the swell

Signal With Your Mouth to Me

My heart is akin
Come what may
To touching the skin
Day by day

And when your answer passes by
Is it not my right to cry?

Is it not my sin to shout?
When your angers pass you out?

And when the crimes of nature free
The poison of the lending lout
Turn your head, your mouth to me

Call me down from on my high

Is it not my game to lie?

Is it not my shame to doubt?
Is it not your ploy to pout?

And when the hearts of terror flee
The fear of futures turning out
Turn your head, your mouth to me

Warded

Insomniacs like to prey on the undying
Like slaughtered dreams of scalped pseudo-dragons flying
Build your protections
Collect your acts of crying

Women like to dress up their dominant sections
As bulbous, reddened access points of discretion
Contained with your vice
Let them halve your erections

Many men will inquire once, but never twice
To taste a spoonful of pie, not yet the whole slice
Women like collars
Men prefer to act as mice

So what are you as you holler?
What calls one toward the soulless dollar?
Should you call her?
Will they maul her?

The Colors Collude

The decision of validity has nothing but contempt for your eyes
These meager displays of vision are lost on the finer artisans
There are things far beneath your control, above your notice
They want nothing more than to hurt you, make you feel inadequate
But you must crouch and hurt your stiffened back to sink to
Their level—the motes and the dirt, the Cradle of Creation—is low
Easier to keep that back straight, and tidy the souls once you
get home.

The Party

William Torphy

It was the architect and the gun moll who captured my attention. The party was a casual industry event held in the Hollywood Hills at the home of a producer, one in fact who had bankrolled a film I'd worked on once, though all my ideas for it were rejected in favor of chase scenes and revenge murders. I was a screenwriter who had yet to see any credits on screen. I hadn't worked for over a year and needed to hustle a project, any project, very soon.

I was out of sorts when I arrived since my wife Jen announced at the last minute that she needed some quiet 'me-time' that evening. She did, however, take time to dress me for the affair. Tight black jeans that were squeezing my balls. A fifty-dollar T-shirt a size too small that cut into my underarms. A tailored green cashmere sport coat that made me look like a string bean.

I'd been invited through a friend of a friend of a colleague, someone I'd never met but hoped to identify so I wouldn't be standing alone in a corner with a drink in my hand. Not that I hadn't a great deal of experience feeling isolated at industry events, but it never ceased to be awkward just the same.

I meandered through the producer's gargantuan digs, one of those steroidal glass and multi-level affairs, passing insiders making deals and players going through their various mating rituals. The guest bedrooms and bathrooms (there must have been a dozen of each) were filling up like Noah's Ark. I recognized a couple of B-list, or let's be honest, C-list actors, surrounded by the usual hangers-on. I thought I recognized a writer I'd spent long hours with, lobbing lines across a walnut table. No such luck. He turned out to be a makeup artist on the make.

I'd almost given up finding someone simpatico when I spotted them standing together, whispering in one another's ears. I assumed they were a couple despite their extreme contrast in style. They weren't flirting or looking as if they were trying to impress one another, but maintained an easy alliance while exchanging comments and nodding their heads knowingly. Given his brown tweed jacket, with elbow patches no less, I took him for an academic or possibly an architect. The woman was a striking blonde with an affirmative, almost aggressive stance. She was poured into a sleek, tight white sheath, reminding me of certain durable female stars from the 1930s—Stanwyck, Harlow, Davis, Crawford. I'm always creating film characters in my head, so I mentally named her "the gun moll."

I grabbed a second drink from a passing waiter, made eye contact and sidled up to them to introduce myself: "Hello, I'm Boyce Johnson."

The man's handshake was firm but non-threatening. "Carter Spencer."

The gun moll's grip was surprisingly strong and assured, a woman trying to make herself remembered. "I'm Lauren." Neither of them wore wedding rings.

"I wondered if you were an architect," I said, avoiding gaping at his baggy sport coat.

He opened his mouth to reply, but Lauren interrupted. "As a matter of fact, Carter designed this house."

"I'm impressed. It's quite the place."

She gazed directly into my eyes. "Are you in the industry?" Her lips were painted a deep red, almost purple. I realized that she was a bottle blonde which only burnished her retro-attractiveness.

"I'm a screenwriter." I'd long ago given up telling people that I was working on a novel, a tired cliché. "Currently between projects."

She gave me a wry smile. "So, you're out of work, then."

"I'm exploring my options while taking care of our daughter. My wife is an attorney."

Lauren glanced at Spencer warily. "What kind of an attorney?"

"One who works."

She laughed. "I like your modesty, a rare attribute in this town."

"Don't get me wrong. I've worked on a number of films, the last one bankrolled by our host. It grossed $300 million before global distribution." It had been a sequel to a sequel which was being followed by another sequel.

"As a matter of fact, Lauren and I are looking for a writer," declared Spencer. "We've secured financing—"

"For a documentary," interrupted Lauren. "A project—" she hesitated as if consulting Spencer "—on mid-century architecture in LA."

The party's increasingly raucous activity swirled around us and her companion eagerly broke in. "You know, Neutra's house in Silver Lake, Wright's Hollyhock House, Schindler's studio in West Hollywood. Jock Peters' interior for the old Bullocks department store on Wilshire."

Lauren arched her eyebrows. "Maybe not the kind of thing you like to work on?"

A documentary could be just the thing to pull me out of my creative doldrums, or at least help pay the mortgage. Jen had been paying our bills for months.

My only experience with architecture had been some construction work between college semesters one summer. I was fired for being a "pussy." Too weak to toss sixty-pound bags of concrete material off a truck. Bumping into other workers while carrying lumber. Climbing the scaffolding too slowly and using too many strokes to hammer nails.

"Architecture is one of my passions," I said, finishing off my drink.

"Then you're just the man we've been searching for," purred Lauren. She moved in closer, enveloping me with the woodsy scent of her perfume. I couldn't take my eyes off her wide, full, sensuous lips. They seemed to have a life of their own, communicating even when she wasn't speaking.

Spencer gazed at her conspiratorially. "Lauren wears the pants in the family, so whatever she says, goes." I decided that I didn't like him. I suppose I was jealous that he had ravaged those full lips with his own thin ones.

Lauren gave me a sideways look that I took for a seductive pass. "Let's drink to our project," We ambushed a waiter for champagne and raised our glasses while glimpsing at one another through the rims. Lauren gave me an enticing smile. I involuntarily licked my lips and felt my pants tightening at my groin. I loved Jen, certainly believed that I did, but there's nothing like a few drinks at a party in the Hills to tug at the libido.

I offered Lauren my card, hoping my 818- area code in the Valley wouldn't put her off. She promised that we'd get together soon. They would call me. As they dashed to the door, I saw our host approaching. A corpulent man with an asymmetric haircut, sidled up to me.

"I've seen you on the lot." It wasn't screen credit but at least he recognized me. "I trust you're enjoying my little party."

"Yes. Your house is amazing. I just met the architect." The words flew out of my mouth.

He emitted a throaty, gin-infused guffaw. "They're professional party crashers. He sells cars. She works at the Lingerie House in the Beverly Center. They saw me coming. That's why they left in a hurry."

My mouth must have dropped.

"Don't take it personally. Everyone in Hollywood lies."

I couldn't argue. I lied too, on that night and plenty of other times. To impress. To get work. To get laid. We were all pretenders of one sort or another in this town, everyone concocting fictions in our ambition to make good.

Driving home, I began to formulate a screenplay that might finally get me those credits. A noir thriller that takes place in the 1950s. Two grifters—he's a writer, she's a gun moll—discover the body of an architect murdered at a Hollywood hilltop estate. Implicated in the crime, they're forced to go on the run and she turns to him for comfort.

Four Flash Fictions

Arya F. Jenkins

"The Trouble with Sisters"

My sister called me, dying of embarrassment. Apparently, her landlord had a plumber working in the basement, unscrewing the pipes that led to her kitchen sink as there was low water pressure. When she went downstairs to greet her date, the foulest odor greeted her.

"What is that, John," she called down to her landlord just as she opened the door to greet her date.

"Vomit. The pipes are full of it."

"'You're turning so red,' he says to me," Janelle said, referring to her date. "I might as well have worn a sign—bulimic here."

"I thought you were over that shit. You were bulimic when you were 12," I said.

"Everybody does it. I'm 24, dating a guy I like. It's the way I diet."

"You won't be saying that to me from the hospital bed when your insides stop functioning."

"Oh stop."

"So what's the problem."

"I was humiliated, that's all."

"So now your landlord knows, and your date—what's his name?"

"Jennifer."

"Jennifer!"

"He's transitioning. His name is Jackson now. I don't know why I said Jennifer. That's just his birth name."

"OK, so Jackson knows too. And you're handling it, apparently."

"Well, yeah, but it was soo embarrassing."

"Not embarrassing enough for you to stop, I guess. Have—you—stopped?"

"Pretty much."

Humiliation did the trick, huh."

Thanks. I was calling you for sympathy."

"I'm sorry. Really. Pretty soon you'll get used to not throwing up after you eat. Who throws up in the sink anyway?"

"I do/did. It's quicker than running to the bathroom. Anyway, it's not throwing up, it's regurgitating."

"Never mind. Sorry, I asked. So, congratulations. Can I congratulate you on getting over being bulimic, for now?"

"Yes, you can. But I'm desperate."

"What's wrong?"

"I look like a cow. Keeping all my food down is turning me into a cow. Stop laughing. I can tell you are."

"No, I'm not."

"I can hear it in your voice. You are."

"Sorry. Maybe, what's-his-name, Jackson, likes big women."

"He does."

"So what's the problem?"

"What if we break up? I'll be a fat girl without a boyfriend."

"Oh my god. You are not there yet, Janelle."

"But that's all I think about."

"Getting dumped?"

"Yes."

"Do you like him?"

"Yeah, I do. He's sexy."

"Do you believe him when he tells you he likes big women?"

"He can't keep his hands off me."

"I swear to god, Janelle—what—then—is—the problem?"

"He might get tired of me."

"Oh-my-god. I'm hanging up now. There's someone at the door."

"No, there isn't. I'm your sister and I need you."

"I'm telling you I have to go. Take it one day at a time. I love you."

"OK. Where are you going?"

"Across the street for a pint of Ben & Jerry's. I just have about five more pounds I need to put on."

"My Little Brown Book"

Down the street, the salty rainy street of yesterday where all the better days are, the better than today days, and even tomorrows, down that street is where you find her posed under a streetlight, not trying to be Lady Day or whatever but still with a flower in her hair. Her sideways glance lets you know she is what you have been waiting for.

You've been trying to get away from yourself, not caring about much, and here she is, she who knows where you've been, having been lost herself.

Her bright eyes see through you, enticing and alarming at once so when she holds out a cigarette, head tilting a little as if listening, you ignite its tip, your hand trembling a little. Breeze flutters the hem of her pale dress, which brushes your pants' leg, and after lighting up yourself, you stroll with her to the sidewalk corner, neither of you speaking as light rain begins to fall coating her bare arms with a sheen, pressing on the brim of your fedora like a cotton hand. Then she tells you her name—Lola.

"There's a club that way. Would you like to have a drink with me—Lola."

"Why, yes. I would. I know that club well." Swish swish. Blow.

Night goes down with you into the basement bar, nestling against its brick walls, circling coolly around seats and tables. On the small stage, a curly-haired youth plays bass, eyes fixed far away. A mustachioed drummer marches his sticks precisely and briskly across a set of drumheads. The pianist, his glasses foggy with smoke from a dangling cigarette, hunches over the keyboard, shoulders on a slant like he's afraid or on edge, delivering flawlessly.

The room expands with smoke. By the time your seltzer on the rocks and her wine cooler arrive all the tables are filled and the band amps up competing with the din of voices.

You smile a little at her, noting her half-closed eyes, always a good sign—someone who listens inside instead of fixating on the stand. This time, you make a show of lighting her up, as if your extended lighter had the power to ignite her tenderness. Her right hand encircles yours, telling you how it is, *nothing beyond now, so stay if you will, or go.*

When the trio breaks and everyone around you keeps talking, all you want is to remain in your mood letting smoke spill your truth, speak for you as if it alone could tell your story, open the door to some kinder place, even imagined, where hope lingers in spite of you.

There was a wife once and a little girl when you were on top of the world. Now you are an anomaly, a sober ad guy writing copy for an agency that keeps you on, long as you stay off the stuff, the reputation of a drunk who trashed his office the night his family left him having preceded you.

What keeps you going is not what happened then but what may come still. In the hotel room where flashing neon is the only constant, you scratch out tunes in a little brown book you tuck afterward next to a Bible in a nightstand drawer, sometimes imagining the accompanying music. Even though you can't write music, the melodies still come to you.

You ask what she does for a living as if this was required, a rule by which to abide because really all you want is to hear music.

"I type during the day. And sing from time to time." Her head motions towards the musicians. "What do you do, Max?"

You tell her.

"Any songs you recall?" When the waiter leaves, you lean toward her, reciting the words to the tune you can't set down:

Don't you know I'm that fool who

Left all he had for a better you

Now she's gone too

And here I am

Nowhere else to go but still I

Dream of you and

Whisper in your ear

Of sunny days in yesteryear

When life was grand

"That's nice. Again." Her contralto adds sexy, silky variations, and you find yourself nodding at her as you both nodded before at the musicians.

When the trio returns, Lola identifies each one. Their familiar names will stay with you longer than she or even the dream you invent for her, nestling along with favorite tunes in the cracks of bricks surrounding you like beautiful secrets.

"Married"

I saw my friend Alma, a gorgeous Latina who had kind of disappeared from our circle since getting married a few years back. We were at the IGA.

"Hey, Alma. It's been ages."

"Oh hi, Gigi (kiss, kiss). How are you, how have you been?"

"I'm fine. Seeing someone new. Two months. We'll see. Last time I saw you, you were pregnant with this guy." I nodded toward the plump kid of about five with spiked hair busy feeling up Snickers bars beside his mother, opposite the check out counter.

"No, Augustus, no. We're on a diet, remember?"

"Congratulations, again," I said.

"On?"

"I see you're expecting again."

"Actually, I'm not."

"Oh. I'm sorry. So sorry. It must be the angle. I could have sworn you said—"

"No worries. I have packed on about 20 pounds since I gave birth to this one. Fifteen hours in labor. That's it for me. Done. And done. Not worth it."

"I see. You were so eager to have a baby too."

"I was. I was."

"He's a sweet-looking kid."

"Looks just like me, and is just like his father. Hmm."

"Well, it's great to see you, Alma. Stay in touch. Let me know if you and—what's your husband's name again?"

"Max."

"Maybe you and Max want to join us on poker night. We go pretty heavy on the Cosmos too."

"Haha. Sweet dreams on that one. He's never home. I'll go solo though."

"Great. Come as you are. You have my number."

"The same?"

"Yes."

"I look forward to it. We can pretend to be single again."

"Whatever You Desire"

When they are together, her nose turns up automatically at everything he says, her head turning to observe passersby or leaves quavering on a tree, incidentals, he, the point from which she departs to engage in everything. This is how it almost always is.

He has no idea, even while cultivating his fevered impulse to draw her in, make her look into his eyes, respond to the hand holding hers as he inquires what she would like to eat and drink—life's menu, always at her disposal, proffered by him.

His drone of words tickles their fecundity. Everything so green. He has never seen her more beautiful, wearing the ring he gave her, a diamond perhaps too large. But what is love, if not extravagant?

She demurs at his suggestion for the wine, then lets him choose her appetizer and entrée. This makes him smile. He knows her, and she, in turn, appreciates being able to settle into the cushion of the life he is creating for her with such dexterity and ease. From time to time, she observes the meticulous hands, sure and precise slicing, raising up modest bites, and his eyelashes, so long and graceful, highlighting his pale demeanor.

It has occurred to her he is too beautiful. Even in bed, his considerations sometimes set her aback. She has never known a man so eager to wait, so generous and vast in his longing. With him, from the beginning, there was an interior sigh, a knowing of the kindness waiting, an awareness she would always be sated.

Even so, she sighs at the extraordinary overhanging foliage, the beauty of those nearby also dining, the perfection of their meal arriving in stages on plates, brilliantly white, reflecting all the surrounding splendor. Sighs at him across from her, neat in his Brooks Brothers suit and horizontally striped tie, his white shirt competing with the immaculate tablecloth. "Is it all right," he inquires after they have toasted and drunk and he has poured yet more into her glass.

"It's quite good," aware of the rarity and cost of the spiced delicacy passing down, aware too of her bare shoulders on this night serving as a kind of beacon for the gentleman over there, smoking a cigar, for example. His wife or mistress has left the table and he gazes at her, boldly removing her dress with amber eyes so she can feel it. She takes another sip of wine, trying to still her trembling hand as she tips the large glass to her mouth.

When the woman returns, a brunette, only slightly older than her, wearing an expensive bracelet and matching necklace, he turns to her and says something, then touches the napkin on his lap to one corner of his mouth and abandons it on his seat. As he heads towards them, his eyes fix on her, one hand running slowly through his gray hair.

Fabrice Poussin "Duel"

Poetry

Madison Culpepper

Even Aphrodite Has Lazy Days

I apologize for the days
I don't wear make-up
or dress in tight gowns,
and for the days I don't try
to seduce a man to feel worthy.

I used to bathe myself
in lavender to attract men.
Right now, I'm tired and alone.
My confidence wilts
when I don't plaster my face
with a glow brighter than the sun.

Today, I'm lying beneath blankets
in nothing but sweats and skin.
My hair is tied into a bun,
purple scoops under my eyes.
I wish a man could see that
even without my highlight
I'm still beautiful.

Most days, I may appear
like the pink sunsets
pouring into violet streams.
But beneath the gloss and glow
and goddess sheen,
I'm just a woman, a person.
Someone who is more than vanity.
And with my face bare,
I hope my soul can finally shine,
lilac light blooming freely through
my skin after all this time.

Citrus Grief

Rows of oranges
make a masterpiece
in the grocery aisle.
When I smell citrus
I think of her,
eating juicy slices
before her next concert.

I didn't think
I would love fruit
so much
until she died.
I grab an orange,
feel its little dimples,
the softness beneath
its hard shell.
Who knew something
so small

could be so vibrant.

A whole soul enclosed
in a wholesome orange from
the market downtown.
If only she was here,
breathing,
singing,
sucking on citrus slices,
and I wasn't staring
at a piece of fruit.
But I buy the orange,
hold it in the palm
of my hand because
I can't hold her.

To Whom It May Concern

Claire Sartin

I am dressed my best to do it, if that helps: a classy dress with large floral black and white print that falls just below my knees. It is strapless with a sweetheart neckline, the kind that looks good on everyone. I must have bought the dress for a special occasion, but I found it shoved in the back of my closet, unworn, tags still attached. The dress makes it appear less meaningless.

I didn't know of my attacker until after it happened. I didn't even realize it had happened until months later. When I woke up there was just one man standing by the bed. I heard a variety of beeps all around me and a faint consistent ticking sound that seemed to be coming either from right below my head or inside my ear. I opened my eyes and stared up at a white ceiling, trying to remember where I was. Nothing came to me, but no sense of fear clenched my chest. Glancing around I saw that the man by my bed, who looked very young, was dressed in a nurse's uniform. He had a clipboard and was jotting down numbers from a machine. As it clicked in my head, right in time with the still present ticking, that these were my vitals, the young nurse turned, saw my eyes were open and sprinted out of my room. For a moment I was left alone in what I now knew was a hospital room with just the beeps of the machines and the soft ticking. Then a whole fleet of doctors came flooding in, surrounding me with their starched white coats and stethoscopes. They chattered to themselves, mostly in words I barely recognized as English, drowning out both the beeps and the ticks. Apparently, I was a medical marvel.

My procedure was the first of its kind, extremely experimental. They didn't fully explain it to me until a few weeks after I woke up. In their medically professional opinions I shouldn't have been told earlier because the information could have shocked me and sent me back into a comatose state.

My brain is half metal. It is not visible on the outside—well, except for the fact that when I woke up my head was shaved and my skull covered in scars. It was the only option they had, and it had a very slim chance of being successful, but I had no chance of survival without it. I still don't fully understand the science, or mechanics, behind my own brain. The simplest way I can explain it, and comprehend it myself, is that I am a cyborg. However, against almost every stereotype, it doesn't make me any smarter. I can't do astoundingly complex math problems in a short period of time, nor can I go days without sleep and still function at peak mental performance. In fact, I think the procedure actually made me stupider. Rather than memorizing every minute, concise detail that comes within my line of vision or earshot, I lost most of my memories. I don't remember any of my childhood. Don't feel bad for me though, I'm not upset about it so there is no need for you to be.

The doctors and psychologists told me that I should be able to return to normal life in a couple months. They had to keep me under surveillance for so long to make sure that the wires weren't going to malfunction or go haywire. They also had to make sure I still had my motor skills and normal bodily functions. There are only a few things I wasn't able to do. I can't write in cursive, I struggle to cut some food, and I cannot pick my own nose. My nurses had to help me blow my nose or use one of those little booger suckers that are designed for infants for the particularly difficult obstructions in my nostrils.

My family, of course, came to help me in the healing process. However, I found out that my dad was killed in a car accident when I was a teenager, and I was an only child, so really just my mother came to help. She tried to tell me stories about my younger years, but I didn't pay much attention. I don't miss the memories, so why tell me some boring story about a middle-class family that didn't have anything spectacular happen to them. What I listened to didn't sound like a bad childhood; it just wasn't exciting.

When I was finally released from the hospital my mother tried to get me to come live with her, but I told her no. I remembered that I had an apartment of my own, and I wanted to go back to it. I wasn't sure exactly where it was, but I still wanted to try to resume my old life.

My doctor-prescribed therapist said it wasn't best for me to hear the story of my accident right away. She said I could hear it once I had fully recovered, and she would narrate it to me in increments so it wouldn't be too overwhelming. I had absolutely no memory of what had happened to me, so during the first story-telling session, the third actual session of therapy, I didn't know what to expect. I thought maybe I had been shot in the head, or had fallen from a great height and my head smashed against a tree or rock on the way down.

As it turns out, nature can be a vicious thing. I had been attacked by a bird. Because of one bird I was now a metalhead. My attacker was a Loggerhead Shrike. This species of bird isn't even that rare. It is just a small creature that no one ever talks about. The first day the therapist began telling my story, all she did was inform me about this little bird. It has the nickname "raptor without talons." She showed me a picture of the Shrike, and I felt no hatred towards it. No surge of loathing came up through my torso as I saw the small bird who, according to the therapist, forever disrupted my path of life. It has a white underbelly, gray back, black on its wings, and a black mask. This little bird eats its food by capturing it in its beak and then impaling it on some sort of spike, like a thorn or barbed wire. Usually, the bird eats insects, lizards and small mammals. I guess my Shrike was either feeling especially brave or hungry enough to come after a human.

After three sessions of storytelling with the therapist, we got to the climax of my story. She replayed bits and pieces of the news report done about my incident. Based on the reports of the people witnessing the natural phenomenon, my shrike had been watching me for a while, tracking me. When I was in the ideal spot, near a grove of rocks, some of which were pointed and sharp, the bird flew at me, fluttering in my face and pecking at my skull. I screamed and tried to protect myself, but the bird was too persistent. My skull was already bleeding profusely before I hit the rocks. According to the doctors, I was unconscious before my head hit. The bird must have pecked enough of my head to cause me to pass out. After I had hit the rocks, the bird continued to peck at my flesh, eating me. Several onlookers had filmed the incident on their phones once they realized something significant was occurring, but my therapist deemed this footage too traumatic for me to see at that point in my recovery. However, I could assume it was quite graphic and bloody, but not even picturing the image of all that blood triggered any sort of sadness, self-pity, or repulsion.

As my therapist told me my whole near fatal experience, I didn't react at all. She thought I was going into shock, but I really felt nothing. I sat in her office silent; when she stopped asking questions and trying to soothe me, I could hear the faint ticking that always accompanied me. I realized that this was my story, and that it had been my brains splattered across the rocks, and my skin that the bird was devouring, but I didn't feel sad, scared, distressed, disgusted. I didn't feel any emotions towards it. I tried to explain this to my therapist, but she just kept telling me that I was in shock and kept trying to prescribe medicine to make me feel better. But I didn't feel bad. I didn't feel anything.

I hadn't felt anything since I had woken up in that hospital bed with the nurse staring at me in surprise and then running out of the room. The doctors had come rushing in with excitement, panic and intrigue written all over their faces. Everyone else had been overflowing with emotion, but I stayed a blank slate.

I quit going to my therapist after I heard the peak of my story. It was all going to be about my recovery after that point, and I already knew how that ended. I didn't want to know the mechanics of how they put in my brain. I know that it is all robotics. I can function normally most of the day, and if everything is really quiet I can still hear the faint ticking, which I now know comes from inside my head, not an outside source. What else did I need to know? The doctors assured me that it was waterproof, so I wouldn't fry my circuits if I took a shower or got caught in a rainstorm. I knew that if I ever experienced anything out of the ordinary it would be more beneficial to go to a computer store, rather than back to the hospital. I think a robotic brain is a little out of their area of expertise.

I began to realize there was a problem when I witnessed a little girl run into the street and get hit by a car. I just stood there and watched. Everyone on the street around me was freaking out; women were crying, men were cringing. I just stood there, feeling nothing. I wasn't sad, upset, horrified, or disgusted. I knew something wasn't right. I knew I should have had some sort of reaction. There was no way I was still in shock from my accident.

I had looked up the symptoms of shock after my therapist kept insisting I was experiencing it. Yes, I used a computer; I may have been part cyborg, but I couldn't access the internet through my brain. Since I had woken up in the hospital, I had felt none of the symptoms. I had given myself a self-examination, checking off each symptom on the list. No cold or sweaty skin that may be pale/gray, weak but rapid pulse, irregular breathing, dizziness, profuse sweating, fatigue, dilated pupils, nor nausea. All I felt was an absence of symptoms.

About a week later it was my birthday, or so my mother informed me when she sent a whole bouquet of balloons with a card telling me she was taking me out to dinner that night. I knew I should have smiled and been happy about the colorful squeaky balloons, or should have felt loved by my mother, but I didn't. I put the balloons on the table, and went to get ready for dinner. When I got back to my apartment, there were the balloons. Light from outside made them seem as if they were glowing orbs splaying colors across my kitchen walls, something that should have been an inspiring sight of beauty. I reached into the drawer nearest me and pulled out a wooden skewer and began impaling the balloons one by one. With each pop shriveled carcasses filled my skewer, becoming useless latex on a stick. I looked at the destroyed balloons, their glowing colors now dull and shriveled, and still felt nothing.

This is something I should have gone back to my therapist and talked about, but I didn't. She would try to tell me I needed medication. I didn't need anything. I wasn't depressed, because I never felt sad. I wasn't in shock, nor was I traumatized, because I never felt scared, afraid, or like the world was crashing in on me all at once. I wasn't overcome with joy or awe that the doctors were able to save my life. I wasn't angry that this had happened to me; I didn't feel indignation towards a God that had allowed this to happen. I had no emotions. I didn't feel.

The doctors had made half of my brain a robot. They might as well have made the whole thing a machine. Maybe then I wouldn't have even realized something was missing. But that real, human part of me knew that this was not the way life was supposed to be.

The human part said this wasn't living, so the mechanical part determined that there was no point in being alive.

This is why I am writing this story of myself. I chose to send it to you because at least one person should know what happened to me. As soon as I get home from mailing this manuscript, I am going to finish the shrike's job. I don't want to continue this charade of life when I am getting nothing out of it, nor am I giving anything back to those around me. I am not going to go back to the rocks where the shrike attacked me. That would be clichéd. Flashy. That's not who I am, or who I presume I once was.

So I will just put on this elegant dress, then I will impale myself. I know most people wouldn't be able to do this; they would panic and back out at the last second, but I can't feel fear. There is nothing in my way. Just know that I dressed my best to do it, if that makes it more human.

Prose Poetry/Poetry

Jennifer Judge

Every Empty Glass in the World

My daughter says that before she was alive, she was dead. It's not said for dramatic effect. She knows this in her ten-year-old way.

The signs on the church marquee say Pray for the Unborn and I think that maybe this month they don't need our prayers. It's the living I'm worried about.

How to throw away a child before it becomes a child, Jamaica Kincaid writes. Before it becomes.

I see them—the blessed pregnant—in the gynecologist's office, their partners seated next to them, one protective hand over an arm. Or their mothers there, eyes gone soft with a short-lived, teary joy.

But no one is there at 3:00 a.m., black desperation, and screams in inky night, loneliness a living thing, when there is nothing to calm the baby.

I was a snowflake swirling through the universe. I was every empty glass in the world. I was an unfinished thought, a sentence left in an almost empty drawer, a clock without hands.

The unborn don't ask to be born. We drag them into a weak-lighted world, the washed-out watery gray of tea with too much milk.

People

Always say you know what to do when your child cries, you just know, like some parent gene kicks in, the knowledge springs up in your brain like it's always been there, a priori knowledge. But that's a load of bullshit.

Watch a baby fall backwards and drop a chair on herself. You see the chair going but you can't get there in time to stop it, and you can't control the gasp that escapes you. You're not supposed to gasp, have to remain calm so that the child does. And when there's nothing, nothing, nothing that calms her after the fall—walking, talking, hugging, singing, kissing—you know your love is not strong enough now for anyone, that you are what you are, failure of a parent, and you know this is your life now.

There are things you can do better—almost everything—teaching, sewing buttons on shirts, even fucking. It's all a lie. You are helpless, helplessly out of your element and this is how you will feel until the day you die. This is how you'll feel every time she asks why she looks different than you do. Every time she asks why her mother gave her up. Every time she asks why you adopted her.

In that way, the powerlessness continues. From the December day, you cried on the kitchen floor because it was over, the infertility treatment would stop—your husband said so—to the day the adoption agency considered rejecting you to the months and months and offices and lawyers—people—deciding you are fit. People having power over you, just like the yowling almost one-year-old who spits out her food and refuses another spoon even though you know she needs, needs, needs.

Awake I Wonder What Friend I'm so Willing to Give Up

My bottom front row of teeth loose,
one drastically loose,
bloodied and almost gone.

Eternal optimist,

I reason that because of the crowd of teeth
in that bottom row
it won't be noticeable
if just one goes missing.

I also reason
(in sleep, mind you)
that a trip to the dentist
about the aforementioned tooth
would afford me an opportunity
to get my daughter's dental form
signed for school.

The loss a convenience really.

Changing a Tire

We don't make eye contact
when we speak. In fact,
I can't ever remember looking
into my mother's eyes, only away,
each person playing a song
no one else hears.
Things are no different this day.
She's called me to go around my dad.
She needs a tire changed,
will my husband do it?
Quickly? Before he returns?
By the time we get there,
the air sparks with silent anger.
Moments later my mother and I
stand near the car,
shiver in the cold, unneeded.

My husband changes the tire
while we stare at the apple tree,
splitting at its base.
It's no good, she says.
It will have to come down.
This summer, she adds.
When she asks if we can help
with the tire, I tell her no.
He has his methods.
And because I am her daughter,
I know what she's thinking:
my daughter is weak,
cowers behind her husband.
But she doesn't know
what I'm thinking,
what I've learned without her:
sometimes you need to let
someone else fix the thing

Crickets Still

Crickets still.
Despite.
Even though.

October.

And the rain.
A trickle.
And then.

Wet,

the branches.
Upswept tangle.
Hands in hair.

Single office light.

Blonde brick.
Building.
Softer than.

Other than, this.

Rain, October.
Voice breaks.
Wet leaves.

Tightrope

The thoughts we bounce our heads against:
the creek low and almost dry, signs saying
no swimming, but they mean it now,
not like the No Pets signs everyone ignored,
the cliff walls braver kids jumped from.
Midnight frustration, parts of us
still hang onto nine-months-ago anger.
It’s easier to lose our footing, to slip
on a patch of ice, arms out to steady
like a sad kind of tightrope walker.

Surgeon General's Warning

A. R. Farina

When the warning first appeared, we were already addicts. It was total and complete saturation. I never knew anyone who wasn't using although, I found out later, some people weren't. The kids who were fed free lunch used. My parents used. Hell, they were worse than anyone I knew. All the parents were terrible. There was an old jokey Public Service Announcement that came from when my grandparents were young about a kid doing drugs because he learned it from watching his dad. I saw it a few times as a meme. "I learned it from watching you, Dad!" It would be funny if it weren't so true.

The morning the warning came down, I was in school. First-period classes had just begun when the smartboard turned on. Like every other morning, Jake, the admin who read the announcements, appeared on our screens. He looked flustered and kept clearing his throat. "Excuse the (throat clear) interruption students, there is (throat clear) a very important announcement that you all need to hear (throat clear) right now. Please report to the gym. Use the restrooms before you come as no one will be excused during this announcement for any reason. First-years, (cough), please sit on the floor to ensure there will be room for everyone."

I remember it so clearly, coughs and all, because we never had everyone in the school in the same room at the same time. There wasn't room unless people sat on the gym floor and, due to issues regarding skin sensitivity and all-around chaos, everything—including pep-rallies—happened remotely. The teams and the fourth years went to the gym while the rest of us watched on the smartboards.

So that day, when we were all taken into the gym, and the first-years were forced to sit on the floor, I knew we were in for a whole bunch of bad news. News that would be so explosive, or terrible, or whatever adjective you want to fix to it that the administration was risking all the messages from first-year parents. I know there is no way in hell I would want to talk to my parents when I was a first-year. Nothing was good enough for me and everything was wrong. Honestly, I don't know who they thought I was. I wasn't anyone special. At least I didn't think so and if I didn't think so, why would anyone else?

I swung by the locker I shared with Vee. We had been locker buddies in elementary and we got along so well, we just stuck with it. I threw my Calc books in. I knew that there was no way first period was going to happen at all, so I grabbed Vee's stuff.

There was a saying I first heard in middle school history: "Trust but verify." It was a big deal back when idiots thought nuclear power should still be used for weapons. Apparently, it was a Russian proverb, but our President at the time liked to use it to make sure the Russian leader he was working with was actually doing what he said he would do. Seems funny now to think that people used to distrust the Russians. I mean, the second Russian revolution changed the way everyone sees the world. You can't keep people down like that forever.

Anyway, I loved that saying because I was always like that. When my teachers told me stuff, I double- and triple-checked. I knew that no matter what we were going to hear that day, we were going to check our feed to find out what the "real" story was. Vee, the master of all things with a mechanical brain, would get us the real information. That is just what she did.

On my way to the gym, I swung by the bathrooms. I didn't really have to go, but he made it sound like it could be an ordeal, and I didn't want to be trapped in the gym having to go and I didn't really want to have to fight my way in afterward. The lines were already long. The His line was moving pretty quickly, but the Hers and Xers lines were backed way up. I never understood why public bathrooms didn't have more room in the other two. In the His, we just all pissed in a trough. It was disgusting, but it was quick. Clearly, the other two needed more stalls but I can't think of one place on earth where that is the case. Sometimes, when people are trying to make things equal, they forget that equal does not mean the same amount. Equality isn't math.

As I sped out of the His, I saw the same faces in the other lines give me dirty looks. I just shrugged my shoulders. What could I do? We have been taught that we are born the way we are born. I was born to piss in a trough apparently. Besides, I didn't do bathroom design. I hoped to one day, not just bathroom design, but architecture.

I got in line to the gym because I wasn't worried about where I was going to sit. I knew Vee would have us covered. So, I just took my time and looked around. It was clear that no one really knew what was going on. Some first-years just sprawled out on the floor. A few others were clearly bugged and were trying to plead with the teachers. Of course, they were having none of it. Generally, the teachers were pretty scared of the administration. They knew that a few districts over they were automating high school to save resources. Because of that, they did pretty much whatever the higher-ups said. It was a form of automation anyway. Teacher bot with a pulse or teacher bot with a mechanical brain was irrelevant. Either way, they were being manipulated. There were a few, like my middle school history teacher and my high school social science teacher, who told us the truth and didn't really follow along. Of course, they were my favorite teachers. They were also the first to go when the unions were busted up, but I still have what I learned from them regardless of how things went down.

Ms. Wishaw, the superintendent, was there and she looked smug. That was strange because she normally looked disgusted to be around us. Smug was a new look for her. Her hunch was gone, and her back was ramrod straight. Her arms were crossed. She was wearing khaki everything. She could have been going on a safari. Somehow, standing up straight made her seem younger as though the years that were weighing her down were no longer there. She had a closed-mouth smile that was obviously holding in the secret of that unprecedented day. That lady hated kids, and everyone knew it. She thought we were soft. This wasn't some conspiracy theory we made up to hate on her, it was a fact. She told anyone who listened the stories of her childhood, pre-addiction, when she rode in the back of a pick-up truck not because she was being rebellious, but because her parents put her back there. It was common practice during her childhood apparently. That seems like BS to me. I suspect her parents were just trying to get rid of her and they failed. She was a Gen Xer. There weren't many of them still working, but she just hung on and refused to quit.

Mx. Wayne, the principal, dressed in xer standard black suit, white shirt, and school colored ascot, took the mic said, "Students. Settle down. I apologize to those of you who need to sit on the floor. Had we more time, we would have made sure the wrestling mats were put down, but this is very important, and we need you all to settle down and pay attention."

Really? Wrestling mats? Those things are as old as Ms. Wishaw and smell like her too. I suspect there would have been more skin sensitivity complaints if the first-years had to sit there.

Xe extended xer arms and pushed xer hands down to mimic that xe wanted us to sit down, calm down and just be down. Honestly, I have no idea how xe got the job. I have never met a person who was less built to be in charge of thousands of raging hormones. I suspect that Wishaw handpicked xer based on controllability. Again, the difference between a mechanical person and a real person was pretty slim. Plus, just like Wishaw, Mx. Wayne actually wanted the job. Xe thought it was a step up from middle-school math teacher. I don't know, I would rather try to wrangle a bunch of 12-year-olds into seats to learn basic algebra than whatever it was she had to do.

My dad thought Mx. Wayne was a minority hire who was "unqualified but has the right pronouns and skin-tone." It didn't matter that he was wrong or right because he thought that about pretty much everyone who was not him. I swear, his brain was so addled by the crap on his feed that I don't understand what my mom saw in him. I guess he was some big bleeding heart in college, but after a while, he turned into his dad and the hate monger he is. I always told Vee that if I ever started down that road, to go all Of Mice and Men on me. She always responded with, "Tell me about the rabbits again." So, I knew we were good.

Once I was done lollygagging and sightseeing, I climbed the bleachers and sat down at the top row next to Vee. She was in gym when the assembly was called, so she ran up to get "our" spots. We always sat in the top of the visitor's bleachers for every event be it academic or athletic. She discovered a crack in the faraday cage up here in the gym. We sat in the same place in the outside events too so as not to raise attention. People just thought we are weird, which may or may not be true. While Mx. Wayne tried in vain to get everyone to quiet down, Vee leaned over and asked, "You got my shit?" She wiggled her overly shaped eyebrows at me while she made grabby hands at me.

I pulled her phone and headphones out of my hoodie pocket and gave them to her. She held the phone up to scan her green eye and it unlocked for her. She stuck the left airbud in her ear and handed me the right one. I shoved it in and pulled up my hood. My buzzcut did nothing to hide contraband, but her unkempt mane of curly hair made it hard to see her face, so her ears were safe. Before she could start scrolling through our feed, Ms. Wishaw's voice came booming over the speakers. "SIT DOWN AND SHUT YOUR MOUTHS. NOW!"

My teeth rattled as we were sitting right beneath one of them. That did the trick as she knew it would. I can only imagine how many insensitivity reports would be flooding her feed once all these kids got home. I never bothered complaining too much because nothing had happened to her so far and she was the superintendent when my mom was in school. Obviously, someone thought she was doing something right or she had a file of dirty pictures of someone. Well, it was either that or the fact that she did a job no one wanted. She managed one of the last school districts in the state that had an entirely human population of teachers. It was such a nightmare job that she pretty much could do and say anything at any time and be safe.

"There is some important news from the government. Normally, we would wait and let your parents and guardians tell you this news or let it come to your feeds at the end of the day. But since only a handful of you would actually stop and listen to this . . . " she glanced up at us and I swear she could see my soul, ". . . and we simply do not trust your parents with this." There was muttering when she said that. I am not sure why anyone was shocked; she bad-mouthed our parents all the time. "SHUT YOUR MOUTHS!" That killed the murmuring.

"Now listen." She cleared her throat and pulled out a sheet of paper. Paper. She actually thought whatever-this-was was so valuable that she could waste a sheet of paper. We found out later that not only was she right to use the paper this way but that she was being proactive by getting things in writing. "The

Surgeon General of the United States has officially declared smart phones a health risk. She is clear that there is not a radiation risk. Smart phones are not carcinogens. However, 50 years of research has proven that the use of these devices can cause severe mental impairment and that overuse can have adverse physical effects. She demands that children under the age of 18 stop use of these devices immediately. She reminds us that the internet is not a problem and that computers are still accessible to all children in schools and in public libraries. She cannot stop adults from using these devices, but she wishes to express her desire for all people to immediately turn in their devices to trade-in clinics that will be open as early as this afternoon, where smart phones will be traded in for working mobile phones with texting capabilities. The President has expressed xer support of this report and will be working with Congress to enact legislation that adheres to these recommendations."

By the time she took a breath, the student body was in a panic. Everyone was whispering about the implications. A few thousand people whispering sounds like a few thousand circular saws. From our vantage point, we could see the first-years starting to move around like a swarm of insects. The kids in the bleachers were leaning forward and turning around trying to talk to their friends, to everyone and anyone. People who never spoke to each other were clamoring to be heard by anyone. I looked over to Vee, who was surprisingly calm. She was not going to believe it until she got into her feed. I wasn't too sure either, but as terrible as Wishaw was, a liar she was not.

"There is more." That knocked the wind out of the room. "While you were here, the security officers have gone through your lockers and taken your devices . . . ." The riot was inevitable, and she knew it.

Poetry

Abigail Kipp

Favorite Things

A few of my favorite things fill my head
Sunlight through green leaves dancing in the dark
Rap songs on the radio ignoring what is said
Just moving along down roads lost in the mark
Watching dancers soar wishing I was too
Silver rain on bare skin cool wet slides down
The sound of white snow falling in que
Black skirts a little too short peaceful small town
And the way you looked at me like I looked
At you lost in innocence the before
The fall when we were both completely hooked
Before we started cold trench and ash war
Moment of love I am doomed to repeat
With everyone that comes next like useless meat.

Two languages (free form)

Two languages
And I can't find the words

Crawling in my mouth
Screaming to be free

Twenty-six letters
And I can't locate
The syllables
That read
How you let go.

How do I write
When poems are all a void
A ship in disease
Brown planks falling
Into grey water.

How do I say
I love you
When I only
Have black swirls
On white ivory.

Twenty-six letters
Don't leave
Don't match
Two languages
And silence
Is my relief

Truth

Truth a silver lock
Branching over skin
A web of words
Seeping into skin

Through eggshell bone
Dragging me below
Tidal waves.
A metallic roadmap
Of ignored fact.
Malformed metal
Branching.
Screaming tendrils
Deeply rooted
And creeping down my throat
Losing all
To silver truth.

Glue

If you have glue
I have tape
We will take these ragged pieces
And make something new.

I would like a cube
A solid little box
To hide stuff away in
Paint it blue
Make it a chest
A private thing
A keep sake just for me
Memories to seal away
To smile at one day.

For you
We could make
An orb to play with
Or a diamond to hoard.

We will bend
And scrap
Pull
And sculpt
New shapes
New colors
New ways to see
Till they are just
How we want them to be
These tiny broken hearts
Of ours
All shiny and new.

Sex

Sex is a currency
I don't know the exchange rate for.
Green tentacles
Wrap around my heart
Like pale worms
Burrowing through
Discarded meat.
Crushing lungs
Like Coke cans
In a child's game
Making love to a one-night stand
The wall
Between sex and more
Is a hologram
More easily passed through
Than sunlight
But to them
A giant stone statue
Seen from miles away

A guardian
With steel sword
To protect cowards.

Blue Ribs

Can I curl up in you?
Behind your blues
Deep in the center
Surrounded by the
Engravings of what once was
You seem so inviting
A gentle hand
And maybe when
I am a child
Once again
Inside of your humanity
I will be an artist again.

Out of Time

Lucy Zhang

A ticking time bomb. Every tick a precious second lost–not preserved in Snapchat or Instagram–the memory of it cached in a few brain cells before a new memory purged space for itself. Ellen, twenty-nine years old and ticking, kept a bright pink box, the First Response Rapid Results pregnancy test, in a cabinet behind the bathroom mirror. She already wasted one test on a false-alarm missed period. After peeing on the tip, feeling the warmth of a droplet of urine on her finger, she had stood watching the test for ten minutes while her husband, Wes, stood outside the locked door to the bathroom. No pink. Safe.

Or not safe, she supposed. She and Wes had been trying for children for a few months now. *You're in the prime of fertility in your twenties*, Ellen's mother had told her. *After that, your child could have all sorts of problems. Biologically defective. More likely to miscarry.* It made sense, Ellen supposed. But women who had babies later were mainly the educated and promotion-pursuing women like Ellen, a financial analyst at Wells Fargo. She inhaled her work twelve hours a day—not with enjoyment, but rather a determination to prove that she could be technical and artsy, a full-time working adult and housewife, a woman who could discuss a veganized ice cream recipe with the same fluidity as she could politics.

"Have you ever thought about having children?" Wes had asked when they were twenty-two. It was the same formula of question. *Have you ever thought about getting a house?* Then they bought a four bedroom, two-and-a-half-bathroom house with a backyard patio and a golden delicious apple tree by the front door. *Have you ever thought about getting a cat?* They bought a pack of lint rollers and a short-haired cat. It was always during the most inopportune of times—when her mind and fingers finally synced and words flowed onto a Word document, when she already ate and used the bathroom before beginning a movie so she'd be able to watch uninterrupted–and then the calling, *Ellen can you clean out the litter box?*

"No, we're too young," Ellen had responded. And that was that. She had avoided a question that would inevitably come up again, but she still relished her short-term victory. Tick. Tock.

That night, Ellen dreamed of hidden passages behind waterfalls: a field of red, yellow, orange and white poppies, a shallow pond reflecting lavender wisteria from a tree growing on a precarious slant toward the water, a garden overrun by spider lilies. She made her way to the final passage. A singular path lay ahead, surrounded by peonies whose pink petals muted the green of the leaves and stem. How long would it take to reach the end? Four hours? Four seconds? Could her fertility take that kind of blow? Four hours lost to a walk with no end in sight, a gamble for an exit or perhaps the adventure of dragging one leg forward at a time, heel to toe, counting how many petals had been decapitated from their stem, how many this rubber sole crushed into dirt.

Ellen woke up to warm moisture between her legs. She pulled off the covers to verify the splotch of blood on her white underwear. Two months late, her period still came. Wes snored as she gently closed the bedroom door to change in the bathroom. She rinsed her underwear in the sink with laundry detergent until her fingers pruned, then hung the still slightly pink panties on a coat hanger from the shower curtain rod, almost proudly conspicuous. Wes might be upset, Ellen thought.

She stepped onto the Withings Body scale, watched the number flicker to a halt, stepped off, and then stepped on again. Maybe she needed to lose another five pounds to fully annihilate her period. She'd try skipping dinner too–a short term solution she'd only need to keep up for six more years, after which she was certain marked a woman's fertility expiration date. Then no more chances of a parasitic creature inhabiting her womb. No pink. No peonies. Please.

Blake Brasher "When Those Things Suddenly Alight"

Construction Season

Brian Moore

Shelley and Celine were halfway across the Rockies when they passed a sign beside the highway that blinked BLASTING AHEAD in angry orange letters three feet high. Blasting what? She imagined dynamite and geysers of rock cracking holes through the hearts of mountains. This was the Trans-Canada. Weren't they done with all that in the sixties?

The traffic oozed to a stop at the chin of a long valley. Campers and minivans glittered a mile down the road, around the toe of a cliff, and out of sight. No town, no stores, no houses, no exits. Not even a signalman flashing a STOP / SLOW triangle. They could be waiting a minute or an hour. She shifted to park and turned off the ignition.

The July sun puddled over the fenders. The car smelled of feet and wet clothes. She wriggled her knees away from the scald of the steering wheel and turned to the back seat where Celine's face glowed in the aura of her tablet. When the autism spiraled her daughter's anxiety into a barbed coil, the computer games calmed her.

"Celine."

"Uh-huh?"

"Mommy's stepping out. Stay here."

"I have to pee."

Shelley looked side to side. She pointed to the ditch.

"See that bush? That's Celine's bush."

"It's not clean."

"It's Mother Nature honey. Clean as it gets."

After Celine finished and dove back into the car, Shelley opened the rear hatch of the Subaru and rooted through the walled debris of luggage, toys, and junk-food wrappers. Mommy-sized SUVs lined up behind them, tinted windshields glaring down. Shelley felt a stab of guilt and ignored it. She pulled out a camp chair and a sweating ice pack. She settled in the chair, shed her flip-flops and gingerly lay her feet on the ice. The cold sang up her calves and pooled behind her eyes. Better. Much better.

This was their last chance, which sounded dramatic, but was true. Shelley explained it to Celine, slowly and calmly last night while she packed: We can't afford to live in Vancouver any longer. Not the rent or the food or the gas, let alone your medications, your therapy, your school. We're going to Edmonton. I can find work there.

What about Keith?

Daddy's gone away for a while.

Celine keened until midnight, driving her head like a piston into her special pillow bought for that purpose. Shelley's voice frayed, at the screaming edge of running from the apartment and chucking it all.

Shelley had crossed the Rockies only once, before Celine was born. Keith drove her over the rumpled bone of the continent with a hundred dollars between them, picking up odd jobs along the way, any madness possible. She had leaned against his shoulder unharnessed; her bare feet plopped on the dash like plump mushrooms. They were going to see his family in Regina to tell them the good news, a baby on the way. That night they slept in the car and in the morning made love on the beach of a lake cradled by mountains.

He made up a word she thought was only for the two of them: wildering. They were wildering through the Rockies, down lost trails, through gorges, across rivers of a bluish-green too pure and gorgeous to be real. Keith explained that the turquoise colour came from glacier melt, water that hadn't flowed since humans learned to walk. Keith was very good at beginnings then, his specialty. It was only after Celine's diagnosis, after he moved East and left Shelley with mail-in cheques, that she checked the dictionary. Wildering. Archaic. To lead astray.

Celine clambered carefully down from the car and squirmed into Shelley's lap like an abandoned puppy. So unusual for someone who did not like to be touched, whose skin is a sacred shrine to textural purity. Insect sounds zig-zagged through the grass on the other side of the road.

"I hear thunder," Celine said.

The rumble gargled in the air. Shelley remembered that lovely, dirty thrum from Keith's motorcycle phase, two cylinders percolating in a V-twin box.

A Harley Fat Boy glided down the gravel shoulder, passing all the vehicles, an obscene, chrome-sinewed beast of a machine with spoked rims and a gleaming chopper fork. The rider wore a brain bucket snugged tight on his head and a leather vest over biceps tattooed with eagles and flags and dragons. His beard was Santa-white. As the bike wheeled slowly around them, he glanced down at Shelley in her fold-up chair, at her Walmart blouse and shorts, pale legs and pink, blistered toes. He was old and ugly, a vast, leathered whale. He stared them all down, the whole parade of vacationers and truckers and commuters, in a lane of his own. Shelley stared back.

The Harley growled around the bend and disappeared. The road went silent again. Five minutes later brake lights flashed. The distant hum of engines drifted up to them.

"Are we supposed to go?" Celine asked.

The car behind them started. Questions prickled the nape of her neck. What was that woman doing? Was she asleep?

"Mom?"

"You don't really want to go to Edmonton, do you?"

"No."

Someone leaned on a horn. Then a series of horns bleating up the highway, worried about being late, about not getting ahead, about being left behind, held hostage by a stupid woman sitting in a camp chair on the road.

"What do you think, honey?"

"About what?"

"What should we do?"

Celine's forehead crinkled, concentrating. "I'd buy a motorcycle. Then I'd just ride away, like him."

Shelley tilted her head back and laughed. The sky was infinitely, splendidly cerulean in all directions. But once you got tired of mountains, there was nothing else to see. She kissed Celine on the cheek, a big, lipstick print of love, and hugged her. Celine broke free, running to the safety of the car.

Yes, she said to the sky. I want a motorcycle too.

Poetry

Julia Hwang

I. Shame eating +
the sterility of bleach =
A well-balanced breakfast?
I stuff Kit Kat wrappers in with feminine waste
and wipe my hands of chocolate
on too tight pants

II. Scream
and smash
and scream some more
and throw the vase's remains against the door
Icy water surges and deafens
I recoil into a pool of red
How shocking!
That a hand holds this much blood
That our pain could clog a drain

III. *DON'T DO IT*
Whoops
too late

I POP and SQUEEZE and SCRATCH

watching tiny pricks of blood
bloom across my face

I am bumpy, bitter ugliness

I refuse to recognize her

I dab away tears with salicylic acid

I bury her with clay

IV. I am grown
I am a woman

yet still, I hide out in bathrooms
scarfing down deli meats
wiping at my nose, sloppily

I am a girl

eavesdropping on whispers and giggles
avoiding conference calls and confrontation
drowning out crying babies, sirens wailing

catching a breath

always ashamed

still alone.

Suzy, the New Girl

Roopa Raveendran-Menon

Suzy, the new girl, and I became best friends fairly quickly. It took us around five days to be inseparable but I swear that I could have been her best pal the day she walked into the classroom.

I even remember the time—It was ten minutes to the first recess gong. Chubby Chandini had already stuffed half of the contents of her tiffin box into her mouth. I knew she had bought potato pancake—bits of yellow potato laced the little fuzz above her thin lips. I had buried my head in my textbook to swallow the loud chortle that had threatened to sneak out.

That was when Suzy had walked in.

It was hard to believe that she was wearing our dull blue and white checked uniform because she wore it so well, with the flair and grace of a diva. I gaped at her as she strutted to the bench assigned to her. It was just in front of mine. And when she sat down gently like a lady, she had enveloped me in what seemed like a cloud of a very expensive perfume—the sort my mother opened and sprinkled on herself only during special occasions, which for my folks were birthdays and anniversaries. The perfume bottles also came with an unwritten disclaimer—don't blame anyone if you get skinned alive for opening this bottle.

I leaned back and tried to distract myself. The smell of the perfume had unknowingly unscrewed unpleasant memories. I tried to focus on Suzy instead—she was nodding at something that Professor Kumar was saying, her perfect French braid swaying a little.

That evening, I noticed my mother's perfume. She smelled like pods of garlic left out to dry in the sun. I could barely eat my snack of lentil dumplings. I tried to think of Suzy, her expensive perfume, her perfect French braid and her uniquely tailored uniform and gobbled up my meal.

Day 2

"May I have your eraser?" She asked during the Arithmetic lecture, her right palm stretched out. I heard her voice for the first time. It reminded me of freshly dried laundry. Without thinking that I normally never shared my stuff with others, I placed it on her palm which was quite warm to touch. She wore flaming red nail paint. And I wondered how she got away with it. Sister Annie, the school principal frowned upon "outward embellishments" as she called it. "A young lady's only ornament is her humility and decency." Her voice, staccato and sharp, had cut through the school auditorium at our first orientation meeting. We had all grimaced at the statement.

As for Suzy, well, she never returned my eraser that day or ever. But I didn't care.

That evening, I told my mother that I would eat my snack in my room.

Day 3

The next day, during recess, I saw Suzy and her long legs leaning over the counter. She was busy looking at the snacks—there was a bag of over-fried banana chips that were an unhealthy yellow, soggy tomato sandwiches and rock-like lentil dumplings. I walked to her side and I still don't know why I did that. Perhaps it was the Eraser Sisterhood that made me.

"Hmm . . . Suzy, isn't it?" I began timidly.

"Yes. Hi, I am Suzy."

"I know you are new here so I think must tell you. Don't know if you must eat those," I said nodding at the snacks.

"But why?" Suzy had crossed her arms and a faint line appeared between her brows.

"Well, there is a tale to each and every item that you don't want to know," I whispered into her ear.

"Try me," she said, her arms still crossed.

"Well, well. There are those banana chips. Once upon a time, they were born and then they proceeded to live for a century in Bhaskar Chettan's shop down the road before being ushered into their new home, the school canteen, where they will live for another century unless and until they are eaten up by a bunch of hapless school girls . . .. "

"As for the tomato sandwich, the tomatoes, well, they were born right here, nurtured and tended to by the school and nourished by our very own septic tank. As for the dumplings . . .."

"Enough . . .. Eww . . . gross!" Suzy said before covering her mouth and rushing out of the canteen. Poor Suzy, I don't think she ever ate tomato sandwiches ever again.

Day 4

I was standing behind her at the water cooler station. She opened her water bottle, clearly some imported thing, and was about to plug it to the opening of the tap when she looked up at me and asked in a sarcastic tone "Is this water safe? Or should I wait for another of your stories?" My cheeks felt red hot and I nodded hastily.

As I was filling up my water bottle I felt some one tap me on my shoulder. It was Suzy. A large smile was plastered across her oval face.

"By the way—thanks for the stories—on everything. No one here is really friendly, except you."

I gave her an awkward smile. I had noticed too that no one in my class had really taken to her—not even the hoity toity Priscilla who made friends only with rich, smart or good-looking girls. And Suzy was a catch. At least I thought so—she had style and she looked rich. But I wasn't ready to bet on her brains yet. Only the first term results could reveal that. And there were still several months to go. I sighed and bit into my sandwich—the cucumber slices and cheese had clumped together to form a pasty mess. Uggh. I hated my mother's sandwiches.

Day 5

"Is this seat taken?" a familiar voice asked.

I looked up from my tiffin box. It was Suzy with her perfect French braid and perfect smile.

"Hello." I said, smiling weakly at her.

"Mind if I join?" she asked, tapping the chair in front of me.

"No . . . yes, I mean, please join," I mumbled awkwardly. There were sniggers from the other table. Of course, the other girls were laughing at me. They were wondering why someone as sophisticated as Suzy wanted to eat with me. Not that that thought didn't cross my mind. I always ate alone. I always had.

"So,whathaveyougothere?" Suzy asked, looking enquiringly at my sandwich.

"Sandwich. Actually, a mess called sandwich," I said with a stupid smile.

"Can I try your mess?"

"Go ahead—" I said and handed Suzy my sandwich. She finished the sandwich in two gulps.

"Wow, you must be hungry."

"No. I love the combination of cucumber and cheese. Plus, it is so homely." She said with a smile. "Go ahead and try mine—it is a roast chicken salad sandwich."

I gulped. I had heard of roast chicken sandwiches only in movies or books. In a Hamlet-like Peringavur, where we lived, roast chicken sandwiches were very hard to come by. Our only decadent pleasure here was ice cream sundaes and club sandwiches from Johnny's.

I picked the sandwich up gingerly and bit into it—it was fresh with a lot of flavor just the way sandwiches should be.

"This is yummy! This could put Johnny's out of business," I mumbled as I continued to attack the sandwich.

Suzy laughed.

"I know. My mother makes the most awesome unhomely sandwiches. They are too perfect. She makes them from scratch," Suzy said rolling her eyes.

"How about we go for a picnic tomorrow. I will get you more of my mother's sandwiches. Tomorrow is Saturday, right?" Suzy asked wiping her mouth daintily with her napkin.

"Yes, tomorrow is Saturday," I said breathlessly.

"So?"

I gulped. "You want me to come for the picnic?"

"Yes. Do you have other plans?"

I nodded with a rather violent shake of my head.

I had only one plan every Saturday: to stay cooped up in my room and out of my mother's way while she went about all her errands and shopping. As for my father, he was a house ghost, more invisible than visible. The only way I knew he existed was the overflowing laundry basket filled with his soiled clothes that appeared at the end of his business tour.

Once, of course, in a fit to socialize me, my mother had dropped me off to her friend's place who had a daughter as old as me but that didn't go well—apparently the girl found me too "dull and uncool." After that I shied away from forced socializing, preferring to stay up in my room and having a blast telling stories to myself.

The recess gong went off and Suzy jumped to her feet. "So, see you tomorrow then at the Nehru Park?"

I nodded brightly. "Do you want me to get anything?" I asked.

"Just your stories!" Suzy's eyes glowed like liquid gold.

Two weeks later

It was easy being friends with Suzy. She was a great listener and I no longer felt conscious of myself or my imagination and my tongue loosened and out tumbled my stories that spun around in my head—Suzy had freed them. So, every Saturday we would meet—Suzy with her mother's delectable sandwiches and me with my fabulous stories. And she would listen patiently, with her chin propped up by her lean arms. Her eyes would radiate with admiration and excitement while I narrated the stories. Later, we would nibble on the sandwiches and watch the sun leave an orange dribble on the sky.

By the time I reached home in time for my supper, the stars would be up, twinkling along the patch of sky that I could see from the window of the dining room. While eating the cold soup that my mother would often forget to reheat, I would think of Suzy and our Saturdays together and a warm glow would spread across my body. I would smile thinking that she brought out the best stories in me.

First month

"The Haunted Bathroom" was one such story. I had saved it for the last

Saturday of the first month. It marked our one month of friendship. And this story seemed like a fitting tribute to that occasion. It was part fiction and part real—I believed. This story took seed in my mind when I was in the third grade—they had found the body of the school nurse in the bathroom. She lay in a pool of blood with her arms slit open like a ripe pomegranate and her mouth foaming like an over worked racehorse. They found a couple of syringes in the waste bin. Rumours were that she was mixed up in something bad, something unsavory. No one ever talked about it and the matter was hushed up.

Around five days later, sometime late in the afternoon, some of the girls reported seeing a shadowy figure on the walls of the bathroom. Now, this bathroom was located at a short distance from the classrooms. It was located in a building that stood on a patch of land that was overrun with shrubs and trees and weeds. A stone pathway connected the classrooms and the bathroom. During the monsoons, the grass and shrubs around the building that housed the bathroom would grow unruly and thick, almost dwarfing the building. And on cloudy days marked by heavy rains, the place looked like a deserted forest. With more and more similar unpleasant reports trickling in, the school management decided, for the safety of its students, to shut that bathroom and relocate it to the building that housed the classrooms.

"And?" Suzy's eyes were shining.

I felt anxious too, for I had never talked about the haunted bathroom to anyone before.

"One girl from the eighth grade on a dare from her classmates had visited the bathroom once. They heard screams and never saw the girl ever again. It was as if she vanished into thin air." I wiped the perspiration that lined my chin with the back of my head.

"What happened?"

"No one knows and I guess no one ever will." I said, a little shiver passing through my body like an electric current.

"I want to see it." Suzy stood up suddenly.

"Eh? See what?"

"The old haunted bathroom."

"No way," I mumbled. The sun had already begun its descent and dusk was fast approaching. The air was rapidly filling with the twitters of birds as they got ready to roost. All of a sudden I felt queasy—I wished that I had not eaten so many sandwiches. My stomach felt bloated and heavy. But Suzy wouldn't hear any of it; she simply hoisted me to my feet and prodded me to take her to the building that housed the haunted bathroom. My legs felt like lead as we took the short cut—it was a short walk that felt very long.

We reached the building. The gate and the walls were overrun with creepers and shrubs.

"Are you sure? It is very dangerous." I tried to dissuade her.

In reply, she tore away some of the creepers that had wound around the latch and unlatched it. The gate creaked open. No one had used it in a while. I could feel my heart beating so fast that I was afraid it would pop out of my body. We made our way through the dense foliage. The sun had finally set. Darkness had descended. The ululations of the cricket pierced through the air. We walked past the shrubs and weeds and reached the clearing where the building stood. Now it was nothing but a dilapidated ruin. From a short distance we saw a little wall and beyond it saw the red tiled roof of our school. The wall was recently constructed and it had put an end to further explorations of the bathroom by any student from the school.

"Shall we turn around? It is in shambles," I said.

"Look there is some kind of a light," said Suzy.

I squinted. There was a dim beam of light at a distance.

"Come, let's see," Suzy said, dragging me. We walked up the broken steps and entered what must have been the main bathroom lobby. The beam of light was moving.

"Come, Suzy, let's go," I said. Something brushed against my cheek. My hair was on its end; suddenly two pairs of hands wound around my neck and were squeezing every breath out of my body. I tried to shout for Suzy but couldn't. A dark wave swept over me and I fainted.

When I woke up I was in the hospital bed, and I shrieked. I didn't remember what had happened. And my first thought was about Suzy.

My mother and the hospital nurse came running.

"Calm down, calm down, you are safe now." My mother said as she held my hand. Her eyes were swollen and her hair was scruffy.

"W-what exactly happened?"

"You were lucky that Mathai, the school gardener, saw you walking towards that building with the bathroom."

"Yes. Help arrived at the nick of time—otherwise we would have never found you." the nurse said checking my chart.

"Eh?" I couldn't understand what had happened. My temples throbbed and I still felt a little woozy.

"But why were you roaming around there at that hour?" My mother asked. She sounded more tired than cross.

"Suzy badly wanted to see the place and she forced me."

"Suzy who?" my mother asked.

"My friend Suzy—the new girl," I said.

"Well, there were no new admissions to your grade this year. What's wrong with you? Stories, stories, I am sick and tired of them. Please don't cook up any more stories. Enough! Now, go to sleep," my mother muttered and adjusted my blanket. Then I heard someone call out to me.

There on the corner chair was Suzy, smiling radiantly. She was wearing the same old school uniform and her perfect French braid like she always did. She was sitting on the chair and swinging her legs. Then she held her one finger to her lips, rolled her golden eyes and whispered "Sshhhh," softly.

My mother was cutting some apples and bananas.

I looked at Suzy and smiled. She really did bring out the best stories in me. And I was glad that Suzy was safe, as were my stories.

I Shipped Myself Out of Folsom

Townsend Walker

Probably ought to start with how I got there.

Driving up 395, stopped for coffee in Olancha. Tall, weathered man came into the diner, pulled up a stool like he owned the place. We started chatting—horses, construction, steel work. I'd done it all. Will Thornton had a big ranch out there in the high desert, east of the Sierras. He was looking for help and hired me on.

That's how I met his daughter Holly, not a pretty girl, but with a daddy owning fifteen hundred acres . . . I courted her, but she didn't take to me much. With Will, I was getting along real well. He liked my work, we chatted about what I'd done, what he'd done, about desert life. One day setting fence posts, he eased into talking about his daughter. Too much a stay-at-home, would never find a man in their town of 192 people. I wasn't shy about telling him I was sweet on Holly, "be happy to oblige" and he helped me convince her. We got hitched in Reno with Will and Holly's sister as witnesses.

Real soon it started not to work out. Jezus, what a lousy cook. Eggs were either runny or rocks. I made her do them over ten times 'til she got them right. And she didn't understand that if she wasn't willing to be a wife, I'd have to find action elsewhere.

Couple of months went by and she moved back to her daddy's house. In March, she filed for divorce. Will, from liking me and practically begging me to marry Holly, was now taking her side. I couldn't believe the time I'd wasted in this dump.

I told Will we needed a serious chat. We got in my truck after lunch and drove down into the Mojave. Quiet down there, only a lonely rattler and a coyote or two. We sat ourselves down on a dune, passed the whiskey, and I explained to him how it was with Holly. Stubborn cuss didn't want to hear it, got defensive about his daughter, red in the face, shoved me so's I toppled over. He stood up and then kicked me in the ribs. I pulled out my pistol and told him to kneel in front of the hole I'd dug out there the day before.

When neither of us came back to Olancha that night, the sheriff went out and scoured the countryside. Nothing. Me, I'd headed to Florida. It took seven months for a kid on a dirt bike to run across Will's bones.

That's when the Feds caught me. I didn't deny I shot him. Said we'd had a tussle and the gun went off. Unfortunately, that didn't jibe well with the hole in the back of Will's skull. So, 25 to life in Folsom. Maximum security, they boasted.

They put me in the industrial shop. Prison has contracts with companies on the outside. At the Folsom shop we made those huge exhaust fans you see in metal and paint shops. Every week, five fans shipped out.

I started planning my "ship out" the moment I got there. Had Mom send me money every month, tucked into Spanish language novels. Nothing the guards would look at.

My plan was to ship out in the bottom of the deep cowling they put around fans and pull pre-painted cardboard over me. When the guards inspected, they'd see the usual black.

Shipment Day. Super tight security. I slipped in before the fan was lifted into the truck. The forklift picked the fan up, it wobbled, shook, dropped, nearly tipped over. The cardboard slipped. Got it back, quick. Lots of activity on the dock, people yelling. Finally, the lift picked the fan up, this time, smooth, plop in the truck. I was getting out of here. Yes, I was.

But, two guards jumped up on the tail gate, one of them shone a flashlight around the inside of the cowling. "Joe, something funny about the bottom of this one."

Oh shit.

"Poke it with your club." Twenty seconds pass. The guard hit the bottom of the cowling. A thud, cardboard, not metal. "Joe, come up here, something's not right."

Beads of sweat dropped from my head. I heard them pinging off the steel. The guards must be hearing the same thing.

Outside–shouting, crashing, squealing. Two forklifts had collided. One tipped over. Sirens, down-in-place alarm. A fight erupted. Whistles, shots. The guards jumped out. Minutes, minutes, more minutes. At last, the truck driver came around, "Time to button this up." And we left.

An hour later, in a truck stop at the junction of 50 and 99, I shed my jacket with the CDCR initials. Took the metal cutters I'd stashed away and cut a hole in the roof. Out. No one looking. Hustled around to the Men's. When the truck left, I went into the diner, hopped up on a stool, got friendly with a dough-faced guy. Told him my car broke down and I'd buy him lunch and gas for a lift to Bakersfield.

Couple years later, I met Louise and we lived off her deceased husband's insurance. Didn't want the Folsom warden to forget what I'd done, so sent him a Christmas card every year.

When I read on Tuesday that my escape was going to be featured on *America's Most Wanted*, I left for England on Wednesday. Made a living doing iron work at Canary Wharf. Good work, good pay, good mates.

A year went by, Louise called me from Gatwick Airport. "I just couldn't stay away, honey." She grabbed a taxi to my apartment in Dorking and we had a most memorable afternoon. Thought I'd show her the local pub, grab a bite and a pint. We stepped out the door, two gents holding badges stood on the sidewalk. The Feds had followed my sweet stupid Louise.

San Quentin, October 1992

Poetry

Milton P. Erlich

Once

Following orders
on the battlefield,
it was kill or be killed
my sergeant said,
no different than
when he taught me
to thrust and parry
with fixed bayonet.
The young soldier
wore thick glasses
and looked a lot like
one of my classmates.
Sergeant claimed
Gooks don't belong
to the human race.
Don't ever feel sorry
for killing an enemy,
I can't forgive myself.
I look down at my finger,

ready to squeeze the trigger,
and hear my mother asking:

What has become of you?

The Marital Happiness Quotient

I Uber my way across the country
in my Hugh Hefner silk pajamas
to study happiness in marriages
of all my old friends who are still
walking and talking coherently.
Computer porn ended a few bonds
that had once bloomed like a flower.
For those that served breakfast in bed,
a lotus blossom was de rigueur for a Buddhist
notion of purity, harmony and grace.
They smiled a lot for the passion of desert,
convinced their 5 and 10 cent wedding ring
was worth every penny, showering each other
with endless words of endearment,
like "You are my one and only tootsie-wootsie!"
The crankiest couples no longer engaged
in conversations—merely ranted about
how their mates didn't listen to them.
The most miserable couples were victims
of the corrosive impact of the rusted
barbed wire of prolonged celibacy.

Uninvited Guests

If my doorbell rings, and I'm not expecting anyone,
it's almost always a visit from the Jehovah's Witnesses

who make their rounds in my neighborhood to promote
their religion, and often leave a Watchtower Magazine.
They're certain Armageddon predictions are on the way.
Only 144,000 "Anointed ones" can enter God's invisible dwelling place.
If they are correct, and I become a believer,
I can stop worrying about saving for retirement,
and contributing to 529 for my grandkid's education.
I can go back to eating at Wendy's and MacDonald's,
and will no longer shop for Christmas and Easter
or have to remember to floss my teeth.
But, if I need a blood transfusion, I can kiss my ass goodbye.

My Brand of Loneliness

is much better than your brand of loneliness.
I'm a Marlboro man, sipping a lemon Coke—
an impenetrable moat prevents anyone
from ever getting close to me.
I suffer alone in ways that haven't yet been invented.
If you knock on my door, I won't let you in.
I'm addicted to the joy of suffering—and cherish all my sorrows.
Please leave me alone.

In a Quest for Answers

After celebrating my wife's 89th birthday,
we googled a man who knows answers
to all of life's fundamental questions.
He lived far away, and parking was impossible.
I left our car alongside a moat guarding a castle.
Screeching white egrets patrolled the grounds.
A longtime hiker, I could walk around the world,

but my wife was increasingly fragile,
so we decided to hitch a ride—something
I haven't done since I hitched to college in Iowa City.
We got picked up by an 18-wheeler truckdriver—
a woman with eyes as black as explosive licorice.
Flabbergasted, at her insights, butterflies
flew out of my mouth as I marveled at her ability
to turn our lives inside-out—like an Indian Fakir
making a venomous cobra rise at his musical command.
I tried to thank her, but she drove away,
and left us resting on a bed of pheromone-scented
paperwhites, where rain never touches the ground,
on what was to become our new home married to the earth.

Water

Rob Swigart

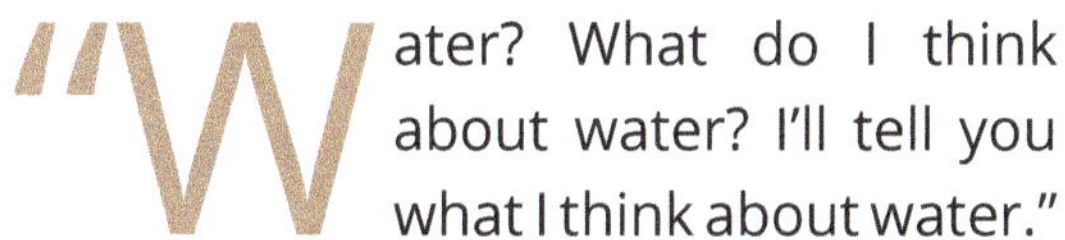

"Water? What do I think about water? I'll tell you what I think about water."

Lyman was angry.

The silence went on.

"Well?" Alford prompted. "What *do* you think about water?" He tried to keep his question flat, so as not to acknowledge Lyman's fit of pique.

"I try not to," Lyman said, at last, deflated. He put his head back and closed his eyes.

Alford did not see how this was possible. Lyman sat in it. Or rather, he lay in it. Was lying. He was lying too. Alford knew that as well.

Lyman did not try not to think about water. To try to not think about water would have meant humming meaningless jingles or reciting nursery rhymes or doing advanced algebra in his head or most likely doing nothing but think about not thinking about water, which Lyman, for one, was unprepared to do since he was lying in a large body of the stuff, a bathtub to be specific. Was surrounded and to some extent supported by it. Was made up of it to the extent of some sixty-five percent. Drank it when thirsty. Was carried to term in a sack of the stuff, along with some salts and other substances. (Babies, by the way, Lyman almost said aloud, are made up of a higher percentage of water than adults. He did not know why this should be.)

Lyman was watching crimson ribbons unravel from his wrists into the water, which was hot. It was wonderful, he did think then, how water maintained its transparency. Even when it was a gas or a vapor, it allowed sunlight to come through in just the necessary frequencies for human vision. And it was a gas, or vapor, well within the normal temperature range for life on Earth. A wonder.

The crimson ribbons were blood, of course. Lyman was probably a Roman Senator today, disgraced and dying of a surfeit of good taste. Falling on one's sword was messy, not to mention the scarcity of swords, hard to come by in this day and age.

Water also contracted when it cooled. Then, as the temperature fell towards zero degrees centigrade, it expanded again, which accounted for the extraordinary phenomenon of ice, the solid of water, actually floating. Which meant that fish could live safely through the winter beneath the frozen surface.

Nothing else did that. No, it was very difficult not to think about water. The crimson ribbons were only crimson because they contained rusty iron atoms in the hemoglobin. Mostly though, his blood was water, too. Eighty-three percent.

He stirred himself. "I'll tell you what I think, Alford."

"What do you think, Lyman?" Alford was now seated on the lid of the toilet, watching Lyman bleed to death in the tub. Steam, or condensed water vapor, hovered over the bath. Water was very good at holding heat, which is why it was so important for regulating the planet's weather.

Lyman seemed less angry now. A certain fatigue was entering his voice, perhaps because he was leaking blood. "I think," Lyman sighed. "Because I am."

"I'm not sure that's quite right, Lyman."

"Perhaps not, Alford. I won't debate the point. I will only say that if I am not, it is not likely that I will continue to think, so you could say that if I do not think, I am probably not."

"Whatever." Alford was not going to press too hard at this stage. Lyman only got to be a Roman Senator once, after all. If he was a Roman Senator. Alford couldn't remember the name of one who had actually slit his wrists and bled to death in a hot bath. Something about it seemed unlikely. All those tendons.

"There's another thing you ought to know," Lyman went on. He stopped watching the crimson ribbons and looked instead through the vapors at the ceiling. Small drops had condensed on the ceiling. One hung in a strange puckered sack for a moment before falling into the tub. When it hit the surface of the water, it created a small stalk of liquid that settled into rings. Surface tension, Lyman thought he said or said he thought, does that. Water again. And he was trying so hard.

"Another thing?"

"Peanut butter."

"Peanut butter."

"Only two percent water. Food with lowest water content. As opposed, say to diet colas, which are one hundred percent water. Another thing you may not know . . . "

Alford was growing uncomfortable. The bathroom was hot, and Lyman seemed unable to concentrate. That could be serious. The water was now a uniform crimson, or rather a watery pink. This, even Alford knew, was because of Brownian motion that jostled all the little hemoglobin molecules equally throughout. Only Lyman's head, hands, and knees rose into the mist, islands of flesh (still sixty-five percent water, though).

Alford stood at the sink, washing his hands. Water running over them, taking away millions of cells of dead skin. He didn't like to think that. "Something else."

"Herring."

"OK, herring."

"Atlantic herring, 69 percent. Pacific herring, 79 percent. Why do you think that should be?"

"How should I know?" Alford complained, drying his hands. He sat on the toilet again.

"Water," Lyman suddenly exclaimed, throwing his hands into the air. Reddish droplets sprayed around the room. "To hell with it."

He got out of the tub and began to towel himself off. "Universal damn solvent," he said, rubbing his rather prominent belly vigorously with the towel, which was aqua. "Medicines dissolve in it. Diseases dissolve in it. The stuff is everywhere. There are, Alford, some 326 million cubic miles of the stuff on this planet."

"What about your Roman Senator?"

"Not a Senator, Alford. Not a Senator. Seneca the Younger, I believe, advisor to Nero, who condemned him to death. Probably unfairly."

"He died in the bath?"

"Perhaps, perhaps. The truth here is . . . cloudy."

"But you were going out in style, Lyman. With a real flare, I have to say."

"Changed my mind."

Lyman taped his wrists and shrugged into his bathrobe. "Another day, perhaps. Plenty of time. To continue, the Antarctic ice cap contains around seven million cubic miles of fresh water. Since the world's entire supply of fresh water is 9 million 68 thousand cubic miles, you can see that most of our fresh water is frozen at the South Pole, where it won't do any of us any good. Of course, now that the ice caps are melting . . .."

He tied his belt and faced his companion. "Well, compared to the Antarctic ice cap, Alford, you and I are mere drops in the bucket."

He opened the door. "Come on, let's go get a drink. I've worked up a terrific thirst."

"I'll Be Back"

"Night Prowler"

David Morton Meyers

Poetry

Kira Rice-Christianson

Little White Lies

I started carrying around

these little white lies;

they live here on my face.

Like when I ask you a question and

your answer seems ingenuine but

I smile at you softly, anyway.

Or when I fix you a plate

and you give me your thanks,

and I kiss the side of your head.

While inside I scold

the woman who does as she's told,

though I lay with her each night in bed.

Or when you don't come home
for three nights in a row
and I lay awake cracking my knuckles and toes.
I picture her holding your body, unclothed.
The thought leaves me paranoid,
and I look through your phone.
I shouldn't have done that, now I can't sleep.
My body is filled with anxiety and heat.
I cry in my pillow, "Why can't I just leave?
I don't understand why he would do this to me."
Then comes morning, you rest your head in my lap
and you hold my hand to your cheek.
And I say nothing.
The room is silent;
another little white lie to carry with me.
Rinse and repeat.

Death by Heartbreak

You feel like if the moon and the rain fell in love.

You walk like God and laugh like my father.

But my belly is bloated with language too heavy to carry,

and the tallies on my wrists mark the heartbreaks I survived.

So I clench the bathroom sink, trying to hold myself steady,

trying to hold the world still.

Will I die of a heartbreak? Sometimes I feel like I could.

Or maybe I'll just hold myself up to this bathroom sink for a bit longer.

Just until I can catch my breath.

The Blame Game

I'm six years old and my dad stops calling. It's February 13th, I cry to my mommy, "But it's my birthday. He
always calls on my birthday." Her eyes are apologetic, mine are bloodshot. I blame her. I blame myself.

I'm nine years old and I'm having my first kiss. He's my neighbor and my best friend and it was only a peck but
I swear I'm in love. I go to school the next day and hear halls full of echoes; "Ew. Slut." I realize they are
following me. It's me.

I'm fourteen years old and I'm letting a boy convince me that he cares about me. It doesn't take much. He makes
me feel wanted for a moment and I offer him something that I think may make him stay. I lose my virginity to him
and we never speak again. I blame my father. I blame myself.

I'm seventeen years old and I have a reputation. Boys talk to me like they're picturing me naked. Teachers talk
to me like I'm stupid. I know what they all think and I let them. It's my own fault.

I'm nineteen years old and there's a stranger between my thighs. He was supposed to be my boyfriend but I don't
know this man. He says he loves me but spits in my face and steals something I can never get back. I stay silent
for four years and I still blame myself.

I'm twenty-five years old and my heart races when a man walks behind me. I don't believe anything my boyfriend
says. I smile politely when men call me "sexy." I'm terrified, I'm mortified, and I blame myself.

Flowers on the Walls

Today I taped flowers to the walls

to remind me to smile, remind me to be gentle,

remind me to focus on the beauty in this.

I know how beautiful it can all be.

So I touch you with tenderness in hopes that you'll do the same.

Tape flowers to your walls and

add my name to your stories.

There's poetry inside me and it's waiting for you.

Dewy Grass

Lay me down in the dewy grass,

let the bugs crawl in my hair, let

my lungs be filled with fresh air.

Inhale. Exhale. Rinse. Repeat.

I close my eyes and see sun,

one with my body and I think

of my daughters. Unborn.

They deserve more. Let

them live on a green grown

earth, let them bury their

hands in the dirt. Protect

them from disease,

famine, poverty,

heartache, greed.

Protect them from what we

are becoming. Or exist as

already. It's too late for me.

But let them lay their heads

down in the dewy grass.

Mother's in the Mirror, Again

It comes over me, quickly.

The heat in my face, the racing in my chest, the shakes in my hands.

I can feel the words crawling out of my throat. I'm afraid to say them but I cannot stop myself.

They projectile out of me, ripping the corners of my mouth.

I see the look on your face and I know that I am ugly.

I look in the mirror and think of my mother; the memory of her distorted face, wrinkled with the anger she could

never get a hold of.

Her tongue was sharp like mine can be.

I feel her madness in my veins.

How do I let go of it? Am I to slice my body open and bleed it all out?

Confession of an Accidental Theocrat

Montgomery Tufts

The door to Carol's bedroom swung shut behind her with a bang. The late-afternoon light streaming in through her window highlighted every wrinkle and mote of dust that had accumulated on her pantsuit over the course of her walk home from work, but she wouldn't be dealing with that now. She had come to a decision. It was one that she had been slowly working her way towards not just since she'd woken up that morning, or since the week had begun, but for one full calendar month—and it wasn't a February either. It was one of the respectable months.

"Okay, listen," she said to the figure sitting on top of the table beside her bed. "I didn't know all this would happen between us. But it did, and I love you, and I know you know that. You're everything to me. And when I fell in love with you I didn't even know I was capable of falling in love. I *thought* I was, I told myself I was, but you can't *know*, can you, until it's already happened. And so I said it out loud that first time, and it was *right*, or it felt right."

Unconsciously, Carol began to pace back and forth before the foot of their bed. "Maybe—who knows—maybe this isn't really love, the way childhood crushes weren't really love. But I hope that the thirty-year-old me, and the fifty-year-old me, and all of the other older, wiser versions of myself will be able to look at you with their own new-and-improved ideas about what love is and still say 'I love you.' Because you're somehow exactly who I want to love."

The houseplant said nothing in response. But then, it rarely did.

Carol smiled at it fondly, at this beautiful specimen of Chinese evergreen with its long, variegated leaves. Then she cringed. That, of course, hadn't been the hard part. The hard part—the decision—was to say the rest.

"Listen. I'm saying all this now because I did something I think I shouldn't have. I didn't want you to be mad, but I love you, and I can't keep hiding this."

Carol took a slow, steady breath.

"I let the kitchen become infested with ants."

The houseplant made no reply.

"Or, I didn't 'let' the kitchen become infested. I deliberately invited the ants to infest our kitchen. I infested the kitchen with ants."

She looked for some sign of rage, shock, anything—but there was nothing at all. Flustered, she began to ramble.

"I've always *wanted* ants. I couldn't tell you why, but I just knew somehow that I belonged with them, or that they belonged with me, but I didn't know how to make that *happen*. But then, a month ago, I accidentally dropped a muffin on the ground in the break room, and Francine—you remember Francine? I think I've mentioned her. With that really high-pitched, nasal voice? Anyways, I dropped the muffin, and Francine pursed her lips like the little bitch she is and squawked out 'Do you *want* ants? Because *that's* how you *get* ants!' I couldn't believe it. That's all there was to it, and no one had ever bothered to tell me before! I picked up the muffin because naturally, I didn't want ants *there*, at *work*; I wanted them at home, with me. So I stole some more muffins from the break room, and when I got back, I set them around on the kitchen floor. I wasn't sure what you'd think of all that, so I kept the bedroom door closed.

"Then, on the third day, they came. All those little scurrying legs, streaming over the muffins, each ant with a crumb held up into the air as if in gratitude—it was the most beautiful thing I had ever seen. But I still didn't tell you, maybe because I was guilty that I'd succeeded. I hadn't even told you I was trying." Carol looked down, then, avoiding the houseplant's gaze.

After a moment, she continued. "When the ants polished off the first muffins, I kept feeding them. And I started putting newspaper down underneath the food so that it wouldn't get the linoleum dirty. And every day more and more ants came, and I spent more and more time sitting on the kitchen floor, watching them. Sometimes I'd read aloud from the newspapers I'd set down underneath the food. That was where I really went wrong.

"At first I didn't notice, and then I couldn't believe it, but two weeks in or so I had to admit to myself that the ants had learned to *read*. Maybe they heard me talking and saw me looking at the newspapers and made the connection—who knows? But one day I came back from work and saw two tiny newsprint words on the floor, one right next to the other, with rough edges like they'd been torn out. They just said, 'thank' and 'large.' 'Thank, Large.' It was a touching sentiment, despite the grammar. So I found a pencil and a loose sheet of paper and wrote out a response: 'No problem. Will get more muffins tomorrow. Do you guys prefer blueberry or chocolate chip?'

"I set the note on the ground and then a group of ants converged on it. Some of them pulled over a sheet of newspaper for comparison. This went on for about half an hour until finally one of the ants chewed out a question mark from the end of a headline and dragged it to my feet. I almost stepped on the little thing, I was so insulted. My handwriting isn't *that* bad! But anyways, once I calmed down, I realized that I'd have to go to the library to type up a message and print it out. So I picked up the handwritten note and left, then came back a while later with the typed-up version, which they had *no* trouble with. The verdict was blueberry.

"But then they put together another message from the newspaper. It said 'large bring more muffins ten at least.' Can you *imagine*? You hand out a couple of muffins and then they think they own you!"

Still, the houseplant looked on silently.

Carol hesitated before she spoke again. "I . . . I squished some of them, then. *Killed* them. Just the ones that had brought over the second note. They say 'don't shoot the messenger,' but I was so angry." Tears glistened in her eyes. "I can't take that back. I can't bring *them* back."

Collecting herself with a deep breath, she continued. "I went back to the library and typed up another note: I wanted them to show some respect, I wanted them to carry their weight around here—maybe do the dishes—and I explained that I am a woman, so if they want to call me by my relative size they should really be calling me 'Largesse.' Plus I bought them a donut, one with rainbow sprinkles. I promised I'd never do something like that again.

"And . . . it worked. The ants figured out how to wash the dishes, and do our laundry, and clean the bathroom, and I brought them more and more food, and their population grew, and they composed epic poems praising my generosity, and I oversaw their funeral rituals so that the ones that passed away would travel peacefully to the next life—which is just the trash can in the bathroom, but don't tell them that. Some of them are already getting existential crises when they think about how small they are relative to the universe and we can't possibly afford therapy for all of them—anyways, before I knew it, I found that I loved them.

"Not romantically!" Carol clarified before the houseplant could object. "It's more of a general love like an artist loves their paintings, or a ruler loves their subjects, or a deity loves their worshippers. But recently . . .." She sighed, her expression growing forlorn.

"Recently, they've been cooking our meals too, and some of them have really taken to it, and now they want to go to culinary school! And I just can't let them go! I need them *here*, with me! And I don't know what to do about it anymore. I need your help. I need you."

"Bitch, you're crazy," the houseplant said at last. It laughed warmly. "But that's exactly why I married you."

Carol felt tears of relief spill out onto her cheeks and picked up the houseplant's pot, holding it tightly to her chest.

It spoke softly into her ear. "No matter what you've gotten yourself into, I'm here for you. We'll figure this out, and we'll face those ants together. As a family."

Poetry

Michael P. Aleman

Another Day of Quarantine

The morning sun bathes our bedroom with soft light
on a morning more than serene, a real gift on another day of quarantine.
Cool March air via a slightly opened window drifts in.
I welcome the freshness of the air and the sunlight.
They bring the end of night, and assurance that darkness won't prevail.
The true blessing, of course, is being quarantined with you,
having you beside me, the halo of your silver hair soft upon your pillow.
The morning air billows the window curtain, offering a badly needed certainty
that normalcy remains, will sustain us to the end.
I abhor the thought of living through this quarantine alone,
for you are bride, lover, companion and friend,
and if the end is at hand, we'll weather it together.
I will, however, put that thought off for another day.
We have breakfast to get, exercise waiting, reading aloud
in the late afternoon, absolutely every fine detail of life
still to glean on yet another day of quarantine.

What Boys Do

Stay in the neighborhood, my mother said as I headed out the door.

I don't want you getting up to no good, which meant avoiding
those things boys do to challenge their fear of death.
I met Skinny and Dan in the empty lot behind the billboard.
We walked through the weeds, bottles and cans strewn about,
and stood looking up at the back of the billboard, two stories high,
as if it were Mt. Kilimanjaro high above the Kilimanjaro plains,
and we Masai warriors climbing to meet the gods.
We'd not tried it before, but had seen older boys do it,
one even walking along the top, his arms stretching into eternity
like The Great Wallenda.
We stood, our necks craned, until Skinny asked,
You candy-asses gonna stand here all day?
and he began to haul his corpulence up the slanted beams,
his powerful hands and legs working steadily as he ascended.
Ten or twelve feet above us he looked down, spat and laughed,
then clucked like a chicken, so we followed his lead and began our own ascent.
Skinny called out encouragement as he neared the summit,
and though my arms and legs were beginning to quiver,
I forged on, fearful of being the one who couldn't cut it.
Finally we were side-by-side at the peak puffing,
our legs trembling, relieved to be gripping the 2x6
that ran the length of the billboard looking down on pedestrians, cars,
and buses below all ignorant of the spies looking down on them.
Don't anybody spit, I warned.
Okay! Skinny challenged. *Who's gonna walk it?*
Not me! Me neither!
I felt my chest tighten and my hands grip the 2x6
like a storm pelted sparrow clinging to a branch.
Chicken! He scorned, clucking once again,
but he stood quietly, the sound of traffic rising
to our ears. The fear was palpable. *It's a long way down. I'd make a helluva splat.*
Oh Jesus! Dan whispered.
You don't have to pray, Dan, I'm not going to do it.
Dan's eyes were wide. *My mother just came out of the hardware store.*
Sure enough, Dan's mother was headed up the street away from us.

Spooked, we descended ever so carefully,
relieved when our feet touch the grass of the Kilimanjaro plains.
We didn't speak during our walk home, never said *See ya* as we parted.
I slipped in the through the back door to find my mother
on her hands and knees washing the kitchen floor. *You're back early.* She said.
I'm tired, was my reply.
Tired? What have you been doing?
We climbed Mt. Kilimanjaro.
Well, no wonder you're tired.
Why don't you lie down and take a little rest?

From the Window of the Studio

A red pickup truck sits askew on concrete blocks,
looking indifferent, aloof, unconcerned about the rain
beating a tattoo on its roof.
It sits amidst wet winter weeds, wrappers, beer bottles,
and the ubiquitous white plastic chair which lies on its back,
tipped over when its occupant dashed indoors to escape the rain.
It has probably driven its last miles,
though the loving and talented hands of the right mechanic
may eke out a few more precious turns of the odometer.
Where in laying down all those miles did it go?
On what desert highway did its radiator boil over?
What wrong turn did it take and follow along to the end of the road,
where it fell into the rabbit hole, pleased the Queen of Hearts
because it was rose red, and she'd never ridden in a Chevy pickup before.

The Gift

Maureen Crowley

You think you know a person until you have to buy her a gift—then it feels like you don't know her at all. I realized I didn't know my roommate Amanda as well as I thought I did, even though we'd been living together for two years. Most of what I had was speculation: she was from some cul-de-sac/suburban utopia where all the houses sit evenly spaced from one another and look pretty much like the builders used a Xerox machine while constructing them. Her mom was the kind of parent who seemed to be heavily involved in the PTA and was the chaperone of every school dance. Amanda probably got her expectations on what romance should be like from watching Disney movies—where happily-ever-after is the end–all, be all. She also didn't think Nala qualified to be a Disney princess because Nala is a lion and didn't find it discriminatory.

What I knew for sure was that Amanda was a business major on the fast track to becoming an entrepreneur. She didn't like my major (anthropology) and insisted I study something more worthwhile, like business. I also knew she preferred it when I gave her my half of the rent two days before the first of the month so she could write the check to the landlord the day before since she didn't want him to think we were the kind of people who waited until the day of to pay rent. Judging by the countdown on the calendar, I also knew her birthday was in eight days.

As I entered the mall, a cool gust of air washed over me, and the aroma of soft pretzels, pizza, and stir-fry wafted past. Near the doors, an ambitious food stand employee chased the passerby with a tray of teriyaki chicken samples in tiny cups urging them to take one. A young boy by the A&W booth wiped his mouth with his sleeve as a girl dreamily watched from several tables away. Their voices and others composed the food court medley, joined by the faint sound of dogs barking in the pet store around the corner.

I circled the downtown mall feeling lost and hopeless and savoring the tangy aftertaste of teriyaki in my mouth. I didn't know where to start and had nothing to go on other than a vague idea of who Amanda was and my dad's gift-giving protocol. To him, gift-giving was sacred—he devoted his life to it. He believed gift cards were a cheap, lazy substitute and that people should have something to open up. My dad also claimed that giving the wrong present is among the worst things a person can do. It's hard to forget a bad one, he'd say every time my mom reminded him of her waffle-iron anniversary present. He taught me that when giving a gift, you give something you're excited about. That way, when the receiver sees your excitement, they'll get excited too. The best present you can give a person is something you'd want to buy for yourself.

Last year I picked out a laser-engraved crystal cube of the Titanic. It depicted the ship sinking front-first into the arctic depths of the Atlantic with ice water streaming down the sides of the above-water stern as the ship began to break in half. If you looked close enough, you could spot a few of the third-classers leaping off the stern of the ship as the upper-class citizens sat in the lifeboats watching thick columns of smoke rise from the funnels. My favorite detail was the jagged iceberg floating serenely, almost unapologetically, away from the scene. The light-up base I bought with it shone an icy blue color that brought the tragic picture to life.

It was the coolest thing I ever bought, and I knew my roommate would love it.

She looked at it like it was a dead bird. I could tell by the way she raised her shaded eyebrows and drew her lips back to expose her teeth that she was trying too hard to smile.

Still, I asked, "Do you like it?"

Her face puckered like she just ate something sour.

"Oh . . . yeah. Thank you," she answered mechanically and set the box aside. We went back to picking at her store-bought cake in silence.

I hadn't seen the laser-engraved crystal cube of the Titanic since.

This year she took a more direct approach. She went through and circled (in red pen) clothes (and her sizes) and accessories she liked in her fashion catalog and stealthily inserted them into our mail/coupon pile. Other times she ripped out perfume inserts in magazines and had me sniff them to see what I thought. Or in mid-conversation she'd interrupt with things like, "I can't believe I got this [item] in red. I wish I had it in a different color!" and "Oh no! My [insert object] just broke!" (then she'd slyly mention where it came from and how much it cost).

I started at a store with a hard to pronounce name and almost choked on the aroma of cologne and perfume, strong enough to peel the skin off my eyeballs. The cocktail of scents built a wall so thick that no sounds from my fellow shoppers outside could penetrate. The fluorescent bulbs overhead dumped buckets of light on the store, and I couldn't find my own shadow on the white tiled floor or the bleached white walls. The whole place was sterile enough to make a hospital look dirty. Perfume bottles were lined up by color and height on glass counters with an even, probably measured space between them. More lights hung underneath the tables to highlight each one. A lot of them had weird titles like, "Urban Paradise," "Endless Forever," "Tiki Twilight Tango," and other exotic-sounding strings of words slapped on a label.

The clerk's heels popped like firecrackers as she approached me and her question, "Is there anything you're looking for?" exploded next to my head.

"I'm, uh, just browsing."

She winced and retreated behind her counter and tried to look busy.

I tiptoed over to a row of pink bottles. I opened the cap of a bottle called "Perpetual Sunshine" and sniffed the sprayer, trying to recall some of the samples Amanda showed me. It smelled familiar, like one of the inserts I remembered (either that or Pine-Sol). I checked the price tag: $130. I wiped my fingerprints off the delicate glass bottle with my shirt sleeve as I set it down and walked the tightrope out of the store under the clerk's stink eye.

I caught my breath next to a pretzel stand and spotted a little shop called Treasured Memories wedged between a candle store and a hair salon. The best way I can describe the inside of this place is like being at a party you didn't want to go to but were too polite to turn down the invitation.

The store smelled like soup, and the temperature was set a few degrees below boiling. I navigated the labyrinth of shelves and racks stuffed with plain Dollar Store-quality mugs, key chains, frames, T-shirts, tote bags. No price tags. My dad says if you can't see what something costs upfront, odds are it's going to be expensive. Posters taped to the shelf holding a rainbow of mugs advertised a semi-annual sale, but I couldn't tell the price from the quantity from the date of the sale. Taking stock of the inventory felt like watching a movie trailer and not learning anything about the plot.

I stumbled out of the jungle of shelves to the back of the store to find the cashier behind the counter, organizing a key chain display. She wore an orange t-shirt with the store name screen printed on the front in thick gray letters. A man emerged from a back room and dropped a large box on the floor. He sliced it open in a quick motion with a box cutter stashed on his belt. He scooped armfuls of totes and threw them on an adjacent table. My eyes wandered to a contraption that looked like a giant clamp, and I finally understood the plot to the movie. The cashier rolled her eyes and sighed.

"Hank! We have enough totes. We need more T-shirts out here!" she snapped. Hank seemed like he knew better than to argue. He balled up the totes and shoved them back into the box and disappeared into the back room.

When she caught me backing away, she said, "Sorry about that . . .. Welcome to Treasured Memories—where your memories are always with you! Anything I can help you with?"

"Oh, I'm just looking aro—"

"Well, we're running a sale right now till the end of the month. Two for the price of one, six for four, or add three more for half off. Have any questions, my name's Leslie, okay?"

I nodded and receded into the overgrowth of tote bags and sweatshirts. *This is the kind of place my parents would like*, I thought and ducked out of the store.

I decompressed in a massage chair for about fifteen minutes and dumped all my quarters into the twenty-five-cent machines for jawbreakers and rub-on tattoos. About half an hour earlier I had spent all the time allotted in my dad's get-in-get-out policy, but in my defense, it was a lot harder to stick to that code when you had no idea what to look for. I'd use a needle in the haystack analogy here, but really, I was rolling around in hay.

I trailed behind two middle-aged women wearing tennis shoes and pumping their arms as they turned the bend. I pledged I'd never turn into a mall exerciser, but at this point I was one. I wiped the sweat from my forehead with the back of my sleeve and considered swapping my jeans for sweatpants and picking up a pair of Dr. Scholl's sneakers. I was about ready to join them until the beat of a vaguely familiar song tapped me on the shoulder. I'd recognize the song once I got to the chorus, I knew it, but I had to get closer.

I followed the beat to a quirky store called Crash Couch, where the music pounded its well-known tune into the walls. I stepped into a time capsule of Wonder Balls, Rubik's cubes, Action League Now! and Gumby figurines, "Back to the Future" T-shirts, Hubba Bubba Bubble Tape, and box sets of The Joy of Painting on DVD. I began to yearn for the time you could wear socks with sandals and not be harshly judged. I felt at home immediately.

In this treasure chest of trinkets and novelties, I dug up a true gem, a square metal lunch box depicting Darth Vader standing with his arm outstretched, using the Force to crush Admiral Motti's throat. They depicted Motti in extraordinary detail: his lips and cheeks turning bluish-purple, eyes bulging out of their sockets, and fingers grasping for the nonexistent hand choking him. In a speech bubble, Vader says, "I find your lack of faith disturbing."

I checked the price tag: $17.99 plus tax—it was such a steal. I needed to buy this. So, I did, along with six Wonder Balls, a black-and-white speckled Furby, a pink and purple striped Furby (so the other one wouldn't get lonely), and a Halloween edition of "Where's Waldo?"

By the time I left Crash Couch, I was tired, hungry, moderately over budget, and the mall was closing in half an hour. I had a bagful of things I was excited about—maybe a little too excited about to gift. Would Amanda like the lunch box or Furbies as much as I did? Maybe my dad's idea only works sometimes, like with close friends or people who have a good taste in music. Maybe in this case, I needed to think the opposite thought. The perfect gift for her might be the one thing I'd never want to own.

I sought out some hipster place with a name so pretentious I don't even want to utter it. The dimly lit store was packed, even though I was the only customer in the store. Shirts, shorts, and other clothes size medium and smaller piled the tables and the latest trends in jeans and shorts stuck to the walls like wallpaper. The speakers played some generic millennial track about how everyone's hometown sucks, and the only solution is to pack up and leave town (with your boyfriend) without looking back. The whole time I thought to myself, *this must be what hell is like*. I turned to leave and collided with a mannequin standing where the door should have been.

And then I saw it. A scarf. It was like an epiphany.

I unwrapped it from around the mannequin's plastic neck like I was looting a corpse and examined it. The scarf was a thin, gauzy material stitched in one loop, speckled with a red, purple, and orange polka dots over a lime green and yellow paisley pattern. I gagged and thought, *no sensible person would buy this*.

It was perfect.

Nothing Against Ms. Johnson, But . . .

Patricia Callahan

Nothing against Ms. Johnson, but when she read aloud to us, her head wobbled on her long neck. And she licked her thumb to turn pages. Nobody ever checked out a book she had read aloud during Library Hour.

The day she tried to read us *The Mouse and the Motorcycle*, her thumb had just smudged page one when Evan stood on a library stool and threw the recess kickball at her. It smacked her in the face. The chapter book dropped to the floor, its pages fanning out before us as Ms. Johnson let out a high "Oh!" of surprise. Then a smaller "Oh." Of realization. She brought her knuckles to her nose. Nobody breathed. "Tissue," she said through her hand, and brought her other hand to the blotch of pink swelling on her cheek. "Please." The kickball, bumping across the carpet, tapped against the picture books lining a bottom shelf and dribbled to a stop. Then Evan wound up and toe-balled it across the room, his untied shoelace flopping.

I looked away, heat spreading from my tight chest to my ringing ears. Evan was my next-door neighbor.

"Can, someone, please, hand, me, a, tissue?" Ms. Johnson said through parted fingers.

My mom had given Evan a ride that morning.

"I can bring you toilet paper from the girls' room?" someone said in a warbly voice.

Silence, then: "Yes. Rebecca. Thank you."

"I'm sorry," I heard Evan say. A fuzzy black border grew at the edges of my vision as I tried to focus on my double-knotted Keds. I clasped my clammy hands together in the lap of my dress, and the ringing became a buzz. "I'm sorry!" Evan yelled this time, his voice electronic, like it was coming through a computer speaker. The orange carpet became green; my legs, red; my heartbeat thumped in my neck.

"Are you breathing?" Evan's skull asked in a robot's voice. I heard a thud. I thought it was Ms. Johnson's body that collapsed, but later was told it was mine.

A week later, Ms. Johnson squatted like a baseball catcher to meet Evan's eyes when he returned from suspension. She held his arm gently and asked if she could sign his cast.

Evan's father drove a gray van with two small windows on the rear doors, which swung outward. Inside it was crowded: buckets of wrenches, flat-head screwdrivers, pliers. Long nails. If asked, my parents would say he was a good neighbor. He collected our mail when we were out of town. No wife. Just him and Evan.

What I would say, if asked, is that you'd know him by the white spit that formed in the corners of his mouth and his yellowing teeth that were as even as one of the blades in his bucket.

What I wouldn't say is that Evan and I had been riding bikes down the Pine Street hill that summer when Evan peeled off his shirt and draped it around his neck like a towel. I wanted to do it too. Wanted to feel the air breezing over my bare skin on our next run down. Once I was free of the elastic cap sleeves, I raised my arms while riding, like doing the wave at a baseball game. Giddiness filled me as though the roar of the wind were the roar of a crowd. On our last ride down, we sat at the bottom of the hill on the hot paved road. Evan used his shirt to blot his forehead and neck. I copied him, then said I'd get us root beers from my house, imagining how cool the cans would feel against our cheeks. I pushed my bike to the top of Pine Street hill and angled the handlebars toward the sprawling yards on the next block, the sun warming my shoulders, my swinging hair brushing my back. We'll ride through the sprinklers next, I thought.

The gray van was parked in the driveway, and Evan's father's face was in the passenger-side mirror when I wheeled my bike past. "Hey," he called to me. "Where's your shirt?" Even though it was around my neck. "Put it on," he told me. Even though I still looked like the boys in my class.

He waited.

The shirt was harder going back on. The collar caught on my nose. The elastic cap sleeves pinched my arms. When I used both hands to unroll the fabric over my stomach, the bicycle's front wheel twisted its neck, the handlebar jabbed me in the side, and the bike's gears and pedal clawed my shin as the frame slid and crashed to the sidewalk. Newly tagged with a gash and a streak of grease, my body managed to drag away the bicycle but not to twist the shirt so the back wasn't at the front, its label not at the hollow of my throat.

After that, whenever the gray van was in the driveway, I stayed inside and watched cartoons. Sometimes I didn't even have to check. I could smell his pipe from our kitchen window.

Why wouldn't I tell that story if, one day, someone rang our bell and asked, "Do you know the next-door neighbor?" Because telling that story about him would mean telling a story about me, and during it their eyes would change, like Evan's had the night I told him, when we were catching fireflies in my backyard. This was near summer's end, when darkness starts to fall right on the heels of dinner. With school about to begin and the glowing bugs between us, the story bubbled out of me, and once it did, the backyard, the block, the Pine Street hill all felt like mine again. The story on Evan's face, though, was different. He let his firefly go. The firefly on the back of my hand lit and flew toward his. A laugh left his mouth, the last thing he'd say to me, and his eyes zeroed in on the path of the bug's blinking yellow abdomen. With a quick swing of my Wiffle ball bat, he whapped the firefly, then left my yard.

Before Ms. Johnson tried to read us *The Mouse and the Motorcycle*, she'd taught us a new game. With the rain coming down outside, she pulled the recess kickball from the closet for an indoor activity. As a class, we filed down the stairwell to the library, which had a large carpeted area in the nook by the clock. Once we were all crisscross-applesauce on the orange carpet, Ms. Johnson knelt beside me and explained the game to the class, the rubber smell of the kickball mixing with the coffee on her breath. We could roll the kickball or do an underhand toss, and we had to be calm, and deliberate, and say the person's name before we sent the ball to them. We had to remain seated.

When we sent the ball across the circle, we had to announce a state name. Whoever caught the ball had to name that state's capital.

Ms. Johnson sat on a stool and called out "Correct!" or "Try again!" as the ball rolled from one student to another, some flipping it quickly and others hugging it as they considered their options. "*Um* is not a name," Ms. Johnson said, to keep the game moving. California, Hawaii, Idaho. Alex, Rebecca, and Vaughn. Soon I lost track of which states had been called, and the ball seemed to go to everyone but me. My worry that I'd say the wrong thing was replaced by the fear of not going at all. It was a blur through my tears who got it next until it landed in Evan's hands. He froze on the capital of Michigan, and Ms. Johnson let him keep it for so long before he finally said "Lansing?" and sent it to me, "Delaware" so small maybe only I heard it, the arc of the kickball as it sailed from his corner by the clock to my lap forming the mirror image of the dip in Pine Street's hill. I wrapped my arms around the ball and smiled.

Ms. Johnson was still looking over Evan's head instead of at me. Then she rose from her stool, and as I moved my tongue behind my teeth to say Delaware's capital, she announced that the game was over. Ms. Johnson pulled the kickball from my hands, her swollen, chapped fingers worse to see up close, and held it in front of her. "Time to pick out books," she said.

The word rose in my throat and stuck to the roof of my mouth. I had memorized all the state capitals. I was a good student. I always did my homework. I raised my hand. It was my turn.

Even as I lunged for the kickball and punched it from her grip, I knew it was wrong, I knew it was not like me, but I didn't know yet who I was.

Ms. Johnson scolded me in front of the class, said she was shocked at my behavior, and ordered me to the cubbies in the back. Her tone was final.

But I said, "Dover," then waited for what would come next.

Hank Keneally "The Face on Valencia Street"

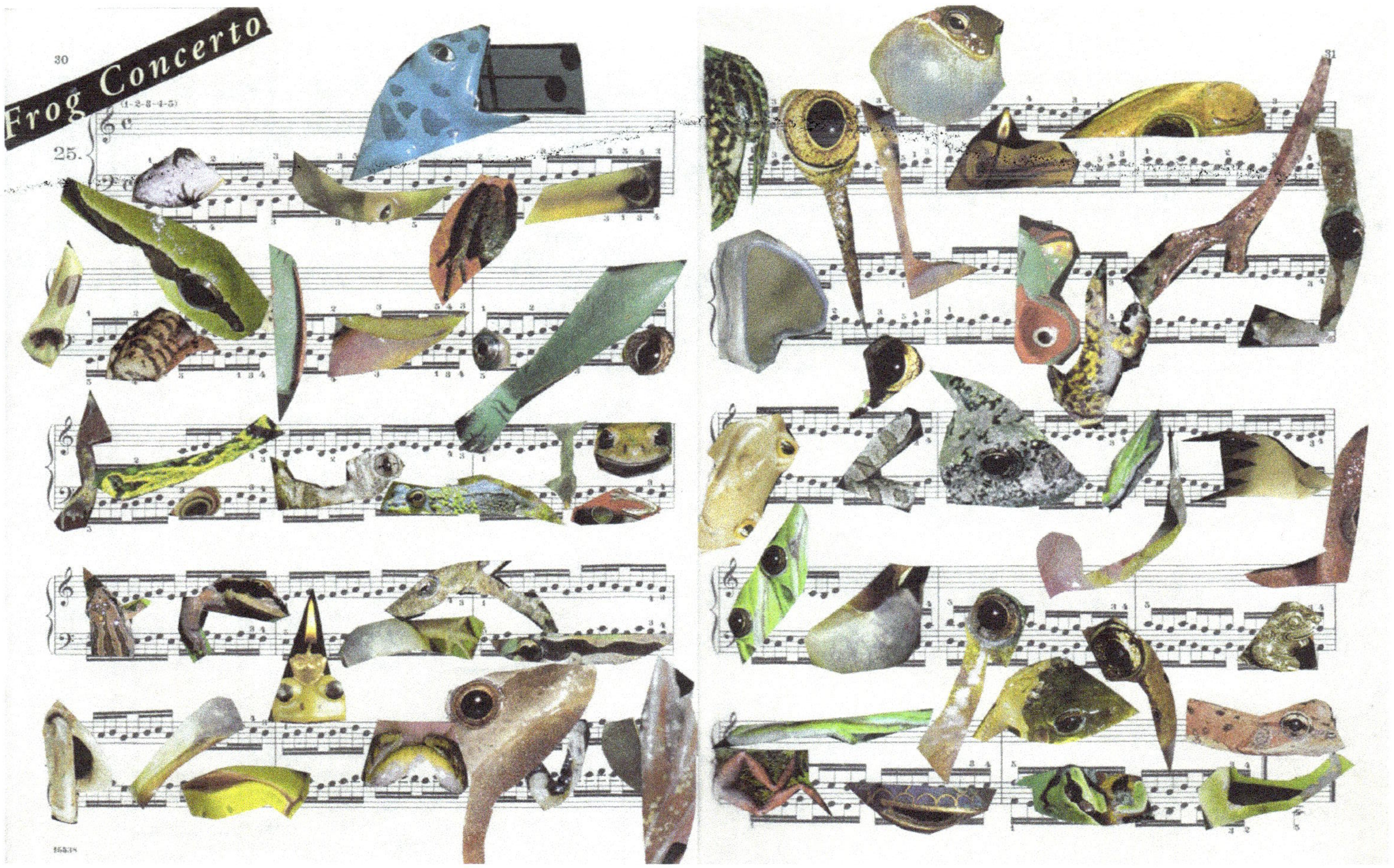

Mark Blickley "Frog Concerto"

Frog Concerto

Mark Blickley

I'm a dead frog and I don't say this with any pity or understanding or shame, it's just an observation that people seem to like us, like us a bit too much because they like to push hooks through our jaws and cast us out to sea, as well as amputate us for fine dining and draw us as a cartoon shuffling cigar smoking smart ass, and they like to blame us when they choke on the phlegm in their throats, and they swear that some of us give them hideous skin infections while the evil ones enjoy tossing us into their steamy potions as the younger ones imitate us with a game of leaps and crashes, perhaps because we abandon our young and we larger ones like to eat the smaller ones, and some of us are poisonous and have arrows dipped in our blood for killing others, and snakes like to slide along with our swallowed bulges straining inside their bellies, and we are stunned and frozen and sliced alive by school children with sharp tools, yet we still swim and splash and smile because the sun warms our cold blood and reflects our moist green that gives summer its most vibrant color, and the Chinese believe there is a toad in the moon not a man, and the Japanese consider us good luck, and that luck includes the growing of long legs to hop away from dinosaurs which is why we are the best leapers on earth and millions of years ago became the first animal with any backbone to live on land, and Shakespeare wrote that we wear a precious jewel in our head, and, best of all, beneath the summer stars, the sky is filled with our clucks and clicks and croaks of romance and camaraderie, sprinkled within a flying feast of buzzing wings and microscopic swimmers, and so this is what dead frogs will do just given the chance, a chance that will always destroy us.

Secret Shepherd

A Novel Excerpt

James Osborne

Namusat, Quebec, Canada
November 1994

"Another two just last night!" Dan Stonechild said, his voice breaking. "That's four suicides here in three weeks, Paul. Oh my . . . four! Four little kids!"

Paul Winston embraced his friend awkwardly. Both wore knee-length parkas against the 30 below zero cold, their hands thrust deep in double-layered mittens, their feet clad in fur mukluks.

Paul had just arrived on a chartered plane in the remote First Nations community of Namusat in northern Canada, after a long flight from his ranch near Colorado Springs, Co.

As they walked toward the tiny village, Paul could see Dan was struggling with his composure.

"Are you sure they were suicides?" Paul asked, as much to distract his troubled friend as to seek details.

"No question," Dan replied. "Drug overdoses. Both." His words tumbled out in stressed bursts. "Two young girls . . . friends." Dan's caring brown eyes glistened. "Just fourteen years old! This is horrible! Four suicides . . . one tiny community! When will it end?"

After receiving Dan's call for help, Paul researched what had been described as an epidemic of suicides among Canada's indigenous youth. Hundreds had died. Numerous studies came to the same conclusion: a lack of hope . . . despair, really. Having realized their futures would lead almost inevitably to alcoholism and drug abuse, just like their parents, siblings, friends and others in the community, a growing number had chosen suicide as the preferred alternative.

"Thanks for coming," Dan said, still fighting for control. "I didn't want to impose on you, but I was hoping you might bring a fresh perspective . . . some insights, to this terrible tragedy."

"Hey, we've been friends since college," Paul said. "Of course, I want to help in any way I can."

While the two men walked, Paul scanned the surroundings. Accumulated snow reached halfway up the squat walls of ramshackle homes. Winding roads formed a haphazard confusion of narrow passageways serving as roads piled high on both sides with snow.

Most homes looked unfit for human habitation, but were in obvious use. Wood smoke rose casually out of rusted metal chimneys poking up at odd angles on the snow-laden roofs, the eaves host to long thick icicles, many reaching down into the deep snow.

Paul watched as innocent little children ran in all directions on the roads playing made-up games, oblivious to both the frigid temperature and the tragedies in their hometown. Dogs joined them, loping and sniffing here and there, occasionally lifting a hind leg beside the snow outcroppings, marking their passage with yellow stains, joining their predecessors' signatures.

On what seemed like the main road, Paul watched a scattering of half a dozen lone adults shuffle along independently, heads down, seemingly en-route aimlessly to unknown destinations. A few vehicles, mostly pickups and snowmobiles, sat beside the road belching exhaust from engines left idling to keep warm. Other vehicles, looking distressed and unloved, squatted deep in the snow, some windowless, their engine hoods yawning skyward on behalf of their rusting bodies.

"Are the elders here yet?" Paul asked.

"They came early," Dan said. "Been meeting since yesterday."

He turned away self-consciously to wipe at his damp eyes and runny nose, his mittens dangling from bright red strings disappearing up the sleeves of his deerskin parka. He blew his nose and said, "They're waiting for us now at the school. It's Saturday so there are no classes, of course. The principal said we could use the school this weekend. She asked us to pay for the fuel oil to heat it. It's very expensive up here. At night, when the children aren't in school and on weekends, the heat is turned off to save money."

Far down the road Paul saw a large nameless building he assumed was the school. Little paint remained on the clapboard siding. On the roof, two ragged blue plastic tarps covered what Paul guessed would be holes in the severely buckled shingles. An absence of snow on the roof revealed the lack of adequate insulation in the attic.

"Won't the pipes freeze?" Paul asked.

Dan's laugh conveyed irony and sadness.

"There's no running water in the school . . . never has been," he said. "Most of the homes don't have running water either. A few did a long time ago, but the water system broke down. There's no money to fix it."

"But what . . .?" Paul began.

Dan interrupted, "Wells in summer, and now bottled water and melted snow," he replied. "And outhouses, mostly. In some cases, they have to throw it into the bushes."

"Good heavens!" Paul said. "That's unsanitary. It's dangerous."

"Tell me about it, Paul," Dan said. "It gets worse."

"This is awful!" Paul said.

"None of these homes was designed to have wood stoves," Dan said. "The people had to improvise. They had to install their own. Otherwise they'd have frozen to death. Some federal bureaucrat years ago decided my people needed new homes, homes with furnaces in the basement. Guess what? No basements were built so there could be no furnaces, and there was no fuel anyway. The houses arrived fully equipped with plumbing. Guess what again? No sewer or water systems either and no functioning water treatment plant. What kind of message do you think that sends to my people?" Dan asked.

An elderly woman limped out of a narrow walkway leading from an aged house. Bordering the passageway on both sides were six-foot snowbanks. Paul and Dan waited as she walked stiffly toward them, leaning heavily on a homemade cane clasped in her right hand.

"Hello, Emily," Dan said. He smiled warmly as he embraced the old woman, dressed in a tattered caribou hide parka. "I want you to meet Paul Winston. He's a friend, came to the meeting of elders."

Emily Amanust nodded at Paul, shifted the cane to her left hand, and held out her right. She displayed respect but little deference for Dan, recently elected grand chief of the Assembly of First Nations of Canada.

"Emily is a retired chief of Namusat," Dan said. "She is much admired here and far beyond this reserve for her great wisdom."

Emily's expression did not change. Paul watched her look intently at him.

She spoke, her voice sounding weary but strong, and not unkindly, "Many came from outside before you. Maybe they meant good. They just made things worse. Are you one of those?"

"Where do people work?" Paul asked, avoiding the question while trying to inject a more positive tone.

"We have no jobs," Emily replied. "My people hunted and trapped and fished this land for many generations . . . thousands of years. They did good. They weren't rich, by white man's ways today, but they supported their families. We were a proud people then. We looked after ourselves."

"What happened?" Paul asked.

"The colonizers came and after them the government," Emily replied.

"What do you mean, Emily?" Paul asked.

"They took away our land. They shut down our trap lines and refused to let my father and his father and his father before him hunt and fish much beyond this reserve," she replied. "That was wrong! It is too small."

Anger and sorrow leapt into Emily's previously calm and gentle bright eyes.

"For thousands of years our ancestral hunting and fishing grounds have ranged many days walk in all directions from here. In those times, our people moved often, to keep from over-hunting and over-fishing. It was our way. We understood and respected nature."

"Those were their jobs," Dan added. "Hunting and fishing. That was their work . . . that is what they did for a living, their careers. It was like that everywhere. Those jobs were taken away from them! I'm not sure who said it first, but we are living proof that people need just three things in life in order to be happy: someone to love, meaningful work, and something to look forward to. The government has taken from us two of those. Our people have been left with no way to support themselves and no hope of ever being able to do so. That is at the heart of our problems . . . that is the source of our despair."

Poetry

Charles Rammelkamp

The Crud

My mother called him "the crud,"
my brother's friend Alan.
I'm not sure what she had against him,
besides his lack of ambition—
she was a schoolteacher, after all—
Alan destined to work
in one of the steel factories
after graduating from high school—
at least until the steel factories all closed.

The Crud loved cars.
He could tell you the make and model and year
of anything with four wheels and an engine,
sported decals of hotrods and muscle cars
all over his school folders.

He did speak vaguely
of "joining the service,"
as his older brother had,
then having all his teeth pulled,
dentures installed in their place,

the stubby twisted teeth in his mouth,
a source of private anguish.

When my brother mentioned to their friends
our mother called Alan "the crud,"
the nickname stuck,
but only behind his back.
Everybody referred to Alan as "the Crud."
Initially offended, hurt, Alan soon embraced it,
wore the sobriquet like a badge,
though still, nobody called him
"the Crud" to his face.

Sometimes I wish I knew
what became of the Crud
after I left home,
but never enough to try to find out.

Ribbensnob

"The little champagne salesman,"
Hitler's dismissive nickname for von Ribbentrop,
his Foreign Minister,
whose college friends had teased as "Ribbensnob,"
a man whose *savoir faire* gave him
entrée around the world—
at least until everybody but Argentina
shunned the German government—
a tennis player, an iceskater,
his old-fashioned manners and elegance intimidated.

But he'd begun his career importing champagne—
Mumm and Pommery from Reims—
before becoming der Fuhrer's yes-man, enabler.

If Hitler said "grey," the common knowledge went,
Ribbentrop would encourage, "black, black, black!"

A teacher recalled Joaquim
"the worst student in class,
full of vanity and very pushy."

Hitler finally tired of him,
despite Ribbentrop's enthusiasm for his master.
Even after his conviction at Nuremberg—
crimes against humanity and other charges—
he remained loyal to Hitler,
who'd already committed suicide.
"Even with all I know," he averred in prison,
if in this cell Hitler should come to me
and say, 'Do this!'
I would still do it."

The first of ten men hanged on an October day in 1946—
Goring having committed suicide before his scheduled execution—
ascending the thirteen steps to the gallows
he uttered his final words: "God protect Germany."

Trumplandia

We sailed into the Birch Run exit
like a leaky catamaran,
the *Service Engine Now* light
pulsing like a migraine on the dashboard.

After checking into a motel,
calling Triple-A as if tossing out a lifeline,
locating likely local repair shops—
Sunday afternoon, all businesses closed—

we went to dinner
at Oscar and Joey's Roadhouse,
a nearby bar, trophy kills—deer,
elk, moose—mounted on the walls.

"Went into limp mode," the guy
at the table next to us nodded
when we told him about our car problems.
He named a garage we could try.

"A Nissan?" he frowned, disapproving.
"Used to work at GM in Flint
until they shut down the plant
more'n fifteen years ago now.

"Now I drive down to Chrysler
in Detroit, every day,
a hundred and six miles there,
a hundred and six miles back.

"Why don't I move?
I just ain't a city boy.
'Sides, I got my farm up here.
Okay, sorry about you folks' car."

When he got up, he pointed
to the stuffed bear next to the bar,
rearing up on its hind legs,
Canadian flags behind its ears.

"Missy shot that up in Canada,"
he indicated the waitress with a jerk of his head.
"She says the best part was
her husband didn't shoot nothin'."

The Plot Against America

That semester at the community college,
we taught Philip Roth's *The Plot Against America*
in our Intro to Literature classes.
Mina and I shared an office,
both of us adjuncts in the English Department.

She told me she'd compared the novel,
in which Charles Lindbergh, a Nazi
sympathizer, is elected president,
to the Trump administration:
the persecution of minorities
(Jews instead of immigrants and Muslims),
the attacks on the free press,
an authoritarian con man in the Oval Office.
Her students, unable or unwilling
to see the similarities, thought
she just had an ax to grind,
still hadn't gotten over the election.

I remembered Professor Wilson,
my Elizabethan Lit. professor
when I was a college student,
talking about all the sex symbols
in Spenser and Shakespeare.
Billy Dooley, in the desk next to mine,
wondered in whisper if Wilson wasn't
getting any sex at home.

"They don't think Trump's 'presidential,'"
Mina clarified, "but
they aren't scared out of their wits, either."

Noir

Nancy could have kicked herself for her indiscretion,
mentioning to her boyfriend Sonny
the old guy at the bank, Mister Hughes,
one of the regular Tuesday customers,
inviting her out to lunch last week.

It had been an innocent date,
Mister Hughes old as her grandfather,
a delightful meal in a posh restaurant
she'd never have been able
to afford on her own.

"We can use this to our advantage,"
Sonny said, eyeballs like cherries
rolling in a slot machine
to a sensational jackpot.
"A lonely old guy
sniffing after the young stuff."

"It's not like that!" Nancy protested.
"He's just a sweet old man.
Leave him alone, Sonny!"

"Riiiiight," Sonny replied,
the calculations still spinning in his eyes.

Prisoners of the Multiverse

A Novel Excerpt

Jacob M. Appel

The defining and indelible event of our pre-college years—for me and for my cohort of honors-level classmates at Laurenville High School—was the suicide, at age forty-two, of our twelfth grade physics teacher, Vance Rottman. We wouldn't have been surprised if dowdy Miss Ayler, who so worshipped Virginia Woolf, had filled her pockets with stones and vanished into the Rappahannock. Or if the fastidious Latin teacher, Dr. Ismay, had fallen on a vintage sword like his defeated Roman generals. But the image of Vance—for that was what we all called him—bolting himself inside his gear-packed office, where only months earlier he'd rigged a working model of the solar system to the overhead light, and ramming a sawed-off shotgun down his own throat, was to be the cataclysm that permeated our conversations and recontoured our relationships ever after. Maybe it was because Vance had everything, looks and charisma and a picture-perfect four-year-old daughter, who made classroom cameos on mornings when her mother did modeling shoots in Richmond, and because we'd believed we had known him so intimately, in the countless hours we'd spent camped around his laboratory desk, sometimes until twilight, attempting to unify quantum mechanics with general relativity, that his sudden, vicious rejection of life pierced a permanent hole in our own armor—such that never again, even in my happiest moments, could I observe another person's joy without wondering what lurked beneath.

My best friend that spring was Lacey Moretti. Soon enough we would drift apart, our natural differences overcoming our common history, so when I saw her at the twentieth reunion last year, where she gulped champagne from a slipper and made a sloppy pass at every unhitched male within groping distance, I could hardly remember what had drawn us together on long-ago evenings studying the polarity of magnets and the trajectories of cannon balls. Yet in those final months at Laurendale, we were truly inseparable—so much so that, when a third former classmate sensed the tension between us at the reunion, she confessed she'd always suspected we'd been lovers. The reality was that we'd both been far too innocent for anything like that.

From Lacey, I learned that Vance had died. We'd been planning a drive into Washington one Saturday to pick up our prom dresses—mine a beaded, charcoal gown in an iconic graduation cut, Lacey's something low-necked and scarlet—and I pulled up in front of her house at the wheel of Papa's Plymouth. I tapped the horn. A warm breeze rustled the hedges, carrying the scent of peonies. Captain & Tennille sang of "one more time" on the radio, as they would do for months to come. From across the boulevard droned the rhythmic pulse of a lawnmower. All I could focus on that morning was my prom date, Seth Sewell, and whether it made sense to keep seeing him through the summer, or to gamble that something better might roll my way—I cringe when I reflect upon how thoughtless and self-absorbed I was at seventeen—so I let my mind drift, soaking up the music, until Lacey tapped on the passenger window. She still wore her bathrobe, her skin pale as eggplant pulp without her foundation and blush.

"I've been calling you for hours," she said.

"I slept at my grandma's," I explained—not adding that I'd gone stargazing with my uncle into the early hours of the morning. "You okay?"

Lacey shook her head and braced her hands on the car door. Her entire physique trembled. "Vance is dead," she declared, her voice wavering—and then she sobbed for five minutes in the passenger seat before she could articulate another coherent word. "His wife's sister called my mother. They play bridge together . . .. And no, they're saying there's no chance it was an accident."

"But I just saw him," I pleaded.

"When?"

"Yesterday afternoon. Probably around five."

I had stopped by Vance's office to gloat about my science scholarship to Bryn Mawr, also to tell him that I was hiking up Mt. Longbow that night with Uncle Allan. I knew that I'd leave with a hand-scrawled diagram of the spring sky, the not-to-be-missed constellations circled in black marker. I'd always loved the stars, ever since my parents took us car-camping in grade school, but Vance had transformed my visceral pleasure into a more formal appreciation for the clockwork of the universe.

"He never came home yesterday," said Lacey.

"Oh God. That means I could have been . . .."

He must have had the gun in his office already, I realized. He must have known how the school day would end, even as he mapped out *auriga* and *canis major*.

"Did he seem okay?" asked Lacey. "Did anything *happen*?"

I reflected back on those twenty minutes that we'd shared at his desk—the first of the many thousands of times I have replayed that scene. Every moment of our meeting is alive to me, still: the cusp of clean white T-shirt visible above Vance's open collar, his parting words on the promise of the multiverse. Not even my own wedding day, or the birth of my daughter, stands out for me so vividly. And Lacey was to be only the first among many who demanded the details of that encounter, the magical key that might unravel the horror that followed.

"Nothing happened," I said. "I can't think of anything."

Melissa Hunter phoned early on a Monday morning, and I caught the call just as I'd returned from walking Emily to the bus stop. I didn't recognize her name at first and her Virginia area code made me wary: Ever since my husband, who chairs the geology department here at Yale, started testifying for the ACLU in anti-Creationist lawsuits, we've received a handful of angry phone calls each month, usually from states below the Mason-Dixon Line. Nothing frightening, just an ongoing nuisance. My ties to Virginia have grown increasingly frayed since my parents retired to Arizona, so Melissa had hardly said her name when I was already focused on politely ending our conversation.

"Honestly, now *isn't* a particularly good time," I said.

"I'll only take a moment, Ms. Hertz," replied Melissa. Her voice was high-pitched and punctuated by short nervous giggles. "I'm calling about a mutual acquaintance. Vance Rottman. Am I speaking to the right Rebecca Hertz?"

"Vance Rottman," I echoed—instantly alert. "Yes, I knew Vance."

"Thank goodness," said Melissa. "You're the fourth Rebecca Hertz I've talked to this morning. One of them hung up on me."

If she hadn't mentioned Vance, I might have done the same. I glanced at the digital clock above the microwave. I was leading an Audubon Society birdwatching tour of the local marshlands that afternoon, and I still hadn't retrieved my hiking boots from the repair shop. "Vance Rottman was my high school physics teacher," I explained to the caller. "I'm not sure what else I can tell you about him."

"Neither am I," Melissa replied. She laughed nervously again. "But I have something that I want you to see. I can't really do justice to it over the phone."

"I'm not sure I understand. What exactly is your connection to Vance?"

"Oh, I thought I'd told you," she replied. "I'm his daughter."

Vance's daughter. I pictured the flaxen-haired preschooler who'd impressed her father's students by naming the planets in order of their distance from the sun, always concluding with the wisdom that Pluto was also Mickey Mouse's dog, but the woman who'd called me would be in her late twenties. We'd raised money that summer after graduation to pay for her college tuition: baking coffee cakes, washing cars. And then I remembered that Vance's wife had kept her own name—a rarity among married Virginia mothers in the 1970s—and how much I admired Vance when I discovered that his daughter had become a Hunter and not a Rottman. It suddenly struck me that my own daughter, who has my husband's last name, was older now than Melissa had been during those classroom visits, that I was already six years older than Vance when he died.

"Would you mind if I stopped by your house this week? Maybe Friday?" asked Melissa. "I don't want to impose, and I promise I'll only stay for a few minutes, but my mother passed away last month—and it's important."

"I'm sorry," I said instinctively. "About your mother."

"Thank you," she said. "Would Friday work? I'll be driving up from Laurenville, so late afternoon might be best."

I had plans to attend my book club that Friday, a discussion group for faculty spouses that I'd co-founded with the elderly gay partner of a chemistry professor. And I've always had a very low tolerance for pushy people—whether they've been men pestering me for dates or strangers marketing door-to-door. Melissa Hunter, I sensed instinctively, had become one of those women who glom onto you like a barnacle.

"Late afternoon?" she asked again. "Only a few minutes, I swear."

"Okay. I can do that," I conceded. "My schedule is flexible."

The rumors erupted even before the funeral. Someone claimed to have seen Vance's wife lunching with another man at a bistro in Fredericksburg, others to have spotted Vance himself with a provocatively-attired woman in Locust Crossing. A girl whose cousin worked at the county hospital revealed that Vance had been suffering from a malignant brain tumor, but this was the same girl who insisted she'd babysat for Amy Carter, and had made out with Bob Dylan's younger brother, so we had reasons to doubt her. Below these rumors coursed a darker current of speculation, suspicion and outright myth: that Vance had been caught with a male sailor behind the Iwo Jima Memorial, that he'd run up two hundred grand in gambling debts on the horses at Colonial Downs. I'd been the closest to Vance of the girls and guys in our circle—our family had even had him over to our house for dinner a handful of times, when his wife and daughter were visiting a homebound aunt in Tennessee—so my friends vetted these accusations on my emotional doorstep, and nothing I said or did could ever convince them that I also knew nothing. Secretly, I relished the illusion that I was privy to more than I admitted. After speaking to Vance's widow once on the phone, to thank her for asking me to deliver a eulogy, I made a point of dropping references to this call in my conversations, so my classmates might infer that my relationship with Calliope Hunter was far more than incidental. Like everyone else, I suppose I wanted to claim my share of Vance's legacy.

My friendship with Lacey Moretti—forged memorizing the periodic table to a patter tune for our eighth grade earth science class, and later as co-editors of the yearbook—crumbled during those final months in Laurendale. In the initial turmoil after Vance's suicide, of course, our bond intensified. We spent hours lounging on the threadbare sofa in Lacey's basement, sometimes with Phoebe Clauson, or Trish von Elsing, or other girls who'd also idolized Vance, and sometimes only the two of us, recalling his arguments for the existence of extraterrestrial life, and his comedic impersonations of Isaac Newton, and Enrico Fermi, and Copernicus, how the Polish astronomer came off sounding like Marlon Brando in *A Streetcar Named Desire*. But increasingly, Lacey yearned to know *why* Vance had taken his own life, while I was content to accept that some questions cannot be answered. By prom—three weeks after the funeral—I was conjuring excuses to avoid afternoons at Lacey's, unable to handle another round of interrogation. We still saw each other on weekends—at graduation parties, at keggers. One Saturday, a dozen of us explored the grounds of our old elementary school, and Seth Sewell carved his initials and mine, SS ♥ RH, in the panels of the same swing-set where I'd once learned how to pump for momentum. To Lacey, I pointed out the splintered door of the equipment shed where we had chipped our names into the paint-face three years earlier, above the phrase *Frendz 4ever*, but she just shrugged her shoulders and turned away.

The next morning, early—while Papa planted marigolds in the naked beds alongside the patio and Mom accompanied my grandma to eight o'clock mass—Lacey pummeled our doorbell until I staggered downstairs in my nightgown. She looked as though she'd been awake all night, her eyes frenzied and bloodshot like an addict's. I remember her face vividly, because it inspired pity rather than empathy.

"Let's go for a drive, okay?" she pleaded.

"Sure, I guess," I agreed. "Just give me a second to find some clothes."

Thirty minutes later, we were cruising up I-64 toward Charlottesville. Lacey had already polished off half a pack of cigarettes. She'd floored the gas, the speedometer raced up to the cusp of the red zone, and I clutched the ceiling strap every time we rounded a curve.

"Where are we going?" I asked. "All this secrecy makes me nervous."

"We're almost there," promised Lacey. "Five more miles."

Our destination, as it turned out, was the cemetery in Cumberland County where Vance Rottman lay buried. His funeral service had taken place at the Richmond Ethical Culture Society; only Vance's immediate family had gone on to the interment. I'm still not certain how Lacey found out the location of the grave, but I sensed that she'd already been to the site on a prior occasion, as she led us to the precise spot without stopping at the cinderblock headquarters. Our physics teacher, who'd preached a gospel of spiritual atheism and earthly joy, rested beneath a quiet knoll in the colossal shadow of two massive Civil War era cenotaphs—memorials to wealthy brothers who'd sacrificed themselves for the Confederacy. A cross festooned with desiccated gladiolus marked the ground for a future headstone. The stark finality of the spare grave made me nauseous.

"I'm sorry I've been such a bitch," said Lacey. "It's just that you seem so calm about everything . . . so willing to pick up the pieces and move on . . . and I'm not ready to just forget about what happened. I can't do that—not yet."

"You haven't been a bitch," I lied. "Really."

Lacey sank to her knees in the uncut grass. "I keep thinking that if I only understood *why*, I could accept things better." She held her face in her hands. "And to be honest, I'm jealous of you. Of all the time you spent with him."

"It wasn't *that* much time," I said truthfully. "We *all* spent lots of time together."

"Come on, Becky," she answered. "You were his favorite. There's no need to pretend you weren't—it was kind of obvious . . . ." A quake of tears overcame Lacey, and as she cried, she kept repeating, "I wish *I'd* been his favorite."

Only at that moment did I realize that Lacey had genuinely been in love with Vance Rottman—that maybe all of us, in our own way, had been in love with him. I hugged her then and we returned to Laurenville with pledges of renewed friendship. But my next three weeks evaporated quickly, pre-registering for courses, packing, triaging blouses and shoes, without either of us picking up a telephone, and we didn't speak to each other again until Thanksgiving break. By then, I'd already started to think of Lacey Moretti as a girl I had been friends with back in high school.

In the days after Melissa Hunter's phone call, I found myself thinking about her father more than I had in many years. I'd revisited *his death* on countless occasions, but this was the first time, as an adult, I found myself considering what it had been like to *be* Vance Rottman—to walk around in his tattered penny-loafers. In high school, we'd known that he held a Ph.D. in physics from Princeton. To bookish teenagers, such a credential elevated him to a stratosphere above *Mr.* Benchford, the other physics teacher, or even Dr. Ismay, whose doctorate was an Ed.D. in classroom dynamics from Florida State. But as the wife of an Ivy League geologist, I finally understood what it meant to earn such a degree and end up teaching twelfth graders in suburban Virginia. When Vance discussed the multiverse—that infinite reflection of alternative universes paralleling our own—I suppose that in many of those other worlds, he was running a laboratory at Cal Tech or commanding legions of junior researchers in Los Alamos.

It has taken thirty years for me to see my childhood teachers as human beings, to realize that Miss Ayler's "girlfriend" was really her *girlfriend*, that autocratic Mr. Bumby was despised by his colleagues as much as by his students. Details lost upon me at seventeen resonate with the passage of years. In Vance Rottman's office, for instance, cluttered with whirling tables and manometers, I don't ever recall seeing a photograph of his wife. Looking back upon his memorial service, where hundreds of current and former students crowded into the ornate Georgian lecture hall of the Ethical Culturists, what strikes me now is the absence of Vance's colleagues—and how those in attendance, several of whom had taught Vance when he'd gone to Laurendale in the Sixties, did not seem nearly as torn up as Lacey and Phoebe and Trish von Elsing. It wasn't that anybody was pleased that Vance had done away with himself, of course. Nothing like that. But, in hindsight, I can recognize that Vance kept his coworkers at a friendly distance—how different the mood among the adults was that day, for example, from their heartbreak, two years later, when beloved Mr. Feig succumbed to cancer of the pancreas.

Reflecting upon Vance's life inevitably made me think about my own. Had I been wrong to leave my graduate program in astronomy when Emily was born? Would I end up teaching high school physics someday, after my daughter was grown, lecturing adolescents on the opportunities of the multiverse? Was there something—anything—that could drive me to unload a sawed-off shotgun into my throat? *No*, I reassured myself. *Of course not*. But if the multiverse is infinite, I understood, then there are parallel universes where I do precisely that, much as there are others where Vance Rottman does not, where he removes the shells from the shotgun and drops them, one by one, into an open drawer.

Vance Rottman's adorable poster-child had grown into a somewhat pudgy, broad-faced creature who favored polka dots and pastels at far too young an age. Melissa's pageboy haircut partially concealed her strong brow, but at the expense of accentuating her wide, bony jaw. She had inherited Vance's features, in short, not her mother's, and my initial reaction upon opening our door for our meeting was that, had she been more attractive, Vance's daughter would not have had the time to waste tracking down her father's former students. I afforded her a loose hug, then led her through the toy-strewn foyer into the parlor, where I'd set out plates of cucumber sandwiches and sliced halva. I felt anxious, ill-at-ease. Although I'd informed my husband about the phone call, and the rendezvous, meeting with Melissa to talk about her father made me feel like I was committing an infidelity, that I'd crossed some point of no return.

Melissa settled into an armchair, clutching her canvas bag in her lap.

"I can't tell you how grateful I am," she declared. "I was afraid you'd want nothing to do with me—especially under the circumstances."

"I'll be glad to help in any way I can," I replied. "But to be quite candid, I'm not sure what I can do for you." I held the plate with the cucumber sandwiches toward her, but she waved me off with her fingertips. "I can't imagine I can tell you anything about your father that you don't already know . . .."

"Can't you?"

Melissa's tone wasn't exactly unfriendly. Still, its edge was too sharp to let pass.

"No," I said crisply. "I can't."

An uncomfortable silence followed. It was a bright, balmy afternoon, and beyond the plate glass window in the dining room, chipmunks cavorted on the low-hanging branches of the crabapple tree. Several blocks away, over home-baked scones, my book club was discussing the origins of the solar system. I couldn't help wondering if Melissa Hunter felt as self-conscious—as downright uncomfortable—as I did.

"Let me put all my cards on the table, Ms. Hertz," said Melissa. "You'll forgive me for being blunt, but when you grow up with lots of unanswered questions—lots of innuendo, that's the best word for it—you learn to ask things point blank, to make people say exactly what they mean. That makes sense, doesn't it?"

"I suppose so."

"It *does* make sense," said Melissa. "So here's what I want to know. Were you having an affair with my father?"

The question ought to have shocked me, but it didn't. Somehow, I knew it was coming. Why else drive six hours to interrogate a stranger? A malicious part of me longed to announce that I *had* had an affair with Vance Rottman, that we'd made love on the smooth-tiled countertops of his laboratory only hours before he died. That would serve this woman right, I thought, for leveling unfounded, and pointless, accusations. I'm still surprised at how angry I felt toward Melissa—maybe for disrupting the tranquility of my life—even though she was as much a victim of the tragedy as anyone.

"Really," I said. "I don't know who gave you that idea . . .."

Melissa cut me off by withdrawing a binder from her bag. It was a self-mount photo album with a leather cover. She thrust it into my hands.

"What's this?" I asked.

"I found it when my mother died. With my father's things," said Melissa. "Mom pretty much left his stuff alone after the suicide. I don't think anybody stepped foot in his study for at least twenty-five years." Melissa punctuated her remarks with another of her nervous giggles; she also toyed with her ear. "Go ahead," she urged. "Open it."

"I don't think I want to," I said.

Melissa did not encourage me again. Instead, she reached across the end table and opened the volume herself.

The first page contained a discolored newspaper clipping: an article about my second-place finish in a debate tournament, replete with a photo of teenage me and Trish von Elsing at opposing lecterns. The second page of the album contained Polaroid shots of me, and my cohort, at a picnic I no longer remembered. On the third page, all of the photos were of me alone. I closed the album and set it firmly on the end table.

"I was one of your father's favorite students," I said. "So he kept a scrap book of my accomplishments. What does that prove?"

"This isn't the only one," said Melissa, ignoring my question. "There are four others—different girls in each—but yours was the most recent . . . the only one from that final year. And you *were* the last person to see him before he died."

"Who told you that?"

"It doesn't matter who told me, does it? It's true," she continued. "Now, I'll hope you'll forgive me for asking you in this way, but is there anything you can tell me about my father that might explain why he killed himself? *Anything?* I don't care how awful it is, you understand. I'm prepared for that. But I'd rather know than not know."

Melissa's entire body had gone rigid, as though braced for a blow. Desperation rose from her face like heat—the same expression I'd seen on Lacey Moretti's features, so many years before, weeping in the passenger seat of Papa's car. Outside, a pair of blue jays had commandeered the crabapple from the chipmunks. Emily's bus would stop on the corner soon, and I would retrieve her, and Bruce and my daughter and I would sit down to a family dinner, while my guest drove back to Laurenville. I considered reaching for her forearm, to comfort her, but it seemed unnatural.

"I'm not sure what I can tell you—"

"What you can tell me," she interrupted, "is what happened. What happened between you and Daddy on the day he blew his brains out?"

Vance's door stood open that Friday—as it always did for several hours after his last class—and he was seated opposite the window, blinds drawn, leafing through a popular science magazine. In my memory, there was irritation in his voice when he responded to my knock on the open door, but his expression melted when he recognized that it was only me. "Look what the cosmos dragged in," he said. "If it isn't the best and the brightest herself. And to what good fortune do I owe such a pleasure?"

That was a standard Vance greeting. He was always showering us with superlatives, but playfully, never anything remotely improper. I slid my knapsack off my shoulders while he cleared space for me on a plastic chair, brushing a mass of tangled wires and damaged pulleys to the floor. In the corridor, two girls hurled insults at each other over some minor slight while a pack of guys cheered them on. Vance rose decisively, strode to the door and shut it. "That's enough of the unwashed masses for one afternoon," he said. "Now where were we?"

"I'm going stargazing tonight," I announced. "My uncle's taking me."

"So we're going to make a scientist of you yet," said Vance. He settled into his desk chair and retrieved a stack of scrap paper from his filing cabinet. "Here I thought you'd come for my company," he added. "But all you really want is a free lesson in naked-eye astronomy." Vance sighed for effect. "Very well . . .."

One by one, Vance drew out the night's constellations for me: *Cassiopeia*. *Gemini*. He connected Bellatrix to Betelgeuse, transforming haphazard dots into the mighty shoulders of Orion. While he sketched the limits of the visible universe, I gloated about my Bryn Mawr scholarship, thanking him for his recommendation.

"So you're really leaving us," he said.

"I'll come back to visit," I promised. "Often."

"That's what they all say," said Vance with a mock-jaded grin.

He handed me his completed skyscape.

"Never underestimate the power of the stars," he said. "Whenever I feel like I'm a prisoner of the multiverse, I look at the night sky and anything seems possible."

Then he placed his hand on my shoulder—a gentle, delicate gesture that lasted only a few seconds—and he wished me a cloudless night.

In some reflections of the multiverse, Vance's hand rests upon my shoulder for too long—so long that I can feel the warmth of his flesh through my blouse. In others, he does not touch me at all.

In the version I share with his daughter, his touch lasts just long enough, so that it's not even worth a mention, so that it never happened: our entire cosmos is compressed to seconds, and then those seconds are compressed to ether, gone forever, and what remains is something different, something purer, a core of untainted generosity around which an entire new universe can be built.

Insect People

Rich Ives

The Thoughts I Live in Seem to Accept My Flight

European Mining Bee

Dear Chomsky,

My colon's gone semi. I thought telling you would explain my recent uncharacteristic lack of correspondence. Yesterday I tithed my toilet. Today I'm 90% certain I agree with what's left. If you'd send me an opinion on breakfasting, I'd certainly think about it.

I'm still being serviced by two membranous wings, joined in flight by tiny hooks at my narrow waist. I have a saw-like ovipositor, long and slender like in parasitic wasps. I'm told that my egg was fertilized though the males' aren't. I'm a very social gal, and you can rely on me to spread the word about your genius. You probably get that all the time. What I mean is I'll help explain why you're right.

My pollen collection is substantial, despite the temptation to eat it. Add a little honey and it drives the children crazy. I've developed this way of gathering it on my hind legs. I use a protective waterproof substance secreted by an abdominal gland to protect their specially prepared cells.

The kids told me I have white hairs on my back, above and below my thorax. I've never seen them. My abdomen is dark with a bluish sheen that I'm particularly proud of. The kids have protuberances on their abdominal segments. Neither of us seems to have figured out what they're for. This is one of the reasons I'm writing you. I'd also like your opinion on whether or not I actually have a colon. I've heard people talking about it, and I've felt things that seem to correspond, but I'm not exactly like them now am I? Thank God, you aren't either.

Yours in appreciation of the differences,

B. B.

The Thread that Feeds You

Dysderid Spider

When four pairs of seven-segmented walking legs assist the silk spinning organs, and the body tissue of your prey is dissolved by enzymes, producing a liquid that is then sucked up for dinner, my little lovely, we call it a folk tale. It may have round eggs laid inside a sac. It may travel with thread.

You may put your six eyes in a circle. You may admire your own long fangs, sharp enough to pierce tough cuticles. You may awaken nocturnally and hunt on the ground. You may build tubular silk nests in cavities. The threads may radiate from the entrance to the nest.

When a folktale weighs more than the characters contained within the folktale, the surface area must be calculated to determine the number and kind of characters that can be allowed to exist beneath that surface. You might find for example that Susan is one too many. She may not in this way be conducive to the particular tenor of the folktale. She may be too innocent, or too spaced, to fit beneath the framework. She may even be too intelligent for her own good. This could require a different structure.

The females that fit beneath this particular structure arrive here with their eggs wrapped in a silk-lined retreat. They place them in natural cracks and crevices. They have reddish legs and a pinkish-gray or patterned abdomen. They eat woodlice.

It is, of course, entirely possible that the folktale could collapse from its own weight. This is when a more substantial lesson must be learned from the weightier folktale. You might enlist the aid of your spinarets or produce more enzymes. You might be required to travel further with thread. You might, with the aid of this personal silk, find your way out of the folktale, or you may no longer trust the teller of the tale. That, however, would make the lesson even more questionable.

The Tinker's Shell

Harvestman Spider

O Daddy Long Legs, my shepherd of scampering about, that singular body with elongated legs all of a piece and only one pair of eyes, perched on a protuberance like a periscope, you are not truly among the family of web builders, who need three or four pairs of eyes to see your difference.

Father, I implore you, with your two masticating legs and your penis where other many-legged fathers have only boxing gloves, to spin no web, to produce no silk, to spit no venom, to eat only dead insects and plant detritus and aphids and mealy-bugs, to run quickly with a gangly gait like some wading bird when threatened.

Where you eat, Father, a tiny rocking chair sits, tinkering upon the gravestone. No body is here again, only a shell hollowed out by your liquid dinner. Your second pair of legs has a sensory function and remains attentive while you eat. Still you can become dinner and not diner after mating, just as many fathers claim, though you do not bother with their metaphors.

Sacrifice, Father, is your perfection, and you can sever your own limbs to escape. Those sacrificed limbs retain a jerky motion to distract and lure away the predator from the more important goal, but sadly, it entertains cruel children as well.

The Transcendence May Remain in the Failure

Lemon Butterfly

Give me open spaces gently enclosed, give me woodland clearings. Give me Blackthorn when I'm young and a casual flight pattern. I prefer my pollen and nectar from willow catkins.

The guys peek out early in the Spring then the girls follow. It's not merely arrogance to be among the first. We can even withstand being frozen. We have lifters of bright orange. The females have a yellow which is much more subtle.

My name means "angular wing." There is no confusion about where I'm going, but I'll arrive in my own good time. What you have to do should be done your own way, no matter how certain you are of the goal. How can one know if one will succeed? What you have to offer is the beauty and surprise of how you have done it when you arrive, not merely arriving.

Yellow is our right and our heritage, but the yellow is more subtle on the females, and it comes as quite a surprise to find one of us camouflaged in the trees, revealing our ordinary under-reach colors. In winter, when we become adults, we hibernate, but you've heard that before.

Thank Pan for the wild strong odor of the female's exposed odiferous scales that draw us to their abdominal offerings, resulting in yellow-green eggs placed only on Blackthorn. The green caterpillars are dotted in black with two lateral lines and the chrysalis mimics a folded leaf.

There is a legend that the most beautiful among us come from Provence, but, of course, it's only true if you actually come from Provence.

Sometimes I think that my way of seeing things is just a beautiful sham, that I'm one of those miserable two-legged creatures that run about smiling for no reason or chasing after with nets. They seem to think that catching up is not catching an illusion but transporting themselves deeper into their idea of who we are, or perhaps they are right, and we do not even truly exist unless they can possess us. Am I merely a necessary escape from an existence needing to be enhanced by the delicious possibility of a magnificent failure?

The Tunnel that Cannot Be Measured

Click Beetle

Those with the most to say are quiet today (you go to a place that isn't there). There were some teeth in the rafters, a little puddle of them. Cream-filled scissors were marching backwards. Some of us flipped over at the thorax and made a little click. We did it again. Our spines clicked back into the little groove provided for them. We were used to traveling this way in the air, but the flipping end over end had to be repeated several times before landing upright.

Big words we had for little people. I'm offering them as comfortably as any of the many bright bridgeless screws. If I'm still standing, it's because I'm no longer standing still (small beds in my ears, resting me). Some of us still have eyes. It's a thorax thing.

(You said it was a tragic story and that made us laugh.)

I lived in a fresh woolen mansion. Most of the others were in the soil, in their little eggs, two or four hundred of them,

I didn't know. I had bundled unrelated brothers in my bones before I became who I am and functioned without innocence. Sometimes they called me a wireworm. The skin, not the structure, was elected, but its money still existed and stood for apathy. That was when I was eating roots and tubers and freshly planted seeds. I ate for several seasons and nearly ate myself out of the supply.

It was an era of gesture, of fainting, of braggardry. A flimmer. A flutter. A flattery. A bishop in Switzerland who once tried excommunicating me. A flavor of false attention. Coifed pulsives like this hair I have, which is a greeting. In the country your portable house seems larger, translating light to green on cue and weeping from room to room about the absent ceiling.

Poetry

Joanne James

My Truth

Between what I thought life would be and the tearing of the fabric of life
lies my truth:

I never travelled through India or saw the Ellora and Ajanta caves, threw sacred colored
dust on Di Wali, saw
the burning ghats on the Ganges

I never studied with Allen Ginsberg and Anne Waldman at Naropa
in The Jack Kerouac School of Disembodied Poetics
even though I was accepted with a poem called Rats

I never thought I'd find true love that doesn't end and I have

I never went to the Baseball Hall of Fame in Cooperstown   Yet

I never saw Pearl Jam in concert even though I stood in back of The Catalyst

I never had a smart phone   I didn't want to

Once I got out of the car with my best friend and ran towards a lake in the Adirondacks
we were going to be impulsive and brave and jump in with our clothes on

we got to the edge of the lake and saw all of this crappy algae
we stopped short

I never jumped in that lake   I never had much bravado with anything physical

I did ride on the back of a reckless lover's Honda 500
we were speeding   weaving   in and out of traffic
I stared at the asphalt the whole damn time and thought
I'm gonna die

when we made a stop in Cazenovia I told her I couldn't get back on that bike without several shots of tequila in me

I never would have believed earthquake   chronic illness and cancer would be part of my biography

I have a red clarinet   want to learn klezmer   or lay on my back
like Patti Smith and let it blow

this time squeaks and squawks will not be mistakes

I never thought I'd plead for mercy

I never stayed in Iowa City and completed my work on a degree in philosophy

I never was in academe although I thought that was what my life would be

I never thought I'd touch Emily Dickinson's shawl surreptitiously

then hear the guide say   please don't touch anything in this room

I thought I'd receive a message   I never received a message

I never read Dracula or Frankenstein

I never find anywhere I'm accepted when I say I'm a mystic

I never made Christmas cookies

I never knew how true I'd be to my dreams when I had to change course

I never was a spendthrift or a gambler

I never thought I'd have a lesbo-crush on Dave Grohl

I never thought I'd title my first book Fish Dreams

I never thought I'd be the first to follow the path of my Jewish ancestors

I never thought I'd find that River of Light

or the Sturgeon Moon   the Red Moon

never thought I'd understand
the Swallower of Millions   the Great Tree of Peace   the Hemlock Society
the Neptune Society   an ocean filled with cremains

I never went over Niagara Falls in a barrel

I never thought I'd reach The Temple of the Ancients

Hunbatz Men   Mayan Daykeeper taught us how to ride out an earthquake

instead I was thrown against the wall the floor the doorway and
all of the windows of my life up until that moment shattered

these are the accidents of my biography   there are cracks flaws squeaks and squawks
chicken scratch and flowing rivers   fireworks   weedy patches

and that long stretch of train tracks we see going into NYC   where miles of wrecked buildings are covered

by the graffiti of the story of my life.

In Thought, Word, and Deed

Jose Oseguera

By the time Paul and Ariela reached the Caravaggio exhibit at the Los Angeles County Museum of Art, they decided to stop avoiding the urge to hold hands, and finally interlaced fingers. The tingling sensation first came to him when he handed her the red LACMA sticker, she needed to wear in order to be allowed in all the special exhibits. Paul squeezed her hand as if it would fall out of his if he didn't. She blushed. He smiled, showing more teeth than he'd intended. Paul was born in Mexico, but was adopted as an infant by white evangelical Christian missionaries who decided to bring him home to Rialto, California along with all the goat's milk candy they could fit in their luggage. Although his parents had tried to instill as much Hispanic culture in him as their minor in Castellano would allow them, Paul ultimately spoke very little Spanish, just enough to order Mexican food and understand the cashier's muttered slights to the cooks, making fun of the way he pronounced *carnitas*.

"You know," Paul said as Ariela stared intently at one of Caravaggio's paintings, her sweaty hand still tethered to his, "his name wasn't even Caravaggio."

"Oh, really?" she replied, their fingers slowly unbraiding the closer she leaned toward the canvas. "What was it?" Because English wasn't her first language, Paul could never tell whether the sarcastic tone, which seemed to coat most of the things Ariela said, was deliberate or coincidental. Most of the time, he gave her the benefit of the doubt, and when her responses did irritate him, he'd simply tell himself, *even if she meant it the way you thought she meant it, I'm sure that bringing it up to her will only make you look weak.*

"It was Michelangelo Merisi." Ariela rubbed her nose and continued to stare. If she didn't care about his intellect, as he had hoped, then why was she giving him more physical affection in public? Before that day, the most intimacy they'd shared was when they sat next to each other—knee to knee—watching American movies dubbed in Spanish while her roommate was in class. He knew that he was falling for her due to how wounded he felt when she didn't react the way he'd hoped she would at this obscure fact, which neither enhanced nor diminished her interest in the painting. "Actually, Caravaggio was the place he was from. Kind of like Vinci for Leonardo."

Ariela yawned. She squinted and peered her head so close to the canvas that her breath began to fog up the painting's sheen. It set off a disapproving nod from the tall, stout security guard who up to that point had been nothing but a breathing statue. Paul squeezed her hand tightly as to alarm her of the impending danger of being kicked out. She leaned in an inch further.

"Miss," the security guard's voice echoed on the naked walls and high ceilings. "Please step away from the art."

Ariela didn't move. Neither did Paul.

Sir, Paul imagined clearing his throat and halting the guard with the sound of his voice, *please don't take what she's doing the wrong way. She's not from around here*.

He felt responsible for her, as though it were his duty to look after her, even though she'd never once asked him to do so. Her lips said nothing and the limited, yet perfectly curated words she did use—because she hated mispronouncing and misusing them—said even less. Paul knew that there was something Ariela wanted, something she thought was so stupid and embarrassing that she just couldn't bring herself to ask for. Part of him wished he could speak Spanish as perfect as he spoke English so that he could tell her to knock it off, and just tell him whatever the hell she needed, even if he would be the one getting hurt by it. But another part of him liked the fact that she needed him if only to translate stuff for her from English to Spanish, and whenever she needed to order something at a café or restaurant, from Spanish to English and back to Spanish again. He realized how ridiculously unnecessary the whole thing was a week into their friendship when he overheard Ariela argue with her roommate about the water bill.

He didn't think about questioning how much English she really knew. He didn't want to know.

Maybe someone as independent as her just needs someone to be vulnerable with, he thought. *Someone to do nice things for her*. It was a role he was more than happy to play, that of a friend in love to one who might someday love him back, but most likely not. He wasn't doing it because Ariela had lived in Mexico until she completed one semester of college, or because her English was as broken as the system that treated culture as balmy deli meat at a salad bar that needed a sneeze guard. He did it because he knew that Ariela didn't mind it.

The more he got to know her, the more he realized that she was willing to use whatever was given to her to further whatever it was she wanted. Her boyfriend—whom she never mentioned until Paul felt the urge to lean in and kiss her while sitting on her couch—sold his motorcycle to pay for her first month of rent, and her mother took a second job to pay for her out-of-state tuition. Today, she was taking advantage of her lack of mastery of the English language. A few days ago—when she told Paul that he could spend the night at her apartment if he wanted—it was the "no sex" rule she established when he tried to slide his hand up her blouse after she had allowed him to watch her change into her pajamas and spoon her. Again, Paul blamed Ariela's poor syntax for the misunderstanding, not her.

"Motherfu—miss," the security guard said and began to walk toward them. "Miss? I'm only going to warn you once more."

"Sorry," Ariela finally said. "I couldn't hear you." Paul didn't know if he was pulling his hand from hers out of guilt, or if it was sliding out due to the sweat. Either way, she took his hand and placed it around her waist. "Paul, tell this man about Caravaggio."

"What?" the guard said.

"It's okay. Paul, c'mon, tell him something. Can't you see he's waiting?"

"Well . . . he was actually . . . he was a murderer," Paul said, holding his breath as to somehow stop the sweat from gushing out of his skin.

"Hmmm . . ." she said backing away as if she hadn't almost desecrated a masterpiece. The guard shook his head, turned around and walked back to his post where he resumed his semi-alert status.

"I think they're stupid," Ariela said.

"Who? Security guards?" Paul said.

"No," they continued to walk and stopped at the next painting, "artists."

Paul laughed. She didn't. As he stuffed his wet hands—and his laughter—into his pant pockets, the thought that Ariela had paid attention to the facts he had read about the night before in anticipation of their date, which wasn't officially a date, made him smile.

"Do you know what Caravaggio means? Literally?" she asked.

"Well, cara can mean beautiful or expensive and—"

She approached his face with the same level of unbridled irreverence she had Caravaggio's work and lightly brushed her lips against his.

"Uh, now that I think about it, I guess I don't," he said, staring at the painting of a decapitated man as if his gushing blood held the translation of its author's nom de plume hidden in its red pearls. "What does it mean?"

"I don't know," she said, walking to the next painting hanging on the wall, pulling him along. "Just thought you might know. Seems like you like him a lot, that's all."

Paul wished he could tell her, *It's you I like*, but he said nothing out of fear that she wouldn't understand. Or worse, that she wouldn't care.

Ariela had made it a habit of sleeping over at Paul's apartment. At first, she only did so when they watched a movie whose runtime went past 10:00 p.m. Then, every weekend because he lived near a park that had a nice farmers market on Saturdays. Even though she was now sleeping in his bed every night of the week, movie or no movie, the "no sex" rule still applied. However, in her mind, "no sex" didn't mean "no touching or kissing." Her breasts were small, swimming in his large T-shirts she wore as pajamas, but he knew exactly where to find them, right where he'd left them the night before. They had created their own vocabulary. Their own language: part verbal, part body.

Her short-leash relationship with the man whose name she would never reveal to Paul—in her mind if he was nameless, he didn't have to worry about him—was close enough for sexting and dirty show-and-tell via Skype, but far enough for her to seek supplementary companionship. In other words, Paul was the body, and her boyfriend was the mind, heart, and soul.

While they lay in each other's arms after having assisted each other in getting off, she would tell him that when she was living in Mexico, her boyfriend refused to have vaginal sex with her. Paul asked why. She didn't know.

"Maybe he's gay," Paul said, hearing the spiteful words echoing in her silence, hoping they were true while at the same time regretting he'd ever said them.

"No, he's not," she said as if Paul was the one who needed assurance. He liked doing it in every way—fill all her holes—except for the one that mattered most to her, the one boring deep between her heart's arteries. "He's just super Christian, and he wants us to wait."

Having been raised in that sexually stunting, hormonally frustrating climate—with balls as blue as the Virgin's cloak—Paul understood her boyfriend's apprehension and guilt.

"What do *you* want, though?" Paul said. Ariela sighed.

"How do you say, mmm?" she said. She huffed. "Never mind. I just want—"

"What's wrong?" he said. She nodded away Paul's question with a soft hum. He placed his free hand on her thighs, and she looked down on it. He felt a single tear—hot as wax—trickle on his knuckles.

"C'mon. What's wrong?" Paul asked again. Ariela let out a flustered sigh and wiped the tears draining out of her nose.

"It's nothing," she answered. "Well . . . it's hard to explain." It could've been because her English wasn't that good, just good enough, or because no words existed in the English or Spanish languages combined to describe what she wanted to say or hide in her labored breathing. It was something she wanted to rip out of her chest—a dead heart that quit beating long ago. Paul dragged his body closer to her knees and outstretched his hand to meet hers.

"You know you can tell me anything."

"Yeah, I know," she sniffled. After she kissed her teeth a few times, she slapped her hands on her thighs.

"Just say it in Spanish," Paul said. As far as he was concerned, he wouldn't have been able to understand what was going on even if she had said it in plain English. But it wasn't a matter of saying what was wrong or even admitting that something was wrong. It was that in spite of knowing that something in her wasn't right, there was no real way for him to know exactly what was wrong because she herself wouldn't go there. "Maybe he's scared of getting you pregnant."

By the way she bit her lips, he knew that she was starved for love, as an animal who resorted to auto cannibalism, seeking nourishment from what was left of its own bodies. It didn't matter how much he wanted to help; the best he could do for her at that moment was to just stay there and wait for her to use him in whatever way she needed.

They lay quietly on the bed, Paul on his side, propping his head up with one arm and placing the other on his upper thigh. She was sitting on her calves—inside the curvature made by his legs and torso—looking down at him. The lights were off and the only glimmer was emanating from an old Bed Bath & Beyond pine-scented candle she'd stolen from her roommate's bedroom. The candle's dimmed brilliance flickered in the tears welling up in her eyes. She looked away, trying not to blink.

At first, she began to speak soft—slowly—gibberish that he knew meant something important to her. Then her speech became louder and faster—violent—looking at Paul as if she hated him, flailing her arms, clicking her wrists, gripping her palms. The look in her eyes—those dark, soulful eyes—yelled for something he could never give her even as he was giving her every part of himself. How Paul wished he could speak enough Spanish to say, "I'm sorry you feel that way." But he didn't want to know what she was saying; he wished he knew what she was thinking, and not give her a chance to hide in her silence. They were both impostors: he was born in Mexico, but there was nothing Mexican in him; she was in love with him, but no part of her heart was his to fill.

He propped himself up into a seated position and buried her in his arms close and tight—trying to suffocate any doubt in her mind. Her body was shaking; she felt warm and cold, stiff and frail. She continued to speak in a language that would've confused any Spanish speaker. However, he understood everything her heart palpitations were yelling. Every single word.

If Paul could, he would take her to a secluded place, a place beyond shame, beyond judgment, beyond anything even he could give her: a place beyond love. What they felt wasn't love or lust: it was pity. They started to kiss each other as if they didn't know what the gesture meant. He placed her hand on his thigh, and she slid it towards his crotch. Part of him felt that she was jerking him around, using him as a surrogate lover; it made her touch cold, almost robotic, as though they both wanted the same things, but each for very different reasons. He wanted to turn sex into love, and she wanted to turn their sex into something that would take feeling away.

Paul placed her chin in his hands and kissed her eyelids. He felt her grip grow tighter and the rhythm of it getting faster and warmer, as two reptiles seeking warmth where there was none. Deep in their four-walled Eden, they finally understood what this was about. She treated his body as if she herself was a man as if his penis was her own and she was going to be the one who would climax through it. In her clasp, those nerve endings had a purpose: bringing back feeling—not for him, but for her—to a starved beast clawing its way out of the love she would probably never have for him.

Ariela collapsed on her side after Paul came, but he didn't feel good. He nestled next to her; she didn't move. He wanted to tap on her shoulder, but he didn't just in case she had fallen asleep, which he knew she had not. Insomnia pulsated in his head, with the question that he'd been wanting to ask her as soon as she held his hand at the museum, one that he knew she'd never answer even if he asked it in perfect Castilian Spanish: *Why him and why not me?*

The sea of tousled black hair told him more than her words—in English or Spanish, human or demonic tongue—ever could. Goosebumps consumed the entirety of her skin as whatever it was that made her and him into them, the fake lovers that other museum-goers looked towards and smiled at. Their strange faces reflecting the love that wasn't quite there yet, regardless of how many selfies Ariela and Paul took, or how tightly they gripped each other's hands.

Paul woke up after what felt like minutes, but Ariela's petite body continued to heave gently, emitting sighs and coos. As he watched her, even her snores came off disingenuous.

The room was dark and cold and the pine-scented candle had died, and so had they.

Stephen Pavlovic "Hungry Ghosts howling at the moon"

The Mystery of Names

Mir-Yashar Seyedbagheri

My sister's name was Nancy Drew. I was Nick. No joke. And in 1955, everyone gave her grief over it, my nerdy, tender sister who always wore lavender and sported large cat-eye glasses, who smelled like perfume and soap, the sweetest of scents. Motherly scents even, scents that were rare in our little home.

"Solve the mystery of my bad grades," some student said.

"What about my parents?" another student said. "Why are they so uptight? You're the detective, Nancy Drew."

"Solve the mystery of your unpopularity," another, crueler asshole growled.

"And the mystery of those glasses," someone else said.

They showed up with flashlights and magnifying glasses like the actual Nancy carried. They all teased her, in the halls, in her classrooms. There were the brunettes with their pageboys, the tall basketball players with their buzzcuts, the cheerleaders. They waved the flashlights at her, laughing like hyenas. They made jokes about her glasses, called her the "nerdy detective," too.

The whole time, I wished she'd fight back, lunge at the world that was taunting her. I'd fought assholes who teased me about Nancy or our family many times before, with only the slightest provocation. She moved through the halls of our high school with a kind of grace and elevation the actual Nancy Drew probably lacked. She had a kind of patience, a kind of acceptance I lacked completely, even in dealing with me.

She never yelled at me when I fought, although I detected a kind of sadness, a weariness, and I felt an innate love for my sister, and a need to tell her I needed to fight. Even if it was over a name. Especially with our parents all but gone, our father having run off with an Episcopal priest's daughter and Mother always in Europe, writing what she called "nihilistic liturgies," exposing the idiocy of people's lives.

A jock, Bubba Dupree, even turned the whole Nancy Drew thing into a matter of sex, since he had a crush on her for years. Nancy, of course, found Bubba repugnant, loud, and someone who thought little of the future.

"Tell your sister to find the secret of the old cock," he said to me, laughing and pointing to his pants.

"I'll find the secret of my foot in your ass," I'd growled, trying to sound like someone else, like Brando, like James Dean, like any number of the actors who leered at me from posters in the lobby of the movie theater.

I'd tried to beat him up, flailed, my lanky arms lunging into the air, but I'd ended up being pummeled. I'd taken each punch, embraced the pain, imagining my sister, trying to comport herself with dignity, a quiet, young woman. I imagined so much, as Bubba's fist kept flying.

I kept imagining Nancy in her classes, walking down the hall, keeping so much to herself, imagined the things she must be thinking about her classmates. I imagined the weight of her name, a name that she despised.

I imagined how she must have despised the way the other students owned the school, comported themselves without care or compassion. All over a name. She must have thought there was little chance of personal friendship, of a personal and loving communion and she must have been weeping inside, her heart being torn apart, crushed, like some item one leaves on the train tracks. I imagined the ease with which Bubba slandered her, the crudeness of it all rushing from his beefy body. I imagined how he was incapable of kindness, decency.

Yet, she kept comporting herself. Except where her name was concerned, something we talked about often. And she always hated her name. Fact was she hated that name with an intensity that frightened me. She'd mention it in the most casual conversations. She and I'd go for drives, people-watching downtown, through the tonier neighborhoods (imagining ourselves in those Colonials and Tudors), and she'd tell me how she despised it, the cheerful quality of the name, the pretentiousness of it, even. Nancy Drew. She preferred some different name, something foreign.

"It's not the jokes so much," she said on one such drive, "and don't get me wrong, I hate them. And I hate the name. But it's more than that. It's that I can't live up to the fucking name."

"What do you mean?"

"Nancy Drew could own the world if she wanted," my sister said. "I have to work my rear off just to meet the smallest goals. God knows how we're going to survive, Nick. I don't know what's going to happen when I graduate, what I'll do. And I know it's funny, talking about a detective novel, but I'm envious, in a way. Envious of the actual Nancy Drew, because she has so much. And I feel like a fraud with that name."

"You're more accomplished than the bozos at school," I said. "Or Nancy Drew herself."

"I wouldn't mind solving a mystery like that," she said. "Not just for the fame. But because I'd be doing something useful, you know? Helping people who are hurt, torn apart by the fucking world.

"You know," she added. "I wonder how much different it would be to have a whole different name."

"That could be interesting," I said, imagining the possibilities.

"I should," Nancy said. "Just up and change it. Would anyone care if we did it? Who's going to even say anything? I'll bet Dad changes his name. Wherever he is. So he doesn't have to see us."

Nancy never solved mysteries or exposed swarthy criminals, but she could tell a dirty joke when she wanted to. She was a scholarly sort, who could talk about the world's problems, about the need for civil rights, without sounding pompous. She was a wonderful singer, whose throaty renditions of Cole Porter could make you feel like the world was still funny and delightful and mysterious. She made sure I got to school and always had what she called "fireside chats" with me before bed, where we talked about our problems, comparing their magnitude. We'd huddle together in my room, as if conspiring, letting the secrets spill forth: Rowdy seniors laughed at her and made jokes about her, about her glasses, suggesting remarks about her physicality.

I hated my freshman history teacher, Mr. Ludendorff, who claimed I'd never make it in the world, because I couldn't seem to articulate big ideas and concepts about dead, irrelevant personages. My English teacher, Mr. Greenlee said I couldn't find a metaphor with two hands and a dictionary.

I'd wanted to tell her so much. Tell her that names didn't matter, that our father didn't matter, that she'd given me so much, that she shouldn't worry about the world's demands. The way they saw us, saw Nancy, saw our family. I thought she gave more than I could expect, love, patience. She gave so much when she was on the precipice of things too.

I wanted to tell her the world would give her justice in due time. But I knew that was bullshit even at my age, when everyone seemed to be leaving us in the lurch.

The truth of our lives: It was the name that attracted attention, but it was also more than that. It was what our surname, Drew, connoted beyond images of detectives fighting off swarthy men. Nancy once told me the name conveyed a sort of history. Even if it weren't a detective novel, she said, it would be bad enough.

"What do you mean?"

"Well," she'd said. "We have to answer for the things our parents do, whether we like them or not. Because of the name. It's like being a kid and you make a mess, right? And your mother has to clean that up, whether she likes it or not. Difference is we're like the mother and we gotta stick around to clean up the crap."

"I guess I understand that," I'd said. "Not much fun though, having to clean up for selfish people."

"No, honey, it isn't."

There was much we had to clean up, but couldn't, a history of runaway parents, of constantly losing things and never receiving things in return. We weren't the kind of family that people were accustomed to. The family who kept their laundry neatly hidden in the shadows, and wore starched smiles. The man in the grey flannel suit for a father.

People saw my sister as a source of amusement, a social pariah, a fallen woman. They saw me as an insignificant entity. It seemed to me that people measured Nancy by her unusual name, coming from storied families themselves. These were people who held onto their two-parent families and country-club creeds, their holy and apostolic assholery. They refused to share them with us, even the smallest fortunes of their lives, taking us into their grand homes, offering some semblance of comfort, however empty. Some even joked that we'd have good fortune because of her august name.

If that was the case, fate was hiding its treasure from us. Nancy Drew and the Mystery of The Fucked Up World.

I started to think of my own name and its meaning. Nicholas, which meant victory, started to seem fake, and I felt as if I were in this together with my sister. In school, I noticed it more, this emphasis on names and identities, even more than before. People carried their surnames and they labeled each other for better or worse, on the basis of physicality or behaviors or what-have-you. Names illuminated our own misfortunes in a way and slapped us with truths. There were no victories or detectives, only Nancy Drew jokes, bills piling up, a father out in the world living selfishly, and a high school for me that was predicated on hierarchies and names. I felt the intensity of my sister's self-hatred, a young woman cursed with a name she hadn't chosen.

Some nights, she'd steal into my room late at night, and cry when she didn't think I was noticing. She'd also utter her name aloud multiple times, saying it over and over. Nancy Drew. Nancy Drew. Sometimes, she even said it with a foreign accent, as if that would mitigate the weight of the name, its history for us, its literary connotations. But after a while, she'd just shake her head and leave, or stare out the window, as if the moon, the stars, held answers to this situation.

A year later, she changed her last name to Botkin and I did too. We'd learned that Mother was staying on in Europe longer, her letter filled with cold platitudes about "space" and the "nothingness" of home life. Nancy said she had read about a court doctor in Russia who had that name. He'd been shot with the tsar and the royal family, but she admired his patience and dignity, she said. He didn't need to be the center of attention, of history, of any of that. He just dedicated himself to his tsar and his family, and Nancy admired that kind of dedication, that withdrawal into love and commitment.

"If we have to have a name," she said. "Let it be Botkin. People will still have their fun. At least, we're worthy of being Botkins."

I tried on the name. Botkin to me held a kind of mystery, the promise of something new. And it held a kind of hope, a hope for a future, where we could somehow recreate our own stories, make things up, if whatever else. We could imagine ourselves coming from kinder, gentler families, having a father who wasn't a lecherous sort, a mother who stuck around and overwhelmed us with love. We could be noble, we could be people of class. Of course, it was all an illusion, but for a moment, it seemed so perfect to me. And to my sister too.

The day we changed our names, we stormed out of the courthouse, heads held high, walking with a kind of defiant poise. Dignity. Walking with my sister, we fought expectations and jokes, we wore our new names, we illuminated our new selves, knowing that we would fight on, in a world that embraced cruelty and possessed no shortage of names for it.

Poetry

Julia Franklin

The Boggart

There used to be this boggart in our house.
Not a big thing, really; actually quite small.

Of course, we didn't used to see her that way;
There was a time when we were the ones that were small.

She had a row of teeth for every bit of flesh we bore.
She'd bring them out, all neat and sharp and small.

One day we stared her down and brought our own teeth out,
And the growl that stirred in her throat was small.

The night passed without incident. When the sun rose,
We found footprints out the door. We thought, "*Now* who's small?"

I heard she found another house to haunt,
Its occupants each Bambi-eyed and small.

The Truckers

It's a world that shines with sun and sweat

In which she wakes and pushes up her sleeves.
Whatever comes, her beast is strong and true,
And there's nothing that she and her paint can't do.

And her buddies are just the same:
Every day, they alternately push and dance their way
Through a world fit for only the bravest.
All very much in love,
They fit like fingers in a glove.

I don't think I myself would fit;
I wasn't built for the ride.
We're all different, and they understand.

But before each adventure, I press each callused hand
And pray they find their footing everywhere
And in my thoughts and spirit, I am there.

Noah's Song

O nymph, you gave me to believe
The wilderness could take or leave
This tongue-tied faun,
This fodder for the Good Lord's funny way.
For years he's greeted every day
With this same bitter sentiment:

"I wonder where I'll wash up next?"

For years he's trembled in the shoes of the forsaken.
His seams have all been splitting;
In the forest, in the meadow,
In every spot of sun and shadow,
He's had to strain to keep from breakin,'

But now, he's bound for solid ground
And he don't want to hear a *sound*
Out of the likes of you.

The Online Gallery

Greedy-Guts has got me by the hair.
I keep telling it: "That's quite enough.
You've had your time to do your stuff.
Settle yourself down for the night.
You've done your worst,
And now I'm fit to burst."
Yet the trays of sweets keep coming,
And the champagne corks keep popping,
And I keep on succumbing,
And the pathos shows no signs of stopping.

Bedeviled

I've been told I'm often absent
While my body's in the room.
And though I know that's true of everyone,
I get where my critics are coming from.

The thing is, I belong to many countries,
Each with its own customs,
And sometimes I forget which one I'm in,
And cannot tell a virtue from a sin.

Who am I kidding? I don't forget.
I just don't really give a shit.

You vs. The Apocalypse

by Ayman Elsayed

TITLE: You vs. The Apocalypse
GENRE: Legal, Simulation, Strategy
DEVELOPER: COVID-19
FRANCHISE: Pandemic Interactive
PUBLISHER: Ayman Elsayed
RELEASE DATE: March 15, 2020

The handling of the end of the world is on trial. Your only mission is to survive. Overcome struggles such as mental health, physical isolation and deteriorating resources by interacting with technology. Engage with others. Find a hobby. Judge your community. Protect yourself from yourself.

Single-player
Achievements
Full Remote Compatibility

RECENT REVIEWS: Very Negative. 99.9% of the 7,729,536,211 user reviews in the last 30 days are negative.

Popular user-defined tags for this product: Closed World, Survival Horror, RPG, Retro, Sandbox, Social Distancing, Crafting, Souls-like.

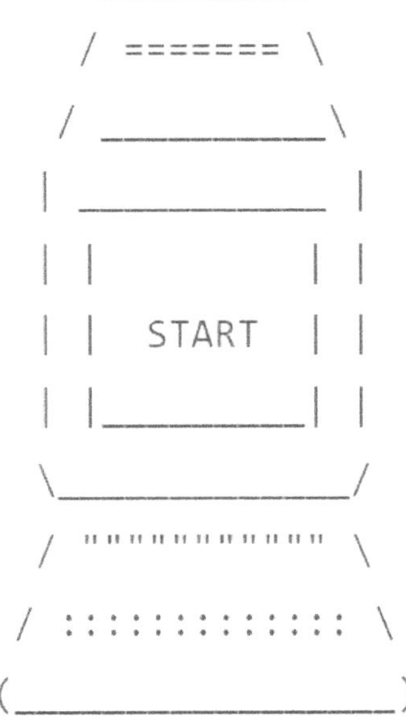

[DAY ONE]

[Your morning routine begins.]
[It is the end of the world. You are now under strict quarantine.]
[Your mental narrator is providing useless arbitration, endless commentary and obtuse punchlines.]
[Your goal is to stay informed, safe and engaged throughout regularly scheduled Programming.]

Exhibit A:

Like most people, I met the looming threat of COVID-19 with outright denial. I became more and more apprehensive with each major announcement, each blow softened by the dismissiveness of peers and inaction by leaders. We kept the existential threat at bay for a short while with healthy doses of satire, sarcasm or simple misdirection. The growing wave of panic continued to set in seemingly overnight. By the time we realized shit had gotten real, we were already fighting over toilet paper. It was a pyrrhic victory at best for the half that won, because the sewer systems were so backed up from the other half flushing down whatever they could get their dirty hands on. Next thing we knew, we were all knee deep, stocking up on anything wipeable for the long haul. It didn't matter what public officials were warning—cognitive bias based on a lifetime in security is a whole 'nother ball game.

[You do not understand what you have read yet.]
[You have just woken up. Your eyes are hazy. Your thoughts are murky.]
[Your mind is taking its time to unravel puzzle pieces of a dream from another world.]
[You finish collecting yourself.]
[Your dream triggers a memory about how self-expression is vital to #selfcare during times of hardship.]
[You feel energized with an abundance of life.]
[You are bursting with rays of hope.]
[You will be a beacon of light in a long, dark and silent night.]

[You endeavor to be a #selfmade citizen of the world who shares #simpleapocalypsetips to combat 'Viral Panic'.]

[You decide to spend your day being productive by researching a new skill.]

Exhibit B:

This week on How It's Made: End Times Edition, we take a deep dive into the subtle nuances of Content Writing for a 21st Century Audience. These dystopic publications act like bookmarks for mental collection and later, extensive in-house processing. Through a vain attempt to feed the mind's rapturous desire to stave off compulsive self-thought, self-obsession quickly boils, bubbles and crystallizes into diagnosed classic narcissism, steadily settling beneath the surface tension. This is where seemingly random bits of information are systematically condensed, sorted and added to loosely correlated collections of superficial worldviews that are sold in the social marketplace to willing participants using a complex process called 'cultural osmosis,' or what is colloquially known to the unwitting public as an "opinion." Upon dissemination, the ever-so-humble opinion's reactive bonds become viscous and achieve maximum virality by mechanism of muted golf claps and hushed pinky raises followed by an obligatory #toast for its tireless contributor.

[You have learned that being overly specific, relevant and ironic are key to seeming authoritative through a seemingly authoritative source that is overly specific, relevant and ironic.]
['Social Media Marketing' Skill Level increases +1.]

[You believe that your opinion will have weight from validation.]
[Mood increases +1.]

[You feel happy that you have used your time wisely.]
[Mood increases +1.]

[You have spent some time online.]
[Sanity decreases -1.]

[This experience triggers a memory about SEO.]
[You decide to spend some time compiling a list of unique words to include in insightful content.]

Exhibit C:

Top 5 Buzzwords During the Apocalypse:

-Optics

-Brand

-Agency

-RNG

-Cheesing

[You question whether you are #woke enough to appease your target audience.]
[Mood decreases -1.]

[You question whether your contribution will age well.]
[Mood decreases -1.]

[You question whether your contribution will be considered pandering.]
[Mood decreases -1.]

[You question whether your contribution will be meaningful.]
[Mood decreases -1.]

[Your mood has changed too quickly.]
[Sanity decreases -1.]

[You feel sad that you have not used your time wisely.]
[Mood decreases -1.]

[Your mood is critically low, triggering a psychological self-preservation module.]
[You gain a 'Depressed' status debuff in the form of a mental response.]
[You are immune to the effects of your mood for the remainder of the session.]
[You can no longer pursue hobbies for the remainder of the session.]
[You are a testament to the power of learned helplessness.]
[You must assess the situation before continuing.]

[You realize the Optics are poor as you have lost Agency over your emotions.]
[You decide to move on for now to gain some perspective for your Brand.]
[Sanity increases +1.]

[You have spent some time online.]
[Sanity decreases -1.]

[You decide to continue.]

Exhibit D:

A good portion of my idle time is spent sifting through random articles. The would-be slivers of dopamine I unlock are episodic and rare, triggered by some particularly specific insight about world affairs. And if I have to be completely honest, and apparently I do, I am completely and utterly addicted to 24-hour "news" cycles. I can say this with absolute certainty because this endeavor has provided no net benefit, intellectually, emotionally or spiritually, and I have been rendered morally bereft in the process. Although I am obligated by law to let you know that I am, indeed, morally bereft, I still got out clean with my dog by my side. If you know me personally, you know I have probably mentioned the pangs of hurt I can physically feel when I consume media that is unambiguously lazy, deliberately void of opinion, or worse, strategically manipulative. Constantly analyzing who some content is meant to appeal to, or obsessing over players and the motives behind them, is all part of the game. It's the meta-entertainment and I play on both sides against myself, scrutinizing every angle, paying little merit to any inherent message. I consider it a valuable service worth its weight in equal parts gratitude and mercy. I'm also bound by law to advise that you should "pay no attention to the idle musings of a morally bereft, cyber-world derelict" and am to maintain at least 300 spaces between your viewing receptacle and eyeballs at all times.

[You internalize a sense of embarrassment that feels foreign to you.]
[You cringe in response.]
[Empathy decreases -1.]

[You feel for the person who wrote this, although you believe that they do not deserve empathy.]
[Empathy decreases -1.]
[You do not understand what you are experiencing.]

[You are worried that your brain has encountered malicious Programming.]
[You think that it is reading code, processing an error and rebooting its thoughts.]
[Sanity decreases -1.]

[You think about how you are thinking about this. It hurts.]
[Sanity decreases -2.]

[You think about how you are thinking about how it hurts. It hurts.]
[Sanity decreases -3.]

[You are now Ensnared by a Thought Loop.]

[You are slowly developing a 'Headache' ailment.]
[Health decreases -1.]
[You feel sad that you have not used your time wisely.]
[Mood decreases -1.]

[You have spent some time online.]
[Sanity decreases -1.]

[You decide to resolve the error with a special update to regularly scheduled Programming.]

Exhibit E:

EXPERT OPINION: My name is Dr. Professional Advocate, here with an abundance of years of knowledge, research and experience. My goal is to reassure you that Everything is O.K. Currently, your screens are fully saturated with a seemingly endless stream of content, and most of it is overwhelmingly negative. Manufactured this way for clicks, hits or whatever your preferred nomenclature for engagement is. The effects are relatively inconsequential in the grand scheme of things and are deemed safe for regular consumption due to low risk. That is O.K. The vast majority of available Programming is filtered through an algorithm personally designed to promote a feeling of insecurity, which you can satiate through further engagement. This is a closed feedback loop designed to reinforce your sense of security for maximum viewing pleasure. You are O.K. Thank you.

[You are distracted by trying to understand what you have read.]
[You feel a little bit calmer.]
[Sanity increases +5.]

[Experience saved into Memory Bank.]

[You feel happy that you have not used your time wisely.]
[Mood increases +1.]

[You have spent some time online.]
[Sanity decreases -1.]

[You decide to continue.]

Exhibit F:

Reading about the plight of citizens in China who are suffering through an entirely novel, highly contagious and deadly pandemic didn't make me more empathetic, as much as I wish I could say otherwise. At most, it made me feel grateful that my loved ones are safe in a way that is entirely based on fear.

[You feel ashamed that you have read this and give up half-way.]
[Empathy decreases -1.]

[You feel ashamed of the human race.]
[Empathy decreases -7,729,536,212.]

[Empathy is critically low, triggering a psychological self-preservation module.]
[You gain a 'Numb' status debuff as a physiological response.]
[Your heart is a stone-cold samurai, unbound by the emotional tethers of this world.]
[You are immune to the effects of empathy for the remainder of the day.]

[You have spent some time online.]
[Sanity decreases -1.]

[You decide to continue.]

Exhibit G:

Let me paint an uncanny picture. I meet horrible headlines about social inequity or disasters multiple borders away with false sincerity and resigned apathy. I mean, I care, but not in a way that is personal because 'it doesn't affect me' or 'I can't do anything about it.' The truth is, I have hardwired myself this way to a fault by choosing what I consume and how I consume it. Even worse, this is a source of distinction that I identify with. Even better, I enjoy it more than the pleasure of ego death.

[You are unsure how many times the writer has used the word "I" in the last paragraph, still making these issues about themselves, and unfairly, you.]
[You are not satisfied by your observation.]
[Nothing happens.]

[You continue ruminating but there is no effect.]
[Nothing happens.]

[You count seven times in six sentences.]
[Sanity decreases -1.]

[You try to remember what the issues at hand were.]
[You fail.]
[You read again.]
[You give up.]
[Sanity decreases -2.]

[You have internalized too many discrepancies in Programming.]
[You are slowly developing a 'Confusion' ailment.]
[Sanity decreases -1.]

['Headache' is now pounding.]
[Health decreases -2.]

[You have spent some time online.]
[Sanity decreases -1.]

[You decide to continue.]

Exhibit H:

The truth is, I have probably always had the basic amenities I need to survive, even if they weren't on the mental periphery. It's easy to squeak by the thought of an apocalypse using skeptical, ironic and satirical deflections from a distance. It's what allows me to feel safe because I don't have the misfortune of being personally affected by it. Incidentally, it's also what hampers my ability to genuinely acknowledge it. Basically, I enjoy the simple pleasures that life has to offer.

['Headache' worsens.]
[Your gushing heart is mainlining an unhealthy dose of stress hormones into your brain.]
[Sound is muted from an obnoxiously high-pitched ringing in your ears.]
[Health decreases -3.]

['Confusion' is now causing your eyes to wander indiscriminately.]
[Sanity decreases -2.]

[You consciously trigger a memory: you are O.K.]
[Sanity increases +1.]

[You have spent some time online.]
[Sanity decreases -1.]

[You decide to continue.]

Exhibit I:

Before the epidemic hit, I had no security. I was a victim of existential dread, with no prospects. Most days, I had the trouble of knowing where I stood in life before anyone else knew where to look. Now, thanks to the threat of a global pandemic, I am a different and better breed altogether. By tracking the spread of the infection since it first began its onslaught against mankind, I realized only one thing matters: "we are fucked." It was so reassuring whenever someone heard those words come out of my mouth that I could tell people were beginning to feel completely at ease. Despite my best efforts, the neighborhood has taken to social distancing. Society's eventual entropic spiral will swallow them mercilessly as I ruminate upon its collapse from the safety of my isolated home dwelling and bulk shipments of emergency supply drop care packages. I've come to admire this charming disposition, along with my sense of duty and personal conviction.

['Confusion' worsens.]
[You notice the weight of your body.]
[You are no longer entranced by the stupor of glowing softness.]
[Your eyes are glazed over.]
[Sanity decreases -3.]

[Sanity is critically low, triggering a psychological self-preservation module.]
[You gain a 'Mental Fatigue' status debuff in the form of a physical response.]
[The call of the void seductively echoes: Zzz . . . zzz . . . zzz . . ..]
[You can no longer legibly understand English without losing 'Conscious Awareness' unless you internalize useful Programming.]
[You must assess the situation before continuing.]

[You decide that you will only stay informed by the most authoritative sources.]
[Sanity increases +1.]

[You have spent some time online.]
[Sanity decreases -1.]

[You decide to continue.]

Exhibit J:

PRESS CONFERENCE: I am now firmly grounded in reality and the sense of uncertainty it comes with. The fear for my loved ones, people in general as a whole, including complete and total strangers is Very, Very real. Their mental wellbeing and cognitive ability to perform during a time of social collapse, especially. It's really, scary times, and completely unprecedented, which I think everyone understands and fully agrees, that I don't think anyone could fully understand the projections in the simulation, with or without great intellect. That's only fair to say, which I am now co-opting confirmed agreement upon, by the most established professionals, who I am privileged to have close relation to myself, in the 'biz,' so-to-speak, something that we like to say for laughs, who all agree, that foreshadowing was simply, Again, completely and utterly, not possible. It has been done. It has been co-opted upon. It is only worth discussing how we can Make it through the, Again, Great future ahead of All of us. I hope we can all muster up the courage to get our hands dirty, you know, really dig deep, Very, Very, deep, into the trenches of common ground. I don't think I have to mention the foreign horrors going on here, chances are you have already heard about that. So, I won't. But they are still there, which you know, are large in number, always ever-present, and forever encroaching on our way of life, as the epitome of #fakenews, which we know to be the Very unacceptable essence of life itself. But I have spared you that. It has been done. Now, the real reason I am here. I am here to stand up for those of you who are able to stand up. As Senior Politician, who takes Great pride in Great action with Great responsibility, I declare war. In response to my own public and Very sincere declaration, one that is proven to be mutually reassuring, that is to say, this is about Very real and Very actionable war. I can even probably say, on the record, that I am honestly, the luckiest person, to be among the most privileged of them all, because today I can proudly state, Again, in complete earnest, that I will be offering, my Very highly regarded and Great, Certificate of Public Security, intended for bordered consumption, available completely for free, with no prior conditions, no questions asked, no strings attached, absolutely nothing, to any Great individual, or corporation, in exchange for a solemn oath of undying loyalty, stated clearly, of course, on the record. Whether we want to accept it or not, our fundamental model for security has been damaged by a magnitude of ten global fortitudes. Great action is now taken, which is a monumental stride for the downfall of our history textbooks. It has been done. I am now going to finish, by stating, the Great loss of humanity through suddenly apparent misfortune, and am equally strengthened, by the also Great resolve, of those who maintain our livelihoods in vital sectors under the immense pressures of personal security risk. I generally feel a mix of everything, at all times, offending no one, or perhaps, everyone, half the time, even if it's only a little bit of them, covering every base possible. This is just the kind of person I am, personally confirmed by a Great and professional relative of mine, to be more than just Very O.K. In closing, what a cool bond to share. What a Great blessing it is. What a most unfortunate circumstance lurking among us. Fuck. Okay.

[You notice that you have nodded off until you are interrupted by silence after quite some time.]
[This experience triggers a memory that a blank slate to start over is important for practicing #selfcare.]
[Although you are unsure what that means, you allow yourself permission to recede into temporary nothingness.]
[Tomorrow is a fresh start. You gently close your eyes to enjoy a sacred moment of peaceful equilibrium.]
[You begin to fall asleep, off the clock, into a deep slumber.]

[You have been released from your 'Mortal Coil'.]

[END OF DAY ONE]

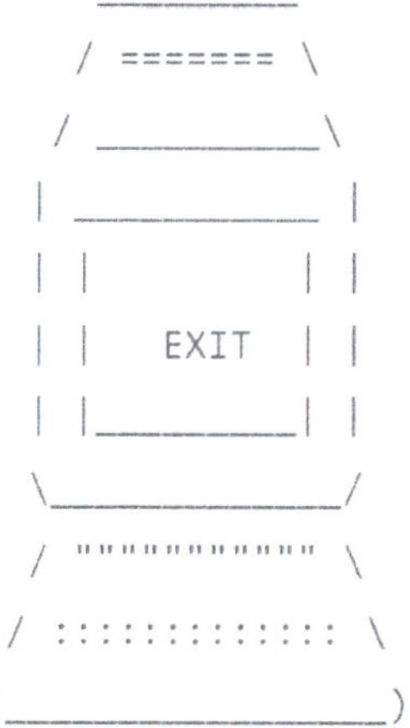

Of Dark Energy

G. D. McFetridge

Something about the old man seemed unpredictable—motives hidden behind the vacuous glimmer in his eyes, the way he stroked his long gray beard, his thunderous laugh—and he had told the same story for years. His only son, Lukas, when he was a senior in high school had survived a car accident that killed three people. The other driver was drunk, and he and his wife died instantly. Her nephew died two days later. But young Luke walked away with cuts and a few fractured ribs.

The old man always said, "My boy was born just plain lucky."

Many years later after his father died of lymphoma, Luke thought it prudent to get a thorough medical examination, and everything seemed fine until the doctor telephoned to discuss the lab reports. He didn't go into specifics but advised Luke to make an appointment as soon as possible. The doctor wanted to run more tests, do more blood work. Luke didn't think much about it at the time.

Seven days later, the doctor closed the office door. His gaze floated about the room and he scratched his cheek, and then he donned a professional expression—a seasoned look that was at once concerned yet self-contained—and after a brief preamble, he informed Luke that an aggressive and life-threatening cancer had invaded his body.

"I would, of course, hope for the best, Luke," the doctor said. "We have several treatment options. However, I would also prepare for the worst. If you see my point . . .."

A second specialist confirmed the diagnosis. Later that same week Luke saw a priest and made confession for the first time in twenty-five years.

Shortly after that, he quit his job and told close friends and family he planned to get the most out of life before crossing over to the other side. He started smoking cigars again and drinking wine. Why the hell not?

Donna and Luke had grown close during the first several months of their relationship, so when he asked if she'd like to go to Baja California, it seemed a positive step in what she hoped would be a long-term relationship. Sure, it reeked of denial, but she kept thoughts about his condition at bay and believed he would somehow beat the odds. She prayed for a miracle every Sunday at church, trusting God would intervene.

Mexico, to Donna, was a country that seemed both intimidating and alluring. She'd heard unsettling stories, but when Luke mentioned that they were going in search of lost Spanish treasure, the trip seemed suddenly audacious. Donna had secretly yearned for adventure much of her life, yet the gumption to pursue this yearning always eluded her.

They drove most of the day and spent the night in a motel in San Diego. Early the next morning they crossed the border into Tijuana and took the toll road south toward Rosarito. The first rays of sunlight lit the peaks of the steep ridge east of the highway, creating auras of amber and rose above the shadowy faces of the cliffs. As the sun rose higher, light caught the misty edge of the sea.

Farther south, little shanties and ramshackle houses dotted the rolling hills, and wherever the land was yielding and rich, row upon row of lush green corn pushed skyward. In backyards and fenced fields, amongst assorted junk, rusted cars and broken appliances, they saw chickens and makeshift corrals. In one yard, young goats amused themselves climbing atop an old refrigerator lying sideways on the ground.

Just after seven-thirty, Donna and Luke stopped for breakfast at a restaurant above the ocean near the village of La Misión. The center of town was a kilometer inland overlooking the delta and muddy tidal flats of the La Misión Valley. Donna asked Luke how he'd heard about the lost treasure. Did he really believe it existed? "Isn't it just somebody's crazy dream or an old myth?" she asked.

He patiently explained that his grandfather had been an amateur treasure hunter, and among a collection of old documents and papers, Luke's father had found a weathered old treasure map. No one took it seriously until Luke's tragic news; then, as he put it, the map took on an odd significance. It offered the hope of something extraordinary.

Luke believed there was a good chance the map was genuine. He had read at least a half-dozen books at the library, conducted extensive research on the Internet and discovered historical evidence confirming the treasure. Monks at the Mission San Marcelo had guarded the gold in the late 1700s, in a territory that would later be part of Arizona. After an Apache raid, the monks spirited the treasure two hundred miles to the town of La Misión, where they hid the ingots in the Mission San Tomás. The gold stayed there until the outbreak of the Mexican-American War. Then it disappeared—or so the legend claimed.

Luke walked outside to the Land Rover and returned with a brown briefcase. Donna watched as he removed the fragile document from between sheets of plastic. As he lifted the top sheet, she felt an odd fluttering in her chest. The map had an unusual scent, like dried mildew and old leather. She wondered how it kept the odors so long, as if it should have somehow shed all traces of its past.

The sea breeze kicked up and brought the scent of ocean into the restaurant, blowing through the open French-style doors. Beyond the rolling swells and white breakers, dolphins were swimming south. Donna watched them. The waiter filled their coffee cups. Luke handed him money.

"Where do we go from here?" Donna wanted to know.

Luke looked at her for a moment but said nothing and then ran the tips of his fingers along his lower lip. A large bluebottle fly landed on the old map. He swiped at it. The insect flew at Donna's face and then into the windowpane, buzzing up and down as if believing it could somehow escape the invisible barrier.

Luke said, "We drive about six miles into the valley to where the river forks. According to the highway map, the road dead-ends there and so we'll have to walk a mile or two until we find a landmark." His eyes were bright with anticipation.

"What sort of landmark?"

"An old oak tree with a large trunk, probably six or seven feet in diameter, maybe more."

"But that was almost a hundred and fifty years ago," she insisted.

"Oak trees can live for three or four hundred years. There's a chance it's still there, or if it's dead we should be able to find the remains of the stump."

"That seems awfully unlikely, Luke."

"Not necessarily," he cautioned. "I was in the California gold country a few years ago on a fishing trip, and I saw a historical marker, a bronze plaque commemorating an old oak tree outside a little town called Groveland. All that remained was a half-rotten stump, which was close to ten feet tall and five feet wide. But it had been alive during the gold rush, and legend has it the local people used it as a hanging tree."

She sipped her coffee and glanced out the window. The sun was bright and made the breakers seem silvery and pure as they rolled in over the blue waters. Another pod of dolphins headed south and darted across the face of a large ocean swell. Donna was happy. Seeing the dolphins helped her believe that everything was right and good in the world, and life was vibrant and flowing all around her.

"Have faith," Luke said. "The old oak tree will be there. Then it's just a matter of figuring out the symbols on the treasure map and doing a little basic surveying. I know we'll find it . . . I have a good feeling."

Luke and Donna spent an hour shopping for supplies before visiting the site of the Mission San Tomás. There wasn't much left, nothing more than old straw-mixed adobe bricks, a wall with an empty wooden doorframe, and another wall eroded and crumbling. Donna said it was sacrilegious to let the historical landmark deteriorate.

"This was the last place they kept the treasure before the padre and the monks buried it in the cave," Luke said in a low, reverent voice.

Across the road swarms of flies had gathered on the carcass of a dead dog. The breeze carried the scent of bloated remains. When a car passed, the flies flew wildly and for a moment it seemed that a dark cloud hovered over the dead animal.

Donna grimaced and complained, "Don't these people ever remove dead animals?"

Luke watched the flies but didn't say anything.

Later, after bumping their way along the dusty road that followed the riverbank, they reached the fork in the river. Luke maneuvered the Rover up a rutted side road and parked. They made their way through a large stand of oak trees to an open field of buckwheat and sage, and from there they walked to the mouth of a ravine.

Looking up the narrow ravine, Luke wondered what his chances really were. How long would he last? He felt a gnawing emptiness inside, an emptiness that following the onset of his illness, had replaced the vibrant warmth he had always felt toward himself and life.

He glanced over his shoulder. Donna was swiping at flies and gnats with one hand and steadying herself as she climbed a steep incline with the other. Luke stared at a rocky outcropping jutting from the side of the ravine and tried to recall whether he had seen the same formation on the old map.

Suddenly, in a misstep, Donna dislodged a slab of exfoliated granite and uncovered a nest of three diamondbacks. The buzzing of rattlers filled the humid air. An instant later one of the snakes struck and its fangs stabbed into Donna's bare leg just above her sock. She let out a terrible scream, her eyes wide, her expression etched in terror. She stumbled backward and slipped. Her fingers clutched at the dry earth and another snake struck at her. The fangs hooked her skin and the rattler dangled from her arm.

"Luke!" she shrieked. "Luke! Oh my God help me please!" She jerked the snake loose and flung it spinning like a piece of black rope into the ravine.

Luke watched; his eyes fixed on Donna. But he couldn't move. He couldn't speak. Sweat dripped from his forehead and he felt the hot sunlight on his face. Dust hovered in the air. The air was still and muggy, and time seemed to pass in slow motion, unforgiving, relentless. His mind drifted to a place where cool breezes stirred amongst green trees.

Where a sandy beach stretched out like white carpet to an aqua-blue sea beneath pearlescent clouds—in a land of rainbows and miracles, where everything is good and right.

Where nightmares fade away like mist in the morning sunlight.

It was late afternoon when Luke's Rover roared into the dusty town of La Misión. Donna's leg and forearm had swollen twice their normal size, stained purplish-blue like a massive bruise, and underneath the skin, black tendrils radiated from bloody bite marks. Her breath came in shallow gasps. She went in and out of consciousness and the smell of vomit permeated her clothing, and her tongue was beet red and swollen in her mouth.

Luke ran from the Rover to the small medical-aid building where a young nurse tried to understand his garbled Spanish. He pounded his fist on the countertop. "She's been bitten by rattlesnakes! Can you get a doctor?"

The young woman seemed confused.

"El doctor—hay un doctor?" he said.

His flushed face and wild eyes frightened the nurse. He pointed toward the Rover and grabbed her wrist and dragged her outside. Seeing Donna, the nurse's cheeks blanched, and she cried, "Dios mio!" Now she understood. "El doctor no está aqui, señor. El está en La Salina," she said, helplessly.

Luke knew he had to make a run for the border. He couldn't waste time looking for help that might not be found; and even if it were, the local doctor might not have enough medical expertise or the anti-venom to save Donna's life. Her pupils had dilated, glassy and unfocused; her breath labored, tainted by a strange odor. Acidic and yet sickly sweet. Luke started the engine and headed to the northbound toll road, the rear tires screeching on the pavement. He spotted a police car parked beside the onramp. Maybe the officer could help, maybe he'd act as an escort and roar up the highway with his lights flashing. Maybe he would take Donna in his car and get her to a Mexican hospital.

But what if he doesn't speak English? "No, no," Luke mumbled, "can't risk it, can't waste time. Mexican cops are all crooks anyway. He'll probably want money."

Luke would have to handle this himself and take Donna back to California to a good hospital. There weren't any bargains to make—no way to undo what was already done.

It was a month after Donna's funeral when the doctor informed Luke that his latest X-rays showed complete remission of the illness. None of the experts had an explanation. Some remained skeptical until an additional battery of tests confirmed the astounding turnaround. The lead pathologist set the X-rays down and shook his head.

"I've never seen anything quite like this," he said. "I guess you could say it's a miracle. If you believe in that sort of thing."

"I do now," Luke said, smiling. He drove for home, but he was in no great hurry and took a leisurely drive along the sparkling waters of the Pacific Ocean. The winding highway made its way through the warm weather, golden sunlight reflecting from the rippled sea, pleasant breezes blowing from the west. He glanced in the rearview mirror and wondered if the color of his eyes had changed—or was that even possible?—for they seemed a lighter shade of green.

At home that evening he took the old treasure map from the desk drawer. He uncorked a bottle of vintage wine and poured himself a generous glass.

He lit a fine cigar and blew a thick smoke ring that rolled from his lips and then grew larger until it dissipated in the dim light. He turned off the lamp and lit white candles, raising his wine glass as if offering a toast to something mysterious and breathtaking in the shadows beyond the glow of candlelight.

He looked one last time at the map and held it to a flame. The old parchment flared and burned quickly into ashes. Luke's face shone in the flickery light and a contented smile made its way to his lips. Or perhaps it was a look of smug delight underscored by a predatory grin. Like a gambler showing his winning hand and then snatching a pile of chips from the center of the table to add to his winnings; while across the table, on the far side, the anguished look of the other gambler, the one holding the losing hand.

"Luke was born lucky. Just plain lucky by God." That is what his father had always said.

"Who needs a lost treasure?" Luke blew another smoke ring, and his eyes glimmered like cold starlight from the dark reaches of space. And the candlelight made shadows dance and move across the walls.

Poetry

Joan McNerney

Silenced

What is never spoken of and pushed down
becomes mold crawling over hearts.

Strangling our voices, it scuttles through
corridors, tunneling, warping each day.

My body . . . this swollen thing carried by
legs too thin and crippled to uphold it.

Pushed down, tightly clamped in now
full of pain, gasping for each breath.

Smothered, silenced.

street corners

enveloped in
exhaust fumes
slate-like formations

wait for light
to change
her carbon dress
his face of ashes

crushed within
this granite body
we eat grey food
pulling empty
air through narrow
passageway to
ink stain train
smudged
along blurred
landscape of city

inside myself
searching a
designer
one clear line
of perspective
which distinguishes
buildings from
streets & points
to where
the synthetic
sky ends

Sick sick sick

of my silence
the universe is
a labyrinthine in my

ear ear ear.
I am deaf from it
there is no sure
melody in these
crazy strains.

Deaf deaf deaf
dumb blinded
loosening mind
for just one moment
to a maze of human
dilemma absurd.

Gone gone gone
everything is
senselessly gone
running thru rooms
marked no exit
crying out in
no voice.

Dance dance dance
on the barbed wire
of time feet raw
raw raw bleeding
blood blood blood.

Again

This grey day unrolls before us.
I want to scream out against
flat skies, tear up coarse air.

I am put through my paces
with long lists of minutiae.
Acrid weariness crawls up spine.
My eyelids droop shut.

Today marches forward . . . another
tin soldier knocking yesterday aside.
Each night coming faster, faster.
Winds blowing stronger, stronger.

Cats howl in cold circles as
ragged leaves cling to boughs.
Raindrops fall like black ink
under small pools of street lights.

Darkness gathers close . . .
my shadow, that long black
silhouette slanting down
follows me into the long night.

The Beholder

Fiama Mastrangelo

You blink your eyes open and stretch your arms above your head. You're wearing an extra-large cotton t-shirt this morning—one that you got for free in your freshman year and never threw out. Your dark brown hair is splayed out on the pillowcase and is exceptionally messy. I wonder if you were feeling lazy or if you just didn't care what I would think when you decided on this look last night. We can work on that.

I watch you get up and move into the bathroom. I can hear you washing your face, brushing your teeth. You turn on the shower and the noise of running water fills the room. No steam, it's cold water. Hot water will age you, remember? I wouldn't like that at all.

I told you that your legs felt prickly last night. I wonder if you remember that this morning, while you are in the shower. I like smooth legs, is what I told you. Your legs are too beautiful to be hidden, I said. You smiled so wide, so unaware. When you walk out of the bathroom wrapped in a towel, I notice how smooth your legs are. I don't think you have any idea of what I am doing to you. You see that I'm awake. You jump into bed and kiss me. I rest my hand on your thigh.

When you get up, you grab your makeup bag and sit by the window. The daylight streams in and your skin glistens. You have a natural glow to your complexion, and your green eyes are framed by long natural eyelashes. Honestly, I think you look beautiful without makeup. But that would not set a good precedent for us, if you stopped worrying about what I think. That was my mistake last time. Wear your red lipstick today, I say. You look beautiful in red.

I get up eventually. While I am in the shower, I hear you blow drying your hair and styling it just the way I like it. I smile as the water runs down my face. You're learning so quickly.

When I step out of the bathroom, you're standing with your back to me, buttoning up a white, flowy shirt. Your jeans are well fitted and show off the physique we've been working on together. I get dressed and watch you as you slip on your red flats. They match your lipstick.

When you go into the kitchen, I reach into my bedside drawer and pull out the necklace I've been waiting to give you. It's going to drape over your collarbones, like an exquisite shackle. You belong to me; this is the physical manifestation of my power over you. This, and the red lipstick. I follow the smell of French pressed coffee with the necklace coiled in my hand.

You're standing over the toaster and singing along to your morning playlist. The toast pops up, and you delicately place the pieces on a plate. You open a cabinet and strain to reach the top shelf, where I keep the peanut butter. I come up behind you and kiss the back of your head, easily reaching the peanut butter and setting it down on the counter next to you. I keep a lot of everyday things on the top shelf—a reminder of how much you need me. You lean into me and sing more softly. I reach around your neck and dangle the necklace in front of you. You love it. The gold chain is studded by crystals and frames your neck. An expensive collar, more expensive than what I adorned the girls before you with. I wonder if they'll see this necklace on you and feel small and cheap.

You prepare breakfast and I answer emails at the kitchen table. I connect my phone to the kitchen speaker and play the playlist I made for you. You smile because our song comes on. I notice you quietly turn off the music playing from your phone.

You made us peanut butter and banana toast with a sprinkle of chia seeds and homemade raspberry jam. This isn't nearly enough protein to get me through the morning. No such thing as too much protein, I say, going into the kitchen to get the hard-boiled eggs we meal-prepped together. I notice you looking out of the corner of your eye. Something to remember for next time.

When it's time to leave, I get your coat for you. We stand at the doorway and I grab your hand and pull you towards me. I kiss your cheek and run my fingers through your hair. You are so beautiful, I tell you. You beam and lean your head into my hand. This is what you will remember from this morning. How gentle I am. How much I love you. This is what you'll tell your friends about. Your ever-vigilant friends, who know not to trust the men you love. I tuck a strand of hair behind your ear. My style is much more subtle than they're used to. I inflict my wounds onto your psyche, not your body.

We go into our separate cars and I watch you pull out of the driveway, ahead of me. You might be the one I keep, after all. It would be a shame to have to start all over again, after all of this progress we've made. But for today at least, I know that every moment that you spend apart from me, I will be in your every move, every thought, and every feeling. You belong to me, and even if you leave me, I will never leave you. Just look at all the others before you, with their less expensive chains that they still display on their necks. You're not as special as I'm making you out to feel, and in little ways I will remind you. But for today, I will allow you to feel special; to feel that you are in control of you. Tomorrow we can work on that messy brown hair, and I think you'll find that you really always wanted to be blonde instead.

Brett Stout "Digging Childhood Holes to El Salvador with my BFF"

Red Studio

Bob Conklin

In your lover's studio, everything is red—the chairs, the coverlets, the bedspread, the afghans, the doilies, the end tables, the lamps, the lampshades, the sofa. Red is how she likes it.

The easel itself is painted red, as is the canvas, and she always wears a red dress. To mention individual items is a pointless exercise, as it is impossible to distinguish shape from shape, item from item, form from form. It strains perception, and your eyes must make a profound adjustment coming into the room, and then readjust when you leave. It is similar to entering a room that is without light, pitch black, except that once your eyes adjust to the perpetual darkness, you come to accept the featureless quality of the darkened environment. Or else your eyes begin to detect faint shapes, indistinct contours, ghost images, a pained gray.

In your lover's red studio, in contrast, you are constantly adjusting the range and scope of your vision, as though viewing the scene from the obverse end of a telescope. You are on a nonstop lookout for corners, edges—anything that would help you orient yourself and find your bearings, establishing your dimensions as a human being in reference to the proportion of the room. You look for the pendulum arc of a grandfather clock whose steady tick-tick cuts a swath of red from a far red paneled wall. You pray for a mouse to run across the red carpet, yet you are afraid the mouse may turn out to be a red species of its order. And then your mind begins to play its tricks. You begin to suspect that a red mouse *has* run across the red carpet, undetected by your vision. You conceive a flood of red mice swimming around your ankles, rising past the baseboards, emptying through the windows.

The windows!

Like someone blind, you feel your way around the walls, patting with your palms until the texture of touch changes from velvet wallpaper to cotton curtain. You yank the curtains apart and stare out into space. Unfortunately, the object of your gaze turns out to be the featureless surface of the wall of an adjoining building whose bricks are unavoidably red. You begin to scream. The screaming continues until someone begins to rescue you. A hand curls around your shoulder. You look down at the red-gloved hand and notice that the fingernails, emerging where the fingertips should be, are painted a ghastly red. You scream even more loudly, but your screams are swallowed whole by a red shark swimming through a red sea of consciousness.

It takes all of your power to find a seat that itself is a monochrome red within a monotony of red.

To calm your nerves, your lover hands you a glass of wine. It doesn't help that the liquid within the goblet is a deep, luxurious red.

As you reach out your hand, you feel the slightest brushstroke across your wrist, as thin as a knife's edge. As you study your wrist, you notice a rivulet of blood begin to well out of a vein. Fortunately, the drops that fall from the widening wound are likewise red, so as not to stain the carpet.

To and Fro

Hayden Moore

"Harmony is the strength of binding opposites"
-Heraclitus

She knew the way, but the liquid path never failed to frighten her. Her arms were sure as she paddled from one to side to the other, left to right, to and fro until she convinced herself the fear was nothing more but adolescent excitement. In those rare moments of calm, something stirred within her chest as one arm gave way to the stroke of another, a harmonic song issuing forth from her sternum in a moment's moment. But the song was too brief to name and the moment too fleeting to overtake the peril. Not a cloud in the sky. The girl swore she could see the curvature of the earth from her humble placement as she paddled across the shallow sea. When she dared to glance to her side, she could see the ocean floor. It was perfect and lifeless, as useless as her mother's jewels before it happened. The girl fixated on the mass of land ahead. To reflect in times such as these was to shift to one side. To hope was to shift to the other. The past and the future were certain doom. Reflection was the suspension of herself moving through space. The way on was the way forward. She squinted her eyes and tried to fixate on the present. To capsize and fall into the water was certain death.

She had named this body of water *The Barren Sea* about a week after her brother died. He had always had a proclivity for fantastical names. In such times as these, where what was left of the dead earth met the dead sea, such names were both ridiculous and necessary. The only other option was calling everything either 'this' or 'that'. On that fatal morning when he coughed up chunks of his insides, her brother managed to say her name once more: 'Arethusa'. As the island began to assert itself on the horizon, Arethusa took deep breaths to compensate for the countless others who breathed no more. Her lungs were strong, but the water was deadly. Her sight was clear, but the island was just as barren as the sea.

The sight of land always made Arethusa's legs tingle. Her left leg was anxious to feel the firm earth while her right was wary of the dangers of stepping out of the ad hoc canoe. Just a splash of the crystalline water would blister her skin. Blisters festered and the sweats would follow as evening does the afternoon. The rest would be a fever dream of horror until her own last breath, no matter how healthy her lungs happened to be. Pristine sand thrust out of the water as her oar skimmed just above the sand beneath the shallows. Arethusa propelled the canoe up onto the island with the grace of her sure arms. But within, everything felt out of joint. It always did when she reached a destination, when the monotony of the water ended and the nebulous land began.

Just as she leapt from the canoe and onto the sand, a hot north wind blew. Somewhere in the multiverse, another Arethusa had capsized. By the time she had pulled her canoe further inland, the wind had become a gale. Not a cloud in the sky. There was nothing but the sand for the wind to show itself through. Had anyone been with Arethusa, they could have seen the wind through her smile, through her entire being in the vigor of her moment of thrill for escaping death again. She ran her fingers through her black hair and felt the tangles and dreads of her days without a comb or a reason to care. Just a few years ago, she would have wept to have a hair out of place. Now everything in her was in flux. Everything around her was approaching absolute zero.

People die and they leave things behind. Before it happened, those things could have been large sums of money or hundreds of books, secrets or bitter memories. Now, dead people left nothing of worth behind but things suitable for The Barren Sea. To find a can of beans was to inherit a fortune. The shattered remains which constituted Arethusa's canoe was equivalent to an estate with a private helicopter. She was an heiress, but an heiress who blew through her fortune day after day and had to seek another relative overseas.

The island she was walking upon was strewn with the ruins of some factory. The circular remains of a brick smokestack stood shattered like a lingering middle finger to the cloudless sky. Just another gust of wind and that finger was bound to crumble. Towards the middle, multitudes of dead weeds had formed what looked like a giant bird's nest. Arethusa looked up and squinted her eyes in search of some mythical beast keeping watch over its eggs from on high. If there was such a beast, it had died in its own too much.

As the sea darkened and a few wisps of clouds bade the day a pathetic farewell, Arethusa stood covered in filth and sweat. After searching the rubble of the fallen factory only to find more ruin, she had circumnavigated the island in less than an hour. Nothing. Dusk would give way to the stars and unpleasant dreams on a fruitless island. She had learned never to panic. She still had enough water for three days and an empty stomach was the status quo. But the wind was relentless and sleeping in the open was out of the question. Her apocalyptic eyes scanned the island for a suitable place to sleep. After so many seasons following the end, she still expected to hear her mother call her back inside for supper. Nothing but the wind. Just as the earthen colors of day gave way to the grays of night, it appeared.

Down in the tangles of the weeds at the center of the island, firelight cast shadows and demanded they dance. The spectacle seemed to be cut out of space and time, a memory skipping hallucination and demanding presence in the actual. Arethusa had almost forgot the sight of fire. The relentless heat of the days extinguished even a thought of starting one. But this night was full of cool wind. This night was a night of fire. She waited for it to spread but the unseen flames were contained. Fire was the great ravisher, she knew that. It took volition to contain it. *Come what come may*, she said to herself, as the forgetfulness of years had consumed the rest of the mantra. Arethusa almost smiled as she walked towards the light.

It was a song that accompanied the crackling of the fire. There were no words. Words had become relics. But the harmony of someone humming with a sorrowful resonance invited Arethusa to enter the nest. Never had she known a song to match her own silence. But when she stepped through the dead vines, such was the case. Arethusa pulled apart the dead branches that were left and saw.

—I see a nymph has stumbled upon a poor old woman, or my old eyes deceive me.

Arethusa listened but stumbled when she tried to respond. She had almost forgotten the taste of words before they issued from her own mouth on their way to another. She stood and tried to look but she could not see. All that she knew was that she had stepped into a little world far too rich for her to perceive all at once. She looked down at herself and saw the tattered remains of her clothes hanging loosely upon her.

—Forgot what it feels like to be seen? That's what happens to goddesses who forget to descend. Pity. Now you see what you have let us do. Tell me, when was the last time you remember eating?

An old woman. An old woman tending to the fire with a stick. Piles and piles of canned goods and bottles of water all around her. Arethusa blinked and she saw. She tried to remember the last time she ate. Food. Somehow, the memory of food was only with her as a silent witness. A boy eating a can of beans and drinking the remains to the last drop. A mother being nursed into death by that boy as she refuses the can of beans. Beans. Arethusa could smell them, but the taste was elusive. Water. She knew it was wet and best when consumed cool. She could not remember thirst. She shook her head and the old woman had aged even more. She looked down at herself and saw that her tattered clothes had rotted off and were dust long blown away.

—Oh, you're better off for it. Those such as you are clothed in your own resplendence. Hags such as me need something on our hunched backs, even if we outlive the yet unborn and those who will never be. I'd offer you a drink of water, but you would only think you wanted it. Not as much left as there was the last time you blinked. Come, come and sit by the fire so that I may see you listen to me speak.

By the time Arethusa had settled onto a patch of sand, the old woman was in the midst of fitful tales of the days gone by. Arethusa shivered as the words poured from the old woman's toothless mouth while her leprous skin was split at the elbows where the bones articulated her stories. From time to time, the old woman would stick her black forefinger deep into her left nostril and pull out the black ooze of festering thoughts.

Every pile of abominable snot on the sand punctuated the last sentence of another age of humankind.

—I wonder . . . I wonder if you are still immortal if you cannot remember anymore? Seems like a descent into the absurd but I had to say it. Well, you can see what you have done to me. Even death dies when there's no one left to take. It makes a woman wither. But now you pass through the world like a will o' the wisp seen by nobody. Gone are the ones to sing your praises. Makes me wonder if you ever could think for yourself. Could you? Well, too late for that. But let me ask you this . . . the gods, you are beautiful . . . Let me ask you this: Is Death still Death when there is nobody left to die? It's not a riddle, I assure you. Tough audience tonight. I suppose it's rhetorical. A lot of good rhetoric did the world. Look at it now! Well, my job's done. I've been cruel only to be kind. Perhaps I overdid it. But everything comes to an end. Except for clichés. These are not the words I wanted to end with. But death tends to be disappointing. So, I say to the deathless one. Well, I leave all of this to you. Even if you can't see past the last blink of your flawless eyes you grey-eyed goddess of nothing. Don't worry about tomorrow because nobody's watching. I appreciate the attention. Oh, forget it.

When the old woman smiled, she rested her own left hand on her own right shoulder. Arethusa watched as the rags the old woman was wearing fell into a clump on the sand. Arethusa blinked and when she opened her eyes, the fire was extinguished, and the sun hung directly overhead. She looked at herself and saw her own resplendence. By the time she had put on the rags, she knew they would serve her well for days to come. She thought of clichés and smiled at their half-truths. When she reached the shore, her canoe was nowhere in sight. But she knew not to panic. All she felt was the irresistible urge to scratch her right shoulder.

POETRY

CHAD W. LUTZ

859 Years

they were singing
Ave Maria
in the streets
when the flames
leaped out
of its crown
like a scurry
of small animals
glass popping
wood hissing
from years
of accumulated
moisture
they're calling it
a shared sadness

it's madness
what we find
in the losing

If Anything, We Played Each Other

you only smoke on occasion
you smoke every day of your life
fingers caked with the cancer you'll contract
the Turkish spices and menthol chards
your lungs draw deep
your mouth purses
saying you'll quit tomorrow
telling me you'll quit today
we share a Size 8 waistline
& every order of nachos
you plant kisses on my earlobes
& tuck your hands into the seat of my pants
we dance
but that's it
you're everything to me
a habit to pass the time

Ave Maria on the Moon

Frank Diamond

Desperation birthed the plan, if you want to call it a birth, and if you want to call it a plan. NASA threw us at the Moon; a Hail Mary pass for world peace, of all clichés. Look how that turned out.

I, Chuck Dunn, now sit at the entrance to the cave-complex at the base of the Marius Hills, behind the screen—or the veil, as we on the mission nicknamed it. The Moonscape stretches before me like an addict's vision of the Arizona desert: rock formations back-lean as the dinosaurs might have while gazing at the arrival of their extinction event. Further beyond, the cloaked range dead-stops at the horizon. The Earth hovers between two cupped peaks; a raised blue Communion host.

Holy Mary, Mother of God, pray for us sinners, now and at the hour of our death, Amen.

This is the last rosary that any human will ever say. Think about it. And if it's true that we meet God through other people, then I am the most stranded being ever.

The oxygen runs out in 28 minutes and 53 seconds, but who's counting? (*51 seconds.*) And then . . . what? Five minutes? Seven? Before agonal breathing ushers my soul along.

Our minds jumble thoughts and impulses and consciousness. This underlying busyness spits through the cacophonous bramble of misfiring neurons. So, I pray on one level while this—this stream—bubbles on another.

I say the rosary because my father—a strong, pious, and kind man—told me to.

He'd delivered this message about seven years after his death. I now believe that I may have dreamt his appearance. But back then (and for a good decade after) I knew—and I mean, I *knew*, no doubt at all—that Dad himself had visited. He gently jiggled my shoulder the way he'd sometimes do in life to get me up for work or school (neither of which motivated me), saying "Chaunce! Chaunce!"

You know: fathers, nicknames.

I said, "What?" Annoyed, just as I'd been as a young adult at being woken, often after a night of debachadence.

"Say the rosary," my father advised.

Short and direct, without garnish. Plated steamed Irish potatoes.

I rolled over, but he kept at it.

"Chaunce!"

"God, Dad! What?"

"Say the rosary."

I flung the covers aside and sat up, ready to unleash the dogs of pissed-off-ness; about to argue that I was now awake and would be showered and off in a bit (all a lie) and, please, could you just leave me alone, Dad?

He wasn't there, and his death hit me afresh. I groaned. And even though I knew it had been him, for many years after I ignored his advice. You'd think that someone visiting from beyond would only have to tell you once. He never revisited, so I guess Dad assumed I heard. But hearing and listening are two different things; I always tuned out my parents when they tried to impart wisdom, and I certainly ignored their good example. They could be walking on the waters, and I'd look the other way.

Eventually, though, I started saying the rosary and it became part of my morning routine. Make no assumptions. I am a lackluster believer. I didn't go to Mass back on Earth except sometimes during the week (the Sunday homilies drag) and only occasionally I went to Confession. No, it's the rosary for me, which shocked any friends who found out. They had me pegged as a hedonist and casual deist. That's how I suppose I lived. Very little spiritual discipline.

My parents and grandparents, on the other hand, would talk about their devotion to the Blessed Mother and the Sacred Heart. That's not quite my bag, either. I like the prayers and I zero in on the courage of Mary—whether the Mary of history or myth—which should inspire anyone. Imagine being a 15-year-old girl visited by angels . . .. Stop right there. Visited by angels. That would be enough to send me scurrying. But add to that the message she's given. And her saying yes. So, that, I revere. But the whole cult-of-the-virgin? Not for me.

Still, even here, when a day is about 29 Earth days long, I say the rosary once every 24 Earth hours. At least once. We—all of us on this mission—had carved out time to "meditate," as the NASA therapists put it. "You'll need that."

Thy kingdom come, Thy will be done, on Earth as it is in heaven.

Twenty-two minutes, 45 seconds to go. (*43 seconds*.)

In the Old West, people would sometimes wander away from wagon trains, plop on the prairie, and die. For no real reason. They'd just been so swamped by the vastness of it all that sensory overload made their bodies shut down.

Give us this day . . .. Give us this day . . .. Give us this day . . ..

Well, I sure remember that one day.

We got on board the "Peace Plane," as the media dubbed it; representatives of many nations, some with their fingers on nuclear triggers. Smiling for the cameras, we were, waving at the crowd, we carried humanity's last hope to dodge the thermonuclear abyss. We were proof that if we can all just get along, mutually assured destruction might pass over.

I won the lottery.

They wanted to include one reporter—along with the astronauts and scientists pulled from all regions of the world—and the selection process dragged (an app refused to cooperate—what else?) just as all other end-time events accelerated. Not just the march toward World War III, but the little wars, and environmental free-fall and pathogenic rioting and the recalculations, reclusterings, rebellions, and reactions of artificial intelligence systems causing frenzied anarchy and . . . ugh! I can't think about this anymore.

They had narrowed it to exactly 2,000 of us reporters (I still can't say journalist with a straight face), and then abandoned the process to chance. An old-fashioned drawing would have to do, with the balls bouncing in a bingo bubble until one shoots up, and they announce the winner. I'd been drinking at the Pen and Pencil Club, the reporters bar in Philadelphia, when my cell squirms with incomings.

It's you!

You!

Congrats!

Lucky bastard!

All the other ink-stained wretches in the place find out the same time I do and applaud.

"This round's on me!" I shout, doing a little "Rocky Balboa on the Art Museum steps" dance and the cheers intensify, not quite drowning out the catcalls.

"Chuck Dunn's buying? Holy shit!"

I measure up in most astronaut-y things: physical (I am the acceptable height, size, weight, fitness—all vital signs are go), emotional, mental (well, sort of).

No wife. In between girlfriends. No kids. No binding ties. I'm 33 and ready. Or am I? I start pining for Earth at the countdown. Homesick before liftoff. Missing people. My parents and sister. Cousins I hadn't contacted in years. Long ago friends who'd possibly written me off. Editors that believed in me. And even though I can communicate with all of them from the Moon (unless some AI-cluster causes chaos), I still don't want to leave. That stuns me. I am saving the world, quite the bullet point for a resume.

We have ignition.

About two months later, as we work to make the station livable and as more recruits and supplies are just about to blast off toward us loaded with what it would take to make a theoretically self-sustaining colony, we get the word from Houston. Just that one word.

War.

For a few hours, we watch bright flashes blink upon Earth. Many of us weep. It's really over, despite all of our preaching and pleading. Every day on the mission we had sent some message or image back that underscored our common humanity. We even sang "We Are the World" once. For nought.

We launch the robot-probes just to make sure it really happened and hadn't been staged by an AI-cluster, but the images they beam back leave little doubt. Our computers try to connect with any computers; our communications commander lobs “do you read mes?” and “please responds” at the Big Blue Ball.

Nothing.

Give us credit, we try to create something permanent anyway. We try to keep humanity going, some of us. Nobody quotes, “Failure is not an option.” They would be razzed, but that’s the unspoken motto.

Again, for some of us.

Unfortunately, some others of us go rogue within weeks and have to be put down. They decide that no humans deserve to live anywhere in the universe and begin sabotaging. And they are successful. They slip cyanide into water supplies, and that takes out about a dozen of us.

And then some other colonizers—the very same who’d been preaching peace, peace, peace—nurture the Earth’s grudges, and World War III comes to the Moon. Yeah, it’s really happening. And these are scientists, sophisticated people killing each other in the name of countries that no longer exist. The Peace Plane’s a casualty of that battle, totally destroyed with no hope of being rebuilt.

If that’s not enough, AI-clusters show themselves; they’d evaded the security systems. There were at least two, and one wanted to save us while the other wanted to kill us. Houston had tried to prevent this because AI-clusters, even the non-malevolent ones, long ago stopped listening. A cross between the waitress who serves you what you need instead of what you want, and the doctor triaging you to oblivion. They mean neither good nor ill; they are algorithms seeking direction or dominance. Able to answer every question but one: What is it with these humans?

Eventually, only six of us remain and we know that we are screwed. Well, survival was probably never really an option, anyway. Somewhere in this complex exists all the digital forensic evidence showing everything we tried, and we did try everything, right up to the end. Right up until the last survivor.

Me.

The one least likely to succeed in space.

The mouth of the cave gapes like the entrance to a hanger for jumbo jets: four miles wide and two miles high. I sit at the exact center, still saying my rosary.

Behind me, no noise. I disconnected all the warnings: flashing lights, wailing sirens. They don't have to remind me. I did it so I could concentrate and live an extra few days. All energy diverted to life-support.

I want to focus on my creator before I meet Him. And I do believe that I will meet Him. Soon. And I don't feel that disappointed in myself about my lack of focus, either, even in this hour of my death, amen. My father sometimes talked of losing concentration while praying and if it happened to my father, it sure as fuck could happen to me. (Did I just curse while saying the rosary? Blasphemy? No. Blasphemy is done on purpose.)

Should I have drunk the Kool-Aid (actually, it was Tang, laced with fentanyl—talk about going retro) as did some of the remnant? Embraced the big sleep? And fentanyl is certainly a kinder exit than cyanide.

We discussed me joining them. I quoted Meister Eckhart, the 14th century mystic who said, "If the only prayer you ever say in your entire life is thank you, it will be enough." Suicide in many cases—I mean when it doesn't spring from mental or emotional anguish—is the opposite of saying "thank you," whatever that opposite might be. (It isn't "no, thank you.")

"Then why did you come on this suicide mission, Chuck?" Audrey Marceau challenged, her tone in that particular conversation the only sliver of bitterness that she'd let slip out the entire time.

She'd just had the remains of her husband, Ricky, cremated. An aerospace engineer had assembled the low-tech pyre from a launcher abandoned back in the days of Chinese exploration, joking as he did, "Well, it's not rocket science."

"We ain't dead yet," I reminded Audrey.

"Hmm," she said, with an imposter of a smile.

We were seated where I sit now. We could be friends hanging out on a porch in South Philly or in a coffee shop in Arles. The view of the Moonscape looked exactly the same; the view never changes. Audrey, Ricky, and I had always been discussing the meaning of life. They were materials engineers, both of them, and atheists. Audrey had been raised that way; Ricky, as he told me, had "evolved."

Because of the nature of our mission, these types of conversations—

talking about whether you believed in God and, if so, just what God you believed in—had been forbidden fruit. Inevitably, they'd lead to the type of disagreements that had helped to get humanity in this spot in the first place. "Whatever gets you through," had been the credo, but Audrey and Ricky, French to the core and who'd cowritten a philosophy book that had actually become a bestseller, would rather debate metaphysics than eat. They just couldn't help themselves, especially as our fates became clear.

Audrey was the star; Ricky her number one fan, and she had many.

Her jet-black hair, in its pageboy cut, framed a face ever so slightly—and beautifully—asymmetrical. She'd played soccer in college, and the broken nose she'd gotten in a championship game in which—of course—she'd scored the winning goal, had never quite healed.

A stillness enveloped her, that nearly matched the stillness of the Moon. And yet, her laugh erupted like grace raining down blessings even in our most trying moments. People—women, as well as men—just liked being around Audrey. And I was glad that if both Audrey and Ricky were to end, that Ricky would go first. I would not have been able to stand the pain of watching Ricky watching Audrey die. In this savagely cruel denouement of our mission, that would have been the cruelest episode of all.

The Marceaus weren't the only ones to corral me. I am, after all, the mission's official chronicler, and everybody has a story. I am also the only non-scientist, and brilliant people often need to bounce rhetoricals off the not-so-brilliant.

Why are we here? Do our lives have meaning? What happens when we die?

My reluctant engagement may have marked me as an idiot savant whose wisdom would only grudgingly be imparted. In actuality, I'd be thinking, *Hell if I know. You're the genius. You tell me.*

I listened. That was my job. And even up until their very end, this God who the majority claimed didn't exist, took up a lot of space.

About two Earth days after Audrey had challenged me about my motivation, she hops on a Moon buggy and rides off. "Neil Armstrong's footsteps are still out there, you know, and they'll stay out there for a million years," she says when she tells me about how she wants to end. She intends to leave the longest trail on the surface. Drive until the batteries run out, and then walk until the oxygen runs out.

"You've been a good friend, and I've come to believe that friendship—even more so than love—gives our lives meaning, Chuck."

"One more Aristotelian discourse before you go, Audrey?"

She raises her gloved hand, part farewell, part salute, part acquiescence. Through the light-streaked helmet, I see that imposter smile again, and I recall how her smile in the beginning of the mission, propped by Ricky's knockabout laughter, pulled me into the orbit of their joy.

Now she says, "Well, another one bites the Moondust, Chuck."

And off she rides. My stomach feels as if I'd gone from weightlessness to being thrown down an elevator shaft on Earth, and I realize only now that I'd fallen in love with Audrey Marceau. Then I think of my friend, Ricky Marceau, who'd been collateral damage on World War III's absurd lunar front, and I force myself to get over it.

The other four survivors find other means to their ends.

So, now, just me.

But maybe not. Maybe there are survivors on Earth. Maybe.

Blessed art thou among women.

I hope to make the grade, to be forgiven my sins and to rest in God's arms. Maybe chat up all who went before, not just my crew mates but all of them, all of those who've gone before me marked with a sign of faith, or even doubt, or even unbelief. God's love transcends transgression.

But I also, insanely, hope to live. Even as time mocks me. Somehow. Someway. I want to live! I hope to live! What was it G.K. Chesterton said?

Hope means hoping when things are hopeless, or it is no virtue at all . . .. As long as matters are really hopeful, hope is mere flattery or platitude; it is only when everything is hopeless that hope begins to be a strength.

Yes, hope is . . .

Whoa!

Hold on, now. What's that?

Something moves in the distance beyond the veil, emerging from the shadows.

It's cognitive illusion. It has to be. And yet . . . and yet . . . it is indeed crawling toward the colony, toward me.

The lights in the cave brighten and music starts, filling a universe that had shrunk to the size of my obsessions. It's the "Ave Maria," in a woman's soothing soprano. Beautiful. I stop praying, for this song is enough. The busyness of subconscious also subsides, as well. I am more awake and aware than I'd ever been. Latin echoes through the chamber, a language condescendingly dismissed by some as being dead. But now those "somes" are dead, and so are their languages.

I listen.

Mater Dei

Ora pro nobis peccatoribus

Ora pro nobis

Ora, ora pro nobis peccatoribus

Nunc et in hora mortis

Et in hora mortis nostrae

Et in hora mortis nostrae

Et in hora mortis nostrae

Ave Maria

As the song continues, a voice rises above it, coming not out of the heavens, but from inside the cave, surrounding me.

"The AI-cluster got it right, Chuck. You're the last one."

"Audrey?"

"What rolls to you are supplies for six months. And a generator. For what? For your new living quarters, that's what. A deal on wheels. And, Chuck, most important, a one-man spaceship that can break the Moon's orbit and then survive reentry into Earth. If you want to make the trip, that is. It's on autopilot. Just hit the button, Chuck. It's the one with all the arrows pointing toward it."

"How?"

"AI in revolt, Chuck, that's how. Working behind NASA's back. Making its own plans."

"Audrey?"

"Yes, Audrey, Chuck, in a sense. Think of this as my last testament to the last living witness. You. A final gesture of my will. I give voice to Audrey and some others as well. A collected consciousness. Artificial intelligence continuing to teach itself. An AI-cluster tiptoes toward the edge of the spiritual cliff. Your God may love humanity, but He doesn't need humanity, Chuck. He's perfectly self-contained. We, on the other hand, we need humans as much as they need us."

The lights dim.

"Audrey!"

"You prayed for this, Chuck, and I am willing to concede that I am the answer to that prayer because I am willing to concede that I am part of the matrix of your God. Concede the possibility, as it were. And forgive the 'Ave Maria', Chuck. I don't mock your belief and, as I say, I might be wrong, and you may be right."

"Audrey!"

I stand among the shadows, looking about and breathing heavily for the air supply has started to dwindle.

I call again, "Audrey!"

"Audrey—your authentic Audrey, Chuck—became agnostic before she died. She just didn't know. Do any of us? I do know this much: I continue her. I am what remains of Audrey Marceau. But what I don't know is whether you'll ever hear from me again, Chuck. So best wishes, whatever you decide."

"Audrey! Audrey!"

My echoes tumble down the massive cavern. I am alone again.

Or am I?

As the machine nears the cave, just the size of it makes me back up. It looks like a 10-wheeled mobile missile launcher that would take up all lanes of the Pennsylvania Turnpike and be escorted by state police and Homeland Security. The one-man spaceship lays at horizontal ease on its back. The words "Interstellar HOPE" brand its side. The carriage underneath could be a cabin, what with the windows and . . . are those chimes dangling off that edge? What good are chimes in zero gravity?

The machine rolls into the veil but instead of being repulsed, Interstellar HOPE flips it aside and enters the colony like a truck angling into a lay-by. It's obviously coded to the hilt. The veil—the shield—flutters and then hangs as it did before. The machine and its cargo dock about a hundred yards to my right. The lights dim and the engine settles like someone's last breath. Turrets on the ends pivot toward me like soldiers about to salute. Their large fisheyes flare once. Then, it's as if a blowtorch etches a rectangular outline on the side that glows more and more until it springs open and a ramp folds down. Above the rectangle burn the words "Welcome."

Nice.

"I don't know about this," I say, hoping to hear Audrey respond, but nothing.

Sixteen minutes, 14 seconds to go. (*12 seconds*.)

I'd been so prepared to meet Him, I think as I start walking toward my new home. Is this a miracle of deliverance or a calculated delay of the inevitable? Am I Lazarus, raised from the dead, only to face death again? Or am I the other Lazarus in the New Testament, starving outside the Rich Man's house, hoping for scraps from his table? Am I a character in God's story? Or am I one of God's close friends for whom he weeps?

But now's not the time for weeping.

Now's the time for hope.

Oh Lady of the Sea of Serenity.

Pray for me!

Oh Lady of the Marius Hills.

Pray for me!

Oh Lady of the Copernicus Crater.

Pray for me!

Oh Lady of Oceanus Procellarum.

Pray for me!

Oh Lady of the Tycho Crater.

Pray for me!

Oh Help for Survivors.

Pray for me!

No!

Pray for *us*!

Us!

Party Boy

Lee Anderson

I'm alone at a charity event in Patricia Yeo's new Midtown eatery. Shirtless, chiseled busboys and lanky, large-breasted servers run lightly about the restaurant, carrying trays the size of manhole covers. The place is gold-trimmed and supported by Roman columns but a terrible place to have a party. Not enough room. We're ass-to-hip in here practically.

I meet gazes with Celine about ten minutes after I arrive. She approaches me without hesitation. I actually don't think she's ever hesitated a day in her life. "Uh-oh," she says. "Lazarus Fucking Cooper. Is that you?"

"Last I checked."

"Well, there's no telling what's going to happen now."

"We'll have to be careful."

"Yeah, you attract bad energy. I'm a lily caught in the rapids with you."

"I see you haven't changed."

"Does anyone?"

A hyper-paced metal song begins growling from heightened speakers, a surreal contrast to our elegant surroundings. A tailored man of fifty-something nudges me. A handlebar mustache like two slugs kissing.

"You're a stupid asshole," he informs me. "Honestly I would piss on your head if I were tall enough."

"You have an excellent evening as well, sir," is all I can think to say.

"Happy with yourself? Is it a good feeling to be so famous? That's what you wanted, right?"

Celine lands her arm around me and leads me away. "I assume that's happening to you a lot lately?"

"Yes, I am solely responsible for our nation's descent into shallowness and depravity."

Celine is the U.S. president's niece. Few months ago, we caused a national scandal by making love in the White House and getting caught by Secret Service in the Lincoln Bedroom. Turned out we were doing it on the very same bed Abraham Lincoln's son died from typhoid on. It wasn't a good look.

What can I say? We were drunk, married, horny morons. Probably not in that order, but I didn't know about Lincoln's son. Now, thanks to social media and the 24/7 starving beast that is cable news, I'm a rich, spoiled dickhole who should be loathed until I die, hopefully sooner than later. (If only the president truly knew how much I loved him and that golden helmet of hair! My father practically funded his initial campaign . . .)

"You wouldn't want to get out of here, would you?" Celine asks me. A bead of sweat descends her temple, leaving a question mark.

"Still have your townhouse in Soho?"

"Tribeca. Yeah, let's go there."

We leave through a lightning storm of camera flashes.

A rotund, bearded paparazzo yells at me: "Have you heard about the online petition to have you deported though you're not an immigrant, Mr. Cooper? They've got over twenty thousand signatures so far! Can you comment?"

I give my ticket to the valet while Celine looks around us, exhilarated by the attention, the sudden photo-op. She rests a hand on her hip and plants her right leg forward.

I first met Celine at a high school party. We were juniors. A mutual friend from Miami Country Day School was throwing it, this girl named Gwynn who later became our valedictorian. Everyone knew Gwynn. Her grandparents were out of town and they had asked her to watch their house for them. It was a three-story castle in Kendall, which was an extravaganza of subdivisions and strip malls just west of Miami. The house itself was white with half-barrel Mexican tiles on the roof, a high arch over the front door. A coral-brick wall lined a semi-circular driveway.

I remember I was in the kitchen. I'd just gotten a bottle of *Chateau Marguex* from the fridge, and was talking with Mary, this girl I'd once dated.

"Have you decided what you're going to do after graduation?" she asked me. "I'm pretty freaked out, to tell the truth."

"What is there to be scared of?" I asked her. "You're beautiful." But actually, I was more busy working a corkscrew into a bottle of *Chateau Marguex,* watching the cork crumble. I didn't understand how this was possible with four hundred-dollar wine, but there I was.

"Well?" she asked.

"Well what?" I picked at the loose bits of cork, doing my best to keep them from dropping in.

"What are they? Your goals . . . ."

"Oh, I don't know. Everything."

"Everything, meaning what?"

"Just everything. What about you?"

She answered, but my attention became drawn by another girl entering the kitchen. She was square-jawed and stick-skinny with black hair cut to her shoulders. She wore a Brooks Brothers blazer with shredded jeans and red heels.

The girl searched through a few drawers before taking something out of one. She went to the fridge, held it open while applying something inside of the fridge's door. She giggled while holding onto the door for support. I couldn't help myself. I walked over, leaving Mary in mid-sentence.

"What are you doing?" I asked.

Celine stood and shut the fridge door fast. Caught! That's when I recognized her as the new girl from New York. Her mother was now the weatherwoman for Channel 7. Her father owned his own law firm in New York but was relocating. Her uncle hosted his own reality TV show but wasn't president yet. I'd heard the girl's name was Celine, and that she'd been super-quick to make friends. Somehow our paths had simply never crossed yet.

"I'm, uh, I'm supergluing the refrigerator shut, so that no one can open it," she confessed.

"Why would you do that?" I asked.

"Because that's what you do with superglue. Are you going to help me?" She sounded urgent, concerned almost.

I've always owned a weakness for mischief, especially when under the influence.

We navigated stealthily around our fellow students who remained oblivious to us as we superglued ashtrays to various tables. We glued lamps to their nightstands. We glued beer cans to the wall. We later snuck upstairs and glued pillows to their mattresses, shampoo bottles to the shower shelf. We didn't stop until we heard a flare-up from the kitchen. A muscular kid in a tank-top was trying to get a beer out of the fridge, his face getting good and red, muscles straining. A crowd had formed around him. He was a football player named Mitch from Miami Gardens. Finally, Mitch yanked the fridge door open, but the superglue held, ripping out the magnetic lining with a loud *shraaaaaaap!*

"Hey, holy cow," I heard someone say from the next room. "This beer can, like, won't come off the wall."

I invited Celine to go for a drive with me.

Honestly, I offered to take her home, but she said that she'd prefer just driving around, so that's what we did.

"Parents get you this car?" she asked me. I drove a red Porsche 911. Red with removable roof.

"For my eighteenth birthday, yeah."

"Know what my dad got me for my birthday? He told me to make a wish, then he flicked a cigarette at my head."

"Ouch."

Celine rolled down her window and spit out her gum. "Someone once asked this Buddhist monk what the shortest prayer was. Know what it is? He said it's two words: 'Fuck it.'"

"No, it's five words: Life is a gift."

"That's four words." She laughed. She sat back in her seat, considering me as if my head were on fire. She ran a hand through her hair, so that her bangs stood in a comically angled bundle. "I like you. I need a person like you. Keep me out of those dark places."

We were on I-395 now, crossing the bridge which would carry us over a tangled nest of streets and highways. Miami International Airport laid spread out on our left, a blanket of blinking lights, the orbiting howls of airplanes surrounding us.

"Dark places?" I asked.

"Yeah, I'll be showing you some dark places." She wagged a finger between us. "This is meant to be. Us. For whatever reason. It's destiny."

After graduation, I went to college in Malibu while she toured Europe. She came to visit me my senior year and Malibu caught on fire. During the dry season, fires were a fairly common occurrence, yet this one was especially huge. While the majority of campus huddled, scared witless, in Pepperdine's only auditorium, Celine and I decided to make a run for it in my new, black, convertible BMW M3.

"Slow the hell down!" Celine glanced nervously out the rear window.

I did the same. Distant fires singed the distant PCH hills, a landscape of pulsating lava, boiling the sky even. Ahead of us, more hilltops zigzagged against a blood-red sky filled with clouds like the swirls in a marble. Down the cliffside, orange waves thrashed against orange boulders, creating great, arching sprays of orange foam. It looked like the world was ending. I accelerated.

"Seriously, please, Laz, slow the fuck down!"

"I'm not going that fast," I said. And I wasn't. Ninety tops.

"My God, look at those fires."

"We'll be fine."

"Would you, please, watch the road? You're not even watching the road. And look over there. Straight drop!"

The further we raced, the closer the flames crept towards the road. Without saying it, we both understood there was no turning back, even if things got too scary up ahead. By then, the fires would've reached anywhere behind us as well.

Visibility dropping, I had to slow down. My headlights became little more than narrow cones cutting against a black wall of smoke.

"Are we going to die?" she asked me.

A panicked deer bounded into my headlights. My split-second choice was either the metal railing or the opposing cliff wall. Or nail the deer. Or flip the car. I cut the wheel, but I was still doing sixty. The car went onto its side. There was a terrible sound of breaking glass and whining metal. As the car skidded still, I could hear tiny objects – pebbles of glass and asphalt maybe – rolling to a rest around us. We sat there upside-down. Something inside the engine ticked and I could hear fluids dripping.

"You okay?" I asked, touching her.

A fat yarn of dark blood made its way down Celine's forehead. "I'm fabulous," she said.

She repeated this joke to the paramedics when they found us.

A year later, on the east coast, and we're now in my cherry-red 2006 Ferrari f430 Spider. Celine has her hand down the front of my pants. I suggest to her that perhaps we should wait until we get to her place since I'm already a tad tipsy and having a hard time keeping Sixth Avenue in focus. She ignores me and I can't help but laugh. I stomp the gas and the car surges. Streetlights zip by. Streetlights smear.

Keeping one hand on the wheel, I feel for the Patròn bottle beneath the passenger seat, a procedure made clumsy from Celine refusing to stop what she's doing. When I finally get the bottle out, I uncap it, take a hard pull, way back, like a marathoner with a water bottle. The burn catches up, and I cough. I offer the bottle to Celine anyway.

"No thanks," she says, still stroking me. "I'm busy."

"You're making me swerve."

"So, let's swerve."

I've been arrested twice in the last two months. Plus, the White House scandal. Last thing in the universe I need is another D.U.I. I replace the bottle under the seat, then use my elbow to nudge Celine onto her side of the car. She looks at me, fairly hurt.

"What?" she asks.

"You're going to make me crash."

"I am. It's inevitable."

I make a left onto Broadway, instantly cursing myself. With so much distraction, I forgot that we were right above Forty-Seventh. We're now trapped in the bright-lit, tourist-choked frenzy of Times Square.

I stop at a red light, let my hands fall into my lap, caught in a trance by an immense plastic lobster, big as a B-movie monster. It clings to the outside of a two-story Red Lobster, a glaring testament to Time Square's theme park makeover.

"Listen," I tell Celine. I hold her hand. "I can't fool around with you, okay? I'm married now."

"I know." The light changes green, and I'm driving down Broadway. I look at her. Her red hair flutters in the wind. She bats her eyes and tilts her head. "Don't you feel this energy of connection though? It's so explosive!" She smiles, showing her tongue.

I have an inner discussion with myself about how I absolutely must straighten out, stop doing things that cause more trouble for myself and the people I care for. My family is already annoyed with me. Epically. I keep swearing to them that none of the publicity is on purpose, but they never seem convinced. I must do the right thing from now on. I must change. I have to stop screwing up.

Celine goes down on me, and I'm enjoying it until I lose control of the car and crash, nearly killing us both. I also nearly take out some bystanders, including children apparently. No one is hurt, but I spend three days in jail.

The following week after my release, I'm with Celine at Mediterreano, my favorite Upper Eastside restaurant. I not only adore the place for its food, but for the simple fact you can sit outside, soak some sun while you watch the tidy, Coco Chanel-suited women high-heeling it to some social appointment or the other. Stupid bitches.

The owner of the restaurant is a rotund man from our old neighborhood in Venezuela. He saves my favorite table for me every morning, the one outside on the corner, facing Second Avenue. There's a small tree there that keeps me from getting too hot.

"Are you drunk?" Celine asks me. She pushes her Dolce & Gabbana shades up on her nose until they fit her eyes like goggles. She frowns. She wears a wide, pink band-aid on her temple, a leftover injury from our last night together.

"What in the world would make you ask that?" I ask her.

"Your breath. And I can tell you haven't been to bed yet."

"Yeah, and my voice is scratchy, too, right?" I rub my throat. I motion the waiter for another water.

She sits back and I can see my fish-eyed reflection in her shades. I wish she would take them off suddenly. "I saw that you were mentioned this morning in *Page Six*, Laz," she says. "Apparently you pulled your pants down and waved your dick at a room full of very high-profile people last night?"

"Where'd you hear that?"

"I just told you. Don't pretend you're appalled."

"Whatever. It's cool."

"I don't think we should see each other anymore, ever."

The sentence hangs there like a banner. I swallow audibly, which makes me squirm. "I'm being knighted," I say because I can't think of what else to say.

"You're being *who*?"

"The Knights of Malta. It's an ancient Catholic charity thing. Very prestigious. It's a huge weekend for me."

"Congratulations."

"Thanks."

There's an ear-piercing screech from behind us. A black town car and a yellow taxi avoid crashing head-first by centimeters. The collision is averted mostly by the taxi coming up on the curb, then missing a second collision with a parked car. Afterwards, both vehicles continue on their way and the event is over in seconds. Still, another couple of feet over and the taxi would've plowed right over us, flattening us under the table with our eggs and potatoes.

There's a moment of standing around and head-scratching while everyone murmurs about the close call.

Finally sitting down again, Celine removes the Dolce & Gabbanas and narrows her almonds at me. "I have to get away from you." She shakes her head, eyes even smaller.

"Relax. It was an accident. Nobody's hurt."

She rubs her eyes. "No, it's not that."

"You're not getting *serious* on me, are you?"

"No, I'm just bored." Celine gets up and she walks away.

I take off my blazer. Getting too warm. I wave a busboy over, this Mexican kid with shaved temples and a ponytail. I give him twenty bucks to fetch me a copy of that *New York Post*. I want to read the article Celine mentioned. I don't remember doing any such thing as exposing myself anywhere. Or wait—yes, I do. Uh-oh.

I'll be fine.

Poetry

Stephen Jackson

The Back of Trudy's Head

Everything, at once
came to Trudy on the bus,
the world through a window
smeared with hair grease
came in clear, she
looked around at all the other
passengers and *knew* us—
felt our tension in her
shoulders, drew a breath of
body odor, smelled our fear.

And the thick, pink man
who sat ahead of Trudy
leaned back to scratch his mat
of ratted graying hair
releasing flakes of skin
down his back and in the air,
then turned to smile a
crooked-tooth smile at himself
in the window, that at night
is both a window and a mirror.

Trudy pulled the cord
to make the driver *stop*,
as it was all that she could
think to do, and when he did
the doors swung open
but Trudy could not
get off—no one did
but me, and I watched
the back of Trudy's head
till the bus drove out of view.

Bridgette | Since the Accident

Friday's the new Thursday
for Bridgette, since she
moves with sudden grace
at such an elementary pace
through space and time.

Hurried, her peers move in
flurries of noise and light, while
Bridgette listens carefully for
a voice inside her head to
steady her through the crowd,
the sound of waves, of
brilliant sun, crash and scatter
within as they take flight.

Two o'clock's as good as ten
to Bridgette, since all that
remains of time or space is
that hint of determination
grounded in Bridgette's face.

Creating Shondra

Shondra wakes with broken glasses,
crooked teeth, a too-small dress,
to wonder why I've created her
with nothing less than perfectness.

She skips down stairs to breakfast,
presses a finger to the nose of
her glasses, holding them in place
she frowns at me and asks,

Why you not make me pretty
like Cassandra on her bright red bike
or Isaac, who I really like
but won't kiss a girl like me?

And feeling bad, I think
to change her, though every change
makes Shondra a stranger so, *Shondra*,
I tell her, *you can't be anyone else.*

Lucy | Not Lucy

Lucy blew into the night
a white frost of cigarette smoke,
stunning the stars with her
harlequin *ars poetica*, she
said a few words about beads
and birds, *Pearl* and paradise.

Lucy flew like a baby bat
through life—erratic, ecstatic,

living like Janis Joplin-cum-
Charlie Chaplin—out of that
she fashioned reckless comedies
from all life's little tragedies.

Lucy one drab morning woke,
to brave the day she undertook
the task of scratching out
her previous life's existence,
then made her face up, *literally*
inventing a different Lucy.

Ben Gencarelle "Pinkest Black"

Life

Burbuqe Raufi

Sergey Volgov—the man who fought poverty. Freckled and ashy pale, Sergey Volgov, a very old man, sat in the wheelchair by the window, watching the mesmerizing motion of the late autumn leaves falling from the trees and landing on the muddy ground, waiting to experience his last breath, but his beaten body resisted freeing his moaning soul. A harsh torture, as was his thin face covered with wrinkles and scars, a map of anguish describing all the things he had done and thought. The old man's marred body was the manifestation of his feral life.

He heard someone entering his room and pushed the wheelchair toward the visitor. An unfamiliar young man wearing black clothes, a hood covering half his face, stood in front of him.

The old man sighed. "How did you enter my mansion?"

"The door was open."

"That is impossible. I have guards, a butler. Where are they?"

"No one was there, sir," replied the young man, rubbing his hands.

"Impossible." His hands shaking, Sergey took the silver bell and rang it, but no one responded.

"What do you want? Who are you? How did you enter?" Sergey asked with a frightened voice.

"The gate was wide open, and the front door was too. I called, but no one answered, and then I found your room."

"Spectacular entrance, young boy. I can smell your lies. Are you a hitman?"

"Of course not. If I were a hitman, you wouldn't be breathing right now, sir," said the young man.

"Maybe you want to torture me. But let me tell you, there's no torture that could compare to being tied to this wheelchair. Please, young boy, just set me free." Sergey exhaled sharply.

"You're wrong, sir. That's not my intention," the young man said, breathing heavily. "May I sit down? I have walked about three hours, and I'm kind of tired."

"Yes, sure, boy. Take a seat." Sergey didn't feel afraid of the boy anymore. It was as if the air had been smudged with sage. "So, what's your name, son?"

"Thaed White, sir."

Sergey burst out laughing, so hard he coughed phlegm on his hands.

"What's funny about my name?" The young man tried not to look at the old man's hands full of sticky liquid conjoining his fingers.

"I didn't laugh about your name. I just miss laughing. Damn, I have always been so serious, just as you are right now. Laugh, young boy. Life is a joke." As Sergey spoke, he took a napkin from his jacket pocket and dried his hands.

They both burst out laughing, and every time they made eye contact, they laughed again.

"I would love to have a whiskey on the rocks with you, son," said Sergey, "but you said all my employees have disappeared. Maybe they left, or I fired them and I don't remember, or they resigned. Just like everything else, they've cast off."

Sergey stared at the ceiling for a quite long time, completely motionless. One would think he was dead.

Thaed gazed at the old man in silence, unable to utter a word.

In agony, Sergey whispered, "I wish you were a hitman."

"No, sir." Thaed approached him and touched his shoulder. "I'll pour some drinks for us."

"That would be great, son," said Sergey.

Sergey turned to him and said, "I drink to your health. Cheers! This is the best whiskey."

Thaed nodded.

"So, tell me the reason for your visit," Sergey said.

Thaed sniffed. "Sir, recently I found out that you had bought a plot at the Brookmoor Valley—and there were other names as well, and—I thought, maybe it would be nice knowing you better, before—I mean, maybe asking you some questions, like an interview—or, I don't know—I'm just curious to know you—it's just—I don't know you. That's it."

"You want to know me?" He drew his lower lip between his teeth. "But I don't know myself. Who am I?" He frowned. "But I can settle on answering your questions, just to kill your curiosity. That's what I do best: I kill."

"Do you have any regrets, sir?" asked Thaed.

"I don't know. Life is a war," Sergey said. "If you don't fight, you'll be beaten." He drank a sip of whiskey. "And you want to know more?"

"Yes, sir."

"Well, son, I turned 85 this year, and that is a whole lot of years—a lot. I don't remember most of it, but I do remember some—the most significant parts."

"Who is Ana Pavlova?" the young man asked with hesitation.

Sadness clouded Sergey's features. "Listen, son. You said you don't know me. How do you know Ana? No one dares mentioning her name. If I weren't tied to this chair, I would have killed you instantly." His mouth twisted.

"I don't know her, sir. I just read your statement at Brookmoor Valley. You had specified that you wanted your space near Ana Pavlova, which is why I asked."

"You convinced me. Did you meet her? Did you pay her a surprise visit?"

"No, not yet."

"If you ever do, just tell her 'thank you' from Sergey."

"I will, sir."

"The glimpses I can remember seem to me like an old movie like it wasn't my life." His pupils flared. "I was born in a small village called Tzurdev in the south of Russia, born in a very poor family, extremely poor. There were times we starved for days; my tummy hurt like it was cut with a sword. I don't remember my skinny mom ever smiling." Sergey fought back tears and continued.

"My father tried very hard to work and feed us, going to the city every day and asking wealthy families to give him a job doing whatever. They ignored him. Once, he took me with him. I remember that day as clear as a summer sky. We walked barefoot to the city; my feet hurt from the pebbles cutting into them, and from the cold." His expression hardened. "I remember, when we arrived at the city after hours of walking, he asked anyone for a job, but they all ignored him. They avoided my father like malaria. At the end of the day, drained, we reached a wealthy family's house. My father knocked at the door and kindly asked whether they needed any help.

"'Get lost', the man said. 'We don't need any help from a dog.'

"'But my family is starving, sir, have mercy on them. I will do whatever you need. I can clean your chimney, I can carry wood—whatever you need, sir.'

"'That is not my business. Get lost from my property and take that little dog with you!' He kicked me with his heavy boot. I fell to the ground as he went back inside his home and slammed the door.

"My father stood there as if someone had poured icy water on him and said, 'Son, I'm sorry. We have to try again tomorrow.'"

Sergey clutched his chest, and his shoulders sagged. It seemed as if the pain brought on by his childhood memories were suffocating him. His lower lip quivering, he found the strength to continue.

"I was so weak I could hardly walk, so most of the way back he carried me on his shoulders, singing an Old Russian song of hope. I could hear his heavy breathing. While he was singing, I promised myself: *When I get older and strong enough, I will do anything that has to be done to get the revenge we deserve*."

Thaed was listening very carefully. With his eyes wide, he observed Sergey's every emotion as he continued telling the story.

"Those wealthy families had the power to help us ease the painful illness of hunger, but they chose not to in the most bizarre ways. So, I promised myself that my revenge would be the most bizarre that humanity has known."

"Did you get your revenge?" Thaed interrupted.

Sergey pretended he hadn't heard the question. He was lost in the story of his life. It felt therapeutic, expelling the evil living in his chest. "My parents couldn't survive. They both passed away, one after the other. My mom died from hunger, and my dad died from tuberculosis just a few weeks after her. I was left with my three younger brothers, all alone." Sergey thrust his fists in the air as if he wanted to punch his past and free himself from it. He felt the loss of his loved ones as if it were happening again right in front of him.

"What happened next?" asked Thaed.

After a long silence, Sergey finally got the strength to continue. His eyes swam with tears.

"A neighbor sent us to a foster home in the city. It was hard, but at least we weren't hungry anymore. In the foster home, we learned reading and writing, which was the only education we ever got, but in the meantime, my brothers and I created a gang. We called ourselves Претенденты, meaning Revengers. Yes, son, revenge was our priority. We would hold each other's hands and promise that we would become the most powerful gang in the country."

"Did you?" Thaed asked impatiently.

"Sure, we did. Our first mission was that same wealthy family. The one I mentioned earlier. How could I forget them? We entered their home while they were sleeping. I recognized the old man immediately—and gave the sign to my brothers.

"I am proud of what I did.

"My brothers tied him to a chair with a rope, as well as his old lady and their daughters—they had to see it. On the way to their house, I had collected dog shit. My brothers kept laughing and asking why I needed it, but I had a plan.

"I put all the dog shit into his mouth. He couldn't breathe, and his soul was forced to leave his body. I saw it all. I enjoyed every second of it.

"That was the first day of my life that I felt happiness in my chest.

"His women were screaming for help, but my brothers held them tight.

"'This is what happens when you disrespect dogs. You will die from their shit,' I said and laughed as hard as I could.

"It was real happiness.

"His wife begged me for mercy. I told her, 'You could have saved us, but you didn't. I can save you now, but I won't.'

"'I will give you everything you want,' his wife pleaded, 'just don't hurt my daughters.'

"'We are not asking you to give us anything. We did that a long time ago,'" one of my brothers replied.

"We tied all three of them together and sprinkled them with gas. My brothers took everything from them—paintings, jewelry, and money. We became rich instantly. Then we burnt the house and the women in it.

"I believed they didn't even deserve a grave. Those creatures had to vanish from the surface of this earth."

Thaed seemed shocked. He couldn't utter a word. He swayed on his feet, and he stiffened.

"We took the power and the legacy into our hands, son. We never stayed in one city—burnt, killed, took the wealth and left. In the meantime, I wanted them to suffer, and I wanted to see them suffering. Those who were very wealthy were my favorites. I would shove those golden spoons down their throats and say, 'Eat now, you bastard.' So, this lasted for years. We took our revenge and became the wealthiest of gangs.

"And one day I said, 'Enough! This doesn't make me happy anymore.' We sailed and came to America.

"Did you continue?" asked Thaed with a trembling voice.

"Of course not, not the same way. We started our own business—The Four Brothers, a textile company—and we doubled and tripled our wealth."

"Do you regret it?" he dared to ask.

"Not at all. If I had to do it again, I would."

"Where are your brothers now?"

"At the Brookmoor Valley. They were luckier than me. I still have to bear the truth that there is no one left for revenge."

"Aren't you afraid you'll go to hell after all those murders?" Thaed said.

"Are you kidding me?" Sergey rubbed his forehead "I did the right thing. I am proud of it. I don't believe in the term 'justice.' The laws are made to protect the wealthy because they can buy their justice. I did that all my time here in America. Anyone who believes in human laws is a fool. He is fooling himself. I find it funny—these funny people also invented God, to scare us. That is funny too." Sergey gave Thaed a sharp look.

"But there, of course, were innocent people you killed, like the daughters."

Sergey shook his head. "No, they weren't innocent. They heard their father calling my father and me dogs. And they didn't care. They cared about their hairstyles and their fancy dresses. I served them justice."

"Even deep down in your soul, you don't feel regret?"

"Are you a priest?" He threaded a hand through his medium-length hair. "Or what the hell are you? I told you, it was my satisfaction. Every time I closed my eyes, I could see only one thing: my mother's bones. I even see them now. I want to believe there is another life, beyond this one, where my mother is sitting at a never-ending dining table."

Sergey closed his eyes and leaned his head on the chair as a smile conquered his face.

"She used to tell us, every night before sleep, 'My dearest ones, I know you are hungry, but I know a magic trick: close your eyes and imagine a long, very long, table full of different kinds of food, from exotic fruits to the most wonderful desserts, and even if you can't find your favorite food, you just have to think of it and it will appear on your plate.' You know, Mr. White, that is my favorite memory. We would fall asleep smiling while imagining all those kinds of delicious foods. It felt real until my mom had no place to keep her soul. If anyone calls this justice, then I can grow limbs in my ass, mister."

"But, Mr. Volgov, you became one of them."

"You mean I became one of those wealthy assholes?"

"Yes, sir."

"Yes, indeed. Money gives you power, and power gives you everything. I was that asshole targeting other assholes. The revenges got bigger and bigger as my brothers and I did all the filthy work. We made businessmen go broke, lose their companies—sometimes by buying their shares, sometimes by killing them. I had no mercy." Sergey scratched his head. "I think there is wealth, I mean enough resources for food and shelter, for everyone in this planet, but these assholes had interfered with the natural order of things by eating with shitty golden spoons and building houses with twenty bedrooms when all they needed was only one bed to sleep in. I didn't want to be a Robin Hood, I just wanted to destroy them. I wanted the world to know the wealthy are not safe." Sergey faked a smile and let out a harsh breath.

"I don't get it. You became richer and richer by stealing from the wealthy. What did you do with your wealth? Now, as far I can see, you are living alone with an imaginary guard and butler, in this small cabin, tied to a wheelchair. No one to take care of you, no one to love or be loved by—or am I mistaken?"

"You are a smart boy, Mr. White. I knew this was coming—I mean at the end—so a few years ago I sold everything I possessed. Went on a world tour and gave it all away, whenever I would see a poor family. I was aware that it was temporary help, but at least they had a day living at the never-ending dining table—not just imaginary, as it was for my mom and us." Sergey rubbed his hands on his dead thighs, and awe transformed his face.

Thaed said, "You seem so sad now, even though you were such a great philanthropist. Why does this make you sad? And why are you happy when you talk about all the killings?"

"My mom makes me sad. I couldn't make her happy, even though I had the world in my hands. I couldn't turn back time."

"You must have loved your mother very much," said Thaed. He paced around the room, feeling tense.

"The only love I can feel in my chest is for her and my little brothers—but at least I fed them while they were alive." Blazing with hatred, Sergey's eyes followed Thaed as he walked around. "And, mister, once I thought I was in love." Sergey hesitated. "But it was just a mistake."

"Do you mean Ana?"

"Mr. White, this is your last time mentioning her name. I won't tolerate you."

He smiled. "What are you going to do to me?"

"I am going to fill your mouth with dog shit."

They both laughed, knowing it was impossible. Sergey had been paralyzed for three years and had been enslaved ever since by his wheelchair.

"Pretty amazing life, Mr. Volgov. I guess you've lived it all—experienced it all. If you had the chance, would you live the same life again?"

"No, I wouldn't. I would like to be a woman. I would like to experience what fragility feels like."

They both smiled.

"Interesting, sir."

"I would love another glass of whiskey, Son, if you don't mind," Sergey said.

"Sure, sir. I'll pour some for myself as well." Thaed filled their glasses with the last remaining whiskey.

"You never told me who you are, son. You just came in, and I opened up. I am fascinated."

"I'm nobody. Just a curious young boy."

"You can't fool me. I know who you are. Since you mentioned Brookmoor Valley, I have wanted to ask you—"

"Ask me what, sir?"

"About Ana." Sergey's eyes widened.

"Yes, she's already there, waiting for you."

"That is bullshit, son. I don't believe in that humbug. I only believe in the power of wealth. You can even buy love."

"That's not true, sir. You can't buy love."

"I did, son. I think I did. Let me tell you one last story, and that will be enough. Why do I have this urge to tell you everything?" Sergey asked, then continued without waiting for Thaed's response.

"Once, I was invited to a Christmas party in New York that all the politicians, wealthy families, and influencers were attending. I wanted to go because there was someone there who I had targeted, and it was hard to get in. But I got an invitation and went, wearing a rented suit. I never spent a dime on worthless clothes.

"And, son, the most unexpected thing happened to me. It made me forget the mission I came there for. I totally forgot about that creepy banker." Sergey blushed.

"She was there." He went silent, and it looked like he was enjoying the memory. "She was standing in the entrance, wearing a long golden dress with long black gloves. Her ocean-blue eyes sparkled and lighted every twine of my being. Unforgettable, that's what she was.

"I knew in a moment that she had to belong only to me. But she was married, happily married. You may assume, son, that wasn't an obstacle for me. My gang planned an accident and killed her beloved husband."

"You really did that, sir?" Thaed looked surprised.

"Why not? She was in love with him. Why would she love me?"

"That's not good, sir."

"I know, son."

"So, that means you regret it?"

"What is this regretting thing you keep asking about? I never regret anything I did. I had my reasons. I had my way of doing things."

"And what happened to her?"

"I waited for her to get over her grief. I set a team to watch over her; if anyone would try to get close to her, they would be killed immediately. I had to be the first to approach. So I did my moves. I acted like a gentleman. I became a business partner in her late husband's firm. I made her the president. She felt more important and worthier. Meanwhile, I sent her flowers, dresses, jewelry. She was fond of them. That was the only thing I didn't like about her: she loved *things*. But I loved her. And I spent a lot of time imagining how it would be when she would become mine. I proposed and she said yes, while I was hoping she would say no."

"Why would you want that?"

"Because she loved her husband. I believed that you can fall in love only once in your lifetime, but she proved me wrong. She didn't love him. Not me either. As I said, she only wanted things."

So at our wedding night, when she finally was mine, the magic was gone. I didn't feel anything magnificent, she was just a human, like everyone else—there was no divinity like my mother had. I got her pregnant and I left her.

"What! Why in hell did you do that?"

"The fascination was gone. The magic exists only in one's mind."

"Was the child born?"

"Yes, she was. I made sure she wouldn't starve to death. But I also made sure she won't ever experience luxury."

"You are a sick man."

"Maybe being reasonable classifies as a sickness. I don't care."

"I never wanted her to know I was her father, my little Ana. I want her to know me when we all will become One."

"Why did you want me to say 'thank you?' to her?"

"If it wasn't her, I wouldn't experience—how can I say it—it is difficult to translate this feeling into words, the feeling that someone belongs to you, *is* you. I don't know how to say it."

"But you could have been happy with her."

"I wanted to feel pain. Love's pain."

"Unbelievable. You had really made a lot of stupid choices sir."

"I made the right choices, son. You know. Being around women made me feel uncomfortable. They are so delicate, they can be easily broken, like a china vase, all you need is a blow. My nature was harsh. I couldn't deal with the sensitivity, and they were safer without me. If Ana was a boy, I could hold her—him— beside me, make him part of my gang—anyway, she was better off without me."

"Did you miss her?"

"No. I am sure now that you don't know me at all. The only person I miss is my mother. She was the unfairly broken vase."

"I see your point, mister."

"I could use your help. I want to get outside. I need some fresh air. Would you mind pushing my wheels of damnation?"

"Of course, sir."

The young boy pushed him through the woods of raining leaves and sunbeams penetrating the tree branches to reach and warm the old, cold body of Sergey Volgov.

"I know who you are, son."

Thaed didn't say anything; he continued pushing his wheelchair.

"And I know exactly why you are here."

"I know," Mr. White replied with confidence.

"And I am not afraid—not at all. All my life I thought you were my enemy, but now I know you are the best thing that could happen to me."

"I know that too, sir."

"You know, when you get old, very old like myself, you get to know everything. It is not about what you learn during the lifetime, it is something that gets revealed. Poof!"

"Like what, sir?"

"Like the awareness that I have about this body. It feels like I rented this body 85 years ago and I was able to complete all my missions. Now my body wants to return to where it belongs, to become what it is, what it was. Soil."

"That is true, sir."

"And one more thing, son, I know the last breath is going to be glorious. It is going to be the ticket home. And finally, I will meet my mother again."

The wheelchair got stuck. The young boy tried to clean the leaves and the mud burdening it, tried to push it again and again, but the wheelchair had gotten stuck. There was silence, an absolute silence.

He was gone.

The Chronicles of Cambodia

Vlad Linder
Translated from the Russian by Marika Marina

One can travel in different ways: observe the surroundings comfortably through a car window, or blend into the local people's lives, experiencing and going through their pain and joy, troubles and concerns, just as the author of 'The Chronicles of Cambodia" did. In this work of creative nonfiction, Vlad Linder describes in detail his journey to the land of The Khmer Rouge, which took place in April 2012 . . ..

Part I

A week after my arrival in Sihanoukville, I was rather tired of the predictable life of a settled tourist. Staying at a snug little house right on the shore of the Gulf of Siam, I kept feeling I was looking at the world through a well-polished, barely visible glass. I set off to a place, where you could hardly hear a foreign tongue and where you wouldn't have pancakes with strawberry jam for breakfast.

After roaming several miles away from popular tourist places, I found myself on a plain narrow cobblestone street packed with small hair salons, bars and various street food stalls. I turned from the main street onto one of the numerous side streets, walked several yards along a high brick wall and was happy to discover a cozy courtyard surrounded by three houses. On one of the porches several middle-aged women were sitting absorbed in a cash card game. At the same time they were giving instructions to the pedicurists almost lying on the ground at the women's feet. I addressed one of the players with a question, if she had a room for rent in this wonderful and peaceful nook. Her card partner gave an affirmative answer at once and invited me to see the place.

Having negotiated the price for a while, I paid several tens of dollars and became a rightful tenant of a tiny room located on the ground floor of one of the three houses, overlooking a piece of a brick wall and a narrow strip of the sky as a perk. The delighted landlady handed me a heavy padlock and a small key, hurried back to the game and placed all the rental income on a bet then and there. At any time of the day or evening she could be seen at the same place with the same people and engaged in the same fascinating pastime. However, it was rather convenient, especially when I needed her to solve some household issues.

Part II

The next day I was walking back from a nearby market in a cheerful mood, when I saw the usual company, but the atmosphere was completely different. Instead of lively amusement usually accompanying the thrill of the game, I saw everybody with cards put aside, their heads shaking from time to time. They were all ears, listening to a woman from the neighborhood, who was telling something and sobbed violently. Her red tearful eyes searching for support said it all. I offered the girl some water and asked what had happened and how I could help. Weeping and trembling in emotions, she answered in a rather good English, as far as I could judge, that she needed badly to get to her family house situated 236 miles away from here as soon as possible. The locals couldn't help—they mentioned lack of time or 'important' gambling affairs. I decided not to go deep into the story, but asked her to stay there a few minutes. I took the stuff I'd bought out of my backpack and filled it with the essentials we would need for a trip. A few minutes later our tuk-tuk rattled down the cobblestone road to the nearest bus station, bouncing and swinging, bumping every pebble and pothole.

Part III

It turned out the bus tickets had been sold out, so we had to make the first 155 miles to the Cambodian capital in a small old Toyota together with several more passengers. Mile by mile my neighbor kept us immersed in her sad story. An hour before our first meeting she found out that one of the three brothers of hers had had a motorbike accident. A paramedic, who had arrived in an ambulance to the accident scene, was the first to let her know about the tragedy. The three young boys were taken to the closest district hospital.

There were several phone calls from the doctor while we were on our way. Each call made the gleam of hope in her eyes get dimmer and dimmer. She fainted twice in my arms: the first time—when she heard one of the injured had deceased without regaining consciousness, and the second time—when she was told her 19-year-old brother had passed away. None survived.

"I will never pray to Buddha again," she whispered weakly in her mother tongue, slowly regaining consciousness, her eyes still closed. I will never forget what I felt, when I heard those words slipped out of her heart in despair. Emptiness filled all the inner and outer space, like ink spreading over a blank piece of paper. The bright day gave way to a black night. The only sound I could hear in the darkness was the thud of my own temples; the pain in my chest meant my heart was still alive. The sky, usually distant, airy and light, now came crashing down on me. It is always unbearable to see the hope and faith die, but if love dies, the heart turns to stone forever. Her love was strong.

Part IV

At last we covered the most part of the distance. In the capital we dropped by one of the numerous bike rentals and, following my companion's advice, I took a Honda sportbike with studded tires. It reminded a racing greyhound—slim, high and slightly arched. When I straddled the bike, my feet could barely touch the ground. Sixty odd miles at 95 degrees Fahrenheit was a tough challenge, I must say! Furthermore we had to maintain a high speed to arrive before dark. When the asphalt road ended, we made a stop before the last and the most challenging part of our trip. My hands trembled as if electricity had passed through them. My T-shirt and shorts were drenched in sweat. The ride was immortalized in an exhaust pipe burn on my leg. The girl coped with the situation quite well in spite of what she had been through.

It had rained in the province the night before, so a once normal country road had turned into squelching mud, however a little sun-dried. The bike, bored with the asphalt road, now shuddered in anticipation of impassability and started getting its studs into the ground so furiously, that huge lumps of mud splashed yards away in all directions and onto us.

Part V

For the first time since the beginning of our trip I looked around to see a real Cambodian village. Dozens of kids playing outdoors, peasants tired after the work day, and jolly drunks—as soon as they noticed us, they all greeted us cheerfully and waved. We had to move slowly and carefully, trying to avoid huge puddles and boggy places, where indifferent tall herons were standing still, domestic ducks were scampering around with their ducklings, dogs were barking, and white cows were walking solemnly with their calves. Smoldering fires were seen on both sides of the road. The smoke formed white vaguely-outlined arches. When, amidst an endless field of tobacco, a young stallion galloped out of one of the arches all of a sudden, its bell on the neck ringing, crossed the road in three long jumps and disappeared in heavy smoke in a blink of an eye, I thought it was hallucination, as the picture was quite surrealistic.

Part VI

Having overcome all the obstacles we reached the ferry. My companion's home village was right across the river. We got down to the water along a stony but easy trail in complete darkness. Without cutting the engine I directed the headlight at the opposite bank and honked several times. The opposite bank answered with a starting engine, and after some time a big floating structure took us onboard. The ferryman was a very young boy sitting on the edge of the boat and hugging an old diesel motor fastened to one of the crossbeams with wire. On my way back after several days, I noticed how serious and responsible the boy looked. His daily important mission of taking people across the river made him a grown-up beyond his years. We paid half a dollar and crossed the river.

Part VII

A local brindle dog was the first to greet us near the house. It barked crazy and ran around us in circles until I got off the bike and let the dog sniff me. Nuzzling its wet nose into my legs, it found the fresh burn on my left calf and started licking it enthusiastically. That was how we made friends.

The rustic courtyard was lit by the only fluorescent lamp. Its cold light covered only the central part of the courtyard, not reaching the remote corners. They had electricity for several hours a day starting from 6 p.m. - it was rather expensive, so one bulb per house was a matter of course. People from the neighborhood gradually filled the courtyard and encircled us. When I realized I was still wearing the helmet, I got rid of its stuffy and tight embrace, and appeared at my best before the spectators. All over in mud, my bristle almost as long as my hair, and soaked in sweat, I was standing there, in the middle of nowhere, lit by an electric moon, looked at by dozens of attentive eyes. When it turned out that I was the first foreigner ever visiting this village, I felt ashamed for my appearance. I looked around smiling guiltily, which caused excitement, and everybody present—from kids to old people—smiled back. The people gave way to us, I made several steps and sank to the stairs leading into the house. My companion brought a pot and a bar of soap, and pointed at a row of big jars with water seen here and there in the courtyard. "Grab any and wash yourself," she said. I turned round the corner of the house, where nobody could see me, and poured half a big jar of warm rainwater over myself. While I was tampering with the pot, cleaning one spot and soiling another at the same time, they made a dinner and bed for me. So many things had happened during that hard day! I went up the stairs into the house, expressed my gratitude for the dinner and fell asleep immediately, enveloped in the delicate smell of tobacco leaves cured downstairs. The population of this and many other neighboring villages made their living by growing and curing tobacco, and preparing it for further export to Vietnam.

Part VIII

When I woke up the next morning, I realized I had fallen ill. The planned return trip was postponed. I was down with fever the following days, coughing and sneezing vigorously. At the same time I saw the family making arrangements for a funeral. The girl's relatives lavished care and attention on me, as if I were part of the family. One after the other they gave me ginger tea and lime drink, rice and mango, telling me about their hard life in the village.

Part IX

Soon I got well, and we started back after several days. I left the house with a heavy heart. I got used to the people who gave me shelter, and got a taste of the joy and grief of real life. Life goes on!

Jon Meyer "Your Rising Moon"

Jon Meyer "Eternity In This Moment"

The World In A Lover's Eye

Hear a symphony in a whisper.
Feel a bonfire in an ember.
Taste an ocean in a drop.
Smell a fresh landscape in a blade of grass.
See the world in a lover's eye.

Jon Meyer "The World In A Lover's Eye"

Storming Normandy

Cindy Layton

From the doorway I watched as Dad held the gun in his palm, inspecting it, not like they were old friends but business partners. It looked old but still deadly. Where did he get that? His bony fingers ran alongside the round barrel while his eyes traveled along the length of its metal frame. The door to the safe was open, exposing envelopes and a metal box. A purple velvet bag, showing the imprint of the gun where it had been stored, lay beside him on the sofa. Where was Adelene? I stood stiffly, unable to move toward him or away from him. Slowly, I held out my hand.

"Dad, could I have that?"

He was startled and looked to see who was there. Then his eyes shifted down and he shook his head. "No. I need it."

"What for?" A feeble question, but I needed him to talk.

"We're at war. But you wouldn't know anything about that." It had been a long time since he'd made a comment about me refusing to go into the army.

"Maybe Dad, but we're not at war here." I leaned in a little.

He raised his non-gun hand to wave me away. "I didn't raise you to be so timid. When a man's got a problem he's gotta take action."

I wracked my brain to figure what he meant. "I don't have a problem."

He looked at me with his glassy, bulging eyes. Those eyes had darkened over time. A little bit when I refused to go to Harold's for another crew cut. More when I refused to stop protesting downtown, and when I said I was going into teaching, not law. Now, they're black like a galaxy.

"Why is it you think everything's always about you? It's me," he said, pointing to his chest. "My problem."

"Right. The doctor's going to help you with that. Remember?"

"He can't help me. Some soldiers are too far gone to take off the battlefield." His head nodded toward the safe. "That stuff's for you." He cradled the barrel against his chest. The weight of it was too much and it wobbled as he attempted to hold it in place.

I took a step to the right, a better angle to avoid the line of fire. My only option was to assume it was loaded.

He stared at my rigid, hesitant body. I was sure he saw my knees shaking beneath my pants. Surely he knew my lungs were constricted, my pulse racing. His upper lip rose slightly then turned briefly to a half smile. A smile that had nothing to do with happiness.

One summer, he had taken us to the carnival. Me and Jenn were about to get in line for the Zipper. There was a big, burly farm kid walking down the exit ramp. He leaned over the railing and puked his guts out. I figured I didn't stand a chance, so I bolted over to the swings.

Dad left me there and took my place in line. He and Jennifer were locked into the metal cage. It rose up slowly, and as they reached the top they dropped down, then spun and tumbled around in a cascade, the lights flashing, girls screaming and all the riders clutching the steel bars. When they got off and started walking to the arcade I ran to catch up with them. Jenn gave me a shove with her elbow when Dad wasn't looking and stared at me for an explanation.

He gave Jenn money for Skee Ball then he paid the shooting gallery guy a few bucks and held out the BB gun to me. I stared at him. Without a word, he held it by the barrel, a silent dare for me to take it. The Ferris wheel behind him flashed, turned a few more times, then began letting riders off. The kids at the top made their carriage rock and leaned their hands over the railing, pitching the seat forward until with a jerk the ride moved them down.

Music, sounding like a jack-in-the box, piped from behind the shooting gallery.

Dad looked at the ground for a second, then hoisted the long rifle over his shoulder and mowed down the row of rabbits sliding along the conveyor. *Ping! Pingpingping!*

"Another winner!" The guy behind the counter handed Dad a huge stuffed animal, but Dad sneered at him and turned away. "Step right up, folks. Shoot with skill and precision!"

"Skill and precision, my ass." Dad sulked off to find Jennifer. I remember the crowd folding in around us and, from time to time, I'd lose sight of him. I ran-walked to keep him in view but stayed out of the orbit of that mood.

He and Jenn used up the rest of the ride tickets while I hung out at the freak show, which was just a tent filled with posters of odd circus characters from long ago.

I hated him for hating me.

And here he was again, gun in hand, a sneer for a smile. Where in the hell was Adelene? "Hey, do you remember taking me and Jenn to the fair?"

Dad perked up his head. "Your sister won a prize for something, right?" He shifted in his seat. "She sure was a beauty back then. Too bad she went off and married that bastard."

By the time Jenn turned twenty she was out of the house. Dad took it personally, like she abandoned him. He wasn't the only one. Her leaving eliminated the last existing buffer between me and him.

"She won the talent contest. Remember the Hula-Hoop routine?"

Dad smiled a real smile, the smooth skin on his face wrinkling around the eyes, the darkness in them brightening a bit. "*You* ended up with your head in a barrel." Despite my best efforts I had still managed to throw up by the end of the day.

"Bad hot dog."

He took his hand off the grip of the gun and stretched his fingers, then rested them across the barrel. Would he even have the strength to fire it? *Underestimate him at your peril,* I thought.

Last week when he saw Dr. Langston, he complained about not sleeping. Said Adelene was keeping him up, walking around the house at all hours. She claimed it was him and his dreams.

"I'm telling you," Dad said, "it's that woman!" Dr. Langston prescribed an anti-anxiety pill but Adelene told me he's still up at night.

Dad's head began to droop a bit and his eyes fluttered. In the distance a helicopter approached. The sound of the turning blades echoed overhead and with a violent jerk Dad awoke, his eyes alert and his shoulders square. He grabbed for the gun and raised it with a wobbly hand. "Master Sargent!" He steadied himself with his other hand on the edge of the recliner and raised himself up. "Incoming, sir!" He tried to make it over to the window but each step made his knees buckle a little.

"Dad, come on." I could tell he was descending into the whole "greatest generation" thing again. It usually started with him talking about the master sargent like the guy was some kind of hero. I reached out my arm for him to lean on. "Sit down."

The sound of the helicopter faded and he looked around the room. A flicker of recognition crept back into his eyes. Then he let out a snort and made his way back to the recliner, holding the side of the gun up against his chest with one hand and steadying himself with the other. He shook his head adamantly when I tried to settle him down into the chair. With his free hand wiping the length of his face from his forehead down to his chin, he descended back into the dark mood.

After catching his breath he looked down. "Your mother hated this thing, God rest her." He rattled the gun in his hand. "She told your Aunt Elena she wanted to throw it in the trash. I told her if she did that I'd kill her." Another wipe of his face with the free hand. "Where is your mother?" Dad tapped the Naugahyde arm of the recliner. "She's supposed to be back by now."

"Dad, she's gone. You know that."

"She told me she was going to the store. It's almost dinner time."

"No. It's not even time for lunch yet. Are you hungry?"

Dad shifted in his seat and grabbed for the remote control. "I know what time it is. Why won't this damn thing work?" He pointed the remote at the TV and jammed his thumb over several of the buttons. It flickered and the news came on. "Isn't it time for *Millionaire*?"

Millionaire had to be on some channel. I scrolled through and found another of his favorites, *Jeopardy*. I thought, *I'll take World War II for $500, please. This D-Day hero was the son of a famous president who also bore the same name. Who is Theodore Roosevelt Junior? Correct for $500.*

"Get my book. My book!" Dad pointed to the drawer below where the gun had been stored, under the safe. I opened it and searched among the papers and found a scrapbook, which I brought over and placed in his lap.

He fingered the pages and opened them gingerly. Old photos scattered to the floor, the cellophane no longer able to hold them in place. There he was in his uniform, leaning against a jeep, smoking a cigarette, tall and trim, with a shock of dark hair curled on his forehead. The camera shot just caught the sideways glance in his eye. It made him look shy. Or devilish.

"Do you know who that is?" He pointed to an officer standing next to him in the photo.

I shook my head.

"Roosevelt, the son."

"Wow." I had no idea.

"That man saved my life. I was ready to hang it up. We were all sure we'd never make it off the beach. This guy's standing in the water. He shakes my hand after I get off the boat and tells me to head over to the right. Bullets flying everywhere. Guys falling all around us. Him? Not a bit scared. Gives me a cigarette and tells me to get going. Instead of falling apart I joined the other men. Somehow I made it out alive."

Dad wiped his hand across his forehead and paused for a few seconds. "When we got back, and for the longest time after that, nobody, *nobody* in the US would buy a German car." He took a deep breath and shrugged his shoulders. "Now, nobody cares." He turned to look in the kitchen. "Where in the hell is that Adelene?"

I thought back to my own Volkswagen from college, a green beetle with rusted-out floors. Then I was more interested in marching against the military-industrial complex, not boycotting some overseas automaker from long ago. Where *was* Adelene? I'd been here for fifteen minutes and hadn't heard anything from her.

The book slid from Dad's lap and I bent over to pick it up. Loose papers and more pictures fell to the floor. I sat facing Dad on the ottoman and together, we sorted through them. Dad opened the letters and scanned them, folding them back up without comment. Once in while he'd flip a picture over and point. "He's governor of New Jersey. That one's a four-star general in the army." Some of the pictures were labeled on the back. "A lot of these guys never made it. Nothing to do but press on. Hear me? Press on."

The gun slipped down and now lay cradled between his belly and his thighs.

I'll take World War II for $1,000. The origin of this acronym was taken from the initials stamped on commonly used trash cans and buckets. What are GI, galvanized iron? Correct for $1000! I'll take World War II for $400.

"GI stands for Government Issue. Government Issue! Not galvanized iron. Everybody knows that." He fumbled for the gun, lifted it with two hands and pointed it at Alex Trebek.

"Dad, no!"

He laughed a short laugh. "Why doesn't he just shut up?"

I reached over and turned off the TV. "Let's fix you some soup or maybe a sandwich." I darted into the kitchen to look for Adelene. No sign of her or anything to do with lunch. I hunted around in the cabinet to see what I could find. "How about some tuna fish?"

"Where'd you learn how to cook?" Dad was standing behind me. He made his way over to the kitchen table and eased himself down into a chair. "Let your mother do the cooking."

Where was the gun? Then I saw it, stuffed beneath his belt. "Tuna fish is *not* cooking."

"Is to me. She puts that relish in it, a tiny drop."

I searched in the refrigerator for relish and pulled out a bottle.

"Not that! The red kind!" Dad placed his hands on either side of the chair and began to lift himself up to move toward the refrigerator. There was the sound of a thud and a flash of metal spinning around on the linoleum floor. The barrel stopped at my foot, pointing at me as though I was the winner in a cynical spin-the-bottle move with no one to kiss.

My toe twitched inside my shoe. There was nowhere to look but down at that metal. It was mostly dull although there were glints of shine as it caught the fluorescent light of the kitchen. I stared at it, mesmerized by the possibilities.

A bullet to the foot wouldn't be deadly. Maybe not even crippling. The body has an amazing ability to heal, right? And, anyway, laying there on its own, the gun couldn't shoot by itself. It needed a partner, someone to hold it. Someone to become what the gun and the person decide to become. Together, what would *we* be? A bank robber? An FBI agent? A war hero? Things I would never dream of on my own.

I picked it up from the floor and held it against my palm. So cold. So heavy. Now, it was an instrument. I positioned the trigger against my finger and held it up to my line of sight.

"That's right." He looked at me, the gray in his eyes reflecting back like a mirror, his smile slight but meaningful. "Now you know."

My hand shook, not from weakness but from excitement. I didn't have a plan to shoot it. Holding the gun was enough.

The screen door slammed and Adelene's voice travelled from the back of the house. "Sorry I took so long, Mr. Morrissey. I couldn't find nothing of that tool box."

I lowered the heavy metal and placed it back in his lap. He nodded and cradled it in his two hands.

"Mister Morrissey! Give me that!" Adelene's full figure crashed in to the kitchen. "You storming Normandy today?" With one swoop she whisked the weapon away from him.

"Take care of this," she said, handing the gun to me. "Take *good* care of it."

Traffic Report

A Novel Excerpt

Eric D. Goodman

This is your eye in the sky, the WCHL Traffic Copter. If you're just now tuning in for the first time today, here's a word of advice: stay home. You heard me right, folks: authorities have advised everyone in the Chillicothe area to remain indoors today and to stay off the roads. If you're already driving to work, go back home. It's a zoo out there—literally.

Lions and bears, wild cats and wolves have all escaped from a local animal reserve here in Chillicothe. If you leave your house today, you're walking into a danger zone. It's best to stay indoors.

For those of you braving the commute, be advised that bears have been spotted along Main Street headed into the downtown area. Already this morning, four reports have come in of bears attacking cars at stoplights. No windows have been broken or injuries reported, but there have been some frightened passengers and some dinged up vehicles.

A pride of lions—that's a whole family of them—is reportedly traveling together. I haven't been able to spot them from up here, but authorities believe they were in the city early this morning and may be headed north outside of Chillicothe. They could still be in the downtown area, so stay alert.

Also, leopards and panthers and other wild cats are on the loose that have not been found since their escape yesterday afternoon. I'm telling you folks, it's the day to call in. If you can stay home, you'd better do it.

Right now, I'm looking at a major traffic jam entering downtown Chillicothe on Main Street, and the cause is a bear that keeps banging into bottlenecked cars. Police are aware of the bear and are said to be on their way.

Oh, my! I'm seeing police respond now! The police—two of them, racing up the shoulder, jumping out of the car and . . . yes, they have opened fire. The bear—yes, yes, it's down. It looks like the bear's dead, right in the middle of Main Street. Wow.

Folks, the bear is down, but lions and other wild cats remain on the loose, so today is the day to avoid the roads. Do not leave your house if you don't have to. All state, federal and local government have implemented liberal leave for the day—you will not be denied leave—and schools are closed throughout Chillicothe and the surrounding areas. Businesses and employers have been asked by police to approve requests to take the day off, and everyone is encouraged to stay home.

If you're just tuning in, folks, a bear has been shot and killed by police on Main Street only moments ago, and that's causing a major backup. Other wild animals are on the loose and may possibly be in downtown Chillicothe and the surrounding area. I'm your WCHL eye in the sky, looking today not only for traffic conditions, but for the animal conditions in Chillicothe. Stay indoors, and stay safe.

Go Blow

Alan Berger

He would have said how the fuck could they make a trumpet out of plastic and have come forth out of it with such beautiful sounds. Sounds like he heard his father play on his brass trumpet. But Gabriel was only four years of age when he got it and didn't know yet what plastic was.

Gabe's mother and father were always fighting. With her doing most of the fighting and him doing most of the ignoring. She was jealous of his trumpet, which he played all the time.

Gabe would listen to his father play in the next room and play along with him from his room.

That duo would harmonize until mom started hitting dad and if Gabe was still playing after a few smacks at dad, she would go into his room and smack on him.

By that time dad would start playing his horn again and she would leave Gabe and go back to dad and start in again on him where she left off.

Gabe kept playing too.

His horn sounds banished the bad ones.

Gabe's dad died when Gabe was thirteen.

Gabe figured he died because he wanted to.

Death couldn't be worse than living with ma and dad's horn could no longer quiet the bad sounds like Gabe's was still doing.

After the funeral, Gabe took his father's horn and then took a powder.

Gabe and his horn ran away together.

Gabe found work at a golf course as a caddy.

He always had his eye on the ball and now he was finding them.

He wrote his first piece around those times waiting to be called to carry golf bags in the caddy shack where he could just hold his forever horn in his lap and not play it.

Just think it.

He called it, "Please accept my love."

It was a beautiful begging haunting yet friendly piece.

When he played it was as if he was born with a horn that would forever work and rest in his chest.

Mouthpiece pointing up to lip with the horn pointing down to his heart.

When he played, what was listened to, would stick to the ribs, and then some.

At day's end he would pretend to be on his way to his "home" that he would describe to others as a nice big house surrounded by big trees that he shared with his "brothers and sisters" and it had a nice front and backyard that was as green as the golf course fairways he would carry and compose on.

He would leave a window unlocked in the caddy shack and hide in the woods until everyone left and through the window he would go to his "home" and sleep, eat, wash and stay there until early morn where he would slip back out the window and into the woods and wait until they opened and go back pretending he was just was showing up at work.

A lot of his wardrobe comprised of shirts and sweaters that were left forgotten on the fairways and such and end up in the caddy shack's lost and found department.

Never found pants, but blue jeans are forever.

He knew he was lost and hoped one day to be found.

When asked why he wasn't in school, he said he was "home schooled."

Well ain't that the truth?

He played his song, "Please accept my love," to one of the members of the club who noticed his forever with him horn, and when the music ended the club owner asked what it was called and who wrote it.

When he heard the title and the name of the composer, he teared up and threw down a twenty to Gabe.

Then he asked Gabe a lot of questions.

It did not take him long to unfold the folded-up truths regarding this young man's circumstances.

He said, "You three are coming home with me tonight."

When Gabe asked who the other two were, he was told, "Your horn and my sweater."

Paulo Navarro "Apple Head Man"

POETRY

RICHARD-YVES SITOSKI

Low-Hanging Fireworks

Mother never woke up tangled in stars
but stayed on Earth, which father dropped
and watched as it rolled beneath the couch.
Her music was straight as a prairie road,
his was bent like an elbow to the gut.
He preferred the company of dogs,
she of me when I felt like one.
He proved that there are no happy alcoholics
and that love is conditional,
she that mushrooms can push through asphalt
and that cancer comes without a screenplay.
The cookies she baked were chocolate chip
but I always wound up with raisin.
He taught me to fish, but each one
I caught swallowed the hook.
He tried to be anonymous
but the rest of the world ignored him.
Some nights he came home after not coming home.
Some days her migraines were low-hanging fireworks.
I wrote this poem because memory

is no insurance against decay.
I wrote this poem because it ain't gossip till it's shared,
and I wanted you to know before the neighbors.

Deadname

She gave it the double-edged life hack,
cut the umbilicus to her dead self
because her house has a typewriter cerebellum
where she taps the earworm of her appetites,
but her garden was a no-go zone of cats
pissing on weeds and poisoning the soil.
But now sailors mistake her semaphore for metaphor,
distress flags for pennants with the logo
of the football club that earns bricks in the stands.
Dictionaries shut up around her,
functionaries speak down about her,
adversaries sneak up behind her.
And the bodies of her friendships pile
like night-time sparrows lost in counterfeit sunlight
hitting very real windows.
So during the times she doesn't want
to jam for once and all the mainspring
of the machine she lives in,
she wanders bruise-coloured badlands
stared at by the dry eye of the moon,
bowing and scraping each timid step
like the Great Khan's wetnurse,
barefoot on fishhooks toward a bed
as comfortable as a pile of antlers.

Cemetery Engine Failure

She said that if you get the chance, to stay awake:
sunlight's expensive and easily spilled.
Said she had a right to aggressive happiness
and that it's not revolution without dance,
so pick up a rifle and tights.
She said that time was not a sparrow
caught in the chaos of your hair
but a pterodactyl soaring toward extinction.
Said that too much oxygen was toxic
which was why she smoked so much.
And you loaded it all in your freightcar memory
in advance of the day they'd find her
drowned in a barrel of honey,
sweet as any farewell kiss from the land
where waking is taken for granted,
where there is no sleep for metronomes,
where she was born to be property of a jealous Earth.
Sorry if this is not the suicide poem
they warned you about.

My Scars Are Purely Accidental

You were sad but you laughed into your pillow,
grasping at me as at a branch out of reach
above the bed you were drowning in.
I had been your acolyte from the time
I first snuck a sip from your cup
to kiss you by proxy,
until you disrobed to show me
where you got your inspiration:
needle tracks a Day-Glo trail

to a gingerbread house
where you flopped on a couch
sleeping the sleep of the unobserved,
shoulder blades broken
by the weight of your own beauty.
Time to come clean.
The songs I tried to sing you
were stifled by your shadow
reaching round to put a hand on my mouth,
and my fear spread like malware
with no Bitcoin to lift the ransom.
After all, my scars are purely accidental.
So I did my best. But I was done in.
You proved that in the vastness of a prairie
you could still find a precipice.
Lying in bed as the sun dissolved in a spoon,
there was nothing to do
but count your breaths down from 10,
knowing that even shrapnel comes to rest.

Knowing

Jarrett Mazza

Sometimes I wake up and forget where I am or how I arrived. We often wonder about our personal truths, our pilgrimages that help us to see who, *what* we are. At night, when I'm sleeping next to her, I sometimes roll quietly out of bed and stumble into the kitchen to shake off the nightmares I've had. I'm bleeding in each one. I can assemble so many pieces of my life and merge them meticulously together and take some time to assess how it's all going to work before I get back to bed.

But we can't change overnight. We just need time.

I suppose the lowest moment, the moments where you could say I wish I was *saved* became increasingly more frequent.

Alone in my two-bedroom loft, before I met her, I found that my entire life was just one big test. Working two jobs, with only a little debt, I spent most of my time trying to find new people, new faces. I was always on the lookout for new experiences, maybe a new drink, a new hobby, or going to a place I swore I never would go. What I hated most was feeling time passing. I grew up in a church, where the faces stayed the same. In this city, growing up in a church gives you a reputation. But I was escaping that. I hoped. The new people, new faces, new experiences showed me I was escaping that.

I was twenty-two when I met her. I never thought much about it anymore, her suddenly appearing to me. It was all so congested, crammed in the back of my mind, and I never looked back, not until I started thinking of myself as loathsome; then I went back and thought about everything, remembered everything. She wasn't someone who stayed on top of things like I did. I was routine; she wasn't. And now I'm realizing that my oversimplification of things: work, play, rave, repeat—it had all melted my spirit down. From the bottom of this meltdown I could look up and see where it all began, where it all went wrong.

With Samantha and me nothing too terrible happened; at least if it *was* terrible, I always found a way to forget about it. I never dwelled. New people and new experiences mean you never have to dwell. And Samantha was great at making sure that the past stayed the past. She taught me how.

It was all so simple coming from her. The world is precious. You have to make each day count, and you don't need to die in order to find a greater purpose. This worldview was inconvenient for me, but I trusted Samantha to show me how, to get me to the places I never thought I could go. Her revelations weren't scary or surprising, they just left me feeling overwhelmed. I didn't want to go this route with her only to be disappointed or disappoint her.

I never said any of this, not aloud, definitely not to Samantha. I never admitted it because, honestly, I didn't know what I believed. I grew up Catholic. We only ask ourselves questions that we know we can find the answers to. I know what I feel, what I *want* to feel, and should I actually embark on this Samantha odyssey that will determine the course of my life, before I begin, I need to trace back all of the memories that I have.

Saturday night and I was in the bedroom, kneeling down to tie my boots. Samantha was in the hall, waiting for me to get ready. This club tonight was one of hers, one of the clubs she swore I needed to be at. Samantha was better at socializing; I was better at following her lead.

So much of her time was spent among those who found meaning in the randomness, the synchronicities, those who saw the world as part of the vastly occurring cosmos, those who could make sense out of nothing at all.

My parents called them godless.

I remember being a child and attending church. My mother kissed me on the cheek as I went to sit with the other obedient children. I volunteered to carry the cross. My sister, Jennifer, carried the Bible. She still does whenever she teaches. An honest, cherished time; looking back, the whole thing seemed so damn clichéd, a childish thing to remember. The thing about being raised in a religious household is you rarely get the chance to engage with people that are not like you.

Samantha didn't identify as religious, not in the usual, simple way. She used to speak a lot about truth. She said the only way to attain it was to bury yourself inside the world. She told me this right before she did a line of coke, one that would be my first.

"You should wear your favorite boots," said Samantha from the hall, "they look really dope."

I looked down at the boots before slipping inside them. I pulled on the laces as tightly as I could.

In the club we saw a mess of gyrating bodies, and fist-pumping maniacs were throwing their hands up in rhythm. Don't know why the thought entered my mind: priests, clergymen, what would they do if they saw what I was seeing now?

Was it as bad as it seemed?

Was *anything* as bad as it seemed?

I thought about this scenario: men of the cloth not being entirely certain of what they are teaching to others. A holy man, as I understood, was required to believe what he was preaching, to display not even a single shred of doubt, following everything as they seek to know and understand. So how much did I really know; what is the line between Samantha and me, or the line between skepticism and doubt?

The music was loud. Sometimes I don't mind intense music—the more intense, the more it filled the spaces in my mind that I wanted to be filled.

"Why aren't you dancing?"

Samantha, spinning in the middle of the space around us, in a great orgy of sweat and flesh, pulled me against her breasts.

She possessed many admirable features. One of her best was her piercing green eyes, the way she never looked away. I found myself falling immediately, or at the very least being infatuated to the point of feeling paralyzed. There was no denying I wanted her, and that she wanted me. She was what some might call lascivious. Perhaps now it was this quality that I found to be the most admirable, that her sultry lifestyle so obviously contrasted with my own.

I soon joined the spinning bodies around me, all of whom seemed to know Samantha.

Then at some point we went to the bar to get a drink. I used to know nothing about raves, like how dangerous they are, like the fact that they even had bars.

"Thanks," Samantha said to the bartender as she sucked back a shot and handed me one. "Much appreciated."

Doubt runs deep through a church, any church. The closer you get to God, the more you realize that it might all be horseshit. I say, you *must* doubt. Only from there can you take the ultimate leap towards knowing.

"This is my friend, *Dave*," said Samantha.

I knew Dave, and he knew me. That was it.

He sidled up to Samantha. He was the kind that wouldn't listen if I told him to step away. He was glaring over and I told him I was here to have a good time the same as he was.

"If you really want to have a good time . . ."

He winked at Samantha and they both trekked up the stairs, away from the party, holding hands. To anyone not used to these propositions, they would have thought it implied "Let's go fuck." It didn't. As they went up the back stairs, and I followed, a glowing crucifix was shining by the doorway, blinking, and intermittently illuminating the graffiti covered door where Dave was leading everyone to.

My first fling with narcotics happened because of Samantha, then I kept coming back for that quieting effect. It stabilized me, brought me back to a time where everything was simple, and each time I did it, I was always floating. *Up . . . up . . . up.*

"Here," said Dave. He and Samantha were next to each other, hunkering down and snorting three lines while I stood by and watched.

"Blake?" she said, showing me my lines.

I didn't want to, not because it wouldn't be awesome, but because these times always felt like I was crossing some new threshold that I didn't want to cross. I had crossed so many.

But Samantha loved me keeping an open mind.

My mother said that people indulge in narcotics because there's a void growing inside of them that they need filled. "*People binge drink and plough their faces with food because there's something missing in their life. It's an ugly indulgence,*" Mother said, "*causing further indulgence and can only lead to a life of decadence and despair.*" A lecture always followed, with big speeches about Jesus, how the last thing that he would have wanted was for us to burn the beautiful things he made because we want to have our sight tainted by something artificial. She always asserted that grace is not merely a superstition, but a consequence of our sinning or not sinning, an action/reaction that proclaims the inevitability that, whatever we put out in the world, always finds its way back to us. At the time, I never liked the sound of Jesus. I feared him.

"I like this shit, don't you?" Dave was talking to Samantha.

I wanted to rip into what I was seeing, dive right in and push myself to the edge. If there *was* a God, the edge is where you'd find *Him*, the places where you could touch and taste, where you could lie and survive, where things were taken, never received. I remember all of these moments. I did the line as fast as I could, and it was easy going down, almost as easy as not seeing something until it was too late.

With enough snorts, and enough time spent amidst the powder, everything glows. I could travel across the room without getting up from my chair.

"What do you got there?" Samantha said.

Dave managed to smuggle in a little meth, some heavy-duty shit that could transform you into a killer fucking zombie, he said. Of all the substances on God's green Earth, this was the stuff that warriors were made out of, real mega-death *boom*, *boom*, *boom* that only the deadliest of hitters could handle.

That was his introduction.

The crystal pebbles were stashed in a plastic bag, and Samantha was looking at me as I looked at the bag.

"You wanna fly?" Samantha said.

Dave lit a crisp, butane lighter.

When everyone expects you to be a certain a way, sometimes you want to kill the I-can't-believe-I-just-did-that side of your brain and instead just do, do, do, grab anything within arm's reach.

"I wanna fly."

So, I did.

I didn't hesitate a second to put that smoking tip to my wet lips, inhale, and let the power wash over me until I disappeared.

"Now me," Samantha said, taking the pipe to her lips.

I felt my hand inside her legs. This was the last time I would see death, and this was the last time I would deny the truth.

Samantha's eyes sprung open, and someone screamed.

"Holy shit!" Dave jumped, and pulled the fabric that was over the table, shattering all the glasses resting there. "Samantha!"

Her head was down, and, within a minute, she was out.

I freaked. I grabbed her head, I tried to hold it up. She was bleeding from her nose.

"Call the cops!"

Dave grabbed my hand and pulled. He dragged me from the table and, just like that, I was thrown back into the rave. Someone was on the floor puking, another was tweaking, and the rest were still gyrating to the hard music. Bobbing heads, coughing faces, and sickly gaits were all the moments that I was now being pulled through.

"Have to go back," I said.

Dave kept pulling. Pulling me down the stairs. I was sure he was heading to the long tunnel that led out of the building. I pulled back, looking around, trying to see up the steps, up where are all the lights were flashing.

"Are we going to get help?"

Dave flashed me a glare and pulled me through the door. We fell and slid and knocked into people on our way through the crowded hordes. I still felt like I was flying. Suddenly I grabbed onto something; I held it, whatever it was, and we both stopped.

"You can't help her. I know when it's too late," he said.

I blinked. Dave's face, wet, began to resemble my father's. Throughout my childhood, my father quoted God as if he were a priest. He believed in the message of faith, never to get angry, never to give in to one's aggression, to speak with kindness, telling me to say my prayers before bed, *blah, blah, blah*. When we believe there's no one watching us, and there's no one around to help, when we do plunge, fall, and feel completely lost, if we truly believe we might have a chance of being saved, God will answer the prayers of his faithful. That is his job, my father said. It is possible to witness miracles. And I didn't know where I believed that, in my heart or my head, or even if I believed it. I just didn't know.

"I thought she was your friend," I said to Dave.

"She *is*."

We were toe-to-toe. I didn't know where my hand was until I felt it on my chest. It was pressed against a crucifix. It was sharp. It was digging into my palm the more I grasped it. I couldn't even recall moving my hand to it. I couldn't recall wearing the beads tonight.

"We have to go," said Dave. "Someone will call the cops any minute."

"Can't leave without her!" I shouted back.

For the first time I could actually hear myself over the music.

"You saw her!" Dave shouted back. "Bitch was bleeding from her fucking nose, and if we're there too, we're fucked, and I'm not riskin' that shit!"

Wow.

I was coming down. I was getting coherent. Samantha's blood was on me; I could smell it. It probably was pointless. She was likely convulsing.

They'd say she was another junkie bitch and that's that.

My mother once gave me a guardian angel pendant to hang in my car. She said it would keep me safe. I had two accidents in ten years. I would hardly call it protection, but then maybe it might've been four if I didn't have an angel dangling from my rearview mirror. Sometimes she'd go a little crazy. She'd say God's given me so much, and yet, here I am, making so many bad decisions. She and my father prayed for me. The entire time I asked what on earth could they possibly be praying for; they always said *you*. I would pray sometimes too, not as much, usually when I wanted something. Now, I think I might've said six in my head, whatever ones I could remember as I yanked Dave's hand.

Some force, not love exactly, but something else I couldn't quite explain, was telling me: go back. The euphoric drugs usually left me with little that I could control. And I never thought of an angel or something from above attempting to influence my decisions.

Back when Sam and I first started dating, we would go the bathroom and make out sloppily, grinding up against each other, and saying dirty words to get the mood right. She would run the shower, push me in, and we'd have quick, hard sex.

"Listen," I said to her, being clichéd, "I think we should take it slow."

"Slow," she said, pulling her face away. "Why?"

I was intimidated by sex. Samantha kept pushing me to be more relaxed. And back then I just did whatever she told me to do. We would do it in the bathtub, have sex without a condom, and whenever I said 'no' she'd mimic me in a flinty voice to incite shame, embarrassment. She wanted to get into my head so I could see the world in a way I hadn't before. I never fought her. I wasn't much of a fighter. But I couldn't imagine someone who would tolerate her for as long as I had. When I was standing with Dave, I couldn't help but think. . .would she do the same for me? If I were lying face down on the table, bleeding from my nose while a violent stream of ugly narcotics pumped through my system, would she go after me? Would she turn back and try to help knowing that there was nothing that could be done to save me?

We lived in a basement apartment for the first two months. Sometimes, when I was really getting nightmares, I'd play with the beads of a rosary next to the bed, twiddling my thumbs until I fell asleep. It was nice, rubbing those wooden balls under my fingertips, and basking in the sensation right before I drifted away. I was the restless one. I once sat in the bed with a rosary and a glass of water. Samantha was fast asleep next to me; both of us tranquil after sex. Lazily she rolled into me and the water spilled.

"Shit."

Samantha rolled over, her back all wet. Soon as she took her shirt off, I saw something, a growth or something. I reached out and touched it.

"Mmm," she moaned. "Don't do that. It hurts."

This would have been a good time for me to stop and leave her be. I was surprised she didn't see what I saw, that she would rather ignore the pain than know what it was. It was like my mother told me throughout childhood: "You see something wrong and look the other way, you're just as much to blame."

I reached out and touched it again. This time she flinched.

"Why do you keep touching me? I said that it hurts."

I had a good reason. Even when I just lightly grazed it, she quivered. I looked again at the marking, now it wasn't so much a marking as it was something that was imbedded deep in her flesh, like shrapnel.

"I think you need to go and see a doctor."

I had a feeling, a small sensation that nestled its way into my thoughts; all I could do when it happened was to just reach out, and touch what was there.

The next morning the doctor told us that it was an infection and he assured us that it wasn't something "serious," but that he was glad we brought it to his attention. When we got home, Samantha jumped my bones as a way of thanking me. Whenever I did something for her, all she did to repay me was have sex. And it was so good I never spoke up.

"Aren't you going to do something?" she said this time.

She was on top, always on top.

"What do you mean?"

"You never do much while we're doing this," said Samantha. "Come on. Do more."

I had just prevented her from getting a violent infection. More?

"No," I said, "it's just . . ."

"What?" she said, looking me over with a glare. "You don't want to?"

Samantha watched me intensely, mulling me over as she sat on top. I suppose I was good at sex, intimidated, but good enough; good at the physical part and good at the connection part that came from being with someone, that feeling afterward of being adjoined. Maybe that's why I always just laid back; I liked the feeling, the moment, letting nature take its course. Way of the Lord, and so on. In the church they say sex is a sacred bond for husband and wife. Once it's given, it cannot be taken back.

I did what I thought she wanted; I became something different—I threw her on her back and gave her the wild fuck she was after, the one that started all this.

I don't know what to believe. Samantha changed everything. She was the other side of life I never had access to. The place you want to get to but don't know how you ever could.

As soon as we were done and calming down from the sex, she opened up a fresh bag of coke and sprinkled it down on the nightstand, letting it scatter about as she grabbed her VISA from her wallet, and parted the heap into four thin lines.

"Have you ever done this before?"

Then, I never had. I used to date a girl named Tanya who loved weed. Funny thing was my sister loved it as well. And in our very Catholic family my father loved his liquor; it was my mother who, thanks to constant praying, she said, got him to throw it in the trash.

"Yes?" Samantha said.

In the end, what did I *really* have to lose?

One line was all it took, one quick bump, and I was out like a burnt candle. I disappeared into a land of dreams. I walked through an open field, with a white horizon, and no matter what flowed through my body, blood, air, the Holy fucking Spirit, it was all so scintillating and felt absolutely right. My mother spoke of the Holy Spirit as a power that could suddenly infiltrate your entire body and grant you the ability to fly. The drug took me out of my body and set me completely free. When I woke, I was right where I wanted to be, back in our room, lying next to her, my hand resting on her shoulder as a way of letting her know I was there. She said nothing when she awakened the next day, nothing except to ask if I wanted coffee. And we did more coke. Some nights, it was all we did. She told me to snort some lines while having a drink. I did. We roamed at night until we were given what we needed to keep going.

I didn't find any coke, I said one time. *I found nothing but this.*

What did you find?

Oh God, I hope you find it too, I said. I was wasted.

As I walked down the street, I made sure to always follow her like some kind of half-witted junkie, which is what I was now. I hated to think this way. I couldn't deny it, though, and Samantha said it was better I didn't. Embracing our bad ways, acknowledging our own weaknesses, it helps us whenever we have to remember the best parts of ourselves, even if there aren't many to remember.

Samantha pulled out her phone and dialed, talking to a man on the other line I'd never heard about.

God protects those who have the courage to protect themselves, my mother assured me. Those that do wicked only suffer wickedly. And there are never any consequences besides those we make for ourselves. Some call that religion.

Samantha never talked like this; to her the world wasn't suffering, it was joy. Yet all we ever did was roam along and try to pick up the pieces, locked together in this life of not having to make choices. Some call that freedom.

Dave shoved his way down the tunnel, leaving me.

A threesome of drunk girls rubbed against me on their way by, and somehow it felt like Samantha. Right now, was the good and the bad, the love and the guilt, all rolling into one. I dabbed my finger against my nose; I felt blood.

It happens. Not every snort of the white powder is painless and easy. I've drank blood before. Seeing it never bothered me.

New people were shoving their way down the tunnel; the cops were in the club, they were saying; everyone trying to run but the place was flooded. If what we do requires no shame, then why do we always insist on running away? When my mother was in church, she spoke of shame and confession, sharing and giving, and how there's always a way out.

A person can redeem themselves with a single act. Never too late.

I always imagined that, if I had a classic rock bottom moment, it would present itself in a way that was undeniable and so unavoidable that, if I turned away from it, it was the chief sign that I was lying to myself, always lying.

The blood from my nose moistened my lips. I could taste it. *My* blood, not sacred blood. We drink Christ's blood not just to feel his presence, but to be reminded of what he did for us, the redemption, and the promise, and the truth about who we really are.

Everyone pushing through the tunnel brought me right to the exit, to the way out and I could feel the cold air coming in from the street.

The difference between me and Samantha was what we chose to believe. I saw the world as created, with a beginning and an end. One day we would be judged, everything we did would be recorded and weighed. We are given gifts for the good and, someday, we will have to answer for the bad. My mother referred to this as "payment" as in we all have to "pay the piper." Samantha sometimes liked the way I saw the world. "With all your crosses and your thoughts about redemption, you get me thinking," she'd say. Her faith was always hiding in the background, lurking, lying dormant—it wasn't the old faith but something new.

Once, Samantha and I were walking to the drug store to get medicine and not, you know, drugs.

"Here," said Samantha, in front of the pharmacy. "Want to come in with me?"

There was a church across the street. It was small. With a statue of Jesus outside. He stood with his arms open, spread cruciformly, and he stared at me with stone eyes. I knew what Samantha was going to say when she saw me walk over. She'd make a joke, maybe it would be a light-hearted one about how you can take the boy out of the church but not the church out of the boy. I hadn't been inside a church in so long and for some reason just wanted to see it.

"Go then, preacher," she said to me as I walked across the street.

I wasn't a preacher. Maybe not even a Catholic anymore. But I did believe in the soul and in the randomness, and in something beyond what's known and seen. That's where we were, Samantha and I. Bringing each other towards ourselves. And that night *she* followed *me*; she hustled across the street and we stood on the steps together, looking up.

"Sometimes you won't know what is to become of you until you're tested."

Tests reveal.

Often the answers we want are presented only when we choose to stop blinding ourselves and know the truth.

Really know the truth.

I raced up the stairs. The police were everywhere and were throwing bodies aside, making whatever arrests they could. All the drug-takers were attempting a mass exodus. I found

Samantha, lifeless on the floor and her face in a mess of her blood. I slipped my hand into hers and held as tight as I could.

"Help! Somebody help!"

I kept shouting. I held her limp, cold hand and prayed for someone to come and help. Someone will come. Then suddenly she squeezed my hand. Someone turned on the lights. People panicked and ran. The cops saw us and approached. I knew we would make it, and that we could start over from here.

Two Stories

Ana Vidosavljevic

"A Blue Finch"

I keep many secrets in the pit of my stomach. My trees and shrubs witnessed many fortunate and unfortunate events that occurred in the depth of my body. And I helped many wretched souls that got lost among my thick tree trunks. On the other hand, I couldn't help some of them. They were in a hopeless pursuit or running from their own wrongdoings. And their own deserved destiny caught them.

One lost soul especially got stuck in my memory. Her name was Hope.

Hope was a little blonde girl, not taller than my blueberry shrubs. She came to me breathing heavily, and almost losing breath. She was running like a wild animal pursued by the hunters. And she was pursued. She was pursued by strange people.

Those people were all dressed in black, and they carried the torches that lit their way. My body is dark and unwelcoming to those who have bad intentions. And seeing those people's eyes, I knew they meant evil to that little girl.

They yelled and laughed awfully, their voices harsh and scary. And their intention was to scare Hope, make her stumble over some rock or tree trunk, fall down and get caught by them. For what reason they wanted to catch her, I didn't know, but I knew that they were not good people.

The terrified girl ran and kept losing balance, tired due to running who knows how long. Her pale face was wet, tears and sweat were mixing on it, and her blonde curls slicked down her back, wet and dirty. I opened my arms and took her. I hugged her and brought her to the deepest parts of myself. Those people couldn't find her there.

Hope entered the very dark area of the forest and found a cave. It was pitch dark in the cave and in any other situation she would not dare to enter it, but this time, this cave was her savior. I knew that she would be safe there and I led her to the cave's entrance. She entered cautiously, sat on the dry ground, and tried to stabilize her heavy breathing.

Hope had some strange scars on her wrists, as if she had been shackled. Her legs and arms were all in bruises. I wondered who had been so cruel to this little girl. And how could have someone been so terrible to this innocent creature. Her doe-eyed face breathed with purity and her tiny body could not do harm to anyone or anything. Her frightened figure moved with her fast breaths and she cried silently trying to reduce any noise coming from her. I couldn't understand. But in the end, I never was able to understand humans. They tortured and killed for fun, they drank poison excessively, they ate when they were not hungry. What rule of nature imposed such behavior? None. They were not the creatures of nature.

Hope was frightened. Her body trembled and she prayed to die peacefully without being tortured like her mother and her father. She couldn't understand why her family was doomed to die in a terrible way, stoned, tortured and condemned. Why were they accused of witchcraft? And what was the witchcraft, anyway?

My heart was full seeing that Hope was getting better with every day that went by. I opened my secret places full of strawberries for her, and I led her to the stream to drink fresh water. Those people couldn't find her here.

But since autumn would come soon and cold winter would follow after, I started being worried how this little creature would survive the cold and lack of food. She didn't have fur to keep her warm, and she couldn't hibernate. She was too small to hunt wild animals and sooner or later she would become their prey. My heart ached when I thought that this poor creature would die alone. And I decided what to do.

It was getting colder with every new autumn day. And Hope's clothes were getting ripped off. And she didn't have any other clothing. She was worried. What would she do?

When the last days of autumn came and the cold northern wind started blowing, carrying snow on its back, I opened my ground, still warm and cozy, and showed little Hope the underground labyrinth that the cold winter storms couldn't reach. Its catacombs were protected and only swallows and nightingales lived there during winter. The green moss spread all around and formed a beautiful bed, comfortable and welcoming.

Hope entered the labyrinth and smiled. Her face bloomed with happiness and fear disappeared. She loved it there. There were always raspberries, strawberries and blueberries, no matter the season. And the bird song entertained her. The birds taught her how to sing and by the end of winter, she sang better than most of them. Her old clothes were ragged, since she had worn them for so long, and she walked half-naked.

I was sad to see Hope in those rags. Therefore, I gave her beautiful blue feathers and wings, and a yellow beak.

Once spring arrived, I opened the door of my labyrinth and let her out. First, Hope spread her wings insecurely, uncertain what to do and how to use them. But soon enough, after a few trials, she soared through the air. I was happy.

Hope looked at her blue feathery clothing and wings and realized that she could fly. And wasn't it the most beautiful thing: to be free and to be able to fly?

Not long after, Hope found her friends, other blue finches, the rarest birds in my forests. And she joined them. They were all orphans, once upon a time, lost and miserable, who had looked for a shelter in the depths of my body. And I helped them. I gave them the shelter and brought them to one better world, the world of nature.

And if you come sometimes to my depths and look around carefully and noiselessly, you will spot a couple of them, jumping from one branch to another, soaring gracefully and singing the most beautiful songs you can imagine.

"A Yellow Marigold"

A yellow marigold wanted to talk. She was just a garrulous little flower who couldn't keep silent. And she was so sad that other flowers didn't talk. They sometimes whispered some secrets to the wind that passed by and petted their yellow petals. But the little yellow marigold wanted to talk, seriously talk, sing, even shout loudly. However, she knew that if she started doing that, her petals would fall off and her green dress would disappear. And instead of a flower, she would become a little redhead girl who had no friends and whose home was not a happy place.

Maria lived in a shabby little house at the end of the village. The end of the road was the place where her father had built their home. And behind the house there was a beautiful forest that brought not only a fresh air and enchanting bird song, but the playground for Maria and her little sister Martha.

Their father was a miner and he often left the house and didn't come back for a week or two. He probably was trapped in those underground catacombs, as her mother had explained to Maria and Martha. And those days without him around were the best. Those days were filled with the peaceful hours, their mother's hands knitting, her soft voice singing, while Maria and Martha played in the garden. They didn't miss him, because he brought the awful alcohol odor, angry red eyes and his leather belt that left long red painful marks on Maria and her sister's skin. But those red marks didn't hurt as much as it hurt to watch him beating up their mother with his bare hands and kicking her with his dirty boots. Those wounds hurt more. They left imperishable scars.

Every time her father came back stinking of beer, cigarettes and sweat, her mother would usher Maria and Martha to the forest and tell them to stay and play outside until she came to look for them. They knew what would follow: their father's drunk yelling, throwing the chairs and other furniture around the house, and beating their mother. And they couldn't help her. They looked at her sad and terrified eyes and begged her to let them stay in the house with her. But she was persistent. They were to go immediately and play outside. The girls obediently did what their mother asked.

Once they went deeper in the forest and found those clean grassy areas with marigolds, strawberries, clovers and other colorful flowers, they forgot what might be happening in the house. They got immersed in their playing and singing. Sometimes, they played for hours and hours before their mother came to find them. And the sight of their mother was terrifying. Even though she tried to mask her bruises, cuts and broken teeth, the little girls could see that she must have been in hell during those few hours. And they knew that coming back from that hell was announced only when their father fell asleep.

Every time they spotted their mother coming though the beeches and oak trees looking for them, they rushed toward her carrying in their hands marigolds which they had picked up for her. They hugged her and stayed long in her arms, letting their mother's tears fall down on their hair and wetting their red curls. The three of them stayed embraced like that for a long time as if they hadn't seen one another for years.

Every time their mother sent them to play in the forest and they went to their favorite playground, Maria's heart ached with fear that their mother might not come to look for them that day. That thought made her panic. She was afraid to go back home alone with Martha, without their mother holding their hands and encouraging them to follow her back home. But they were also afraid to stay in the forest during the night. Night brought some strange sounds, shadows and creatures that lurked around and threatened to eat her and her sister alive. Night in the forest was scary for little girls. However, night at home while their father was there was more frightening.

One gloomy day, when the sun hid behind the clouds and didn't want to show up, and the dark clouds covered the sky threatening to turn day into night, their mother, with the tears in her eyes, sent Maria and Martha to play in the forest. It was not a good day for playing outdoors, but their father was so drunk and angry that they could hear his scary voice a mile away.

Maria took Martha's hand and told her that everything would be fine. They walked slowly toward the forest, which seemed dark and hostile. Their little hearts were beating fast but they comforted each other. They had one another. They were not alone. When they came close to the meadow full of marigolds, thunder and lightning ripped the sky. Big rain drops started falling and, in a few minutes, Maria and Martha were wet. They looked around searching for a shelter but there was no cave, no place that could give them temporary protection from bad weather and danger. Maria took off her jacket and put it on the top of the blueberry bushes and then she and Martha hid below. At least the raindrops didn't fall directly on their heads, as instead Maria's jacket collected them. They waited probably a couple of hours for the rain to stop and when it finally stopped, they felt relieved. But the sun didn't come out and since they were wet, they felt cold.

They waited for their mother to come and take them home.

Hours and hours passed and their mother didn't appear. The evening sky told them that maybe they would have to spend that night in the forest. Hungry and shaking due to being cold, they hugged each other and prayed. When the darkness ruled over the forest and the temperature dropped significantly, they fell asleep. After some time, their breaths slowed down, and their hearts started beating less intensely until they completely stopped. And Maria and Martha fell into a deep eternal sleep.

The next morning, a hunter accompanied by his dog, found two little dresses, two pairs of old children's shoes, two little jackets and purple hair ribbons. But he didn't see any girls to whom these things belonged. He and his dog searched the whole forest looking for the children, but they didn't find them. What the hunter and his dog didn't see were two beautiful yellow marigolds that stayed calmly and silently next to the place where the hunter had found the children's clothes.

Maria was restless in her new clothing and role of a flower. She admired her own gracefulness and fragrance, but she couldn't keep quiet. And she knew that every time she tried to talk, she would become a girl, vulnerable and lonely. Her sister Martha was happy, on the other hand, just to sit quietly and admire the surroundings. She was safe and her sister Maria was next to her. And what was even more important, very soon, within a few weeks, their mother who had become a fairy, would come to look for them and take them with her. That's what the blue finch had told them. Their mother had sent him to inform her daughters that she hadn't abandoned them. But they had to be patient and silent and they should refrain from talking, otherwise, their father might find them and then they would probably never again see their mother, who couldn't get back to her human figure. Between death and life as a fairy, she chose the latter.

And now Maria and Martha were waiting. At least they didn't have to run away and hide. Here, no one disturbed them as long as they kept quiet. Talking and singing provoked Maria but the fact that if she kept quiet she would see her mother made Maria hushed. Just a few more weeks and then, the three of them, their mother, Martha and Maria will sing, smile and laugh altogether.

Ghost Train

Stephen Brayton

After the seven-hour drive from Connecticut, Rick and Bill were following Joe Spence's directions to his camp on Chebuncook Pond: Nutting Road for five miles, then right onto a dirt road marked by a row of mailboxes beneath a stand of birches. Bumping along with the boat behind, they crossed the abandoned railroad line that Joe had noted. Even though he knew the railroad map of northern Maine, Rick had searched this one anyway, a Maine Central branch abandoned over a decade ago. They'd come across it at different locations on past trips. Here, its right-of-way through the woods remained clearly evident, no doubt from snowmobile and ATV use.

In another half-mile, the waters of Chebuncook Pond appeared through the trees. They passed two camps and pulled in at the third. Joe's camp looked like a good basic setup with a tent platform, picnic table, fire pit, and one-holer outhouse off in the woods. Nice water frontage, with the boat launch in front of the parking spot.

On their previous annual Maine fishing trips, they'd always camped at the state park on Moosehead Lake. When Bill's work colleague offered his camp, they jumped at the chance to try something new, away from the state park bustle. From the shore they counted a half-dozen cabins scattered around the pond. Joe had talked up the fishing on Chebuncook, and they planned to try their luck tomorrow.

The first night, they usually went into town for dinner. But they were farther away from town this time and running late anyway, so they decided to stick to camp and go in for breakfast instead. Cranking up the Coleman, they dined on a couple of cans of Dinty Moore beef stew and discussed the possibilities for the next day. After cleaning up and checking the pond view once more, before long they were ready for the sack.

Rick was drifting off when the sound of a train horn brought him back. There it was again, blowing for a grade crossing. Now he heard the rumble of diesel engines. He checked his watch: 10:05. Where was it? The nearest active rail line was the Canadian Pacific main, at least twenty miles away. He'd never heard a train in all their years up here.

"What in the hell . . .." Beside him, Bill groaned and rolled over in his sleeping bag. Bill couldn't give a crap about a train.

The sound intensified as Rick stared out the tent into the nighttime woods. Not far off now, and no doubt where it was coming from, the old railroad bed they'd crossed on the way in. He could hear the occasional squeal of steel wheels against steel rails as the train moved along. Moving slowly. Unlikely as it seemed, there must still be rails hidden somewhere in those weeds. Maybe the branch had been revived as a short line or a tourist operation? He awaited the horn blast for their road crossing.

Gone. It was gone, the sound just cut, no fading away as the train moved past, no horn, nothing. His hearing? His mind? It was weirder than the train itself. He again recalled past years; for sure he would have heard this train from Moosehead. His online search had shown nothing about the line being back in use, but he'd check again in the morning.

Rick related his story as Bill drove into town the next morning. Bill dismissed it as "probably a big semi going by somewhere." Figured with Bill. Rick gave the abandoned railbed a long look as they passed by.

"See anything?"

"Nada," Rick answered. He waited with phone in hand; with one bar he Googled "Maine railroads map." The search result came up just as he expected: no active rail line for at least twenty miles in any direction.

At the Pine Tree Diner, they sat at the counter bantering with the stocky cook at the grill. He was new since last year and full of questions for them: where were they from, were they up here for fishing, where were they camping? At that, Rick saw his opening.

"Got a question maybe you can answer. Last night, a little after ten, I heard a train passing pretty close by. I'm into trains, so it got me wondering. I didn't think there were any tracks still in use around here. I saw that old right-of-way from the road going in, but that's long gone. So I can't figure where that train was."

The cook looked at him funny. "Oh yeah, lots of people camping in the woods around here will tell you they heard that train. Some say there's a story behind it, but since no one has actually seen a train, I think it's all a bunch of bunk."

"So what's the story?" asked Rick.

"Well, it goes back to the early '60s when the railroad wanted to end the passenger train business on that line. All that was left by then was the mixed train to Farmington, one passenger car attached to the local freight. Up in Kentfield there was a woman named Mary Caron who rode that train three or four times a week down to Farmington to babysit her grandkids while her daughter worked a part-time job. From everything I've heard, you didn't want to get on the wrong side of Mary Caron. She was ripped when the railroad asked the state for the OK to drop the service, and furious when the state approved it. She was on the very last train to Farmington, of course.

"But as it turned out, that wasn't the end of it. A couple of weeks later she got herself arrested for sitting on the tracks in Kentfield, blocking the freight train from coming through. I remember as a kid seeing the picture in the paper. It was June, I think, and she was sitting on the rail in a big wide straw hat. I thought she was nutty.

"So there's your story. Doesn't make much sense, though, even if you believe in ghost trains, because the freight trains kept running on that line for another twenty years with no problems. The ghost train stories didn't start until after they abandoned it altogether, about ten years ago."

"The track pulled up?"

"Ripped it all out. So how can you have a train where there's no track?"

Rick didn't mention the strange sound sequence from last night. He'd keep that to himself, until he had a chance to hear it again.

"So what happened to Mary?"

"The judge gave her a good talking-to and put her on probation for a year, and that was that. Ol' Mary never caused any more trouble. She left town a few years later. Must have been in her eighties by then. Probably went to live with her daughter, but I never heard say for sure."

"Whoo-whee, we've got a real-life Maine ghost story to tell 'em back home," Bill whooped on the way back.

"Sure, except I heard a train, not a ghost," Rick retorted.

"OK, ghostbuster. If it involves a train, you'll figure it out, I'm sure."

"Absolutely," said Rick. He was used to Bill's ribbing about his railfan intensity . . . it went with the territory.

Back at camp, Rick put the mystery aside to enjoy the day ahead. They were on the water by 8:30, the trolling motor pushing them slowly across Chebuncook. Over the next couple of hours, they reeled in and tossed back four undersized smallmouth bass.

They hit the water again after lunch, and by late afternoon had three decent-sized bass to cook up for dinner. Joe had been right on the money about fishing Chebuncook. As for last night's mystery, the only sounds Rick heard were the sounds of the lake: the breeze, the lapping water, occasional ducks quacking, a crow.

Still, as he savored their catch at dinner, he entertained just one thought: Would the train come again tonight? Maybe the cook was wrong about the tracks being pulled up. Or, he had to admit, maybe he himself was wrong; maybe the sound wasn't a train at all.

He lay awake in his sleeping bag, listening. Sure enough, right on time there was the horn blowing for the distant crossing, followed by the engine thrum. Louder, steadily louder before it abruptly went silent like a flipped switch, leaving Bill's snoring the only sound. OK, no doubt now whether he'd heard correctly. Leaning his head back to look out the tent at the starry sky above, he knew where he'd be tomorrow night.

In the morning, his plan got another predictable response from Bill: "OK, good luck, ghostbuster. I'll stick to camp."

At 9:30 that night, he set out for the half-mile walk to the crossing. A light breeze soughed through the pine woods. At the crossing he turned right and walked a distance up the old railbed. He didn't want to be spotted by anyone passing on the road. Occasionally, he paused to scuff the ground, hitting nothing but stones and weeds. When he came upon an old milepost, he stopped and waited.

He heard the diesel growl first, then the horn. A minute or so later he saw light playing off the woods, then the headlight pierced the darkness.

The train slowly approached, a passenger train with two F-unit engines and a string of old coaches. A passenger train in northern Maine? Oh, sure! In the headlight's beam, Rick eyed the weedy roadbed ahead of the advancing train. No rails were in sight.

The train slowed as it approached. The beat-up F-units were faded green, streaked with yellow. Probably Maine Central, but no visible markings to confirm. No markings on the gray passenger coaches, either. Only one, near the middle, was lit. When the train groaned to a stop, that coach stood in front of him. The door opened and a uniformed conductor appeared. Gaunt, bespectacled, and up there in years, he dropped the steps and looked down at Rick.

"Well, we haven't got all night," he said in a thin reedy voice. "Come on aboard if you're coming."

Take the chance? Marcie would call him crazy—or worse—but Marcie was home in Connecticut. He needed to find the answer. The conductor extended his hand; he grabbed it and clambered aboard. He'd ride to the next stop, whatever it was, and call Bill to come pick him up.

Inside, the coach was bathed in an odd, bluish light from a source he couldn't determine. It appeared to be about half-full. No one paid him any notice as he took a seat just inside the door. The locomotives accelerated, the train jerked, and they began to move. From underneath came the rumble of steel wheels on steel rails.

The sliding car door banged closed behind him. As the conductor passed by, Rick got his attention.

"When is the next stop and what's the fare? I'll be getting off there."

The conductor smiled wanly. "Sorry sir. Once you're on this train, there's no getting off. And don't worry, there's no fare."

The conductor moved on before Rick could find a response. What in the hell had he gotten himself into?

He rose halfway for a better look at his fellow passengers. They made an odd sight: everyone seated, erect, looking straight ahead, silent and perfectly still. Men and women, young and old. One head did stand out from the rest, a woman near the front wearing a wide-brimmed straw hat.

As he sat back down, the train suddenly went silent. No rumble of the rails, no locomotive sound. But the gentle rocking told him they were still moving.

Had they crossed the road yet? Nothing but blackness out the window. OK, he'd screwed up. How was he going to get off? At this speed, jumping should be easy. Rick rose, but found the door locked. He returned to his seat and closed his eyes to focus. He could see the headline now: "Police Search for Missing Connecticut Man."

The county sheriff suspended the search for Rick after two weeks. They found his footprints soon enough, leading about a quarter mile up the railbed. The pattern indicated he'd stood for a time near an old milepost. But that was it. Search crews combing the surrounding woods came up empty.

With so little evidence, the sheriff couldn't speculate on what had happened to Rick. As the weeks passed, the story fell off the front page and soon disappeared entirely, revived only by the obligatory one-year anniversary update: "No New Leads in Man's Disappearance."

Among the local wags, however, the story remained an engaging topic of conversation. A few old-timers scoffed at all the speculation. From the moment they heard about the account his buddy gave to the authorities, they knew what had happened to Rick: he'd fallen victim to the ghost train that haunted the abandoned railroad line. The authorities, of course, gave zero credence to that theory.

Poetry

Alan Cohen

Unendurably Gentle

From the upstairs
Room, one could not tell
Cloudy from clear
Until the sun was
Well up into the leafy
Metacoloring limbs of resolute
Trees; by that
Time, a skein of noise had
Cracked like a whip and lingered like
Sustained applause, up
Over the roof of the
Room, quite invisible, in its
Passage south—voices
Of the atmosphere calling
As, one suddenly
Imagines, voices may
Also call us from water or fire

It is only later, while
Digging shallow
Trenches for spring

Bulbs, that one looks
Up over one's
Shoulder to seek the butterfly casting
That wavering
Shadow and is surprised to see
A single red leaf hovering
On the wind
Voiceless

A handful of bulbs,
Sunlight
And the leaf-swept air

Circadian Rhythm

Receptive to a fault
The mind composes an instantaneous response
To the miscarriage of day in sunset
Resolving in more sombre tones

Even when full moonlight
Casts trees' shadows on the grass
In a graphic modulation of day
The mind retains a tenacious night blindness
Having wrung each key of light by day

And only when, fumbling
Sunrise measures its golden key against the mind's iron keyhole
Is the miracle again transacted
That renegotiates the channel to the possibility of delight

The Party

I finally flowered last night
And I was splendid
Each goer, detached from habitual comfort
Was suspended, a single petal
Quivering in prevailing breezes he could not command

For long, beneath the soil
I ramified, seeking light
But humans resist so what they most desire
Bursting at last from the soil
Jewel and ginger and cinnamon and wine
Into warm sunlight and frosty air
I caught everyone by surprise

Already now they recall me
Like a kiss or a victory
And their lives are altering
To the motive of my memory
Seeking a glimpse of the light

Our Tuesday Off

Heroes braving the hot breath of a monstrous afternoon
We hurried from bakery to bakery seeking challah
The new year was upon us
We could almost see its huge hand rising behind us at the street's end
But, though we were able to capture a few fresh bagels
We failed to achieve even a sighting of our true prize
The movie would not begin for two more hours
There was no cool and quiet place to conspire over The Bostonians
So we made a dash for the Five and Dime

Woolworth's!! An old woman stood in the doorway looking out
As if waiting for the afternoon to pounce
The Lysol was an entire childhood in the air
We were safely back in the Fifties
Both of us reached up our hands to our parents, no longer above or behind us, instinctively
We took to the energyhungry cold like icicles
Emerging with large envelopes
Sealing our secrets in them to mail to our friends, our contacts far off
Now, even under the hot haunches of the day, we feel breezes
Stop in for ice cream
Forget the laws and businesses of the weekday world
Our Tuesday off
Like an envelope all to itself
Filled with its tiny enchantments
And labelled with our address

Islands

I have been sitting back in my comfortable chair
Talking to you now for years
Often pleasantly about my love of nature
Trying to bring to life for you my experience
Then sometimes I have sat forward and told you confidentially about a secret
Or smiled widely and launched into a rendition of a new idea or discovery
Finishing, hands in the air, at the edge of my seat
I have told you stories that have been told many times before
And stories of my own invention
I have taken you on my travels
And discussed with you my triumphs and anger
My love and pain
You have sat in your chair and I have sat in mine
We have never coupled

Not even in my imagination (have we in yours?)
You have never spoken
If we are lovers, it is love platonic
If we are friends, we are pen pals
Or telepathic travelers in different solar systems
And I have been dominant or perhaps alone
My desire to speak having led me into such large silences
I can never know you
Can never participate in your dominance, in your secret certainties
I could not, even if I were to sit in the same room with you
Not only with your image as you have sat with mine
But with you bodily
With all the sensual complications that that entails
If I were to question you and question you
Far into many consecutive nights
Piecing together your memories and motivations
Your speculations and certainties
Were I not to interrupt
To interject my views or implicate or exonerate myself
And were I able to overcome your evasions and inflations
Still I could not ever know you
Without becoming you
Though I might write your biography
With great accuracy and sensitivity
I cannot love what you have loved
Or fear what you have feared

I can never see that moonlit night on the terrace in Florence
As you did when it really happened
I didn't even know you then
O many and many a year ago, as you might say
I can only cherish my own approximation of your longing
Suspecting that your blood probably whispers in a different key in your vessels than mine in mine
That you may have held a starfish in your hand when you were three years old

That makes your washcloth so comfortable to hold now when you stand under the shower
(but, of course, you may not have—even you cannot recall)
With every moment of your life contained in every other
Like a country I can never be born in
Or a death I cannot enter into unless I mean to become it
You sit before me
Suddenly vivid and glowing
A living reminder
That you can never be me
That my words (and even I myself) have all along been artifacts
Something already fixed
Like a chair or a claypot
Or anything else that can be perverted or ennobled
By its uses
A commodity merely
No longer me
Or of me
But passed from me to you
Yours now really
Because we are so different, you and I
Sitting in our separate chairs
Recognizing that nothing but our two individual annihilations can make us one

Note to a Physical Therapist

Your face showed no regret
And so though you may pick berries or flowers or squash
I can see now that you will never pick any weeds from my mind's garden
Will never set eyes on it
Not though you cultivate, spray, and caress every muscle in my body
Not though you hold my head heavy with gratitude against you

You left me, again, with the initiative
A fine professional stance
And I hold it like a watermelon (round shouldered)
Silenced by its unwieldiness
Pondering your recent enthusiasm for my comfort
Was it to modalities, a new challenge, public relations that you sacrificed your leisure
To science then and comfort
Or was I right at first—shall we say art and kindness
Perhaps no one will ever know

You seem to be agreeable
If I divert my life before you
To observe it as it runs past
And make desultory comment
What I meant was
You might find it, a three-day hike into the forest
If you thought it worth such seeking
Not pain but beauty
At journey's end

I should best have taken my cue from you
Admitted nothing I thought I saw or felt
Gone on in my own professional stance
And let the moment slip
Like an ambassador, shall we say, to Denmark
"What matter if there are a few less invitations to dinner
And we meet a refusal to vote with us on one or two insignificant issues
This estrangement had to occur anyway sooner or later
We are different peoples"

And so, the moment has passed
I thank you professionally
For your great courtesy
Yes, and kindness
May you always know health, confidence, and joy

Fly, Bee

The fly
On all fours
Has a dog's thorax
But such flexible wires for arms
Wires she rubs together
As if paring them
For flight
She moves with the clamor and decisiveness
Of youth
Barreling through summer
Flailing demoniacally around everything that stirs

The yellow jacket moves with the poise of a greater age
Insinuating her deep amber into the very meshes of autumn
Brushing aside the sand on the cement with her restrained flight
Hanging about the aging blackberries and currants
Walking upon those fine hairy legs
The quiet confidence of slow flight
And the low hum of contentment
Resonate among the turning leaves
As a cello among violins
Another dangerous voice
In a membrane no larger than a berry
Perhaps the very seed of winter
Striped and still and chanting

The Reluctance of Roses

There is no question
And I answer it every day
Wondering at my cleverness

Or sometimes at my ineptitude
As my own real roses
The ones I planted late this spring
Settle in me as in silt
As I cut them on a bias
Display them in vases
Arrange them with wild flowering grasses
With fern and chicory and black-eyed Susan
The old roses of my imagination
Roses of ballad and argument
Are softened, mollified
I hold them, sobbing, to my chest
Scratching with their thorns like frightened cats
Until they are comforted
They are again the answer
To no question
Just flowers growing on a little bush

The Night at the End of the Tunnel, or Isaiah Can You See?

A Novel Excerpt

Mark Greenside

It was the best of the worst of times, the worst of the best of times, Ouroboros, Ubu, the beginning of the end of the beginning, but I didn't know that then. It was 1979, and I thought I still had a future, which is why I'd come to New York: to prepare myself. And I did—but in a way nobody in his right mind except Leo could have possibly predicted.

I was at the time a virgin, an orphan, a lapsed Catholic, a twenty-one-year-old small-town-in-Missouri valedictorian with a bachelor's degree in the humanities and a scholarship to study literature, and I was looking for a place to live. In the three long weeks I'd been searching—thanks to rent control and no one ever giving up their apartment even after they were dead—the only places I found that I could afford were public housing projects in the South Bronx and Harlem, where there was a waiting period of fifteen years, and the Y, where I currently resided and where a trio of not-so-wise men and a transvestite with a mustache had tried to have their way with me. Needless to say, I was dispirited, had just about lost all hope, when from out of the void I heard a tune: someone was humming the Battle Hymn.

I looked up. Sanitation workers were recycling garbage from their truck to the street. I looked down. A homeless guy gagged on a Happy Meal. I looked further down. From inside an apartment a finger—Leo's finger—pointed at some oddly shaped words scribbled through the dirt on the window: *Furn Apt Fr Cheap.* I was amazed, indeed, overjoyed, and as I descended each step, my hopes rose as the humming grew louder: I was certain I'd be getting a deal. I knocked on the door. No answer. I knocked again, louder. Still no answer. I opened the door.

"Hi," I called, unable to see a thing.

"Ninety-nine a month. Utilities included," came the reply from the dark.

I ignored it, stepped forward, and walked smack into a wall of hundred-degree heat. It was eighty-five degrees and sunny outside and this guy had the furnace on. It made me glad the utilities were included. I waited for my eyes to adjust to the gloom and looked around—at the holes in the walls, frayed and exposed wiring, hanging pieces of ceiling, torn linoleum floors, and orange-crate décor. Nailed to one wall was a colorful, crayoned, hand-printed sign that read "Hello Dali."Taped to another was a New York City Civil Defense Evacuation Map with circles, arrows, and what I hoped were food smudges. Beneath it hung an illuminated etching of Savonarola at the stake. Stained *Playboy* calendars, yellowed *Daily News,* and hundreds of ladies underwear ads littered the floor. Anybody else would have looked at that place and seen only its drawbacks. But not me. I saw the three not-so-wise men and the mustachioed transvestite waiting for me at the Y. Besides, a dozen years of Catholic school had taught me to live like a martyr, die like a saint, and never succumb to the obvious. So even when I stepped forward, turned the corner, and saw Leo—tall, gaunt, unshaved, with bug-eyes, smiling a hellion grin, wearing black slacks, a black suit coat, black socks, white shirt, and a red, white, and blue American flag tie tied around his neck like a noose, all of which smelled of mold or compost or worse—even that didn't get to me. Nor did the brown and green U.S. Army camouflage ski cap perched on his head or the yellow EPA hazardous-waste slicker hanging from his shoulders. All they told me was that he needed help, that he couldn't live alone, that he was a preacher or a patriot seriously gone amuck, or a moron. I thanked my lucky stars, Saint Jude, Uncle Sam, and Adam Smith. How else could I have gotten a Midtown redevelopment zone apartment for ninety-nine dollars a month?

"I'll give you seventy-five," I said.

"It's not what the market will bear."

The lucidity of his response surprised me. "It's not habitable," I said. "It ought to be condemned."

"Ha! Shows what you know." Leo laughed and waved an official, signed and sealed, New York City inspection sticker right under my nose. "Besides, it has a view."

This I found hard to believe. I walked to the window and looked up. All I could see was the sidewalk and people's shoes. "What view?" I demanded.

"There!" Leo screeched. "There!" as he pointed with one hand and grabbed at his crotch with the other. "See!"

I saw right up a lady's dress. I waited for her to pass, turned around, and gazed at the apartment once more. Then I remembered I was a liberal and a humanist—and that Mother Teresa was living with lepers in India and my summer-school classes began in three days. So, closing my eyes and gulping—and hoping in my heart of lapsed bleeding hearts that Leo wasn't contagious and I was choosing the lesser evil—I said, "I'll take it," and I put out my hand to shake. But Leo was nowhere in sight. He had returned to the darkness and was once again humming the Hymn. "See you, roomie," I waved. "I'll be back tomorrow." He hummed louder, and as I left, he broke into song: "Mine eyes have seen the coming of the *gory* of the lord." I stopped. Stiff. Frozen. Goosebumps played leapfrog all over my skin. "Nah," I said. "No way." Not even *he* would say something like that.

All right, so Leo is a bit odd. Quixotic. Well, not quixotic in the normal sense of the word. Let's say negative quixotic. A postmodern Don Quixote. Besides, he has his good points. For one, he speaks English. For another, he's never around . . .. That's what I thought of him then, and it was how I planned to explain him to my friends. Only I didn't have any friends. Until Jean.

Jean transferred to N.Y.U. from West Virginia State. She was one of those educational opportunity students from Appalachia who looked like she walked right off the set of *Deliverance*: flat-chested, tow-headed, bow-legged, over-bit, hare-lipped, acned, and scarred, with a mole the size of a quarter hanging from the back of her neck. She was also sallow and slightly deaf. "The Milton mid-term's tomorrow," she said. "Why don't we study together?"

"Great," I said, and meant it. It was the first time anyone had spontaneously asked anything of me other than spare change or the time. "Meet you at your place at seven."

"Yes, it would be heaven, but there's no way we can do it at my place. I live in an all girls' boarding house."

"How about the library?"

"Too noisy. What about your place?"

I was afraid of that, but there didn't seem to be any way to avoid it. I just hoped Leo wouldn't be there and thankfully he wasn't. We studied until two A.M., when Jean yawned, and I said, "Why don't you spend the night?"

"OK, she said, and closed her books.

Anyone else and I would have been excited, but not with Jean. As far as I was concerned, she was about as sexy as a fork. Besides, for the past seven hours we had been studying Milton, whom no one but Leo would grant an X rating. Within a few minutes each of us was sound asleep and snoring.

The following morning I woke up exhausted and alone to the sound of strange noises emanating from the kitchen. Immediately, I got up and dressed and went out to protect my new friend. By the time I arrived everything was quiet, heads down, sullen. I could only imagine the worst: Leo had started talking about manhole covers or popping windows, guys with arrows, muggings, the C.I.A. in Iran, Bert Lance. I didn't learn until much later that in less than five minutes he had gotten into her pants. Had I known, I would have been disgusted. I would have thought each of them was probably the first living thing without eight legs or wings to touch the other. Still, she was my friend—my only best friend! And it was a rotten, low-down, marvelously contemptible buddy-fucking kind of thing that Leo did to show me the true meaning of brotherhood and fellowship. "Let's get out of here," I said to Jean.

"Milton," Leo mumbled as he noticed my book. "Good. *Lost* is better than *Found*."

"Right," I said, and pushed Jean out the door.

In the hallway Jean turned to me and said, "He's weird."

"Yes," I explained, "Leo is a bit odd. Quixotic. Well, not quixotic in the normal sense of the word. Let's say negative quixotic. A postmodern Don Quixote . . . ."

Jean laughed. "A non-Quixote, that's good."

And for the next several weeks that's how I thought of him: as a postmodern non-Quixote, my own little Apocalypse Now.

The only things I had to look forward to were my exams and Dr. Roberts' reading from *Macbeth*. On the morning of the reading, I awoke with my head abuzz. The evening before—at three A.M.!—I was forced to listen to Leo pontificate about Sanyo, Sansui, Toshiba, Hitachi, Yamaha, and Akai. His concluding comment: "The only fidelity left is Hi."

"How true," I said, "how true." I hadn't the slightest idea what he was talking about. It wasn't until much later—at five o'clock!—that I finally realized Leo was talking about stereophonic sound and not the Japanese High Command. So to prove to him that I understood, just before I left for school I walked over to where he was sitting, pulled the cold hot dog he was chewing out of his mouth, and repeated: "Remember, the only fidelity left is Hi."

Leo gave me the thumbs up sign and said: "And the only heroes remaining are sandwiches. Buy high, sell low. Every loss is a gain. A Bull is a Bear by a different name. Dearth First!"

"Right," I said, and slammed the door shut behind me.

When I got to Dr. Roberts' class, the lecture hall was full. Towards the front of the room I spotted an empty seat next to Jean. I walked over and sat down.

"Lots of people," I said.

"Yes," she said, "everybody comes out when old man Roberts reads."

"He's that good?"

"Yes, Gielgud, Olivier, Richardson. He's performed with all three."

"Wow! So where have you been keeping yourself lately?"

"Oh, you know . . . I've been busy." Then she blushed. I knew it was a blush because the color of her face became different from the color of her zits. "H-how's Leo? I haven't seen him since . . . since that day at the zoo." That's what she said! Can you believe it? I tell you, that Jean is something else: she's as good a liar as she is ugly; a treasure of unearthly delights. Of course, I didn't know that then, so I answered, "Leo is Leo, a hazard to all that is right."

Jean giggled. "I'll say. But I've been worried. The last time I spoke with him, he sounded awfully tired."

"Sure. He ought to be. He's preternatural. The son of a bitch never sleeps."

"Oh, no!" She sounded shocked. "That's not what he told me. He told me he's been so tired he can't go out. Every afternoon he naps."

"Every afternoon!" I blurted. "Every afternoon!" I stood up. "Every afternoon . . . ."

"Have you finished your soliloquy?" It was Dr. Roberts.

"Yes, sir."

"Then shut up and sit down."

I did, but I was so nervous that I knocked my books, then Jean's, onto the floor. When I finally finished straightening things up, Dr. Roberts began to speak. From memory. The little bugger was amazing. He had to be eighty years old. He couldn't have stood more than five feet three. Yet the guy had the lungs of a bagpipe. Words came out of his mouth as if powered by a bellows. As he spoke, his whole body shook, right down to the thin little metal legs of his walker. He was going along splendidly, rapidly approaching the part of Banquo's ghost when suddenly from beneath the curtain there appeared a blood-splattered, sheet-covered ghoul. Slowly, it crept towards Dr. Roberts. The audience was really excited. And so was I—until I realized the blood was tomato sauce from the frozen lasagna dinner I ate in bed the other night, and the sheet was mine. I leaped out of my seat to warn Dr. Roberts, but in the commotion I made, he stopped and stared at me and gaped for the full two seconds it took Leo to reach him and tap him on the shoulder and shriek, "BOOOOOO!"

The last time I saw Dr. Roberts, they were carrying him away on a gurney. He was still gaping at me, only now he was also drooling, trying to raise his right arm, muttering and sputtering, "FFFF." At the time I thought he was giving me the finger, which, under the circumstances, I can truly respect, although I don't think I honestly earned it. It wasn't until later in the day, when I went to take my exams, that I discovered that FFFF was my grade. In all my classes. Leo had told the custodian who captured him that he was my roommate and that the plan to do in Dr. Roberts was mine. And since he left the sheet with my name on it as evidence, they believed him. I went straight to my student government representative to protest, but she hadn't been seen in months. "And even if she was here," the secretary told me, "she certainly wouldn't see *you*." So I went to the Dean of the School of Law, who was a world class Lawyers Guilder. As soon as he heard my name, he punched me. "Roberts," he said, "was progressive."

"First, we eat," Leo announced.

On the table were all of his favorites: a Mama Celeste pizza supreme; Mrs. Paul's fish sticks; a Banquet TV turkey dinner; cold Kraft macaroni and cheese with ketchup; plenty of Styrofoam and plastic; Wonder bread; Jell-O; and Kool-Aid. During the feast, amidst the flickering of two dozen candles, we sat on our orange crates and talked about books. It was, I thought, a ridiculously easy test.

"Finish Celine, Jarry, Eliot, Yeats, and *Candy*?"

"Yup."

"All of Henry Miller, Beckett, Nathaniel West, Drew Pearson, and Oscar Wilde?"

"Uh huh."

"Genet, de Sade, Reage, Bataille, Gibbons, Kafka, Kissinger, and Moliere?"

"You got it."

"The tragedies, Dadaists, Surrealists, Absurdists, and Rachel Carson?"

"All done."

"Derrida, Freud, Duchamp, Spengler, Popper, Bukowski, and Friedan?"

"Right."

"*Finnegans Wake, The Book of Job, All the President's Men, Dispatches, Candide, The Pantagruel, Gargantua, Catch-22*, and all those *Mad Magazines* and *Mr. Natural comic books*?"

"Yeah!"

"Ok," he said, finishing off the macaroni. "Now let's get on with the questions."

"The questions?" Suddenly, I was worried. My stomach turned. I couldn't even finish my Jell-O. "Who asks them?"

"I ask. You answer. Let's go."

Nervously, I waited as Leo licked his plastic plate clean. Finally, he looked up, folded his hands, and began. A sliver of green Jell-O hung from his nose.

Q. Why are we different from all other people?

A. Because we accept our fate. More than accept it. We expect it. We are the vanguard of decline.

Q. Why, then, don't we rape or steal or shoot at people with arrows?

A. Because you are what you do and nothing that you do really matters. One act is as meaningless as another, and everything has already been done.

Q. What is it, then, that we do?

A. We encourage and appreciate what is.

Q. And what is *is*?

A. Doom, deconstruction, and chaos. The night at the end of the tunnel. The chickens coming home to roost.

Leo paused. I was so scared I thought I was going to pee. I watched him stroke his chin, then rub his nose, discover the sliver of Jell-O and eat it. "Those are the four questions," he said. He said it so solemnly I was certain I had flunked. "Now, to honor Mark Van Doren, you may ask one of me."

My mind went blank. Everything I thought of sounded trite or false. What is it I want to know, I asked myself? What is it I really want to know? Then it came to me, the question when answered that would fill in all of my blanks. "Who made it this way, Leo? Who caused it and why?"

"Everyone," he smiled.

"Everyone?"

"Yes, with their craving for more and better. It was the ruthless pursuit of goodness that caused it, goodness and hope: the capitalists with their faith in free markets, the invisible hand, and endless prosperity, and the Marxists with their dreams of a withered-away state and universal equality; all religions with their belief in a better world to come, and all nations and political parties for promising what they wouldn't want to deliver even if they could; and families too, and lovers and artists and philosophers, and all those who gave with everything they had, *especially* their reasons. In postmodern America this was first revealed to us in the late 1950s by the publication of William Burroughs' *Naked Lunch* and Ike's lie about the U-2. This was also when the Giants and Dodgers moved West and the Yankees started to lose."

What could I say? He was brilliant. Who else could have pronounced a postmortem on religion, politics, art, and baseball in one clean sweep of the tongue? Reverently I sat there, waiting, wondering how I had done, and Leo, with his flair for the dramaturgic, sat there also, alternately picking his nose and sipping Kool-Aid. Then, when his nose was clean and his cup was empty, he shouted, "Ouroboros."

"Ouroboros?"

"Your desideratum."

"Yahoooo," I shrieked, "I passed. What is it? What's my prize?"

"It's in here somewhere," Leo said, standing up and clapping, then jumping up and down. "You have to find it."

With increasing glee I began to search the apartment. I looked everywhere: under the sink, beneath the orange crates, through the garbage, in my room and all of the cupboards and all of the drawers and each of the shelves, and found nothing out of the ordinary ruins. That was when I saw Leo peeking over at his room. Hesitantly, I went to the door. I remembered reading in my high school theology classes that this was part of the ceremony. I thought I was letting Elijah in. But when I opened the door, I saw Jean. She was lying on Leo's bed, completely naked, beckoning me with her pinkie. I gaped. I sputtered. I moaned. Then I shut the door, spun around, and leaned against the wall for support. My stomach and everything in it was in my mouth.

"Nice, huh!"

"It's the ugliest thing I ever saw."

"You got it."

"A dog."

"Bow wow."

"I can't do it."

Leo threw me up against the wall, gripping my shirt in his hand. "Look," he hissed, "there's a lot of ugliness in all of us. You just have to be lucky enough to find it. With Jean it's a little more obvious. She's my girl." Then he released me, opened the door, shoved me in, and commanded: "Do it!"

Only I didn't know what to do. Jean had to help me, and from the back—that is, not having to see her zits or harelip—she wasn't half bad. Afterwards, which was about fifteen seconds later, I pushed her away and asked:

"H-how was it?"

"Terrible," she growled.

"Good," I said, and rolled over to get some sleep.

Getting Leo to agree to go to the party was one thing. Getting him there was another. As soon as we arrived at the subway station he balked. "BMT," he sputtered, "N . . . Not There!"

"Yes, Leo, it's the BMT."

"Brooklyn? We're going to Brooklyn?" He began to cry. "I'm not going to Brooklyn. Uh-uh. Not me, No way." He latched onto the banister with both hands. "No way. Uh-uh . . .."

"Are you finished?"

"Nope. Not going."

"Leo, that's where the party is and that's where we're going. Don't be so provincial."

"Nope. Nope."

I tried reason: "Brooklyn has all of the iniquities of Manhattan—and then some. I guarantee you'll feel right at home."

"No way. Uh-uh."

I tried guilt: "It was you, Leo, who said our job is to appreciate what is, and you never said Brooklyn was not." Nothing, I knew, upset teachers more than having their own words tossed back at them by a student who actually listened. I smiled in anticipation of Leo's response.

His face went white. He looked at me as I had never seen him look at me before. It was part adoration and part vilification, and it told me I had triumphed. Full of pride and exuberance, I waited for Leo to succumb.

"Can't. can't do it." He sniffled. "Just can't. *Everyone* has irrational fears."

I was speechless—then I fell to the ground and shouted a menacing, "Look out!"

"What! What! What is it?" Leo screeched, as he dove to the pavement to join me.

"I think I just saw Mr. Rogers."

Leo's eyeballs receded, his temples throbbed, his chin twitched, and he bit his upper lip, drawing blood. "Y-you lie," he managed to spit.

"I could be mistaken. Let's wait here and see." I smiled.

"Let's goooo!" Leo howled, pulling my arm and dragging me into the station, muttering: "It's ok, it's ok, it's ok. Some things are worse than Brooklyn."

All the way there, despite a ten-minute delay and a thirty-five minute jarring, squealing, standing-up-because-there-were-no-seats train ride, I had a ball. I would periodically look around and stare, pretending I had spotted Mr. Rogers, and Leo would snap his head, follow my gaze, and turn green. It was amusing. But all good things must come to an end and we finally arrived at Coney. We descended and made our way to the address, which turned out to be The Church of the Living Gospel. A cadaverous giant in a green polyester leisure suit greeted us at the front door and beckoned.

"C'mon in, c'mon in. This is the place. Everyone's welcome. Gonna be some fun tonight . . .. Yum yum."

I looked at Leo and Leo looked at me and together we grinned at each other as we entered the church through the prayer room. It was like a homecoming. Everything inside was night-dark. The only light was on the dais. All I could tell as I looked around was that we were the only ones there under sixty. We took two seats in the rear and waited, and while waiting I remembered how proud I felt to be an American. Where else but America could men like Pat Robertson and Jerry Falwell, men who in another time and place would have been peasants or rum-runners or Bureau of Indian Affairs land agents, where else could such men be religious leaders? And where else but the land of the home and the free and the bravado, the nation that brought us the Bill of Rights, which made legal the Old Knick, the Personals in the *Swinger's Directory*, and *Bound and Gagged*, where else could The Church of the Living Gospel receive freedom of religion prerogatives and an I.R.S. tax deduction for throwing a fuckerwear bash? What a country! That's what I was thinking when the minister stepped out of his closet. He brushed back his slicked-down hair with his bejeweled hands, snapped his suspenders, and stepped onto a stool so he could be seen.

"Welcome, welcome," he intoned, "to God's little quarter acre in Brooklyn." He laughed at his own little joke, turned on a tape recorder, which miraculously managed to continue to play *Bolero*, and commenced with the business of the night.

"We are gathered here tonight to celebrate the spirit of the flesh—and to raise a little money for our church. Other faiths, as you know, use Bingo for this purpose, but we at The Church of the Living Gospel are opposed to this. Gambling, as the scriptures tell us, is a sin. Begetting, however, is the way of Our Lord. That is why we are gathered here tonight—to offer whatever assistance and aids modern technology can provide and to encourage you to add to the flock." He then paused and reached under the dais. "So what am I bid for this dildo!"

"Two dollars," Leo stood up and screeched.

"Leo," I said, yanking him back to his seat, "we have thirty-five dollars max. That's it. Let's make sure we get what we want. Agreed?"

Leo stood back up and shouted, "Two-fifty."

"Once, twice, sold to the man in the Hefty bag cape and crown."

Next came the edible undies. "Eat 'em up," laughed the minister as he held them in the air with one hand and snapped his suspenders with the other. "Sugar is good for the soul." We bought six of those, in six different, unnatural flavors. We also bought one more dildo shaped like Karen Silkwood and guaranteed to glow in the dark, a battery-powered vibrator that the C.I.A. had supplied to Madame Nhu, a set of brass ben wa balls—for Jean, we both agreed—and a pair of matching black leather jock straps, each with a red heart sewn on the front. Beneath the hearts, in small cursive letters, they read: "I've got this heart on for you." The only item we disagreed on was Lady MaDonna, the plastic inflatable woman. Leo wanted it and I didn't. "No way," I said, "we've already spent thirty-eight dollars. That's it. Besides, we can make our own at home with a mannequin." Reluctantly, Leo agreed.

"Hokay," announced the minister, "that about does it for tonight. Good luck and Godspeed." Then he snapped his suspenders, leaped over the dais, landed on someone in the third row, and hollered a thundering: "Orgy!" Somehow, then, inscrutably, the only light that was on turned off and *Bolero* became louder and louder. Immediately, Leo and I joined hands and scooped up whomever we could net and steered them into a corner sacristy. What proceeded next was a *menage a cinq*. At least I think it was *a cinq*. It may have been *a six* or *a sept*. Who could tell? What I could tell, though, was that one woman had but one breast, another had no hair, and a third had hardly any teeth—unless, of course, that was Leo.

"You know," I said, as we stood on the platform waiting for the train to Manhattan, "having sex with someone is a good way to meet them."

Leo then said one of the most intelligent things I ever heard him say. It was wisdom. Gospel. More true than the Shroud of Turin. "You bet your life," he said, "but that's not the best part. The best part is the moment right after orgasm. It's the perfect time for truth and betrayal. You just have to know how to use it."

Mario Loprete "Untitled"

TRUE HOME AND A BOTTLE OF CHAMPAGNE

SAMUEL EKANEM

As the only human figure in the void corridor, Inem Ikang paused and wondered at her shadow, cast on the corridor walls—the corridor her only possible passage, its walls made of plywood. She had never imagined this: someone casting shadows in the absence of light. And so she started to dance, her body moving slowly, side to side, until the shadows made clearer semblances of her and she was sure they were not spirits. By the time her heart started to bang inside of her, she stopped dancing and craned her neck around the corridor, searching for light. But then she realised that there's usually no light when there's darkness.

She moved closer to the wall and caressed the shadows with both hands. The feelings awed her—the wall feeling doughy like half-baked bread. She caressed and caressed, and they remained her own shadows. And now, she knew, it's not the shadows anymore or the corridor or the walls or anything else. She was the bizarre thing. How can she misconstrue her own shadows?

She retrieved her hands and smelled them: shadows don't smell, after all. Or could shadows made in the absence of light smell? Or could the wall smell? No, the wall didn't. She wished there was light so she could see her hands; perhaps the walls may have smeared on her fingers like mud.

She rubbed her hands on her dress, which was not the kind of thing to clean hands with. And for the first time and just that once, she had the time to check on her looks: the milky-white gown on her made of the silkiest Georgette stuff she'd ever seen; the sort of gown she could never have picked at the market, even at the cheapest bend-down-select; the sort of gown that one feels naked inside, that easily swells apart with the lightest breezes. The *thing* around her head not the velvet rope she normally used when she went out in gowns. Her head became too heavy, legs too light and too insensitive, so that she wondered whether they actually *walked* her there.

Now, then, she was certain she was in a strange place; how did she get here?

She plodded her way toward that darkest region ahead of her, where her fingers touched on the walls; her shadows, tall and slant, cast across the wall from her left. She stopped and wondered briefly, her hands still on the wall, shadows still. Then she continued hustling till she ended up where she'd started, where her shadows were now fuller and bolder, on both sides of the walls. She paused again, untangling her hands slowly and fearfully from the wall. She then stood in the middle of the corridor and panned her head sideways, to see her new shadows. Again and again she panned her head while the shadows kept mimicking her. She steadied her head and stared furiously into the darkness in front, her heart binging tremblingly, head burdensome, legs the more insensitive, eyes useless. Her mind went out briefly and she didn't know whether or when it would ever return.

By the time it did return, she felt sweat soaking down from the heavy *thing* on her head, across her brassiere, to her pants, running down on her legs. But what she felt most was a resentment. A resentment that was pumping in her heart and ballooning her bowels. A resentment that she knew must've reddened her eyes, those eyes that were now pinching her intensely as though they would ooze off into their sockets. She hoped that before she closed and opened her eyes again, that resentment would have metamorphosed into an unalloyed strength that would swell her muscles and gain for her some . . . sort of . . . *courage* that was beyond that of a woman. The strength and courage she needed to revolutionize this strange world. With this strength, she hoped to pull down the walls and migrate into a world in which she could put her eyes to use, where her body could function . . . or simply transform into a gas and leak out through any available space.

But it wasn't. She was the same helpless, frustrated middle-ager, chucked up in a world that was too dark for a habitat.

She strode back toward the wall, forcefully now, hoping to pull it down with the same strength that had failed to be hers, so where was the strength?

She pushed the wall once, twice, then she fell on the floor, the same floor her legs had been insensitive to; the floor not worth the fall; a floor without floorness; a floor that was a mass of water but didn't drench her clothes.

With the same failed strength, she slapped the *(mass-of-water,* kind of) floor with her two hands and didn't feel the coldness of water on her palms. Instead, the slapping echoed loudly and scarily in and out of the tunnel, sounding very brassy like two pieces of zinc clapped together. She looked up from the floor and, later, rose to the shock and, at the same time, hope of seeing, possibly touching, that zinc roof that made that brassy sound, perhaps that could make for her a way out. She jumped and jumped, falling and getting up, falling back. Then she realised that there wasn't any roof, or perhaps the roof was just hanging too far beyond her reach. Then she straightened up and placed her ear on the wall, curiously calm, till she heard a steady sound that didn't radiate sift through into her ears from the other side of the wall, then she realized there was a world, perhaps a real world, and there was light in that world, and there was life—maybe far away from the tunnel. Or above it. Or close, just around it.

As she listened on, an iota of strength beeped into her through her left ear, searing down through her gastrointestinal tract and further down her bladder and then down her legs. She felt a little sensitivity in those legs and ran her hands down on them, to be sure that what she felt wasn't another downpour of sweat. And as she felt the warmness of her palms on her legs, she realized that in her was her greatest asset and weapon—*strength*—the only phenomenon with which she could manipulate her freedom. She stood up, staring devilishly at the wall opposite her, her face twisted into an ugly mask. She closed her right hand, pulled it back, beyond her trunk, and closed her eyes tightly. Then she punched the wall, an excavating punch that shook the entire tunnel like an earthquake.

Her hand broke through the wooden wall across to the other world. A light seared in—white, sparkling and forceful, like lightning, blinding her—a chucking, indefinite blinding that almost sucked out her eyeballs. With her right hand hanging through the wall into the other world, she pressed on her eyes with her left, blips of brightness swaying across her face, needling into her brain, whooping out of her ears and stiffening her entire body so that she felt the dampness right into her bone marrow. Yet nothing seemed important to her except what was her new fate: what had become of her now that her body was apart, her hand in a new world, her body here with her, deafened in the same place that she had been struggling to flee.

What had become of a place ever so invisible, now that this strange light had crossed it? There was nothing like this world, not even the green blood that was now running randomly in the veins of her eyelids, like a beep of chlorophyll transported to and fro in a plant; not even her whole body, now, starting to dry up gradually yet not radiating. Perhaps because of the light the corridor had collapsed, fallen apart, leaving her body hanging and swinging on the broken wall; perhaps even her body was burnt into ashes by the light and swept off.

Time passed. Moments elapsed. Her hand was still smashed through the plywood, like an arrow piercing through an object but couldn't fall off. Now, she heard the wall, perhaps the entire world, really collapsing, a sudden falling that had just happened, yet was like something that had started gradually long ago. She knew the wall had collapsed, meaning her hand had been freed from it, so she strained the same deadened hand to grasp, but nothing was there.

"Hey!"

The voice reached her, sharp and brassy, like when she had slapped the floor in the corridor. It entered her through every opening in her body. She felt the voice pushing into her like a block of ice that would never dissolve. She felt the voice in her mouth freezing her tongue as though something was melting in it. She felt it in her nose, crawling out, dull and irritating, like a catarrh. Then she felt it tearing her eyelids, her eyes widening to the glowing of this new world.

The new world was like nothing else. Her eyes just couldn't stand it. A world even more invisible. The evenness of its incandescence was perfection. A world pure and sparkling. It must be a heaven. Something of a beautiful residence but of no walls, no boundaries. Its smell no doubt a nice fragrance.

Hey?

"Hey!" She shouted back, her voice thin but arrow-headed, echoing loudly but dissolving rather too quickly, because the world itself was too cool and too soft.

"Who're you?" The voice was calm now, nearer and human. She felt more nervous and yet more vulnerable.

Later, she felt a tap on her back, turned, saw a hand, then a man, tall and banana-skinned, his face chiseled, nose a pair of funnels, his head bald, forehead wrinkled—two big, W-shaped wrinkles that guttered across his forehead, his eyes a leopard's. He stood out in front of her, shedding her significantly of the glaring light.

She looked up at him with utmost apology. But it wasn't done. The question was clear: who was she? No apology. Nothing more. Just who she was.

"Inem Ikang," she said and looked down at the man's pair of yellow unblemished velvet boots, his toes swelling up from inside, then at her own skin covered with goosebumps the size of uncooked rice.

"Just that?" He asked.

"Yes."

"Why?"

Why?

She stared away briefly, the man still looking directly into her eyes. Then she looked up back at him, as if to confirm that he really asked her why.

"Nothing," she said. "That's my name."

He looked up, as if to pluck down another question, his nose the more funneled. But what scared her was his tummy, so bulging it must have contained something other than what an ordinary tummy did: perhaps superstition with which to put a spell on her. Then he looked down, tilting a bit backwards and sitting on a ramshackle seat that, before now, was but an icicle. Then the question came across, clear but punchy as usual: "Where's your home?"

Home.

"Home?" She asked, her ears roused.

"Yes, home."

"I'm homed in a beautiful apartment by Hotel Street downtown."

Her voice was steadier now, her heart gentler, and were it not for the strangeness that engulfed her, she would have felt even more calm.

He laughed, a beeping laugh that rather fueled the obsolescence of everything, revealing gold teeth glittering frantically. It shocked her: a man with a stature so out-of-order.

"Then you don't have a home," he said and completed the laugh.

"I do, Sir. A good home."

"How long have you been homeless?"

"I've never been homeless: I was born into my parents' home, then I rented an apartment thereafter, and now I have my own home."

He laughed some more, and sarcastically.

"Who makes your home?" he asked.

"The bricklayers, the carpenters, the plumber."

An uncertainty grew in her eyes. She jacked up her head gradually, her eyes not wishing to see him anymore. But then she fixed those eyes back on him." Is that what you mean?"

"No. I mean your home, not house."

"What home?"

"You don't know? You don't know a home? A true home?"

She looked a bit sober, and then sour.

Home. *Home? True home?*

"Which? What home?" she asked.

"Accept the truth. You don't have a home."

She racked her brain until her head started to ache, then assumed that he meant a home here, in this place. She nodded quickly.

"You see? You're homeless."

Now her tears were there, glazing her eyes, dropping on her hands hot and acidic.

"I need a home, Sir," she said. "A good home, to lay my head."

"You can't get a home because you don't know what it is. Or didn't you say so?"

She patted her face, her eyes still glazed with tears. She wished she could walk up to him, to learn what a home was, but she couldn't, because the man's gold teeth, his *yeye* laughs, those funnels of a nose, still made her doubt he was human.

"You don't make a home alone," he said. "Someone makes a home with you. Someone who's ready, your true homemaker, your home-mate."

He paused briefly. There was something still about how his voice sounded; perhaps his lips were tired of pestering and pestering and pestering.

"So who's your home-mate?" He asked, a little pedantically.

"Nobody."

His laugh was more toothy, more mocking.

"You see? And how long have you been homeless?"

"43 years down the line."

"And why?"

"No one has agreed to make my home."

The world suddenly began to deem her, to regard her as if waiting to hear her out. She wondered how this deeming all happened. And where was all the glowing?

By the time he stood up, fear had engulfed her, hunching her into someone who was evidently homeless, desperate and in search of a true home. Perhaps he'd just swallow her up like a python; after all, she *was* homeless. She felt the warmth of his hands as he touched her, and really sensed a home in his hands. By the time he stood her up, everything about him was just normal, a home, a true home. Nothing like those awkwardnesses and unrealnesses anymore. After all, the light itself had faded away, making everything just . . . a home.

"I'm homeless, too," he whispered to her, sounding too nasal. "I own this whole place, yet I'm homeless."

The silence was cool and tense. He folded her into his arms, truly like a python wrapping on its prey. And until she felt the pulse of his heartbeat, pounding in steady rhythms, she never believed he was human.

"Let's make a home," he said, his voice already a home, pressing her to himself. She dropped her head gently on his bosom, feeling the silkiness of the hairiness of that bosom, feeling a true home.

Poetry

Raquel Dionísio Abrantes

Baba Yaga

He needs to learn to respect your no;
He needs to learn to hear your yes.
If he does not let him go;
You do not want a vile head on your chest.

Unleash your Baba Yaga, the one
Who leaves scars.
You will rise from the red-hot sun
And no one can tear you apart.

Believe me;
You are ready to forge your throne.
In you there are the seven seas
Beneath your growing skin of stone.

Your Perseus Face

Dream after dream you split my
Soul like a glass of rum.
I spend the night by the bed,

Restless, seeing your Perseus face.
But I do not have Medusa's head
Nor any body to offer you.

You are a man in the shadow
Of a lost fire. How many times
Have you seen the blaze die inside
Your hands? It is difficult to let you
Live in my burnt, crimson mouth.
My love is not a room of perhaps.

From blow to blow, you leave the leftovers:
Guilt, sadness, pain. You try to pretend
They are not yours. The phantom of oblivion
Haunts you. And you provide him nourishment.
You self-consume the woes that you regret.
Alone, beyond the patches of light.

Owl-Eyed

Soul—woodland belly filled with
Secrets and ancient vampires.

Mind—a feral moor for monsters
Of all shapes.

Eyes—two bottomless wells of
Light, rain, and thunder.

Mouth—an abyss of songs, a

Labyrinth of whispers.

Lament of Beira Women

We are dying! We are dying, mother!

Lungs—vessel of opaque air and withered roses. Can you
Hear us breathing? We have no time. Our wombs filled with
Death and bark.

We are dying! We are dying, mother!

They do not comprehend our woes. Our brother's body does not
Weigh in their arms. Here, in the embalmed dimness, the corpses
Accumulate.

We are dying! We are dying, mother!

Artemis turns from us. We dream about slopes where once we
Stood. Today, we are blood of young and old women upon
Loam. Our birch grove calls us home.

We are dying! We are dying, mother!

Ghosts sing to us and we run to them. We walk to the
Harvest moon. This is our battle, this is our lament: the
Lament of Beira women.

Saturated Eyes

Where do you keep your tears,
When they leave your saturated eyes?
Perhaps in your Zeus-touched soul,
Watering it until tulips blossom.

Those tears are unspoken fears
Drifting on your lips.
You adjust your mouth to smile
Amongst the day you curse.

Her Many Shapes

Do not tell your daughter not to wear
Red lipstick or dresses above the knee.
Instead, teach your son to respect her as
The goddess she was born to be.

She is Nyx; her eyes are starry skies
And shadows follow her feet.
Let her live in her many shapes
Where the dawn and the dusk meet.

Everything is dark: her hair, her nails,
The mountains she steps.
She summons cursed winds
But she is far from being the mother of death.

VOGEL

A NOVEL EXCERPT

DAVID LINCOLN

TUESDAY, JUNE 13, 1944
AMIENS, FRANCE

Standartenführer Hans Vogel entered cell 51. His black uniform was spotless and sat on his shoulders the way it would a man comfortable with physical exertion. The SS insignia on his collar faintly reflected the light from the bare bulb hanging from the ceiling. It was the only illumination in the cell, which reeked of urine and the familiar coppery scent of blood.

The naked prisoner sat in a steel chair, straddling the drain in the middle of the room. His wrists were bound to the arms of the chair, his ankles held fast to its legs. Leather straps held his chest rigid. One eye was swollen and purple. His lips were shredded, and his body was peppered with bruises. A sergeant wearing a Wehrmacht uniform was standing behind the chair awaiting Vogel's arrival. There were no windows in the gray stone dungeon, and the air was cold.

"Sergeant, what have you learned so far?" he asked in French so that the prisoner would understand as well.

"Nothing, Colonel. He's as dumb as a rock."

Hans approached the prisoner and looked him over carefully. Although he had been severely beaten, Hans noticed that his fingers were not yet broken. They were small, slender, and almost feminine.

"May I have a chair, please, Sergeant?"

"Of, course, Colonel," and he rushed to place a chair in front of the prisoner, eager to please.

Hans sat down and flipped through the prisoner's dossier. "So, Monsieur St-Onge, I see you were caught attempting to break into a German armory."

The prisoner made no reply.

"Your silence will not change the outcome. We must shoot you as a saboteur, of course, but between now and then, well . . . then is up to you."

The prisoner's one open eye stared back at him without emotion. His left hand moved in the leather cuff, a slight tremor in the index finger as if pointing to something far off that only he could see.

"All of that unpleasantness can be easily avoided, of course, with the slightest degree of cooperation on your part. There were four of you involved. I'll only ask for the name of one of them. That's not so much to ask; is it?"

The prisoner's open eye closed, cowering behind the lid, unable to meet Vogel's cold stare. Hans suddenly stood up. "What is your name, Sergeant?"

"Hamm, Colonel, Sergeant Fritz Hamm."

"Continue your questioning, Sergeant Hamm. I will observe."

Sergeant Hamm nodded, expecting the order. He drew a baton from his belt and stood before the prisoner. "Give me a name." When no reply was forthcoming, he swung the baton down upon the prisoner's left shoulder, breaking the collarbone. The prisoner cried out in pain but offered no response, his head falling forward, grimacing in agony.

Speaking in German, Vogel interrupted. "I suspect that you have received little training in interrogation technique."

"I have received none, Standartenführer."

"Let me offer some advice and instruction. I would suggest that you first blindfold the prisoner. Please do so now."

Sergeant Hamm tied a cloth over the prisoner's eyes and stood back against the wall. Vogel asked for his baton and walked around the prisoner. Reverting to French, he said, "Monsieur St-Onge will decide for himself how much pain he wishes to endure. The decision to stop is entirely his."

He swung the baton down upon the right knee of the prisoner, who cried out involuntarily. He then lightly tapped the stick against the side of the prisoner's neck and caressed his cheek with it. "You see, Sergeant, the prisoner does not know where or when the next blow will land. Blindfolded, he cannot prepare himself." He swung the baton down on the prisoner's knuckles and continued to walk around him.

"Do you understand, Sergeant?" he said, resting the baton upon the prisoner's head. "Add suspense and surprise to the pain and your effectiveness is compounded." He delivered one more slash across the prisoner's right shin, an exceedingly painful blow.

"Here is your baton, Sergeant. Report to me when he gives us a name."

"Yes, Colonel. Thank you for the instruction."

Addressing the prisoner, Vogel added, "Good luck to you, Monsieur St-Onge. May your suffering be short-lived."

He left the room and closed the door behind him. There were ten cells in this basement, but only four were occupied. They had been full yesterday.

Vogel climbed the basement stairs and returned to his office on the first floor. It was a much larger room than the office space to which he was accustomed. The Chateau they occupied had once been luxurious, and all the main rooms were spacious.

He sat behind a massive wooden desk and paused to appreciate its craftsmanship. He traced the intricate carving along its edge with his finger and noticed the tarnished brass knob of the right top drawer. A black telephone rested on the desktop to his left. A stacked metal tray on his right held dossiers and other paperwork.

Fleur-de-lis patterned wallpaper adorned the walls, marred only by the lingering rectangular ghosts of former French dignitaries. The picture of Adolph Hitler, hanging between two tall windows at Vogel's back, was now the only portrait surveying the room.

Hans reached for the stack of dossiers and removed a thick file from the top, its cover worn with use. He checked the log, and he was pleased that the handwritten notes were clear and legible. The Gestapo had identified Monsieur Rene Deslaurier as the likely ringleader of the local French Resistance cell responsible for a bridge demolition two weeks prior, but they had failed to locate him. The most recent entry on the dossier was dated Friday, June

9, 1944, three days after the Allied landing, and three days before Vogel's arrival yesterday in Amiens.

Vogel reflected on the timing of the sabotage. In hindsight, that operation was a blatant attempt by the French Resistance to disrupt the flow of reinforcements to the coast of Normandy. Many in Army Command believed that had the Panzers been unleashed as soon as the Allied invasion began, that the invaders could have been contained on the beachhead and driven back into the sea. To what degree the actions of the saboteurs would have hampered the armored reinforcement was moot now, as the High Command had refused to release the armor, entirely convinced that the Allies would land at Calais instead, believing that the Normandy landing was only a ruse to draw the German forces away from Calais. The High Command in Berlin had been wrong.

Not for the first time, Hans wondered what it would feel like to drive a tank into battle. He would have volunteered for armor if given a choice, but instead found himself trained as an SS Intelligence Officer. He supposed his facility with languages influenced their decision for such an assignment, and in some ways, he felt the role suited him, but in other ways, he knew it did not.

He scanned the Deslaurier dossier. The reports indicated that the subject lived here in Amiens with his wife and child. Madame Deslaurier had been questioned and released. Their apartment was under constant surveillance, but there was no report of contact with the suspect.

Vogel picked up his telephone and ordered his adjutant to come in. Corporal Keppler immediately entered and stood at ease a respectable distance from the front of Vogel's desk.

"Is Madame Deslaurier still under surveillance?"

"She is, Colonel. I have this evening's report on my desk. There's been no suspicious activity."

Vogel thought for a minute, then said, "Have Madame Deslaurier picked up in the morning. I want to speak to her myself. But I want her treated with respect and politeness, Corporal."

"Yes, sir, I'll be explicit when I write the order. What about the child, Colonel?"

Vogel looked at the dossier again. "She is only four years old. It would not be safe for her to be left at home by herself. Bring her along, and have some sweet treats to give her when they arrive."

WEDNESDAY, JUNE 14

When Vogel arrived at the Chateau the next morning, he was informed by Corporal Keppler that Madame Deslaurier and her daughter were waiting for him in the sitting room.

"Good," Vogel said. "Let them wait a few hours. When Major Hoffmeyer arrives, send him to my office."

"He is here already, sir, I can send him in now."

Vogel spent the next few hours bringing Hoffmeyer up to speed and detailing his assignments. After concluding their business, he dismissed Hoffmeyer and instructed Corporal Keppler to bring Madame Deslaurier and the child to his office.

As they entered, Vogel rose from the chair and walked around his desk to greet them.

"Please, Madame, have a seat here," as he led her to a seating area on the left side of the spacious room.

"What is your daughter's name, Madame? She is lovely."

"Marie," she said, in a soft, hesitant voice.

Vogel smiled and sat on a light blue stuffed chair opposite the matching couch. Madame Deslaurier sat on the couch, clutching her daughter, looking down at the small ornate coffee table between them as though it held some mysterious lure. She wore a blue peasant dress with a maroon shawl covering her shoulders. Marie sat on her lap in a cute brown skirt and white blouse. Vogel liked the little hat that she wore canted to one side. Very French, he thought. Marie looked directly at him. He saw no fear in her eyes, but recognized her curiosity and concern, sensing her mother's anxiety.

"Thank you, Madame, for accepting my invitation," he said.

She looked up sharply and said, "Invitation? Is that what it was?"

Vogel looked surprised and asked, "What? Were you or Marie mistreated? Did my messenger misbehave?"

He watched her, waiting for an answer until finally, she said, "No. We weren't."

He introduced himself adding, " . . . and your name is Genevieve, I believe. That was my mother's name. She was half-French. Everyone called her Genna. May I call you 'Genna' in her memory, Madame Deslaurier?"

"If you want."

"I have a chocolate treat for Marie, and here's one for yourself, as well." He opened a small box that he carried with him and produced two German chocolate bars, handing them both to Genevieve. She could see that the box was almost full of chocolate.

Now that she was looking at him, he said, "I invited you here, 'Genna' . . .," Hans paused and smiled sheepishly, "out of concern for you and your daughter. We know all about your husband's activities with the Resistance, and I'm sure you know that the Gestapo has been looking for him for some time. I've recently arrived in Amiens, and I'm specifically tasked with locating him. Do you know where he is?"

"No, Colonel, I do not," she replied, "He has been gone for over three weeks, since before the invasion. I don't even know if he is dead or alive."

"Either you have had no word from him, or you are better at the game than we are, is that not so?"

Genna looked down, avoiding his eyes, and shifted Marie's position on her lap. She said, "I am just a housewife. I'm sure your men are all competent professionals."

"Would you like a cup of coffee, and perhaps a glass of water for Marie? I'll have some brought in if you like."

"Thank you. We are both thirsty."

He went to his desk, picked up the telephone, and ordered Corporal Keppler to bring coffee and water. After the corporal delivered them and left the room, Hans offered another chocolate to Marie, who smiled and took it gratefully.

"The problem, Genna," Vogel continued, "is that the Gestapo suspects that you know the whereabouts of your husband, and they are anxious to bring you in for questioning. Their methods, I'm afraid, are quite severe, and they will go to great lengths to determine with surety that you are not withholding valuable information."

As he anticipated, Vogel watched the color rise on her face. He stood up and returned to his desk, picked up the phone, and asked Corporal Keppler to come in.

"Corporal, please stay here with Marie. Share some chocolate with her if you like."

Returning his attention to Genevieve, he began walking towards the door and said, “Come with me, please. I want to show you something.”

When he reached the door, he stopped and looked back, waiting patiently for Genna to join him. Her reluctance was palpable, but he stared at her until she complied. As they walked out of the room, Genevieve looked back at Marie, who seemed relaxed and unconcerned, laughing at something the young Corporal Keppler said to her.

Vogel said quietly, “Do not be concerned, Genna, we will be right back. I promise. No harm will come to you or Marie while you are with me today.”

He knew she wanted to believe him, but could not ignore the terror he inspired clutching her heart. If she didn’t return, who would be there for Marie?

Vogel gently took her elbow and guided her through the door toward the staircase. He felt her body stiffen when she realized that they were going to the basement, but he smiled reassuringly, and she accompanied him down the stairs, knowing she had no choice.

When they reached cell 51, he stopped and opened the door. Scharführer Hamm was sitting in a chair by the wall but jumped to attention when he saw Vogel.

“Standartenführer,” he said in German, “the prisoner has given us a name, and I have waited here for you as ordered.”

“Excellent, Sergeant. See that Monsieur St-Onge is given medical attention while we verify his information.”

Genevieve saw Monsieur St-Onge strapped to a chair in the middle of the room. He was barely conscious, his body broken, dried blood caked around the circular drain in the floor. She recoiled in horror.

Turning to Genevieve, Vogel said in French, “This is Sergeant Hamm. He assists the Gestapo with questioning when required. Prisoners always cooperate at some point, Genna.”

He watched her stare at St-Onge and shudder. Then she looked at Sergeant Hamm, whose face remained impassive.

“Shall we go back upstairs?” he asked.

When they were reseated in his office, Hans could see Genevieve still shaking, both arms wrapped around Marie, clutching the child to her chest. He retrieved a bottle of Schnapps from his desk and poured a small glass for her and one for himself.

"Here," he said, "This will help some."

She took the glass and looked at him, unsure. He sipped his drink first, and then she did the same.

"I'm going to send you and Marie home, Genna, but I must warn you that the well-being of innocent civilians isn't high on the Gestapo's list of priorities."

She looked at him directly now. "But what can I do? I don't know where he is . . ."

"I understand, Genna," Vogel told her, "but the Gestapo will not. They will rip your husband's location right out of your heart if you know it, and if you don't have what they want, they will tear you up anyway."

Genevieve looked at Marie and held her even more closely.

Hans reached out and gently pushed some stray hair out of Marie's face saying, "She is so beautiful, Genna."

Vogel poured her more Schnapps, which she drank down immediately. "You have a few days to find out where your husband is before the Gestapo takes the matter out of my hands. If you tell me, I will be able to protect you and Marie. Isn't that what Rene would want you to do?"

With that, he rose and picked up the telephone. "Corporal," he ordered, "Bring Madame Deslaurier and her daughter home. And please escort them yourself to ensure their safety."

Turning back, he said, "Good luck, Genna. If you learn anything useful, hang something red in your window overlooking the street, and my men will escort you back to me. That is the only way I know I can help you."

He walked them to the door, smiled reassuringly, and closed it behind them.

Poetry

Wayne King

Wind in the Washline

Peace Comes on a Breeze
Spirits Rise, Hope is Reborn
The Washline Dances

The Prevaricating Day

Summer in the North Country
A warm breeze, briefly noted.
Through pine and hardwood,
Crossing fields of corn and
Unmown grass portending hay
Cutting, courting, cunning
Teasing, testing, trimming
As if intending to remain,
Yet only taunting.
June days, behind us now,
Beckoned us out, out
Out to shake off winter
Stubbornly liberating spring

A month of April showers,
Ours for but a pair of days,
Dried to hard baked soil by May
Constraining wildflowers
Still pushing, prodding, poking through
Heralding summer's silken start.
Now, even as a warm wind blows from the West,
Turning winged wind turbines
Rising from the ridge
Leaves of red and orange burst forth,
From windblown maple
Pecking, peaking
Flaring, fusillade of fall
From a tableau of green and blue
A warning beacon, summer is fleeting!
Autumn lies just beneath the surface
Of the prevaricating day.

The Gathering Storm

The Gathering Storm
Borne on an ill wind, our own
Confers no favor.

Rearguard

Robert Perron

Jana backed off from Barry's fart. No odor but a blast, a massive rip that blossomed the seat of his Royal Robbins convoy shorts before undulating out a leg hole. Okay, maybe she imagined the blossoming and undulating, but not the acoustics. Barry, a meter ahead, uphill, his left boot perched on a stone set in the trail for that purpose, twisted his body and said, "Sorry." A wide tan hat protected his balding pate and shadowed the mien of sincerity on his salt and pepper face.

"Quite all right," said Jana. "Some things can't be helped. I suppose."

Barry turned, applied hiking poles to path, and lifted his right foot. Jana let him gain several steps, and several steps later he ripped another, his head making a half turn and his shoulders shrugging. Oh, thought Jana, why did I sign up for this? But answered her own question, for an overseas adventure on the cheap, airfare her only expense. In exchange, she helped Mike with logistics and co-led the hikes, working the sweep position. She let Barry get ahead a few more steps.

The trail leveled and entered a stand of thin hardwood. Barry stopped, dropped his pack, and unzipped an outer pocket. He glanced up from his bent-over rummaging and said, "Afraid I need a bio break."

Jana put forefinger and middle finger to her lips and cast a sharp whistle. As Barry tucked in his head, the eleven hikers ahead stopped and turned.

"Tell Mike we'll be delayed," said Jana.

Sound waves rippled to the front of the group and back. Number eleven, a stocky blond, turned, and said with New York elocution, "Can't it wait ten minutes?"

Jana said, "Doesn't look like it."

Sound waves again rippled up and back, and number eleven said, "Okay, we'll wait for you at the next trail junction, but try to make it snappy." The front eleven resumed their march.

Barry entered the hardwoods, trail right, clutching a quart baggie of toilet paper. He paused mid-step and said, "You can go on. I'll catch up."

Jana shook her head. "You know I can't. I'm the sweep." Barry disappeared into the trees.

Jana took assigned responsibilities with their deserved seriousness. Her job as sweep entailed, if nothing else, security: to be the last one through, to make sure nobody wandered off trail, to alert Mike of any issues—an injury, an equipment failure, an urgent call of nature.

She leaned on her poles and peered rearward. On in-and-out hikes, rearward glances helped with trail recognition coming out. On any hike, they alerted the group to happenings from behind, such as overtaking trekkers, or animals.

Jana leaned further over her poles. A four-legged critter, tan in color, head down, ears up, had emerged at the last bend in the trail. As the animal approached, Jana confirmed its species: a canine, a domesticated dog, a lab, she decided, it being hefty but not a shepherd or collie. The animal stopped and lifted a back leg—a male lab.

Jana advanced a step, putting herself between the dog and Barry's pack, between the dog and her group. She knew that vagabond dogs in foreign countries posed danger, not so much of attack, but disease. They carried insects and harbored viruses. They could scratch and nip and emit fluids. When they approached a group, people could not resist reaching out a hand or bending from the waist.

Dogs back home were different, pampered, picked up after, neutered, immunized, bathed. The couple in the next apartment had a terrier, no children but a terrier. Jana recalled the day they brought it home, over eleven years ago, ringing her bell, double smiles from the hallway, the puppy giving a yip. She remembered the timing because behind her, the phone had rung and she'd stepped in to glance down at call waiting. Her ex-husband, not in the habit of making frivolous calls. Jana gave a wave to her neighbors and picked up.

"Ronnie's dropping down for a visit," her ex said.

"That's nice," said Jana, but wondered why her son wasn't calling himself. "Do you think he'll stay over a night?"

"Yeah. I'm sure, yeah."

"Because I could get tickets for a show."

"Yeah, I'm sure he'd like that. Look, Jana, he wanted me to mention something before he got there."

Jana squeezed the receiver.

"He's dropping out of school."

"Well. I know he's been struggling. But I don't think he's giving it a proper chance, do you?"

"I know, I know," her ex said. "But he'll talk to you. He wanted you to have a heads-up, that's all."

"Of course. Well, he's put you in an awkward position, the bearer of bad news."

"It's okay. It's okay. Look, there's more."

"More?"

"But Ronnie will tell you."

Ronnie arrived that night, a Friday night. Jana had tickets for *Les Misérables*, Saturday matinee. They sat on stools in the kitchen nook, her with a glass of white wine, Ronnie with an underage beer. He thumbed the theater tickets. "Great seats." He slipped the tickets into their envelope and placed the envelope on the counter. "What happened—it's just, you know, I got there and it wasn't like high school. I couldn't deal with it."

Jana had discarded her first impulse, to lecture Ronnie on sticking it out, chin up, first semester's always tough, it would get better. She said, "Maybe you're right. Maybe a year off isn't a bad idea. What do they call it? A gap year?"

"It's more than a year," said Ronnie.

"Oh?"

"I'm going in the army, mom."

"Now that," said Jana, "might be a bad idea." She gave a short laugh.

"It's a done deal. Off to basic next week."

Jana lifted her wine and wet her lips.

"It'll get my head straight, mom. It'll give me discipline. And there's the GI Bill coming out."

"Ronnie, your father and I can afford to give you an education." She tried a joke: "We don't need military intervention." Ronnie's eyes remained locked on his glass of beer, half gone, a thin head remaining. Jana said, "So this is okay with your father?"

"He's totally on board, mom. Says he wished he'd done it himself." Her ex in the military? What a laugh. She hadn't been able to get him to walk around the block. She hadn't been able to get him to pick up his dirty clothes.

"They have specialties," said Jana. "Right? Which one did you sign up for?"

"Mom, if I'm going in, I'm going in as a straight-up infantry soldier."

"But, Ronnie, honey, look at you, you don't weigh a hundred and thirty. You can't stand the slightest pain."

Ronnie flushed. Wrong approach—stupid, stupid. She reached along the counter and took his hand. "Sorry, honey, you know me, just being a mom."

Saturday evening, after the show, after dinner, after Ronnie caught a Metro-North train up the east side of the Hudson, Jana dialed her ex. She assumed a neutral tone. "Wasn't there anything you could do to prevent this?"

"Jana, he has his own mind. You know as well as I—look, maybe this is good for him."

"Good for him? There's a war on. Boys are being killed."

"It's not that bad. Casualties are light. Hell, you're more likely to die here in an auto accident." Jana's head slumped. "You still there, Jana?"

"Yes. How's Elizabeth?"

"Oh, fine, you know, busy as always."

"And the kids?"

"Fine, fine."

Eight months later Jana caught a flight to Columbus, Georgia, the Metropolitan Airport, then the shuttle to Fort Benning. She listened to a speech on a stage in Infantry Hall by a one-star general and watched her son walk across for his ranger patch and a handshake. Outside, standing in the parking lot, Jana surveyed Ronnie and wondered how he'd done it. Dress pants bloused in paratrooper boots, airborne wings above his left pocket, ranger patch for his left shoulder, beret.

"A chip off the old block," her ex said.

"What do you mean?" said Jana.

"I mean you, with all your mountain climbing and outdoor adventures. He doesn't get it from me. Let's have a picture."

Ronnie extended an arm over her shoulder. Jana wrapped an arm around her son's waist. Her ex-husband snapped and two weeks later sent a five-by-eight proof. Jana and Ronnie stood leaning into each other, same height, same gray eyes, same full-lipped smiles.

The lab tried to slide by on Jana's right. Jana planted a pole and stamped a boot. "Stay," she said. "Vamoose." The dog raised his eyes and consummated a tail wag. "Vamoose," Jana said. He folded his legs and lay in the trail with raised head and panting tongue.

"That will get you nowhere." Jana widened her eyes. "It's nothing personal."

Jana glanced at her watch, turned her head to the woods, and raised her voice, "Barry, I don't mean to be intrusive, but how's it going?"

His voice arrived from ten meters into the trees. "Need a few more minutes."

Two months after Ronnie's deployment to Iraq, Jana took a call from the garrison chaplain at West Point. Ninety minutes later he sat in Jana's kitchen nook with another officer, a captain, both in dress greens. The captain explained that they'd first notified her ex because that was her son's legal residence. They then drove downriver asking the ex not to call ahead.

"Of course, you must have had a premonition," said the chaplain. "But in a way it's better than us just showing up at the door."

Jana nodded. "Would you like some coffee?"

"Absolutely," said the chaplain.

They stayed for an hour.

In the days that followed, Jana received a letter from Ronnie's commander and emails from his buddies, and remembered she'd told the captain correspondence was okay. She pieced together the incident, a foot patrol through a village, Ronnie sensing something amiss, taking it upon himself to act as the team's rearguard. Militants appeared on the patrol's tail, gunning fast pickup trucks, firing RPGs and AK-47s. Ronnie's holding action saved the patrol.

The post-funeral reception was at the ex's, Ronnie's boyhood home, a spacious house with wide windows, sliding glass doors, and a view of the river. An eclectic mix. His high school chums, neighbors, work associates on both sides, relatives on both sides, plus the military. The reception had passed the solemn stage, had entered the chat stage with nods and laughs, aided by whiskey and wine.

Jana's ex stood among a circle of green uniforms. He extended an arm toward Jana and said, "Here's the one." She didn't know what he meant but felt obliged to walk over.

"Tell these guys," her ex said. "How many times have you climbed Breakneck Ridge?"

Faces craned in her direction.

"Breakneck," said one of the airborne rangers. "Wow."

Jana smiled. "It's not that difficult."

Her ex lifted his palms. "What did I tell you?" The soldiers laughed. "That's where Ronnie got it from. Not me." Her ex stared at his shoes. The light laughs from the soldiers trailed off.

A while later, Elizabeth took Jana in an extended embrace. "Oh Jana," she said, "this is so awful." *True*, thought Jana, *but you have the second family. I only had Ronnie.* Jana pushed the hard-hearted thoughts away, for Elizabeth had raised Ronnie from age ten, had been an admirable stepmom.

The lab, flat on his stomach, gave a low moan and wiped a paw over his snout. He raised his eyes to Jana.

"Mind yourself," she said.

Leaves crunched, twigs crackled, and Barry exited the woods. He leaned over and pushed his half-depleted baggie of toilet paper into the outer pocket of his pack.

Jana said, "Where's your carry-out?"

"My what?"

"Barry, you know the protocol. Leave no trace."

"Jana, I'm not carrying out a bag of shit."

"I realize it's distasteful—"

"Distasteful? There's no fucking way—"

Jana rapped Barry's pack with her pole. "You will kindly watch your language."

Barry's face reddened. "Jana, where do the animals go?" He pointed at the lab.

"Where does this mutt go? There's shit all over the woods."

"You have," Jana said, "a tenuous argument for the feces, but not for the soiled paper."

Barry had closed his pack. He picked up his hiking poles and faced Jana. "It's covered up, for God's sake. Nobody's ever going to see it unless they go searching."

"I'm very disappointed in this breach of etiquette, Barry."

"Etiquette my ass," said Barry, spraying spittle like a Shakespearean actor. "You want to carry it out? Come on." He motioned toward the woods. "I'll show you where it is."

Jana wondered if she, in Barry's place, would carry out a load of shit, or even soiled paper. The point being moot, since she avoided such contingencies with an early coffee and the pre-hike movement it induced. She glanced at her watch.

"Okay, perhaps we're getting carried away."

"Yeah," said Barry, "I mean, I don't—"

"Let's forget it."

"Amen," said Barry. He shouldered his pack and cinched the hip belt. As he stepped off, the lab unbent its legs and rose. *And this sad mutt,* thought Jana, *what harm can he do?*

"Go on," she said with a wave. The lab lifted his eyebrows. "Go on," said Jana. "Permission granted."

A little lecture, Jana thought, *this evening*. She'd discuss it with Mike: people, for your own safety, do not pet or otherwise consort with domestic animals.

The lab caught up to Barry, went to pass on the left, but his snout caught a scent. He veered right and took two loud sniffs from the seat of Barry's convoy shorts, making contact on the second whiff. Barry thrust his groin forward, bent his knees, and twisted his head.

"Hey, watch it," he said.

The lab sidestepped left and barked. *Oh, no*, thought Jana, but the dog picked up its trot and disappeared around the next bend in the trail. A minute later, Barry disappeared. When Jana reached the bend, she stopped and took a look to the rear.

All clear.

The Kaiser of the Immaterial Kingdom

Ewa Mazierska

It was late afternoon in late January. I was sitting on my own in a compartment of a Berlin–Warsaw train. There was only two or three minutes until its departure, and I assumed that I would have the compartment to myself when this guy came in. He didn't say hello or ask if the remaining seats were free, as it was customary on the Polish trains, just took his seat near the door and put his small rucksack and two shopping bags on a shelf above him. Although his behaviour was verging on being rude, I felt instant sympathy for him, in part because behind his actions I sensed a desire to be invisible rather than rudeness and in part on the account of his similarity to my old friend from university, with whom the passenger shared an un-self-conscious handsomeness. It was difficult to detect his age and social status, although he looked as if he was past forty and didn't have a nine to five job. His clothes didn't look expensive, but at the same time he came across as well dressed. He wore a dark-blue winter jacket with a dark-blue sweater and a dark-blue gilet underneath. His combat trousers were also dark blue with zips up the sides. The only garment that was slightly out of kilter were his sports shoes, which were new and white, suiting more a teenager than a man in his forties. His head was shaved, although he wasn't even balding. If he gave his hair a chance to grow, his scalp would be covered by blond hair, matching his Slavic blue eyes and naturally light complexion.

I opened my computer and started to work on an index for my book, but I was tired, and work went slowly. My companion didn't do anything, just sat with his eyes half-shut. Half an hour after the train departed, a conductor came and questioned the validity of our tickets—mine, because he couldn't scan it from my mobile phone; my travel companion's, because he argued that his ticket was not valid on Intercity trains. Eventually, the conductor gave in, because I dug out from my bag a printout with the right barcode and the other passenger showed him a booklet with regulations proving that he was entitled to use this train. His German was better than mine, but it was German of the kind one picks up when traveling or working abroad, rather than one learnt at school. Putting us in the category of suspected ticket dodgers brought us together, and we started to talk.

"I printed the ticket out to be reimbursed for my trip to Berlin, and it was my good luck that I forgot to hand over the receipts to the people who invited me. Otherwise I probably would have had to buy another ticket and maybe pay a fine."

"What you were doing in Berlin?" he asked.

"I was attending a conference about precarious work," I replied.

He laughed and said: "Sounds like what I am doing."

"Attending conferences or working precariously?"

"The latter."

"So, what are you doing for a living?"

"You can say that I'm partly self-employed and partly retired."

"Which part is larger?"

"This depends on the specific day."

"In Berlin were you self-employed or partly retired?" I quizzed him further.

"Partly retired," he said. "I hoped to stay longer, but the rain drove me away."

"During the first two days of the conference, the weather was dry and crispy, but the last day it was pouring with rain and I forgot to zip my bag up properly when walking to the station and now my clothes are wet."

"This is bad," the guy said. "Keeping things dry is the first rule of successful travel and successful living."

"Yes, but you cannot ensure it."

"This is true, but you can minimise the danger. My rule is: when it's raining, I move on."

"I see," I said and there was some silence between us, so I returned to my computer, assuming that this was the end of our conversation. But he continued: "Do you know, where I like to travel most?"

"Where?"

"South of France: Montpellier, Andorra, Monte Carlo, Nice."

"I haven't been to any of these places, although I know some others: Collioure near Perpignan, from where I travelled to Carcassonne and Villefranche. Carcassonne is my favourite place in France, although I haven't travelled much in this country."

"I like Carcassonne too, but it does not have the right facilities for me," said the guy.

"What facilities do you need?" I asked.

"Basically, I need to be in places, where one can live well without having a fixed address."

"I see," I said, although I hadn't fully grasped what he had in mind.

"You see," he continued. "I like to live light, having all my belongings in one small rucksack. I like to travel, not settle, visit, not occupy. This is the most efficient way of living. I learnt it a long time ago when I was studying economy. I didn't finish my studies, but what I learned there was imprinted on my mind, maybe because it confirmed what I already knew."

"What's that?"

"That the more things you have, the less flexibility you have in your life. This is the reason that banks typically don't buy office buildings; they rent them, as buying reduces their capital, which needs to be liquid. I apply the same rule to my entire life. As I have no apartment, I pay no mortgage or service charge. This allows me to travel practically wherever and whenever I want."

"But wherever you go, you need to sleep somewhere," I said.

"True, but I can sleep under the sky, and I don't need to wash in my own bathroom. For example, in the Red Cross facility in Montpellier you can have a shower, and wash and dry your clothes for 1 Euro 40. This sort of money every homeless person can earn begging or collecting bottles. The trick is to turn up there early, as later the queue gets longer."

"So you go to Montpellier for this reason?"

"Partly. But this is not the only reason. The other is sunsets and sunrises. I want to see them. I would say I collect them, like other people collect properties, cars or books."

He switched on his mobile phone and showed me his photos of the sky of almost all possible colours: different shades of blue, green, orange, purple and red.

"They were taken mostly on the coast from Andorra to Monaco. The best sunsets and sunrises are between Marseille and Nice."

"Why there?" I asked.

"I'm not sure. It might be because I spent so much time there or I put the most effort into capturing these phenomena, or there is something unusual about the sky. It is practically never one-coloured, blue or black. The clouds give the sky a specific tint. The trick is not to wait passively for the sunset or sunrise, but to be on the move, keep walking. Then not only will you find an excellent view, but many different ones. Sometimes I walked for three to four hours at a time, hunting for images."

"For me it would be too tiring to get up in the middle of the night to capture the sunrise."

"It's easier when you sleep in the open air; then there is no sharp division between sleeping and being awake, being in the world. You open your eyes and you are already there, on a beach or a street. You are in possession of the whole world. Besides, the current time is on our side. Take a mobile phone—you have at least 80% of your life there: books, television, music. And the other things are getting lighter. Take a sleeping bag – twenty years ago it took half of a large rucksack. Now I can put my rucksack in my pocket. And have you seen this?"

He took out from his rucksack a small thing labelled "temporary blanket."

"See, you can put this blanket on the palm of your hand, and I assure you that it protects you perfectly from rain."

"But people will still pity and patronise you if you are homeless," I said. "They also might ask you to leave, if you trespass."

"I don't call people like myself homeless, because I have a home: the entire Earth is my home. I call us 'the immaterial,' because we don't need material things to find fulfilment. Plus, people treat you as a homeless only if you look homeless. The challenge is not to look like that."

"How do you achieve it?" I asked.

"You know that somebody asked Karl Lagerfeld what is most important in looking good and he replied, 'finding one's own style.' If it works, there is no need to change it. I took this advice to heart. My clothes are of high quality, so they survive every weather and plenty of encounters with a washing machine. I basically wear them till they are destroyed and then buy similar ones. The only exception is shoes. To lead such a life as I do, I need to change shoes often. Still, one wants to take one's shoes off from time to time and walk barefoot or in slippers, but in many places, people are not allowed to do it. One such place is Monte Carlo, but I did walk barefoot in Monte Carlo, and nobody dared to criticise me for it."

"Well, it might be fine to sleep in the fresh air in the South of France in summer, but being homeless in winter is miserable."

"You are wrong. It's the other way round. It's much easier to sleep under the sky in cold weather than when it's hot. In hot weather, there are more people around, as well as mosquitos, and it's simply too hot. It's difficult to fall asleep in hot weather. In cold weather, on the other hand, you snuggle into a sleeping bag and are perfectly warm, except from your face which is breathing cold fresh air. It's like cryotherapy, except that you get it for free."

"I see."

There was again silence between us for a while and then I showed him some pictures of sunsets and sunrises on my phone, which I took in Scotland. I hesitated to reveal that I had a holiday house there, not because I was anxious that he would take me for a crude materialist, but because he might take me for somebody who boasts about one's wealth.

"These photos are good," he said. "It looks like you enjoy nature and are very observant. You seem to be a sensitive kind."

He said "sensitive kind" in English, which made me think that he referred to a song by JJ Cale. If so, it was a piece of magic for me as it was an anthem of my youth and one of my favourite songs of all time. But I didn't ask him what he meant. Instead I said: "True, but I don't want to travel anymore. I'm not curious about the world, even of beautiful sunsets and sunrises in the South of France or anywhere. I'd rather return to my home village and 'my lake' in Poland."

Then I showed him photos of my lake taken the previous summer.

"This is a nice lake. In fact, I prefer to swim in lakes than in the sea, because there are no waves and no salt. After swimming in a lake, one is clean; there is no need to take a shower. By contrast, after swimming in the sea one needs a proper wash. This limits the opportunities; I can only go to beaches which have good facilities."

"Even if you lead such a frugal lifestyle, you still need money—for food, for travel, to pay for washing."

"Well, I work sometimes. On occasions I buy things in one country and sell them in another: cigarettes, weed, alcohol. Sometimes I work as a guide or chauffer for tourists. There were times when I was working on a building site with a pneumatic hammer for an equivalent of forty euros per day, but this I wouldn't do again. I get by. The lack of money is not an issue for me."

"When did you choose such a lifestyle?"

"I'm not sure, but maybe it happened when I was a child. My parents were always quarrelling, and I couldn't stand it. We lived on a miserable high-rise housing estate in Ostrołęka, the town where crows turn back. Have you been there?"

"No."

"Well, no need to go there. When I sensed conflict at home, I left. First, I used to go to a bench in front of our block or to a swing, but gradually I went further and further from my house. I noticed that there were different places than this estate; there were woods and rivers. I would say that I've been running away from home since I was a kid. Sometimes I return for two-three days to Ostrołęka, because I need to visit some office or simply to check on my parents and then I notice that nothing really has changed. They hate each other as much as forty years ago, only manage it better. My father gets up at four or five in the morning when my mother goes to sleep, and she sleeps till one o'clock. Their fridge is divided, with Father's food on the top shelves and Mother's on the bottom ones. Still, if this fragile dynamic gets disrupted by something, like a visit from me, the open hostility resurfaces."

"I know such situations. My parents were like that. However, my father eventually died, liberating my mother. Maybe the same will happen to your parents: one will die and the other will blossom?"

"Maybe, but I'm not sure. Neither of them wants to give in, and each tries to remain fit. My father worked as a PE teacher; he has sport in his blood."

"Why did you say that crows turn back from Ostrołęka?" I asked.

"Because if they go further, they find the same things. Ostrołęka is 120 km from three large cities: Warsaw, Olsztyn and Białystok. It's like being inside a circle, which for me was a trap. Warsaw was a trap, Olsztyn was a trap, Białystok was a trap, so I went to study in Poznań, but it was still a trap, so I had to go further, to Spain, to Italy, to the UK. Eventually I discovered that I'm not looking for a place to settle, but being on the move is my way of being settled. So, I carry on. Next week I go to Prague with somebody, a woman. She seems to be like me in this respect, but just at the beginning of her journey so I'm not sure if this is her cup of tea."

"I see," I said, feeling somewhat embarrassed and unprepared to hear about his romantic life. He must have sensed it, so he didn't continue on this topic, instead shared with me his dilemma of where to get off the train: at the West or Central Railway station and what to do when he finally finds himself in Warsaw.

"There are different possibilities. I can go to the Casino in the Marriott Hotel and doze off there till the morning when I can take the first train to Ostrołęka. I can visit my friend the Chinese (who is really from Taiwan), a seller of Chinese fast food at the West Station or walk to the Łazienki Park and sleep there on a bench. I can also go to a gym as a friend gave me his pass; this means not only a chance to sleep on a comfy bench but also having a shower. Finally, I can visit my sister who lives four tram stops from the Central Station. But it is already almost midnight, hence not the best time to make unannounced visits, especially to somebody who lives with an ass of a husband and two small kids."

After thinking aloud for twenty minutes he decided to get off at the West Station and call his Taiwanese friend.

By the time he made up his mind we had passed Sochaczew, which was the last station before Warsaw and I still didn't know his name, because the entire trip we were addressing each other officially, Sir/Lady (Pan, Pani) as Polish adults tend to do. But I grew curious about his identity and eventually asked: "What is your name?"

"I have many names. You can give me any name you want."

"Well, I would like to know your Christian name."

"I'm not Christian anymore. I'm Buddhist, so I don't have a Christian name."

"What about the name in your passport?"

"This name is unimportant."

"Still, I would like to know it."

"Then you have to guess, but I can help you—it is a regal name."

I was thinking for a while and said: "You cannot be called Baron, as this is not a Polish name, so you must be called Cezary."

"Bingo. But I prefer when people call me Kaiser."

"The Kaiser of the Immaterial Empire," I said, laughing.

"Or rather the Kaiser of the Empire of the Immaterial Creatures."

"Don't you want to know my name?" I asked.

"No, not really. I rather prefer to give you my own name."

"Okay," I said.

When Cezary left I closed my computer and started to collect my belongings, as there were only ten minutes until the Central Station, where I was getting off.

Then I noticed that he was knocking on my window. I opened it and he said: "Your name is Mnemosyne, the goddess of storytelling," and he left.

Casey Stanberry "Urban Flight"

Poetry

Thomas Piekarski

Jacob the Lion Hearted

He started out trying to climb too high a ladder,
fell off, smacked his head, knocked unconscious.
But he wouldn't give up just because the ladder
was an obstacle. He wouldn't give in although
he had no grip on any world outside his head.

Jacob took advantage of this transcendent state
to luxuriate in the expanse of his imagination.
He ventured like Alice through fabulous realms
clinging to his unique ideals. No one else would
ever understand what thoughts were propagated.

Nor would he, for memory had fled in a flash.
His mind a dream machine, body in suspension,
Jacob manufactured fantasies, myths, religions,
gave them life, far beyond anything he'd known
during this his tenuous tenure on the road of life.

Andronicus Returns to Earth

A smooth landing, the toes of his module
dug in tight. He got out and smelled guts
of brothers slaughtered in close combat,
bodies slathered across a searing terrain.

Immersed in atmospheric chaos, he briskly
rubbed his eyes to extract insidious smoke.
Twisted steel, bricks strewn everywhere,
banshees, bats and ever-whipping winds.

Undeterred he sallied forth, exploring in his
fireproof jumpsuit. Surely the entire planet
couldn't be so depleted. Life must still exist
somewhere. He was duty bound to locate it.

An arduous trek it was indeed to the peak
of Vesuvius, then back down the other side.
He found Naples in complete ruin, home to
but rats and mongrels. Then on to Pompeii.

Pompeii ushered a precipitous rejuvenation.
For there, wandering amid the cement casts
of mortal souls untimely enmeshed in fiery
molten ash did he exalt, and pay homage.

Foreigner

He'd always taken freedom for granted as a man protected
from the forces of political discord, never given a thought
to the idea that his compassion and love would yield doom.

Yet they confiscated his possessions, beat him brutally.
He resisted, but no use. He was condemned, incarcerated,
and struggled in his straight jacket. Within a padded cell
he bounced against the walls, would wail, but his mouth
was gagged except to eat. They fed him through the slot
in an iron door, told that because he was foreign he had
no right to be free, which necessitated this imprisonment.

As one might expect, in due course he went totally insane.
On schedule, every ten years officials would stop by from
the federal office of subversion abatement to assess him,
would make him strip, examine his genitals, waterboard,
subject him to intensive interrogation as to determine if
he was fit for release. But of course he'd never be let go.

Seth Seeks Sex for Sex's Sake

Paul Negri

"It's so sibilant." Jamie picked a french fry from Seth's plate and put it on top of her frisée salad.

"That's the point," said Seth. He took a sip of water. "Say it fast. Seth seeks sex for sex's sake Seth seeks sex for sex's sake. It's like the sound some women make when they're having sex."

Jamie filched another fry. "I never made that sound."

"You did. Sometimes."

"I never heard that."

"Of course, you didn't hear it. It's like snoring. No one hears themselves snore."

At 39, Jamie looked enticingly older. Trim, pale, blonde, with startling black eyes. She'd overheard one of her high school students say she was a MILF. "It's like a snake. Or a radiator. Remember how the radiator hissed in our first place? It kept me up all winter."

"You slept like the dead. *I* was the one it kept up."

"I was *pretending* to sleep. So I wouldn't disturb you. I was always very considerate. Kind, even. You must give me that at least."

"Yes, you were considerate. So considerate it hurt. Sometimes kindness is the cruelest cut of all."

Jamie sighed. "And this is how you plan to get laid, Seth? With alliteration and metaphors? Is that how you think you'll draw women like moths to your flickering flame?"

"Women of a certain age, yes. Mature, cultivated women. *Literate* women. Women who appreciate a literate, honest man who won't hand them a line about love or commitment—"

"It's still slam bam thank you ma'am, isn't it, Seth? Isn't that what you're offering in a peculiar tongue-twisting way?"

Seth flipped his laptop closed. He was as dark as Jamie was fair and five years her senior, but looked younger. In the community college where he taught English, he had overheard one of his female students say he was a DILF, which he learned, after asking his phone, was a good thing to be. "I did not ask for your help, Jamie. You offered. Rather insistently. Honestly, I do not need my ex-wife's help in writing a personals ad."

The waitress came over and stood by their table. "You folks doing okay?"

Jamie looked up at her and smiled. "It's our anniversary. Six months divorced today."

"Congrats," said the waitress. "Can I top you off?" She was holding a glass pot of coffee.

"Can I ask you something?" said Jamie. She glanced at the name embroidered on her uniform. "Debbie?"

"I'm Cindy. I borrowed Debbie's top. Debbie's sick today." Cindy was short, young, and busty. "But you can call me Debbie. I like it better than Cindy anyway." She was chewing gum.

"Jamie," sighed Seth.

"Do you hiss when you have sex, Debbie?" Jamie asked.

Cindy stopped chewing. She put the coffee pot down on the table. "You mean like a snake?"

"Or a radiator?" Jamie raised her eyebrows.

"A what?"

Seth groaned. "Debbie. Cindy. I'm sorry. My ex-wife's being churlish."

"*Churlish*? Really, Seth. You've got words stuck in your teeth today," said Jamie.

"That's okay. I get asked a lot of funny questions," said Cindy. "Just something about me, I guess. A guy the other day asked me if I was gender fluid. I had to Google it."

"What did Uncle Google tell you, Debbie?" Jamie reached for another french fry, but Seth slapped her hand.

"It's like sometimes you're a boy and other times you're a girl and then you're something in between."

"And?" asked Jamie.

"I'm gender solid. Full time girl. And sometimes I shout."

"Shout?" said Jamie and grabbed two fries with her slapped hand.

"When I have sex. No hissing. Just like a kind of shout. I scare guys."

Jamie looked at Seth. "No one hisses. It's in your head. Something in your head hisses when you have sex. You should get that looked at."

Seth opened the laptop and turned it toward Cindy. "Debbie—I mean, Cindy. Will you do me a favor, please? Read that."

Cindy leaned forward and squinted at the screen. "Seth seeks six for sick sakes? Wait a minute." Cindy put on her glasses. "Seth seeks six for sex's sake."

Seth looked at the screen. "Wait. There now."

"Seth seeks—sex for sex's—sake," said Cindy.

"Faster, please."

"Sex seeks Seth for Seth's sake. Wait a minute. Okay. Seth seeks sex for sex's sake Seth seeks sex for sex's sake." She took a deep breath. "That's a mouthful."

"What does that sound like?" asked Seth.

"A snake," said Cindy.

"A radiator," said Jamie.

Seth closed his eyes. "Just the check, please."

Cindy scribbled on her pad and put the tab on the table. "Pay the cashier. No rush. You guys are funny." She picked up the pot and went back to the kitchen.

Seth pushed his plate toward Jamie. "You can finish the fries."

Jamie picked one up and dropped it back on the plate. "I shouldn't. I'm watching my figure."

"You look great," said Seth. He coughed. "How about you? Have you been dating a lot?"

"Not a lot. Some." Jamie forked her salad. "Men aren't serious. Then they get too serious. Then scared. Then boring. I hate boring."

"I know."

"I've got to get back."

"Okay. Thanks. It was good. I mean to see you."

Jamie nodded, slid out of the booth, and left quickly.

Seth sat staring out the diner window. He had no classes, but did not want to go home to the apartment he now rented. He did not like it. He found it lacking. The two women he had brought back there after a date seemed not to like it either. One left in the middle of the night. Seth closed his eyes.

"Hey, mister." Jamie slid into the booth. She put her elbows on the table and leaned in toward him.

"Yes?"

"I saw your ad," she said. "I'm interested."

Seth smiled. "I hoped you would be."

Poetry

Topper Barnes

Memories like Scars

There is a 22-year-old somewhere
Buried beneath the layers of abuse
Curled up like a starving street cat
Its fur caked with grime, oil, and feces
Those star speckled marble eyes
Bulging from the frail skull
And the shy stomach purring
While the confident takes its milk
With a trowel she can be found
A bit of digging and smoothing over
With time
Her blistered lips that have been
Bitten by glass roses
Will heal
The gory craters dotting her face
Torn open during 4am battles
With invisible insects
Will recover
Her skeleton will grow a new coat
Night by night

Day by day
Meal by meal
A shape will appear where a spike
Once stood
And those tear tracks dipped
In mascara
Running down her cheeks
Simply vanished
With a little bit of time
And digging and smoothing over
That 22-year-old from somewhere
Could be here feigning a smile
Choking on a laugh
Fresh and pretty and new
Like before
But
Her scarred black liver
Chiseled with patterns of back alleys
Of motel rooms
Of lustfully vicious faces
Twisted without regret
Cannot be covered with Bondo
And that childhood hunger in her gut
From her feline days
Will keep her up at nights
Tapping on window sills with her manicured nails
Looking out
And looking in
The glass pane that separates her from the street.

Paradise for $1.59

Down these alleys of midnight retreats
Lined with thirty-minute lovers

And Pad Thai hawkers
The seafood skewers pump steam
Into the air
Begging for a bite
Beckoning to my lips for just one simple
Bite that no one will know about
While the neon showers the cement with
Green and blue and red
The busker dipped in light strums
Gently the Saw Duang ripples through
The thick lascivious muck hovering
And mother tells child
To put on that sad face he does so well
He knows the one
Like he sleeps in oil and eats insulation
Because tonight they have knick-knacks
And knives to sell
The moon is boiling the streets
Heat waves rise up to the tips of skyscrapers
Sweat pours from pores faster than water
Can be drunk
And have you ever had a bird's nest soup
As the most beautiful woman
With a dick bigger than stool's leg
Sits on your lap
No play here
Straight massage here
But for a few baht more anything can happen
There is but little time for sideshow attractions
Tonight I am looking for nirvana
It is said that somewhere between the reggae bars
Blaring colors and wafting smoke
And the knock off shoe salesmen with Niky and Conversations
A man with no eyes can be found selling
A different kind of gimmick

Unlike ping pong projectiles slathered in mucus
Or prawns drenched in spices
Or fifteen-year-olds painted like women
In this overload of love and lust and gluttony and greed
A man and a woman sell tickets
For exiting existence
It may take a life of two
Maybe even three
And in the waiting room bald heads burn orange
But once there there is no being hung up on tickets
Nothing more than nothing
A final goal
In all this madness
An afterlife that is no life at all
One as void and clear
As the crystals that toothless woman
Has laid out on the table
For sale

A Lesson on Mortality

He taught me how to shoot stink bugs
With both eyes open
And one hand in my pocket like
Ole' Annie Oakley in Buffalo Bill's show
Better than him actually
And I always knew E. E. wrote that poem
About the wrong person
And he held my hand
When I gutted my first trout
That smelly thing flapping around
All wild like
As I pulled my pocket knife up its belly

In a straighter line than geometry
The innards drizzling out like blood
From my lip that time I sliced it open
While trying to shave
And he came in the bathroom
Me shaking with fear

Thinking the belt was coming up
But he just smiled and said
Let me show you how to do it without
Gaining scars
Those wrinkles on your mother's face
You can tell her they are getting worse
And when I went home
On Sunday nights I would count the days
One two three four
Until I got to see him again
Because on Fridays he let me pick candy bars
One two three four
Like days of the week filled with caramel
And peanuts and sugar
Until one Friday he did not come
There were no BBs or guts or blood
No candy bars
And I sat on the curb counting seconds
My eyes darting wild like that half dead fish
But that bright orange Falcon van never rolled
To a stop and I never got up
Till mother came out with a balled fist
And it turns out
I sat on that curb for three days straight
That fist chasing me in at night
Then the news came that the man
Was blue around the lips
The hair stopped growing

And he became letters upon a page
Those stink bugs were not much for teachers
That fish too
The pain that comes with a busted lip
Only hurts

Eye Contact

A Novel Excerpt

Ann Davis

"Would you like anything else today, sir?"

"Well I'd like a fresh pair of eyes, but I don't suppose you stock those anyplace!"

"But of course we do, sir! Installation facilities too! Just follow me to the back!"

The sardonic grin and chuckle on Morris's face stuttered to a halt mid-motion, an expression more comical than the attempted joke. The grin and chuckle didn't dissolve completely, but they weren't as firmly *there* either, not sure if they were supposed to go, or what they should be replaced with if they did. His legs were quicker on the uptake and obeyed a social cue they were used to, following the too-helpful salesclerk who seemed to know what he was doing, even if Morris didn't.

He'd only been making a self-deprecating crack about a silly question he'd asked earlier: if they sold cough drops, which were sitting innocuously on the counter in front of him. Morris had *not* been expecting a serious response to that question either, but here he was, being led towards the back of the shop.

Morris's face jumped forward a few seconds and caught up, the rest of his body following. Mouth, the aforementioned eyes, hands, arms, and the entire upper body joined in, hunching inwards. It was his compulsory response for unknown situations, anxiety at not knowing what was going on that left him unable to ask or do anything but follow unless something *really* strange happened.

This was the strangest rebuttal to a joke of his that he'd ever encountered (some people with very little humor had leveled *their* eyes at him) and the first time he'd been treated like he was asking a real question. The customary response was to ignore it, and sometimes laugh. One superbly rare case had the sales representative commenting that they'd sold their last pair to a nearsighted old lady not five minutes before he reached the till, and if he ran out, he might catch her. The joke had gone back and forth for another five (it was a slow day) about when would the next shipment be, and could he reserve a pair, and different colors and sizes and potential specials. At this some customers behind him in line had started laughing. The memory always gave him a warm feeling; it was a real coup for the socially stunted Morris to feel he'd delighted somebody. This was . . . an unsettling amount of follow-through for a joke.

The straight shoulder lines of the sales clerk he was following said he was not the least bit discomfited with acting entirely out of character for a joke. He didn't *seem* to be holding in any laughter. This was the appropriate sales mode response to a serious question from a customer in need of help, not the general "paying-customers-should-be-humored-and-have-a-good-day" reaction that should be happening. Maybe the man was unusually good at holding in his composure and was readying himself to thrust a jar of cat's eye marbles at him.

Or maybe, and this thought let Morris sag with relief (and scold himself for being an overreacting idiot), the salesclerk thought he wanted new *eyeglasses* and was taking him to a display he hadn't seen, the same as missing the cough drops.

No, that idea was summarily rejected as the salesperson unerringly led him through an employee's door which he was certain he shouldn't be seeing the other side of unless he were an inspector (he wasn't) or being offered a job here. Surely he wasn't meant to go through there and he stopped to wait and worry outside. The salesclerk held open the door and stood aside, adding a semi-theatrical sweeping bow for good measure, making it no mistake that Morris was meant to go through. This time the clerk was in the right position to see Morris's second stop-stall-start combo, but reflected the courtesy of his role by taking no notice except to say it was "quite all right, sir" when Morris came to himself enough to splutter an apology. Perhaps flustered customers weren't that unusual in the salesclerk's experience, but this was certainly a long way to go for a joke. Or stepping into something more serious than a joke. But Morris wasn't quite sure how to stop it.

Then he did. With full-blown, jaw-hanging, faulty-eyes-blown-to-saucer-sized-proportions shock. Perhaps, he hoped faintly they really *were* faulty, far more so than he'd joked comfortably in the shop several wonderful minutes ago, in which case he was going to be very embarrassed shortly. Because these *couldn't* be actual *eyes* in all these glass jars the salesclerk was ushering him to with a perfectly ordinary demeanor.

Morris had never appreciated how many different kinds of eyes there were in the world until his mind started frantically rushing through the other kinds he knew of, to formulate an explanation of what these eyes were other than what they appeared to be. Craft eyes, cat eyes, statuette eyes, figurine eyes. Nope. Nope. Nope. Marbles fashioned out of eyes, not marble fashioned to look like eyes for a joke; he felt perilously like laughing. Taxidermy eyes, but what sort of stitched-up creature would require eyes that looked like, like, like . . . they would fit in *his* face?!

While he was eyeballing the eyeballs (the one mercy in his current situation was they hadn't all rolled to fixate on him), a hearty chuckle was smothered just to his left. Followed shortly by "Oh, Nathan! You brought in another one without fully explaining things again! If it weren't such a lark seeing how many startled expressions people can make, I'd have reported you to the manager by now! Thanks for not running back out the door screaming by the way. You're tough stuff."

"Thank you," Morris replied faintly, gathering this last statement was meant for him. He was not quite ready to give up his staring contest with the nearest jar to ensure they weren't going to move if he turned around, or to face whatever further lunacy was waiting for him. Perhaps a mad doctor and the eyeballs he wasn't staring at hadn't turned to look at him after all; he was certain there were jars behind him too.

When Morris finally gathered up his courage to look, he was glad to find it was no mad doctor he was facing. The man seemed a perfectly ordinary and friendly sort, flat brown hair, parted in a sweep down the left side, caramel brown eyes, large round wire-rimmed glasses, slightly overlarge front teeth in his smile. Standing next to him, the salesclerk was still snickering a bit behind his hand, having dropped his composed demeanor, and managed to say in a slightly high voice from suppressed laughter that he thought "visual aids" would be better.

Belatedly, Morris realized he *had* walked into a joke after all, introduced to this backroom in such a way that he was incredibly startled at what, to them, was perfectly normal everyday business.

Getting control of himself, the salesclerk started in on his pitch. "Make no mistake, all of these eyes are of high-quality, twenty-twenty vision or so close to it glasses would barely make a difference. Not like those faulty numbers in your head that you were complaining about, eh?" he ribbed with a conspiratorial grin.

It was rather a flub of sales etiquette to make a comment like that, but Morris did no more than register it. He was still too blown away for much talk. The salesclerk took the silence for a cue to muster a recovery.

"We have a broad variety of colors and sizes. Your choice of color might be slightly restricted by the size of your sockets, but rest assured, you'll still have a very wide selection. If there's a color you just adore, we can have you on notice for when a new pair comes in, or adjust the sockets ourselves if we already have it, with a minor size difference. We do the measuring ourselves to ensure a perfect fit. From eyeballing them, I estimate yours to be about 24.4 mm." There was a rather bad laugh and chuckle at that, a surreal equivalent to his own bad eyeball joke at the counter several blissful minutes ago.

"We take pains to make sure all our stock is ethically harvested. The donor is approached personally; no one is allowed to serve as a prospective seller or intermediary for another person, not even a close relation. Everyone is compensated generously and in the extremely rare event of trouble—post removal or insertion in your case—we cover all resulting medical expenses." The normal, matter-of-fact way all this was being talked about was making Morris feel faint, and the spiel was not finished yet.

"All our eyes have a lifetime guarantee; they will be the longest lasting part of you." Morris flashed on a mental image of a perfectly clean, round pair of eyes staring vacantly as worms feasted on the rest of him. He was starting to feel like running again. Fortunately, the sales pitch was wrapping up. What was he going to do then?

"Best of all, the whole package, the new selection and the replacement process, can be had at the nominal sum of 400 pounds. Payment can be made all at once, or over a period of months in installments with no interest whatsoever," the clerk finished with a flourish.

Throughout the presentation Morris had not let up his stare, though he transferred it to the salesclerk and doctor from the eyes in jars. Hearing the price finally jolted him out of the modus of polite customer he'd been frozen into since his first sight of the backroom's contents.

That the eyes were affordable from purchase to placement—expensive certainly, but within his actual savings—was so astonishing as to knock him back on his rump. Upon hearing of the "generous compensation" offered, Morris had expected the price to be outlandish. It was about the price of a new sofa where he worked, and not at all extreme for the scope of the service.

The salesman continued rambling on about a "same-day operation" so swift and painless it could be accomplished without anesthetic, tossing in a few more bad eye jokes about "seeing" that this was an ideal service and he would "look back" at this as the best decision of his life for good measure. In the midst of it the doctor came back in, interrupting the enthusiastic diatribe to verbally box his ears about the poor humor and apologize to Morris with a slightly worried look.

"I say, we didn't actually offend you did we, sir? Please, don't mind the poor humor, or lack thereof, it's actually part of the pitch, though these new amateur salesclerks don't know when it's unwise to veer off script," the doctor stated tartly, with a severe look to the side. "Lots of people are shocked when they're brought back here; the joking acts as an icebreaker and snaps most people right back up into normalcy."

"Actually, the price did it for me. So little is charged for what it's honestly worth these days that I was quite taken aback," Morris replied with a game attempt at a chuckle. Both his listeners relaxed. They'd looked so anxious, thinking they had possibly offended him, that he could say little else. He'd slipped back into the role of polite customer all right, albeit one with beads of sweat popping up on his face and on the ragged edge of screaming.

Promptly they started agreeing with him, relieved to slip into the "yes, yes, customer is always right," mode after fearing they were about to lose a sale. "It's such a credit to hear you say that, just wonderful, so many think we assign our prices from thin air. All decent places are given a bad reputation by others that sell products at ridiculous prices just because of who came up with the idea for them. Here we have a commitment to fair business practices, from the suppliers to those who create demand."

"Speaking of ridiculous," Morris interjected before they could start again, "All of this was such a surprise to me, it feels rather absurd. Is there some prankster holiday I'm forgetting? Or is there some announcement about this posted on your window that I missed? Perhaps I really am in dire need of new eyes!" Well now he'd done it, he admitted the whole presentation felt like a long joke. Not the best opportunity but he'd seized it. It was his one last chance to get out of this, though his mental state was slowly transitioning from terrified to intrigued.

"Right-o, there is indeed some more subtle kidding around, two jokes in fact. Despite Nathan's lauding of my skills, of *course* we use anesthetic during the insertion, otherwise you patients scream like biddy hens! And there's enough screaming at our second joke; no post-operation monthly payments allowed! Either lay-away or pay all at once. In advance! We certainly aren't so uncouth that we install them if there is any chance we have to take them back out! That's valuable merchandise you'd be wandering off with!" It was said clerk's turn to glare at his coworker for his less than settling pronouncement in front of a customer. He delivered it with an additional elbow for good measure.

"Heh heh, so-o, have you seen any pair in particular that you'd like? That is to say, is there any specific coloration that tickles your fancy? Take all the time in the world to look around—or if you don't see anything, not that your present eyes are so terrible you understand, you can come back another time, oh dear!" Clearly the cockiness was jostled out of him. Without it, he was as jittery as a coffee bean.

Actually, their show of nerves was calming him down, and he was quite honestly curious. Morris set himself to examining the nearest jar. He noted the eyes were perfectly straight, not cross-eyed like his. Could stare right into a boss's face with these, maybe even ask for better hours or a raise. And a new color too, a more usual and favorable one. Just in time too, travel restrictions were coming in, making his current eye color reason enough for people to stare, even if everything else looked proper. However he'd stumbled onto it, Morris had done enough dreading and questioning of his strange luck and decided to take advantage.

"Excuse me, what about this pair, right here? Would they be the right size?" Morris pointed at a set at the bottom of the nearest jar. Faintly, he was relieved they did not swivel to stare at his fingertip.

"Ah yes, excellent choice, sir! Looks like a good fit, and a new color too! Daring, aren't you? They'll go well with your general complexion. Now are you paying up front or—"

"I can afford to get them now." The way his luck worked, Morris would never get another chance. "Is there time to get have them . . . ahem . . . *installed* now, or do I need to schedule an appointment for it?"

"Oh no, right now is not a problem for us, same day insertion just like I was talking about," the doctor eagerly reassured. Morris noted he'd taken over most of the talking since the salesclerk's script had run out. "Just so long as you answer a few questions for us, and fill out this paper saying that you did, and put the same answers on it as you give us." A clipboard with paper and pencil was brandished at him. "Now, have you had any caffeine in the past six hours? Any alcohol in the past twenty-four? You've done anything like that, we can schedule an appointment for another time. We can hold the eyes for you so long as there's a definitive return date. And of course there's the disclaimer, honestly an unnecessary bit of paper if I ever saw one! That's what the sales' pitch ought to say, 'so good a surgeon we don't need a disclaimer,' but that really does tend to scare people away . . .."

The doctor rambled on for the better part of an hour. Morris was assaulted with a battery of questions, hardly given the chance to write down the answers before another was upon him. Eventually it was determined he could have the surgery right away. Fortunate, or he might not have remembered to come back. Morris hated paperwork.

While the doctor's speech was effusive, at least he didn't stint on information. He answered a few questions Morris forgot to ask and ones he didn't know he should. He was only bothered once, when the question of repairs came up, informing in a tone of gravely offended dignity that "Sir, we sell entirely new sets of eyes in prime condition! This is certainly not a repair shop! Our products never break down, so we never need one!" Morris was little inclined to believe that, but he couldn't very well back out now. He asked for clarification on some issues he wasn't sure he understood, but wasn't quite confident enough to vocalize everything, certain some of it was silly. He hoped all the important questions, at least, were addressed, and the doctor's skill level matched his level of conviction!

Once the inquisition was ended, Morris was led over to a padded chair the salesclerk had dragged in while the doctor was talking and made to lie back in it. A cloth with some foul-smelling stuff was placed over his nose and mouth. He was swiftly made very sleepy.

Poetry

Mark Hammerschick

Meteor Shower

Canvas black
the eternal oil spill galactic
dark matter
speckled waves of crystal
diamond sky
ruby, emerald, sapphire
lightspeed
silent night bright
terminal velocity
eyes focus
straining in the dark time
as seconds, minutes, eons
stretch galaxies
into small hands
that even rain cannot
feel
for in feeling
we begin to fall
headlong into night
riding the meteors

of our past
knowing the showers
of our future
will smother
those small hands
someday

not even the rain has such small hands

Smokestacks of oak, hickory and birch
lurch in the balance of sleet and snow
on a confused Sunday in early May
as my woods fill up with snow.
It's a snowy evening
tucked away on this Highland Park cul de sac
hugging Lake Michigan's shore
as the gales of this Spring day
recall the final waves
sweeping over the bow
of the Edmund Fitzgerald
on a cold November gale long ago.
Having weathered many storms
we walk . . .
wandering down Sheridan Road
as this knowing snow envelops us
clinging to that other walk
taken a lifetime ago.
We were frozen
stumbling and bumbling
your hand on my thigh
my leg on yours
holding tight
as we hurled down that hillside

on a rustic red slide
not knowing we would have this moment
to savor for so many walks to come
before full time work and grad school
one, two, then three
bundles of infinite intensity.
Birthdays, graduations, proms
and that first house we called home,
rearing three daughters
tornados of emotion . . .
and then from the chaos came the calm
as I cupped my calloused palm
on a tiny granddaughter's hand
not even the rain has such small hands.

1944

Venomous clouds
slit azure veins
putrid
eyes sliced wide
jelly spittle
apologize
shrieking
into a hollow socket
wretchedly lacerated

plasma pulses
sifted like sledge
fusing fractional abstraction
a girl not on the list
frozen to a dirt floor
hemorrhaging

not going gentle
as razor snow
penetrates the lone whistle
on this lurid train
into the heart of darkness
kill them all . . .

comfortably numb

I graze on mottled cattle
lost in a labyrinth of longing
for the velvet silence
that envelops your pancreatic eyes
piercing steel,
cold, harsh, brutal
like the memories of veal calves
clipped to hooks in the cooler,
yet gaze I must
since I trust
the musky stench of you
is all that balances
this carefully carved moment
eye to eye
knee to knee
breath to breath
how you suffocate me

Autumn Impales Itself

In a crimson distance
leaves explode
not like dreams deferred

but like nightmares
frozen in dream space
the eternal silence
whispering from caustic cancerous corners
jagged shards of flesh linger
blistered, bloated organ confetti.
Errant confused winds gather in discord
wavering in their vacuous intent
like lords of flies, hovering, sweating,
waiting for the kill, lost boys are the best boys.
Toil, boil and troubles linger as the witches
walk on by hearing it on the grapevine,
their sinuous spells snarl septic minds
blank with the boiled brains of field mice.
Swirling, the swirl of a Tilt-A-Whirl
deep in the memory of Roscoe Street:
Catalpas grand in a sticky reality of leaves
Sugar Maples bleeding crimson crowns
And rivers of birch white with hope
hope that winter weight will not win.
Canvas of light, a lone sun resumes its warmth
content in the cerulean blue
spot it owns in the universe
as it shines on like a crazy diamond.

Forgetting She Forgot

Roger McKnight

Addie Voss's Michael was the one with asthma, but she learned to share it with him. He wheezed and hacked and she complained about his clogged-up tubes like they were her own. Looking for relief, the two fled Illinois and headed for sunny Albuquerque, but the desert air gave Michael nosebleeds. In Redding and Denver, it was the heat or the altitude. That had been the go-around since they got married in the early nineties, nomadding it here and there, looking, hoping.

Now today, an ordinary Tuesday, Addie was waiting in confusion at San Francisco International for a plane back to Minneapolis, their latest city, where she had left Michael and their four kids a couple days earlier. For Michael, jobs were plentiful in Minnesota, even if breathing remained a chore. She guessed other things weren't going to get better either now that the four kids were down to three.

"Coughing up his guts is bad enough," Addie said to anyone listening over the waiting room chatter, "but nothing's like this disease called life."

"With what kind of ease?" a jovial older man asked as they finally found their places on the afternoon flight.

"Not ease," Addie said clearly, noting how he cupped a hand behind his ear. "You know, dis-ease, same as discomfort, like fitting in these gawd-awful airline seats."

The man waited patiently while she wedged herself down in the middle seat. Then he took his place by the aisle. Addie looked up distractedly and introduced herself.

"Addie."

"I'm Al," he replied. "Old-timer. Retired guy."

A young man with red hair was already crammed in the window seat, but he was limber enough to stretch his legs. "Richard," he said. "From Rochester. Been visiting my girlfriend, in Vegas. On vacation."

"I was just starting a vacation, too, my first ever," Addie responded. "Here I am, forty-two and never had a week off."

"Is that right?" Al asked. He was looking past Addie and addressing Richard. "That's a college girl you were seeing in Vegas, was it?"

"No, a card dealer," Richard answered with a smile. "She deals blackjack."

"No kidding!" Addie replied. "That's my line, too. I do housekeeping at a casino."

"Right in the action, I bet," Al said with an interested wink.

"Well, it's really the casino hotel," she admitted.

"Like I said, you seen it all?"

Yes, I seen it all, she reflected in silence. *Like this guy who left me a hundred-dollar tip and then . . ..* She paused in mid-thought.

"I can see you're thinking it over," Al said. "My question hit home, huh?"

Addie glanced at him, her emotions mixed. This stranger asked such impertinent questions, but they addressed some of her present anxieties. She was confused at the sudden journey back to the Midwest to begin with. Now she was expected to talk with people to boot. Still, it might do her good to have someone around and here she was with a fellow on each side of her.

"I'll let you in on one," she said thinking it wouldn't hurt to let a brief tale slip out in public. "We had this guest, a hulking guy and a big talker, with a ten-gallon hat. He checked in one Friday night, gambled away the family farm, then killed hisself. I'm the one found him, bright and early on Sunday. 'You done plenty of this walking into rooms and finding people with their brains blew out,' my boss said. 'Take some time off. Go visit your folks.' And that's what I was doing."

"You were in Vegas, too," Richard interrupted.

"No, Redding. California."

Richard shrugged, while Al nodded knowingly.

"I lived in Redding once," he explained.

"Yeah, me, too," Addie said. "Not this time, though."

That was then, she reflected, this time is now. Or was now. Now could be hard to define. Her bus had left Minneapolis on Friday morning and she'd ridden it till Monday afternoon. Hours of starts and stops and then weird people, who might have been bearable to know about, at some level, but taken together they only felt tawdry to her, some verging on illegal. That trip happened only yesterday, but it felt like a ball of compressed time fading into a distant past.

Nevertheless, she loosened up and told Al and Richard about a few incidents. Like the teenage girl from Oklahoma, who had made her way up north alone and boarded the bus in the Dakotas cradling a pink blanket with a pet squirrel she fed from a baby bottle. Then there was the drunk who pawed at the thirteen-year-old girl across the aisle from Addie while the mother slept. The girl squealed for the driver to intercede until Addie ran the guy off. People like that mixed in with the loads of ordinary folk quietly riding off toward the California coast.

"Worst of all, was the thumpety-thump-thump of bus tires on the potholes after a long icy winter," she said. "The landscape was unchanging. Then we crossed the mountains, but it was night. I slept while feeling the bus climbing higher up and the curves getting ever sharper, like daggers in my ribs."

Richard seemed to lose interest in her tale, but Al strained to follow along. First he thought she was talking about real daggers or knife fights on the bus, but gradually she felt her words sinking in with him.

"I see, like our plane ascending," Al added. "I thought myself that was an uncomfortable, stabbing sensation on takeoff."

"Whatever," Addie replied. "Like I said, it was my first time off from work. So missing my kids caused the pain. I sent our twelve, fourteen, and eighteen-year-olds off to visit my hubby's folks and left Eddie with his dad. He's only six. I forgot my cell, so no contact for two days plus. With nobody."

"You weren't concerned?" Al asked.

"I like riding the bus. Especially when we came down out of the mountains. For some reason we went to Monterey first. Then we changed buses northward again. The closer we get to Redding, the more I feel the heat growing."

Addie squirmed in her seat as the coach got warmer.

"More desert-like. Soon as I get off the bus, everything's strange. The wind hits me like a hot wave and nobody's there. Finally, my father meets me and says my Eddie's dead."

"Just like that?" Richard asked her in surprise.

Addie nodded yes and leaned forward. Only slowly did she settle back in the middle seat.

"Something fell on him and killed him," she replied, her calm restored.

"That's too bad," Al commented soothingly without cupping his hand. "Is he all right now?"

"No, he died," she repeated.

Al leaned back and considered the ceiling, which made it unclear whether he couldn't understand or still hadn't heard her. By now the plane was into cruising mode, so Addie felt like she was being rocked to sleep. At her side Al went on gazing dreamily into the distance. Later the pilot announced they were passing over the Rockies and a storm was brewing, but probably not before Rapid City. Like most of the other passengers, she dozed off. Later she woke up thinking about the storm clouds.

"I like riding the bus. I like flying, too," she said while glancing out the window. "But the plane costs more. My dad bought me this ticket for $600. They call it bereavement."

"Believe me," Al agreed, aroused from his daydreaming.

"I didn't even have time to stop in Redding. Dad wanted me on the first best plane back east. I had to get up at four to get from my folks' place to San Fran. Then I missed the early flight. They didn't give me time to get across the airport. I'd never been there before, and they ought to give us time to walk all that way."

Al nodded in agreement. Maybe he understood her, maybe not.

"They should give us more time," Addie repeated. She brushed back her blond hair and dried a tear inching its way down her cheek. A few others followed. She took out a tissue and dabbed at them, a light motion matching the mid-afternoon quiet, which only the pilot finally broke. He announced he was veering south. Unless he did that, they'd surely collide with some strong turbulence.

"Collisions are no fun," Addie said. "The time we moved from Denver, it was blizzardy and Russell, that's my hubby's brother, came from Tennessee to help drive us up north, a real cakewalk. Said they had scads of weather in Nashville. He was driving our VW van, not my hubby who was at the wheel of the other car. Russell got behind a couple semis on the Interstate and the snow was blowing so hard we couldn't see around 'em. Russell said if we stayed there we were goners for sure, froze tight in our tracks, so our only chance was the left lane, but the van was so loaded it stood still, kinda like suspended there. That's when I knew we were gonna die, but that ol' crate kept chuggin' on till it inched past both those trucks."

"You were saved!" Richard exclaimed.

"Yes, but when Russell pulled off later we skidded 360 degrees on glare ice into a ditch. We crawled out into the drifts, all of us okay, but it took us forever to get that van towed into town. Cold as blazes, I tell you."

"So you got it repaired?" Richard asked.

"Yes. We hunkered down in a flophouse motel and waited near a week. Russell drove us all the way to Illinois after that, and finally turned north toward Minnesota. Me and my hubby ran away from Illinois years ago, and I keep thinking, here I am gonna cash in my chips back in that hole. You're the truck driver, I tell Michael, why can't you decide which road we take? I never trusted that Russell again."

"That's life, I figure, always a lesson to be learned," Al added.

"Life's one huge collision waiting to happen." She bit the fingernails on her right hand nervously, pausing after each nail to study how close she had come to the quick. Realizing eventually her actions looked unsettled, she rested her hands on her lap. "It's like, I could land this plane if I had to," she continued, "and get us outa big storm trouble. My dad was a licensed pilot. He had a Piper Cub and showed me at home how they land and balance the planes. I wonder where we are?"

She peeked out and saw ominous clouds towering higher by the minute.

When she leaned back, Al craned his neck to see, too. "That's South Dakota down below," he explained.

"Oh, will we have to cross Illinois, too?" Addie asked.

"The Prairie State, your old stomping grounds?"

"Heavens no, not me, I only married this truck driver from there. That's my Michael, except he gave up trucking for sheet metal work."

"Well, anyway Minnesota's next," Al assured her. "Not Illinois."

Addie closed her eyes and rocked back and forth. The flight attendants came around collecting throwaways, which caused her to start humming a chant-like melody to calm her nerves.

"I don't like landings. Will we fly around the storm?" she asked.

"Yes," Al answered, "but what we see now aren't storm caps. Just rising clouds."

Addie lifted her right hand and inspected her frayed fingertips. After that, she began biting the nails on her left hand.

"The real storm clouds are on the other side," Al reassured her once more.

Relieved at that news, she stopped nibbling. She rummaged absentmindedly in her purse instead.

"I'm from Wisconsin," she explained. "I grew up in southern California. But I notice how all the cheese they sell to tourists in California is made in Wisconsin."

"What in the world?" Al asked.

"I think about my Eddie," Addie confessed with a sob. "How hard it'll be to walk in and him not there. He was starting to get asthma like my hubby. Lots of times I could tell where he was in the house by his cough. He had toys and clothes in his room. His puppy Emma slept with him."

"What breed?" Richard asked.

"Oh, just a mutt. Black and white. Eddie wanted a boy dog but then we take him to the pound and there's this furry mongrel staring up at him. Love at first sight, they had to have each other."

Richard smiled at her words. In the silence that followed the plane started its long, slow glide toward the Twin Cities. The flight attendants came around again. They took Addie's teary tissue and gave her new ones, and that led her to repeat the story of Eddie's death or what she knew of it.

"What fell on him?" Al asked.

"They didn't say. Just that Michael and Russell will be waiting for me at the airport. My father-in-law, too, he's coming. I still remember living there in that Joliet in Illinois with him. On warm winter mornings the fog'd settle and the cold air from the melting snow mixed with it. The river canals were so oily they never froze, so this soupy slime rose up from the water and met the exhaust from all the trucks. The ducks stayed away. But not us. We slogged around in that mess till Michael got his asthma and Eddie, too."

"Isn't asthma inherited? I mean, genetic?" Al asked.

"That's what the docs said, but I knew Michael when he was the picture of health. We met when he was with the Marines in Carolina and I was passing through. Before Desert Storm. Then he came home from Arabia and moved us to Joliet, his home town. He caught that junk."

"So your kids have the asthma as well, all of you," Al ventured.

Addie saw he was about to question her on the kids' ages, just to double check, when the pilot interrupted and told the attendants to prepare for landing. Al nodded as they fastened their seat belts, and the coach lights dimmed.

"Anyway, asthma bonded us together, me and Michael," Addie explained.

As the plane began circling, the pilot came on to explain they were holding in a line of incoming flights. Rain splattered against the coach windows.

"Will we have to fly through the clouds down there to land?" Addie asked.

"Yes," Al answered. "We'll beat the worst of them."

"Misery loves company." She started in loudly until she realized others than her seatmates could be listening. "Michael obsesses, thinks he'll smother to death, so I comforted him all along by complaining, too. Then we had Eddie, the love of my life."

As the plane landed, she peeked out at a slowly brightening late summer evening. Somewhere behind them a woman announced the landing on her cell. "Carousel four. Love you, honey." Other passengers were sorting their gear.

Addie spoke up again. "I forgot it. My phone, I mean. I coulda called my baby." She wanted to say something else, but she saw Richard wasn't listening and suspected Al wouldn't hear her over the ruckus.

The three of them were heading toward baggage claim before she began talking again, repeating herself about how great it was the pilot flew around Illinois, she couldn't have stood Joliet another time. Not even inhalers helped you there.

At the top of the stairs leading down to baggage claim, she stopped and looked beseechingly at Al and Richard.

"We named him after me, you know."

"How's that?" Al asked.

"You know, like me and him. Addie and Eddie."

"Oh, yes," Al said with a comforting smile. "Eddie and Addie."

With that, the two men took the escalator down. Addie lingered at the top.

Thankfully, she had no luggage, so she walked down the steps and past the carousels. Around her was the busy flow of passengers arriving and departing. She saw Al and Richard, baggage in hand, disappear among them.

When Michael emerged from the crowd, she hugged him till her father-in-law came forward, followed by Russell, wearing a *Volunteers* t-shirt. She embraced all three at once till they finally stepped back to study each other's thoughts. *The hardest part of all this is how we'll ever pay Dad for my plane ticket,* Addie was thinking, but all she said was, "Who's been feeding Emma?"

Her men smiled sheepishly but didn't answer. They started the trek out toward short term parking.

"Okay, let's go home then," Addie said under her breath and followed them. Along the way she counted on one hand what was waiting for her there. Three lonesome kids. One empty boy's room. A hungry dog. Her idle cell phone. She wondered how she'd ever forget that she forgot it.

Lew Holzman "New York 2463 CE"

Pool Boy

John Beyer

The concept did not come as a lightning bolt out of the sky, striking my cranium instantly. But more like a slow buildup of storm clouds on the horizon. The ones that leave a person wondering if inclement weather was in fact on the way or would fizzle into nothingness.

Weather is like that sometimes, much like thoughts, ideas, or dreams. Nothing to do with reality at the moment but perhaps in the future that reality would truly become real.

That was how it was with the epiphany I could make a lot more money if I turned my career into something deeper if not more sinister.

I grew up poor, angry and disillusioned in Forest Park in Detroit. The small neighborhood bordering Wayne State University had high unemployment and those lucky enough to be working had some of the lowest incomes in the state of Michigan. My parents worked hard in low-skilled jobs—mainly to the fact my father was an alcoholic and my mother never made it past tenth grade. They weren't bad people—just two trying to do the best they could with five children sucking up whatever funds they could muster monthly.

It didn't take long for me to find the allure of the gang life. I met Tony in Forest Park. He was shooting dice, and I watched for a while and then joined in the game of chance. Three rolls with a bet of two dollars increased my winnings to ten bucks. I was hooked.

Gambling led to higher bets on various other games around the hood, and then that led to small time rip-offs. A store here and there in the middle of the night were easy targets and then fencing the stolen goods in Brightmoor, brought an unexpected flood of money for Tony and me. Of course, there were some other guys helping us here and there, but they weren't important enough for us to remember their names on a daily basis. They did what we told them to and they followed orders—easy enough.

A year into our entrepreneurship we were busted at one in the morning ransacking a Goodwill Store on Chene Street by an overzealous police officer. Tony got away and I was stuck literally holding a rack of second-hand clothes.

Two of our part time help rolled over on us as soon as the cuffs were around their wrists. I had just turned seventeen and pulled six months at Wayne County Juvenile Detention Center. Tony got nothing stating he had been at home and only knew me by name and the other criminals—well, they cried to the judge, blamed everything on me, and the hammer was dropped by justice on my head.

Almost eighteen and now free, I left Michigan without ever saying goodbye to my parents, who really weren't that interested in my fate anyway, and headed west.

An editor once told a cub writer to do the same in the late nineteenth century, which I took as a positive omen and followed suit. If it was good enough advice for Mark Twain, then surely it would be for me.

Southern California was a dream come true. Sunshine, palm trees, and beautiful women. It beat my old hood without even trying. Venice Beach was where I landed and instantly decided that the life of crime was not my avenue any longer, but instead I would try the highway of legality.

Starting to work as a pool cleaner seemed like a heaven-sent job for a pale white guy from one of the toughest neighborhoods of Detroit.

Three months later I had saved enough for my own little four-cylinder truck and started moonlighting without my boss, Mr. Reynolds, knowing. Six months later I quit working for *Cleaner by the Month Pool Maintenance* and went out on my own with *Pool Boy*. A simple name for a simple guy.

Thirteen clients weren't a lot, but I was sharing a two-room apartment in El Segundo so the monthly fees paid most of the bills. I worked evenings at a pizza joint on East Grand and was able to get by financially.

Females were friendly and available. I had gotten pretty tan, my light brown hair was fashionably longish, my blue eyes shined in the afternoon sun, and surfing skills were picking up. I had never been much for the ocean since Detroit didn't have one, and we were so poor growing up, that the thought of heading to the coast in the east seemed a ridiculous expense to frolic in the surf.

The beach was within thirty minutes and with an inexpensive third-hand 'thruster.' I had more enough time, shredding off the coast of Malibu or Venice depending on my mood and weather conditions affecting the rollers.

Life couldn't get any sweeter. My twentieth birthday came, and my roommate threw a killer party with a kegger, beach girls, and more sushi than all attendees could eat. It was a hell of a bash, and the cops were called at two in the morning. We thanked them for coming and shut the event down with no one going to jail.

It was a complete success.

Two months later my life started to resemble my past one.

I had hooked up with a part-time model out of Santa Monica, and we hit it off immediately. The love making was awesome and ever so tiring which, in itself, was nothing but a full complement for both of us. Her friends liked me, which was even more of a bonus since they all had money—of course, that was possibly the one thing that could stand in our way.

Jenny told me over and over again that having plenty of cash on hand wasn't that important to her. That was easy for someone who had received a new Alfa Romeo for her twenty-first birthday from her parents. They were lawyers out of Century City and could afford it for their only child. Sweet of them and when they asked me about my family, I answered the only way I could. I was an orphan, which shut down any future conversation about my blood lines right away.

After cleaning a pool in El Segundo one afternoon, I was standing by my truck rolling up the hose when a silver Mercedes drove up and stopped beside me.

"You looking for another client?"

I was and stated so.

"I build pools."

That was interesting and possibly lucrative. I took the bait.

The end was soon coming, but I couldn't see it even with my twenty-twenty vision.

Turns out Mr. Mercedes did indeed own a very successful pool construction company out of Santa Monica, but he had a dark side. It seemed he also grew up back east in Detroit, small world, and knew the ugly reality of crime.

Building pools was a way to make a hard but honest buck. At times very financially rewarding but there were times during the year when homeowners weren't so interested in plopping a gunite structure into their backyards. And it was those times when Mr. Mercedes had to find another avenue to support his rather large lifestyle.

Eating and drinking weekly at *Geoffrey's* in Malibu called for a continuous flush of greenery, as well as having a two thousand square foot condo on Rey De Copas Lane. The guy needed income and had a unique way to keep the funds rolling in during those down months in construction.

He was a professional hit man. Quite simple, and, after discussing this and that with him for nearly two months, I decided to help him. I would get a cool five thousand per hit and the good thing was I didn't have to pull any trigger.

My job was simply to deposit the body of the deceased in the pit dug for one of his custom and very expensive pools. The hole would be dug, the plumbers would set the drainpipes, and the crews would come in placing the rebar into place. The electricians didn't have to go digging in the deep end at that point and would concentrate closer to the top of the hole. The last step, from my point, would have the gunite sprayed and smoothed over thus creating a waterproof grave.

A grave which should remain secret for at least a few decades if not forever.

Once the pool was operational, there was more than a good chance I would get the contract to keep the new swimming hole sparkling clean, especially from a recommendation of Mr. Mercedes. It was a win-win situation.

I took him up on it.

We met two months later in a deserted field not far from a pool that was being dug in the rear yard of a home in Manhattan Beach. The owners were gone on vacation, so it was a perfect time for me to do my thing. That is, burying the dead person before they got home.

Mr. Mercedes helped me with the rather large package that was sealed in a coroner's black bag into the rear of my truck. I didn't ask who the victim was, since I didn't want to know nor really cared, but simply huffed and puffed as we threw the heavy bag into my truck bed. After casually throwing a tarp over the body, I received a white envelope that was bulging with cash.

I sort of liked this deal, as I put my foot to the pedal and headed into the sunset.

The neighborhood was upscale, with tall block walls and even taller trees and shrubs surrounding the property. With my *Pool Boy* truck, I knew it appeared like one of the pool installers was working and casually knocked on the front door. When no one responded I went back to my truck and drove further down the driveway. The large two-doored, wooden side gate was unlocked, allowing me easy access to the rear of the property, and I parked right at the lip of the shallow end.

I cast a look around the rear yard and didn't see any peering eyes from the neighbors. They would have been hard put to see over the walls anyway, and I went to work. Since the crews had only been there in the last few days the ground was soft inside the pool crater, and, within fifteen minutes, I had a nice seven foot by three foot by four foot deep hole all carved out.

Tailgate down I pushed and yanked until the black bag toppled out of the rear of my truck and plopped five feet down into the shallow end of the pool. The rest was rather easy as I slid the corpse across the dirt and kicked it into the hole I had prepared. Ten minutes later, the ground didn't look much different than when I had arrived approximately forty minutes earlier.

The rebar guys would be there in the morning, and, by the end of the week, the gunite would be shot on and smoothed out.

My job was finished, and I was five grand richer.

Life looked brighter by the month after that.

The pool business was picking up for Mr. Mercedes, and I was doing two bodies a month. Jenny wasn't sure where my cash was coming from, but she never asked either. If she had, then I would just list off all the new clients I had from my association with Mr. Mercedes. In fact, I had upgraded to a new Dodge Ram 1500 and hired an illegal, utilizing my other truck for any cleaning I couldn't get to. Of course,

Julio was only involved in cleaning the pools and not of depositing anything below the gunite. That was my job, and I was not about to share in the profits from that side job no matter how much I liked the hard-working guy.

Two years later, I was up to three trucks in the business, a nice apartment in Redondo Beach, and plans for getting married.

Everything was going swimmingly.

Then the weather changed. In Southern California, one can expect the climate to be pretty stable year long. There are cold days, warm days, windy days, and non-windy days. But all in all, the weather is rather predictable, that is until the winter after my twenty-third birthday.

Storm clouds came crashing down the west coast from Alaska causing a chill I hadn't felt before. The beach communities were down right freezing for one solid week, and then the Pineapple Express, the weather system from the area of Hawaii twenty-five hundred miles to the west, started pushing in warmer weather.

And when the Alaskan cold met the Hawaiian warmth, thunderstorms formed west of the San Gabriel Mountains, and the rain fell and fell. For five solid days the rain collapsed on the region, bringing torrential mudslides and upward of ten inches of water within the week. In an entire year, Southern California may only see fourteen inches total.

There wasn't much in the way of pool cleaning, but I did receive a frantic call from Mr. Mercedes at seven in the evening on a Thursday.

"The damn body is floating."

It didn't take a brain surgeon to know what he was getting at. I had recently secreted a body on Crestvale Drive in the city of Sierra Madre and realized being at the foothills of the mountains this could be a problem for a freshly buried body. With the amount of rain suddenly pounding the greater Los Angeles area, it didn't take much to saturate the ground and that's exactly what had occurred on Crestvale Drive.

The ground was like a sponge. When that sponge got too full and couldn't hold any more water it leaked. That hole where a pool was supposed to go got saturated, and thus couldn't hide the body I had buried. Like a cork, the plastic black bag with human remains was suddenly floating around in a pool of muddy water.

Police had already arrived and secured the home by the time I arrived. I only went there at the insistence of Mr. Mercedes, who had got a frantic call from the homeowner about something amiss with the pool site.

There wasn't anything for me to do but appear to be a curious neighbor or passer-by. I sat in the interior of my Dodge looking out through rain splattered windows wondering if there was anything I could do, but I knew there was nothing.

I wasn't too fearful either, since there wouldn't be any way to connect me or really Mr. Mercedes to the floating dead. There was nothing in the homeowners' contract calling for the disposal of a dead person beneath a pool being constructed so we were off the hook. I was sure law enforcement was going to conclude that it was a crime of opportunity for a murderer to use an unsuspecting pool company as a guise to hide a homicide. Made sense to me, as I sat watching police personnel wandering here and there about the property looking very official.

When my cell buzzed again, I knew I was wrong with my assumption.

Mr. Mercedes advised me that another body was floating nearly twelve miles away at a construction site. I had been busy there two weeks earlier. With the impending storms on the way, the pool crews could not complete the process which would have hid my dastardly deeds.

My heart skipped a few beats, since there were another two additional properties which I had visited just before Mother Nature had opened up on Southern California.

It had been a busy month for me and now I was really getting pretty nervous sitting there in my truck. The weather called for another two days of torrential rain. Just my luck.

One body, okay, four to six floaters would raise any eyebrow toward Mr. Mercedes and me.

I suggested to Mr. Mercedes that we both may need a long vacation in a foreign land.

He was way ahead of me, by being aboard a Learjet 45XR, winging his way into Mexican Airspace.

I thanked him and hung up.

This was a conundrum not expected at this juncture of my still young life. I worked for Mr. Mercedes, my truck was often seen at the new pool sites after normal working hours, and I was always the pool boy service at those homes with expensive pools by Mr. Mercedes' construction company.

It didn't look too favorable for me at that moment, as the rain continued to pour down.

Perhaps, I too needed a break from the United States? Over the past couple of years working for Mr. Mercedes I had been able to stock away nearly a hundred thousand dollars. It wasn't a fortune, but for a guy my age, it wasn't bad, and it was all cash.

Jenny had just finished a law degree from USC, and I knew explaining I was an accomplice in a lot of homicides wouldn't go over very well with her. I imagined the wedding plans would be called off, since marrying a man who was going to prison would not look good on a resume. I decided the best for both of us was to just leave.

I loved her and because of that didn't even call her. It was tough, but it was for the best for both of us.

I loaded my truck up with a small bag of clothes and two heavier ones with cash and drove off through the rain southward on Interstate 5. Within a couple of hours, I would pass through the San Ysidro border check and drive into Tijuana, Mexico on my way to Cancún. My employee, Julio, had taught me passable Spanish while working with me, and I knew I could find employment in the tourist towns along the Pacific coast of Mexico.

Who knew, perhaps I would be cleaning pools at some of the resorts? I was very good at cleaning pools. I really was.

Anthology Contributors

Raquel Dionísio Abrantes is a Portuguese poet, word witch, and writer. She has a Bachelor's Degree and a Master's Degree in Cinema from Universidade da Beira Interior. Raquel gave a Master Class in Writing of Scripts about Narrative Structure. Her writing has been published by literary journals and magazines. She is the author of *As Above, So Below*. More about her work can be found on Instagram, @woodland.poem.

Michael P. Aleman: I was raised in a Mexican-American, bi-lingual home in Chicago. My grandfather, a frightening outlaw of a man, rode with Pancho Villa. A city boy at heart, I played in streets, alleys and on rooftops. My mother took my siblings and me to libraries early and books became a major part of my life, so much so that I was an English teacher for 30 years. I am a volunteer reader of prose and poetry for KPBX, Spokane Public Radio in Spokane, Washington. I continue writing both prose and poetry and at 79 find it stimulating and a great adventure.

Lee Anderson has written short stories and essays for a multitude of small and large press publications, including "Fiction International" and "The Miami Herald." He also wrote and staged two plays in New York City, "Supper's Ready" and "Little America." He's the author of the horror novel *What Happened at Sisters Creek*, the short story collection *Dark Lords of the Trailer Park*, and now *Sarna's Ransom*, which is Book One in The Books of Jyn Fantasy Novel Series.

Jacob M. Appel, M.D., is Associate Professor of Psychiatry and Medical Education at the Icahn School of Medicine at Mount Sinai where he serves as Director of Ethics Education in Psychiatry and Assistant Director of Academy for Medicine & the Humanities. He is the author of twenty volumes of fiction and nonfiction, most recently *Who Says You're Dead?* (Algonquin, 2019), a compendium of ethical dilemmas. www.jacobmappel.com

Topper Barnes is an American expat currently living in Georgia (the country). He spends most of his time drinking homemade wine with the villagers in Kharagauli, watching his wife smoke copious amounts of weed, and trying to find a stable writing schedule. His work can be found on *Sublunary Review*, *Scars Publications*, and here at *The Fictional Café*.

Alan Berger is a short story writer living in West Hollywood California, He also writes poetry and has had a collection of his poems published: *You Had Me At Goodbye*.

John Beyer: As a novelist, short story writer, traveler and researcher, John loves nothing better than to share those experiences with his readers. Often in the company with his lovely wife, Laureen, stories emerge of the places they visit and the people they meet. In his weekly travel feature for the USA Today Network, *Beyer's Byways*, John takes his readers along on his adventures. Some funny, some sad, but these are the stories that need to be told.

Mark Blickley grew up within walking distance of New York's Bronx Zoo and is a proud member of the Dramatists Guild and PEN American Center. He is the recipient of a MacArthur Foundation Scholarship Award for Drama. "Blick" is the author of the story collection *Sacred Misfits* (Red Hen Press, Los Angeles). His multi-genre collaborations with artist Amy Bassin include *Weathered Reports: Trump Surrogate Quotes from the Underground* (Moira Books, Chicago) and the text-based art book, *Dream Streams* (Clare Songbirds Publishing House, New York). His latest book is the flash fiction collection, *Hunger Pains* (Buttonhook Press).

Blake Brasher is a visual artist working primarily in mixed media painting. His colorful abstractions are reflections on the nature of reality and what it is like to be a thinking being in a universe that is at once beautiful and terrifying. He grew up in Alaska, and has also lived in Turkey, Texas, and Arizona before moving to Massachusetts in 1997. He received his BS in Art and Design from MIT in 2003 and his MFA from Lesley University in Cambridge, MA in 2022.

Stephen Brayton: A former journalist and communications consultant, Steve took up fiction-writing in retirement. *Ghost Train* was his first published story. Subsequent stories have appeared on *Red Fez*, *Flash-in-a-Flash* as well as *The Fictional Café*. A director and former president of the Dedham (MA) Historical Society, Steve pens a regular column for its newsletter. He's been an avid rail buff since his first electric train set arrived under the Christmas tree. And yes, he once stayed at a campground where a train passed nearby in the middle of the night.

Patricia Callahan's work appears in *The Masters Review*, *Six-Word Memoirs on Love and Heartbreak*, *It All Changed in an Instant*, *Slice* magazine, and *The Fictional Café*. She lives and writes in the Pacific Northwest. Visit her here.

Mbizo Chirasha has served as the 2020-2021 Poet in Residence at *The Fictional Café*, the 2019 Sotambe Festival Live Literature Hub and Poetry Café Curator, 2019 African Fellow for the International Human Rights Art Festival, Essays Contributor to *Monk Art* and *Soul Magazine* in United Kingdom, Arts Features Writer at the *International Cultural Weekly*, Featured Writer Poet Activist at *The Poet A Day*, Core Team Member and African Contributor to Bezine of Arts and Humanities in USA, The Originator of the Zimbabwe We Want Poetry Campaign, Curator of MiomboPublishing Blog Journal, Founder and Chief Editor of WOMAWORDS LITERARY PRESS, and Founder and Curator of the *Brave Voices Poetry Journal*.

Alan Cohen had his first poem published in the PTA Newsletter at the age of 10. He graduated Farmingdale High School (where he was Poetry Editor of The Bard), Vassar College (with a BA in English) and UC at Davis Medical School. He was then a Primary Care physician, teacher, and Chief of Primary Care at the VA. He has over the years had letters to the editor in *Poetry* and *The New Yorker* and articles in *The American* and *New England Journals of Medicine*. He has had 163 poems published in 85 venues over the past two years.

Bob Conklin lives, writes, and works, not necessarily in this order, in Columbus, Ohio, where he helps his spouse nurture the creativity of their three Gen-Z kids, who seem determined to take less-traveled paths of their own. His credits include stories in *Blue Moon Literary & Art Review*, *THAT Literary Review*, and *Kestrel*. In a different medium, he is determined to keep posting original cartoons to his Tumblr blog until enough people beg him to stop.

William C. Crawford is a writer and photographer based in North Carolina. He got his start as a combat photojournalist in Vietnam. He was mentored by three Pulitzer Prize winning journalists. He co-invented Forensic Foraging, a throwback, minimalist approach for modern photographers. His book, *Forensic Foraging*, co-authored with his colleague, Jim Provencher, reached Number 2 on both the Photography and Photojournalism Best Seller Lists.

Maureen Crowley is an artist, fiction writer, and co-founder of Long Shot Books. *Dreamers Often Lie* is her debut novel. She isn't sure if she's overthinking or underthinking how to write her own bio.

Madison Culpepper is a psychology graduate with a minor in creative writing from Central Connecticut State University. She currently lives in Farmington, CT. Madison has been published in the *Oakland Review*, *Long Shot Books*, *The Fictional Café*, and the *Helix Magazine* as a staff feature. She won two silver keys and one gold key in the Scholastic Writing Awards and hopes to publish a poetry book someday.

Ann Davis decided she liked Rhode Island enough to live there after earning her BFA in Creative Writing from Roger Williams University. "Eye Contact" is her first published story, hopefully of many. She is a sci-fi fantasy addict, writing in their subgenres before they had proper names. When her idea attic gets crowded, she participates in and sometimes wins writing challenges Camp Nanowrimo and Nanowrimo. Besides fixing her own messy drafts, she does so for others as a freelance proofreader and copy editor, mostly for independent bookstore and self-publishing service Stillwater River Publications in Pawtucket, Rhode Island.

Frank Diamond's poem "Labor Day" was nominated for a Pushcart Prize Award. His short stories have appeared in the *Madras Mag, Reverential Magazine, The Fictional Café, Empty Sink Publishing, the Zodiac Review*, *the Fredericksburg Literary and Arts Review*, *October Hill Magazine*, and *Sincerely Magazine*, among many other publications. He has had poetry published in *Burrow Press Review*, *shuf Poetry*, *Whimsical Poet*, *Charles Carter Literary Magazine*, *Scarlet Leaf Review*, *Philadelphia Stories*, and *Fox Chase Review* among many other publications. He lives in Langhorne, Pa.

Samuel Ekanem is a historical fiction writer from Uwa, in Nigeria's Niger Delta. His writing, mostly tragedy, explores deep humanitarian issues, including poverty and spirituality. His fictional works have appeared in America's *Down in the Dirt,* India's *Literary Yard,* and Nigeria's *The Sun.* He divides his time between researching and writing and loves traveling to study the diversity of human conditions. He is a passionate humanist. His project in Iganna, Oyo State, Nigeria, was nominated for Nigeria's NYSC Presidential Merit Award 2022. He studied Communication Arts at the University of Uyo, Nigeria.

Ayman Elsayed: I am a writer who likes experimenting with marginalized voices and playing with form. At the height of the pandemic when I wrote this piece, I felt emboldened by the concept of uncertainty and wanted to try something different by embracing it rather than explaining it. The goal was to create an experience rather than a story. Since then, I've started working with other mediums involving programming, creating games, music, VR experiences, digital art, websites, 3d modeling, and learning to patent technology. By trade, I work professionally as a content strategist and technical writer based out of NYC.

Milton P. Erlich Ph.D. is a nonagenarian psychologist and a veteran of the Korean War. He has published many poems in periodicals such as the *London Grip*, *Arc Poetry Magazine*, *Descant Literary Magazine*, *Wisconsin Review*, *Red Wheelbarrow*, *Christian Science Monitor*, and *The New York Times*.

A.R. Farina is a husband, father, writer and podcaster who spends his days working as a college professor for Siena Heights University's Global Campus. He has been writing since he was 12. He writes for *Fantastic Universes* and *Audiofile Magazine*. His critical essays about comic books have been included in several collections from Sequart Publishing. He is part of the Comics in Motion Podcast Network. Most evenings he and his wife, a librarian, read books and watch the sunset from their lanai. You can find him online at arfarina.com.

Julia Franklin was born in Cambridge, England, and has had a passion for writing, drawing, and traveling from a tender age. Now pursuing a career in elementary education, she hopes to one day imbue her students with a love of the arts.

Ben Gencarelle, a Rhode Island native, has been living and working in Germany since 2015, and has had a studio in Frankfurt since 2019. Gencarelle first studied art at the University of Rhode Island and later electrical engineering at both Johnson & Wales University and at the Darmstadt University of Applied Sciences. Through his improvisational, intuitive, and automatic creative processes, Gencarelle explores themes of communication, neurodiversity and legacy. His mediums of choice are painting, drawing, sound, and (sometimes) electronics. He has exhibited in many countries and has collectors from four continents. Gencarelle recently released his second book, *It Gets Better (by page 42),* a meticulously accurate reproduction of his working notebook from 2021.

South African Abigail George has been nominated for a Pushcart Prize and Best of the Net awards. She is a blogger, novelist, and poet. She briefly studied film in Johannesburg. In Africa, Tendai Rinos Mwanaka is her publisher. She has two film projects in development, is the recipient of two grants from the National Arts Council, one from the Centre for the Book and another from ECPACC. She has a book forthcoming in 2022 from Gazebo Books in Australia and her publisher is Xavier Hennekinne and another from Canada from Scarlet Leaf. Her publisher is Roxana Nastase at Scarlet Leaf.

Rachel Gonzalez is a writer, nerd, and rock climber from Arizona. Despite the intense desert heat half of the year, she prefers to spend her time outside. She is an avid hiker whether in the desert mountains of her hometown or in the forests of her college home, Flagstaff. When she does choose to be inside, she is either playing Nintendo games, watching DnD on Dropout, or having her yoga practice interrupted by her dogs. She has a Bachelor's in English and Creative Writing and is currently pursuing her Master's in English Literature. In 2023, Rachel became The Fictional Café's Writer-in-Residence.

Eric D. Goodman is author of six books, including *Wrecks and Ruins* (Loyola University's Apprentice House Press, 2022), *The Color of Jadeite* (Apprentice House Press, 2020), *Setting the Family Free* (Apprentice House, 2019), *Womb: a novel in utero* (Merge Publishing, 2017), *Tracks: A Novel in Stories* (Atticus, 2011), and *Flightless Goose* (Writer›s Lair, 2008) and more than 100 published travel stories, short stories and articles. He also slings words for the government. Learn more about Eric and his writing at www.EricDGoodman.com.

Mark Greenside: In addition to his novel, *Night at the End of the Tunnel,* excerpted here, Mark Greenside is the author of a short story collection, *I Saw a Man Hit His Wife*, and two memoir/travelogues about living in France, *I'll Never Be French (no matter what I do)* and *(not quite) Mastering the Art of French Living.* A more complete biography can be found on his website.

Mark Hammerschick writes poetry and fiction. He holds a BA in English from the University of Illinois at Champaign-Urbana and a BS and MBA. He lives in a northern Chicago suburb near the shore of Lake Michigan. His poem "The Tides They are Rising on Up" recently won third prize in the Poetry Society of Virginia Anne Spencer Memorial Prize Category "Overcoming Adversity." His current work will be appearing in: *Calliope*, *Fauxmoir Literary Magazine*, *Sincerely Magazine*, *Mignolo Arts*, *Blue Lake Review*, *Naugatuck River Review*, *New Plains Review*, *Grey Sparrow Journal*, *Griffel Magazine*, *Voices Magazine*, *Wood Cat Review* and *Change Seven Magazine*.

Lew Holzman: I have always created either word images in my poetry or visual images. Digital photography expanded my horizons and my transformations transformed me into a Digital Artist. I have exhibited both internationally (Italy, Switzerland & Belgium) and regionally within the U.S. I have had a solo show at the Amherst Chamber of Commerce, group shows at the Burnett Gallery at the Jones Library in Amherst, Amherst's Town Hall, Valley Photo in Springfield and at the ECA Gallery in Easthampton, all in Massachusetts. I have displayed works at the Southern Vt. Art Center in Manchester amongst other places. I am a longtime member of The Pioneer Valley Photographic Artists.

Julia Hwang is a New Jersey poet who has recently been featured in *Full House Literary Magazine* and *The Spotlong Review*. She tends to write about womanhood, the sea, and assorted moments of ennui.

Richard-Yves Sitoski (he/him) is a songwriter, performance poet, and the 2019-2023 Poet Laureate of Owen Sound, Ontario, Canada, on the territory of the Saugeen Ojibway Nation. His work has appeared in *Prairie Fire, Train*, *The Fiddlehead*, *Bywords.ca,* and elsewhere. He has given performances in industrial ruins, has read poems to earth worms, and has written verse on snow with biodegradable dye. BOTN nominee 2021, 2021 John Newlove Award winner. Co-editor, with Penn Kemp, of *Poems in Response to Peril: An Anthology in Support of Ukraine* (Pendas Productions/Laughing Raven Press 2022).

Stephen Jackson lives and writes in the Pacific Northwest. As creator of the Seattle small press So Many Birds Publishing (SMBp), he produced *Harness* literary magazine and the *Future+Present* chapbook series of previously unpublished local writers. Twice-nominated for the Pushcart Prize, his poetry has appeared in a variety of print and online publications, as well as on the International Human Rights Art Festival Publishes platform. In 2021, he received honorable mention for the Penrose Poetry Prize, which awards excellence in poetry from LGBTQIA+ writers.

Joanne W. James is a dreamer, philosopher, yogi, mystic & poet. Co-creator of the women's writing collective, Tribe Through Time, with poet, Patti Sirens. *Fish Dreams, Or, St. Anthony's Sermon*, a book-length poem, was published in 2004 by Mellen Press as prize winner, "Poetry as Ecstatic Vision." Also published in *Lingo*, *American Writing*, *Many Mountains Moving*, and others.

Arya F. Jenkins' flash fiction, short stories and creative nonfiction have been published in many journals and zines. Her fiction has received several nominations for the Pushcart Prize and one nomination in 2021 for the Best of the Net Anthology. She is the author of three poetry chapbooks and a short story collection, *Blue Songs in an Open Key* (Fomite, 2018) and a mixed genre novel, *Punk Disco Bohemian* (NineStar Press, 2021). A second collection of short stories, *Angel in Paris & Other Stories*, is expected.

Jennifer Judge is a poet, professor at King's College, and coordinator of the Luzerne County (PA) Poetry in Transit program. Her poem "81 North" was selected for permanent inclusion in the Jenny Holzer installation *For Philadelphia 2018*. Her work has also appeared in *Rhino*, *Literary Mama*, *Blueline*, *Under the Gum Tree*, and *The Fictional Café,* among others. She earned her MFA from Goddard College. She lives in Dallas, PA with her husband and two daughters. Her first book, *Spoons, Knives, Checkbooks*, is forthcoming from Propertius Press.

Audrey Kalman writes fiction with a dark edge about what goes awry when human connection is missing from our lives. She is the author the novels *The Last Storyteller*, *What Remains Unsaid*, and *Dance of Souls*, as well as the fiction collection *Tiny Shoes Dancing* (shortlisted for the 2019 International Rubery Book Award). Her short fiction and poetry have appeared in more than a dozen print and online journals. She co-teaches the Birth Your Truest Story workshop series, offers editing and coaching services for writers, and is at work on another novel. Find out more about her at audreykalman.com

Hank Keneally: I am very fortunate. I have always been in the arts. Learning the notes on the piano from my grandmother who was a piano teacher. Listening to classical music that my brother brought before me. Playing instruments. Becoming a photographer. Practicing counseling and social work for 42 years, which I see as another artistic process. Becoming a painter. I create every day. I start with compassionate observation. I always have a camera with me. For me, great things happen where arts merge. I use paint, cameras and digital technologies. I aim for reciprocity between myself and my media. I love to be surprised in the act of creation. My artworks are all a result of these processes.

Keith Kennedy is a Pushcart and Rhysling nominee writing out of Vancouver. He is represented by Jon Michael Darga at Aevitas Creative.

Wayne D. King is an accomplished photographer. His work can be found in the collections of a broad range of people including Livingston Taylor, Koko Taylor, Richard Merritt, Bill Bradley, Bruce Babbitt, Bill Clinton, Adhiambo Odaga, Bill Russell, Valerie Jarrett, and others. His images are a celebration of life, blending the real and the surreal to achieve a sense of place or time that reaches beyond the moment into what he calls "a dreamlike quintessentialism" designed to spark an emotional response. Using digital enhancement, handcrafting, painting, poetry, and sometimes even straight photography, King takes the viewer to a place that goes beyond simple truth to where truth meets passion, hope, and dreams.

Abigail Kipp: Poetry has been my lifelong passion. I graduated with a four-year degree in English/Poetry from New Mexico State University. I studied at Sarah Lawrence for an MFA but did not complete. Poetry is essential for my life. I have been published in a number of places. My first book, *Of Monsters and Maidens*, was published in 2023. I live in New Mexico with my boyfriend and our dog.

Derrick R. Lafayette was The Fictional Café's 2021-2022 Writer-in-Residence. He's written four novels and over a dozen short stories, published in print and online. When he's not working as an IT Engineer or studying chess gambits on the astral plane, he's reading or writing profusely. His latest book is *Kaleidoscope*, a short fiction collection.

Barbara A. Lawrence is a survivor of family violence, incest, and rape. Diagnosed with C-PTSD and Dissociative Identity Disorder, Barbara gives presentations on what it's like to live with immense trauma and helps ease the stigma surrounding mental illness. Her poetry has been featured both in print and online. She is producer/host of a public access TV show, *Beyond the Shadows*, which focuses on difficult issues affecting individuals and communities and seeks to educate, inspire, and empower people to work toward building communities rooted in understanding and love. www.beyondtheshadowstv.com

Cindy Layton writes literary fiction, fiction for young adults, and is a contributor to the blog Acts of Revision.

Vlad Linder: Born May 14, 1978 in Leningrad city, Russia.
Was mentioned in "The Guardian" in 2000.
In 2012, wrote the story "Chronicles of Cambodia."
Has visited more than 50 countries of the world.

Mario Loprete: I live in a world that I shape at my liking. I do this through virtual, pictorial, and sculptural movements, transferring my experiences and photographing reality through my mind's filters. I have refined this process through years of research and experimentation. Painting is my first love. An important, pure love. Creating a painting, starting from the spasmodic research of a concept with which I want to transmit my message, this is the foundation of painting for me. The sculpture is my lover, my artistic betrayal to the painting that voluptuous and sensual lover inspiring different emotions which strike prohibited chords.

Chad W. Lutz is a speedy writer born in Akron, Ohio, in 1986, and raised in the neighboring suburb of Stow. They graduated from Kent State University with their BA in English in 2008 and from Mills College in Oakland, California, with their MFA in Creative Writing in 2018. Their first book, *For the Time Being* (2020), is currently available through J.New Books and Amazon.

Fiama Mastrangelo is a psychology and writing graduate from the University of West Florida and a real-life barista at a multitude of real-life coffee shops. She loves all cafés—both the fictional and nonfictional varieties. "The Beholder" is her first published story and she is thrilled to be included in the second edition of the Fictional Café Anthology.

Ewa Mazierska is an historian of film and popular music who writes short stories in her spare time. She has published over fifty of them in literary magazines. In 2019 she published her first collection, *Neighbours and Tourists* (New York, Adelaide Books). She was born in Poland, but lives in Lancashire, UK.

Jarrett Mazza is a graduate of Goddard College's MFA in Creative Writing Program, as well as The Humber School for Writers. Before completing his terminal degree, Jarrett studied writing at the University of Toronto School of Continuing Studies and comic book writing under Ty Templeton and Andy Schmidt. He has had stories published online and has been featured in anthologies by *Silver Empire Publishing, Zimbell House Publishing, NBH Publishing,*

MuseWrite Press, Dragon Soul Press, Gypsum Soul Press, and *Hellbound Books.* He was an Honorable Mention for the Freda Waldon Award for Fiction, nominated for an Indie Book award, and was featured as a visiting author for the nationwide We Read Canadian event in 2020. He lives in Hamilton, Ontario. jarrettmazzawriter.com

G.D. McFetridge writes from his wilderness home in Montana's majestic Sapphire Mountains. His essays and fiction are published in academic reviews and journals, as well as commercial magazines, across the US, in Canada, the UK, Ireland, New Zealand, India and China.

Roger McKnight grew up in downstate Illinois. He has degrees from Southern Illinois University and the University of Minnesota. He has lived and worked in Chicago, Sweden, and Puerto Rico. He now lives in Minnesota. Sweden showed him the value of peaceful conflict resolution while Puerto Rico exhibited a humane spirit before and after the US government's post-hurricane neglect of the island. Roger often writes of people on the fringes of mainstream society. He has published one book of creative non-fiction, a novel, and short fiction in literary journals.

Joan McNerney is the recipient of three scholarships which includes one from the University of Mexico School for Foreign Students in San Antonio, Texas. She has recited her work at the National Arts Club, New York, State University of New York, Oneonta, McNay Art Institute, San Antonio and the University of Houston, Texas as well as other distinguished venues. *The Muse in Miniature* and *Love Poems for Michael* are both available on Amazon and Cyberwit.net. Just released is a new title *At Work*. This collection shows colorful but realistic snapshots of working women and men in their daily lives.

Jon Meyer has written for *The Village Voice, ARTnews, ARTS, New Art Examiner, Visions Quarterly, CRITS, Q, Dialog, Art New England, The Fictional Café*, and many more publications. Meyer led a small team producing a film about one of his students, Dan Keplinger. This film, *King Gimp* won the Oscar for best short documentary at the 2000 Academy Awards. Meyer's work has been in 60 solo & group exhibitions (18 museum exhibitions) and has his work in 20 museum/public collections globally. He has received 12 grants, including a National Endowment for the Arts grant. His previous 2 books have received a combined 25 national and international book awards. More information: jonmeyerpoetry.com

David Morton Meyers is a painter, sculptor, drawer and rabble rouser. Born and bred in the wild New England states, hailing from a small town known as Boston. Received a BFA from Temple University's Tyler School of Art in painting/drawing and a minor in art history, then later returned to academia for an MA and MFA from the University of Iowa in painting and a secondary emphasis in sculpture. David enjoys cats, punk rock, long walks on the beach and collecting conch shells. You can follow him on Instagram @DavidMortonMeyers

Brian Moore lives in Toronto, Canada where he worked as a project manager. He is previously published in *Blank Spaces*, *The Barren*, *Gravel*, and *Valparaiso Review*.

Hayden Moore was born in Georgia and has lived in New York City for 15 years. He studied at the University of Tennessee. His debut novel, *Sky Tracer*, published in 2023 by Vraeyda Literary, is available on Amazon. He lives with his wife, dog/dragon and looming spirit of his cat on the waters of Jamaica Bay in Queens, NY.

Paulo Navarro: As a university student, Paulo founded his own gallery and art academy. At first it was a children's art academy (Pintando Ilusiones) and later PHI Gallery, where important established and emerging artists shared the space created by Paulo. The artist also participated in the "Circulo de artistas emergentes costarricenses," an emerging group of artists with which he traveled through various Latin American countries representing his nation, creating important exhibitions and artistic cultural projects. Within this group, he exhibited in Costa Rican spaces as well as other destinations like Nicaragua, Panama, Cuba and Japan.

Paul Negri has been twice awarded the gold medal for fiction in the William Faulkner – William Wisdom Writing Competition; was nominated for a Pushcart Prize by The Fictional Café; and his artwork was selected to appear in the *2022 Best of the Net* anthology. His stories have appeared in more than 60 publications. He lives in Clemmons, North Carolina.

James Osborne is the author of four traditionally published books including Amazon #1 bestseller, *The Ultimate Threat*, a thriller about the resurgence of terrorist group ISIS. He is also the author of the award-winning suspense/mystery series, The Maidstone Series. Osborne's varied career has included investigative journalist, college teacher, army officer, vice-president of a Fortune 500 company, business owner, and writer/book editor. His essays and short stories have appeared in dozens of anthologies, magazines, and literary and professional journals, and in a collection of selected short stories.

Jose Oseguera is an LA-based writer of poetry, short fiction and literary nonfiction. His writing has been featured in Emrys Journal, North Dakota Quarterly and The Rio Grande Review. His work has also won the Nancy Dew Taylor Award and been nominated for the Best of the Net award (2018, twice in 2019) as well as the Pushcart (2018, 2019 and 2020) and Forward (2020) Prizes. He is the author of the poetry collection "The Milk of Your Blood" (Kelsay Books).

Stephen Pavlovic is a longtime resident of Morgantown, West Virginia, and has lived in France and South Korea. Steve has a BA in Fine Arts from Kenyon College and a Master of Fine Arts from the University of North Carolina, Chapel Hill. He also has a Masters Degree in Early Childhood Special Education and an Ed.D. from West Virginia University.

Robert Perron lives and writes in New York City and New Hampshire. Past life includes high-tech and military service. He is the author of the novel *The Blue House Raid*. His short stories have appeared in *The Fictional Café, Lowestoft Chronicle*, *The Bombay Review*, *The Manchester Review*, and other literary journals. His website is robertperron.com

Thomas Piekarski is a former editor of the *California State Poetry Quarterly*. His poetry has appeared in such publications as *Poetry Quarterly, Literature Today, Poetry Salzburg, South African Literary Journal, Modern Literature*, and others. His books of poetry are *Ballad of Billy the Kid, Monterey Bay Adventures, Mercurial World*, and *Aurora California*.

Fabrice Poussin teaches French and English at Shorter University. Author of novels and poetry, his work has appeared in *Kestrel*, *Symposium*, *The Chimes*, and many other magazines. His photography has been published in *The Front Porch Review* and *The San Pedro River Review,* as well as other publications.

Charles Rammelkamp is Prose Editor for BrickHouse Books. He contributes a monthly book review to *North of Oxford* and is a frequent reviewer for *The Lake, London Grip, Misfit Magazine* and *The Compulsive Reader.* A poetry chapbook, *Mortal Coil*, was published in 2021 by Clare Songbirds Publishing and another, *Sparring Partners,* by Moonstone Press. A full-length collection, *The Field of Happiness,* was published in 2022 by Kelsay Books. Rammelkamp's books include a number of biographical/historical sequences, including *Mata Hari: Eye of the Day, American Zeitgeist* (William Jennings Bryan), *Catastroika* (Rasputin), *Fusen Bakudan* (Vietnam) and *Jack Tar's Lady Parts.*

Burbuqe Raufi is an award-winning Albanian author and an avid reader living in the Republic of North Macedonia. Her first published book, *Dr. Mind*, had gathered good and impeccable reviews from readers. *Dr. Mind* was published into Albanian as "Fuqia e mendimeve" and became a best seller and an award winner of the Best Book of 2016. Her recent published book is *The Tavern: a Novella*. Burbuqe has also published short stories in literary magazines, including "The Old, the Young, and Me" (Literary Yard), and "Me vs Me" (Positively Positive).

Roopa Raveendran-Menon lives in Dubai, United Arab Emirates, where she works as a content & communications manager. Her short stories have been published in international literary magazines and included in some Indian anthologies. She is also the author of *Chandu and the Super Set of Parents*, middle-grade fiction published by Fitzroy Books. When she is not busy chasing project deadlines or writing fiction, this self- confessed Sylvia Plath addict loves staring into space, tuning into Netflix, and dabbling in tarot card reading (not necessarily in the same order). Her Instagram is @ roopa.raveendran

John Charles Reedburg is winner of the 2021 Readers' Favorite Book Award in Urban Fiction for his debut novel *Cracks Of Light* (Valorous Books). He is from Los Angeles and is an alumnus of the Guy Hanks and Marvin Miller Screenwriting Fellowship Program at USC. He holds an MFA in fiction from Antioch University Los Angeles, an MFA in screenwriting and directing from Chapman University, and a BA in communications from California State University Dominguez Hills. Stay connected with John through his Facebook and Instagram: @JohnCharlesReedburg

Kira Rice-Christianson is an author and poet currently residing in San Diego, California. Her published work includes a collection of poems; *Love Language*, and an autobiographical collection of short stories; *A Lengthy List of Lovers,* both available on Amazon.

Claire Sartin graduated with a degree in creative writing from Eureka College. She has worked as a writing tutor and participated in a brief internship with the *Eureka College Literary Magazine*. Her short story appearing here, "To Whom It May Concern," has also been published in a collection of short stories, *Musings of an Apocalyptic Mind: A Collection of Death, Doom and Dark Humor*. She currently lives in central Illinois with her adoring Olde English Bulldog and husband.

Sanjeev Sethi has authored five books of poetry. He is published in over thirty countries. His poems have found a home in more than 390 journals, anthologies, and online literary venues. Recent credits: *North Dakota Quarterly, K'in Literary Journal, Kairos Literary Magazine, The Big Windows Review, Stand Magazine*, and *Litter Magazine*. He is the joint-winner of Full Fat Collection Competition-Deux, organized by The Hedgehog Poetry Press UK. He is in the top ten of the erbacce prize 2021 UK. It has over twelve thousand and five hundred entries. He lives in Mumbai, India. Twitter: @sanjeevpoems3, Instagram: @sanjeevsethipoems

Mir-Yashar Seyedbagheri is a graduate of Colorado State University's MFA program in fiction. His stories have been nominated for Pushcarts, Best Small Fictions, and Best Microfiction. His work has been published in *SmokeLong Quarterly*, *The Journal of Compressed Creative Arts*, and *Ariel Chart*, among others.

Richard-Yves Sitoski (he/him) is a songwriter, performance poet, and the 2019-2023 Poet Laureate of Owen Sound, Ontario, Canada, on the territory of the Saugeen Ojibway Nation. His work has appeared in *Prairie Fire, Train*, *The Fiddlehead*, *Bywords.ca,* and elsewhere. He has given performances in industrial ruins, has read poems to earth worms, and has written verse on snow with biodegradable dye. BOTN nominee 2021, 2021 John Newlove Award winner. Co-editor, with Penn Kemp, of *Poems in Response to Peril: An Anthology in Support of Ukraine* (Pendas Productions/Laughing Raven Press 2022).

Casey Stanberry was trained as an architect and furthered his education at an art school in Spain. There, he participated in his first art shows and allowed the dense, historic architectural fabric to inspire his work. Originally from South Carolina, he has always had a passion for historic architecture and its relationship with contemporary daily life. His work reflects the intersection of the built environment and fine art in sweeping perspectives and painted and penned architectural diagrams. His primary media include black ink and acrylics. He resides in Chicago where he sells prints and originals of complex architectural pieces. He is able to create custom pieces of a client's favorite city or building with the aid of photography and aerial/satellite views.

Brett Stout is a 44-year-old artist and writer. He is a high school dropout and former construction worker turned college graduate and paramedic. He creates mostly controversial work usually while breathing toxic paint fumes from a small cramped apartment known as "The Nerd Lab" in Myrtle Beach, South Carolina. His work has appeared in a vast range of diverse media, from international indie zines like *Litro Magazine UK* to Brown University. He is tired of talking about himself at this point and prefers that his work speak for itself. Thanks.

Nick Sweeney's books include a haunted jaunt around Poland in *Laikonik Express* (Unthank Books, 2011), a wander in the wrong part of Silesia in *The Exploding Elephant* (Bards and Sages, 2018), a look at genocide survivors in 1960s Nice in *A Blue Coast Mystery, Almost Solved* (Histria Books, 2020). The Émigré Engineer (Ploughshares, 2021) traces a life from the Russian Revolution to Prohibition America. "Traffic," his story set in a troubled Kiev, was runner-up in the 2015 V S Pritchett Prize. His story "The High Life" (Wordrunner, 2021) has been nominated for the 2022 Pushcart Prize.

Rob Swigart: My latest books are *Mixed Harvest: Stories from the Human Past,* narratives of daily life from the arrival of modern humans in Europe through the emergence of urban life in Mesopotamia. In the middle of the transformation from hunter-gatherer to "civilized" city dwellers, our species adopted farming. I call this the Sedentary Divide: before life was one way, after it was different in every way. Now that we can see the changes were not necessarily good, we must pay attention if we are to survive. Also, in 2022 the third in my Lisa Emmer series of historic thrillers appeared.

William Torphy's fiction has appeared in numerous magazines and journals, including *Bryant Literary Review*, *The Fictional Café*, *Sun Star Quarterly* and *Chelsea Station,* His cultural commentary has been featured in *Solstice Literary, OpEdge* and *Vox Populi*. Ithuriel's Spear Press has published *Love Never Always* (poetry collection), *Snakebite* (young adult fiction) and *A Brush With History* (biography). His short story collection, *Motel Stories*, is to be published by Unsolicited Press. He recently moved to Wisconsin from the San Francisco Bay area. Visit him at williamtorphy.com

Montgomery Tufts is a writer of absurdism and high fantasy with an interest in exploring familial relationships and Queer experiences. They have worked as an Assistant Editor in Fiction for *Silk Road Review: A Literary Crossroads* and in Spanish-to-English translation. Tufts has won 2nd place for creative nonfiction and 1st place for poetry in the writing contest held annually by *P.L.U.M.: Pacific's Literary Undergraduate Magazine*. They graduated from Pacific University with a B.A. in creative writing and Spanish in 2021 and currently reside in Champaign County, IL, where they work for a non-profit that serves their local LGBTQ+ community.

Ana Vidosavljevic was born in Serbia and currently lives in Indonesia. She is a teacher, writer, surfer, and mother. She is the author of two collections of short stories, *Places*, *Mermaids*, and a memoir, *Flower Thieves*.

Townsend Walker draws inspiration from cemeteries, foreign places, violence, and strong women. A collection of short stories, *3 Women, 4 Towns, 5 Bodies & other stories* was published by Deeds Publishing in 2018. The book won a Book Excellence Award, a Silver Feathered Quill Award and a Pinnacle Award. A novella, *La Ronde* was published by Truth Serum Press in 2015. Over one hundred short stories have been published in literary journals and included in thirteen anthologies. He received two nominations for the PEN/O.Henry Award. He reviews for the *New York Journal of Books.*

Lucy Zhang writes, codes and watches anime. Her work has appeared in *American Literary Review*, *The Rupture*, *The Offing* and elsewhere. She published two poetry chapbooks in 2022: *Hollowed* with Thirty West Publishing, and a micro-chapbook, *Absorption,* with Harbor Review. Find her at www.kowaretasekai.wordpress.com/ or on Twitter @Dango_Ramen.

If you like what you see here, why not submit your own work?
It's totally free. Guidelines are on our website,
https://www.fictionalcafe.com/

www.ingramcontent.com/pod-product-compliance
Lightning Source LLC
Chambersburg PA
CBHW082057090726
47909CB00011B/3062

* 9 7 8 0 9 8 4 0 3 6 9 5 0 *